THE GREAT LOCOMOTIVE CHASE, 1862

The Symbiont Time Travel Adventures Series

Book Four

T.L.B. Wood

Book and Cover Design by eBook Prep
www.ebookprep.com

February, 2018
ISBN: 978-1-947833-19-7

ePublishing Works!
www.epublishingworks.com

DEDICATION

For Henry and Jesse

The supreme happiness of life is the conviction of being loved for yourself or, more correctly, being loved in spite of yourself.

—Victor Hugo

CHAPTER 1

"You want me to do what?" I asked, feeling no need to soften the sharp tone of my voice. I had a sober flash of the realization that a hostile tone, especially directed towards a valued friend, is never a good way to conduct business. Despite a tiny voice nagging from somewhere deep within, I found it difficult to restrain myself. A bead of sweat tricked down my back; with effort, I shoved my shoulders, which had crawled up to my ears, down. The chair I'd chosen was easily the most uncomfortable in the room with an unforgiving wooden seat that made my tailbone cry out in surrender.

"I think you heard me clearly enough," Philo replied calmly. From behind his desk, he reached forward to casually rearrange some papers and pens as if that was more important than my query. A small desk clock ticked softly, expectantly, as the room fell silent.

I sat quietly for a moment, counting to ten under my breath, as I struggled to regain control over my temper. Philo, after all, was my oldest friend, a trusted confidant, and valued advisor. Once we'd been peers sharing a similar casual disdain for the power structure and a slight attitude of defiance toward those in charge. But now, Philo found himself promoted to the leadership chair and I was a subordinate. How would anyone handle that unexpected transition with grace, I wondered? I glanced at Kipp, who lay nearby in an isolated patch of sunlight cascading across the floor. His tail thumped out a slow, steady beat as his amber eyes met mine. In the manner of well-matched telepaths, his thoughts merged with mine, much like water from two divergent streams pours into one, deep reservoir.

There were so many oddities in regards to my relationship with Kipp that one could begin a list at sunrise and still be busy writing long after twilight fell. My work as an investigator of past mysteries had taken me far afield, and on one particularly difficult trip, my bonded traveling partner, Tula, was killed. Without her synergistic balance, I was literally stuck in time, shivering on a prehistoric hilltop, waiting for something bad to happen. Such was the worst thing that could befall a time traveler, to be abandoned in the past with no way home. But instead of something bad coming my way, I was found and rescued by Kipp, who was one of my kind in need of companionship. Somehow, we forged an improbable bond that brought us, as a duo, to my contemporary home. The trust that sort of connection brings is unparalleled.

"I'd hate to be compelled to insist, Petra, but we really need you to do this." Philo raised his eyebrows and added, "And you, after all, work here, right?"

I felt the heat start at my neck with a flush that rapidly moved upwards. Over the many years I'd known Philo, we'd had more than a few disagreements, but those were tiny bee stings compared to how I felt at that moment. It was an odd sensation to actually be furious with him. Kipp, an eternal optimist, privately counseled me to try counting to ten, once again.

When Kipp joined our collective, he brought with him a fresh set of skills, many of which had been lost in antiquity as we evolved and suppressed our natural talents, all in the name of becoming more civilized. Telepathically, he entered my mind and soothed me in ways no one else could. Kipp and I shared a uniquely open method of communication in that we were constantly present in each other's minds. My contemporary peers despised such eavesdropping and had adopted rules of civility that prohibited mind intrusive with one another without an invitation.

Turning my head, I gazed out the large window of Philo's office; it faced north and overlooked the pretty courtyard, which, in spring, was filled with azaleas and hydrangeas. It was summertime, and the crepe myrtles abounded, their limbs bent heavily from the weight of countless blossoms. A large yellow poplar threw its massive shadow against the side of the Technicorps office building which was nestled in the heart of Research Triangle Park. I'd lived in this part of North Carolina–the piedmont with its gently rolling green hills–for many years. At some point, Kipp and I would be transferred out, to live in another collective, and I would grieve the day I left my comfortable home. The humans with whom we worked and lived would eventually become suspicious at my conspicuous lack of aging, since symbionts were naturally long lived.

Our relationship with humans was covert, and necessarily so. With our ability to travel back in time, symbionts can deliberately or inadvertently change the arc of history and alter the progression of established facts. It would be all too seductive for humans to manipulate our skills. As far as my human neighbors on my quiet street knew, I was a reasonably attractive woman in my late twenties who lived with a large, reddish colored dog. They would never have guessed that the dog, Kipp, had an intelligence superior to most humans and skills surpassing all living symbionts.

I gazed at Kipp and again he thumped his tail in response. His large, upright ears swiveled in my direction as he tried to cross his eyes, failing miserably. I knew he was trying to humor me out of my agitation with Philo.

"I know you and Kipp are having an intense discussion to which I am not privy," Philo finally remarked. "Petra, the reason we need to push the issue is that, quite frankly, our kind are losing the skills that make us unique. Fewer of us are willing to become travelers; it's a complicated, difficult life style that pretty much destroys the option of home and family. It's harder and harder for us to create the bond needed to time shift, as you well know. When we find two interested candidates who test as compatible partners, we have to move on it."

"But Peter Keaton?" I began, shaking my head. "He's only fifty years old, with no experience."

"Petra," Philo said, his voice patient but strained, "you once had no experience, either. All learners have to start somewhere." He looked more than a little tired; the gray was overtaking his hair, and his dark eyes were shadowed.

I'd had enough at that point. Philo was correct in that I worked at Technicorps, and if I wanted a paycheck, I'd need to do whatever was asked of me. Globally, our colonies worked to surreptitiously benefit mankind through research in a diverse number of areas. My specific talent was to visit the scenes of past unsolved mysteries and bring lost information to the present. Some was shared, with care, with humans, while most was cataloged by Fitzhugh, the keeper of our history of a species. By no means were we allowed to interfere with humanity or the progression of time as fate had designed.

After a terse goodbye to Philo, Kipp and I made our way outside. It was a late summer day; the sun was completing its predestined arc of the bright blue canopy, and the sky was gracefully streaked with the lavender gray tones of impending twilight. A flock of birds soared overhead, turning suddenly with the amazing ability of their kind to avoid collisions as they twisted and banked on their journey south. Kipp paused, craning his neck back, as he stared at the birds.

"I really don't know how they do that," he said. "I've tried to comprehend their thoughts, but it's difficult because there are so many of them in a tight area."

"Well, I wish I could read their little bird brains, but I'm having trouble just dealing with my own kind right now."

With that comment, I gave Kipp a silent salute at his advanced ability to read, to some degree, the notions of the baser creatures of the earth. Certainly none of my contemporaries could manage such a thing.

"You will make up with Philo," Kipp said, with a confident nod. "Your friendship is too deep to stay angry for long."

Well, of course I knew he was correct. There were two beings on earth who could be totally honest with me: one was a humanoid, Philo Marshall, and the other was Kipp, a dog-like creature referred to within our circles as a lupine and my superior in all ways calculable. Despite our physical differences, we were all members of the family of symbionts.

The warmth of the fading day was thankfully mild. The weather in the piedmont was unpredictable. There could be harsh cold, with snow that impeded travel, while the summers could be so hot as to rival a tropical zone. But those were the extremes, and the waning summer had been gentle, with only a few days when the temperature went above the mid nineties. I'd lived in North Carolina long enough to become accustomed to its climate. Since my birth in 1604, I'd been challenged with different homes, as well as a variety of cultures that required a broadening of the mind and attire that tested my tolerance and adaptability. To this day, I despise a crinoline as well as a corset.

We walked along a familiar route that meandered close to the series of streets that led to my little house on a tree lined avenue. The sidewalks were broken from the roots of stubborn old trees, and despite the city having promised to repave the pathway, they remained a jagged reminder of the past. I, for one, was happy to see them unchanged. My neighbors thought of me as a mildly eccentric woman who gave lectures at the local universities, both Duke and UNC, as well as NC State in Raleigh. My students gave me rave reviews for historical presentations that seemed so real, my listeners could actually pretend they were present for the events described. Little did they know that I had, indeed, visited such times and even participated in some of the events that I subsequently unraveled for them like a piece of worn fabric.

As we strolled past a field where the long grass stood in tangled masses, I smiled and looked at Kipp, who returned my glance. In that abandoned pasture, we'd rescued a kitten which grew into the mighty Lily, now residing with an overly indulgent Fitzhugh. A surge of love flowed through me. Yes, Kipp was mine and I was his, as long as we chose to maintain our bond. There was no room for a mate or children, and that very fact was why so few symbionts would bond as did Kipp and I for travel. I'd had a husband and child, but both had died in an accident many years ago. At this point in my life, I was happy to be Kipp's partner and travel to the past in search of answers to the imponderable.

As I reflected upon those thoughts, my heart squeezed painfully as a series of exquisitely detailed memories flooded my mind, despite my conscious effort to restrain the self-indulgent musing. During my last trip with Kipp when we travelled to London in the late 1800's, I'd allowed myself to become involved with a human man who'd fallen in love with me. There was really no greater crime, if that was, indeed, the correct word, than for us symbionts to become emotionally involved with human beings. There was absolutely no future in such an alliance, and the chance of changing the progression of history was too profound. We were, as a species, to leave a tiny footprint or, more preferably, none at all.

"Is it possible?" I asked Kipp, looking down at him.

He was a remarkably handsome lupine, with a thick and slightly wavy coat of an unusual deep auburn color. His plumed tail was carried proudly over his broad back, while his eyes, glowing amber orbs lined with dark fur, stared back with intelligence and sensitivity.

"No, I don't think we can go back in time without leaving at least a hint of memory behind," he answered, after giving my thought consideration. "I'm certain Perdy remembered us to the end of her days. I'd like to think the same of sweet Alice," he added, dipping his head. He had strong and sentimental thoughts about some of the people we met on our first journey together.

"I think it's just a story told to us when we are learning to keep us on the right path," I finally concluded, feeling pleased with my analysis. Tilting my head back, I allowed the waning rays of sunlight to touch my face; it was a pleasurable moment, and I closed my eyes for just a second.

The concept of being a novice and of learning caused me to consider, more rationally, Philo and his request. I was not completely stupid and realized that the young ones of our kind needed teachers. Perhaps it was selfishness, but I had no desire to take along a couple of trainees as I worked. The journeys were difficult enough without a couple of inexperienced travelers thrown into the mix.

"You are thinking of yourself," Kipp pointed out helpfully, yawning as he stared ahead at a large dog which was blocking our path. The dog, from a distance, saw the equally enormous Kipp as a potential challenger, but he would, as did they all, scamper off when he realized that Kipp was no dog. I'd seen Kipp scare off a pair of hungry wolves; there was no dog who would threaten him. The dog, as predicted, turned and dashed off, plowing through a hole in a ragged hedge in his haste to be gone.

"But, I'm thinking of myself, too," Kipp added with typical Kipp honesty. "The other side of the equation is Elani, and you will recall she has a crush on me." He rolled his eyes as he looked at me. "What am I gonna do with that?"

I was forced to laugh. At least Peter didn't have a crush on me, or at least I didn't think so. I was truly old enough to be his mother, but symbionts aged so uniquely that one would never know. Fitzhugh was more than 1300 years old, that achievement being pretty remarkable in itself. At around 400 plus, I was comfortably young but not too far off from middle age. The thought caused me to think of my Victorian love interest, William Harrow. He'd probably thought I was in my twenties, wondering why I was a spinster at such an age. I'd lived over two centuries and then some before he was born. And that was a sobering thought.

"I'm not sure I want to agree, Kipp, but I don't know how to decline. Philo is correct in that I work for Technicorps…so do you. We may have to quit, and then what would we do?" I looked ahead down the street, watching as a stray cat cautiously crossed the road, his head down as he slunk along, hoping to avoid attention.

"I don't think we can refuse, Petra." Kipp nuzzled my hand. "Philo wouldn't ask us to do this unless he thought we were the best candidates, and he is, after all, a good friend. I'm sure he would have collaborated with Fitzhugh and Juno, too."

In short order, we arrived at my little house; I took pleasure in its familiarity. As we stood on the front porch and I fumbled for the door key, my eyes took in the iron railings that had become weathered, with bits of rust showing through the faded paint. The front door was also in dire need of a makeover, and the windows needed cleaning, inside and out. I was not overly attached to material things, but I confess my home was a refuge of comfort and security. From the chipped ceramic tiles on the kitchen counter to the rooms filled with little bits of what some might think to be useless discards, I was surrounded by the golden warmth of history. I would look at a piece of old pottery and wonder through whose hands it had passed and what had become of those people. As I unlocked the door, the phone was ringing. It was Philo, exasperated I'd left Technicorps without the issue of serving as a symbiont instructor being settled. Yes, we were a telepathic species but there were distance limitations on what could be discerned. Kipp by far had the best telepathic nose, so to speak, and could detect the faint ping of other symbionts even when he couldn't understand the thoughts.

"I'm coming by tomorrow morning," Philo announced brusquely, his tone clipped and impatient. "We didn't get finished today, and I need to report by Monday."

"I've got yard work to do," I replied lamely, crossing my eyes to amuse Kipp–since he managed that sort of thing poorly—who sat at my feet, staring up at me.

"Then I'll watch," Philo responded and hung up in my face.

Tossing the phone on the counter, not caring if it might break, I walked to my bedroom, Kipp following, his toenails ticking on the bruised hardwood floors of my house. Passing beneath a light fixture, I glanced up, recalling the moment I spied it in the dusty, neglected corner of a junk store. It was stained glass–real stuff, not fake–and there had only been one tiny flaw in a pane of amber glass. To my way of thinking, the imperfection only made the piece more precious.

"You have an unusual way of looking at the world," Kipp observed.

Ignoring him, I paused at my dresser. With a quick glance in the mirror, I reached up and carefully felt for the fastener of the delicate strand of pearls nestled against my throat. Just touching them reminded me of Harrow, who'd bestowed that precious gift to me. Looking up again, I wondered what he'd seen when he gazed at me. Staring back at my reflection, I observed an oval face framed by dark hair, hazel eyes and a sprinkling of freckles across a too large nose. Whatever it was, he'd liked my face and eventually loved me. Kipp came up behind me and nuzzled my hand with his soft mouth.

"Let go of the thoughts, Petra. They only make you sad."

With his wise counsel ringing in my ears, I took a quick shower, thinking the hot water running through my hair would help me to feel better. Actually, by the time I finished, I was motivated to get a bite to eat and watch a movie coming on TCM. After feeding Kipp his large bowl of chopped chicken and rice, I took a bag of popcorn to the living room and plopped in my favorite chair just as the credits for "The Champ" began. It was the original 1930's version with Wallace Berry and Jackie Cooper, who had the serious face of a grown man even when he was just a little boy.

Kipp, in his quest to educate himself and better his condition, had actually learned to understand the English language and could read the printed word. If he had opposable thumbs, I'm quite sure he could have managed to write, too. His questions about the movie were endless, most of all his curiosity about alcoholism.

"I still don't get it, Petra. Why do people drink that stuff that makes them act goofy?" he finally asked.

I shrugged my shoulders. Experts had been working on that one for years and still managed to write books with multitudes of theories.

"Some people drink to numb themselves, Kipp," I finally replied. "Symbionts can do the same when emotions are too strong and painful."

"Like with baby George?" he asked, blinking his eyes at me.

I answered by nodding my head. The loss of my baby had been transformative, although I was thankful that Kipp had nudged me out of my place of total denial. Since Kipp had joined my life, we routinely visited the little granite headstone that marked George's last place on earth, where he rested on a quiet, bleak hillside surrounded by other departed souls.

The movie left me pensive and sad, and that was one emotion I didn't wish to visit. Quite honestly, our last time shift exposed me to vulnerabilities that I preferred would have stayed hidden, and I visibly stiffened my back and shoulders as I led the way to the bedroom. I was tired and wished to fall into a dreamless sleep, if that was what fate had in store for me. As I climbed into bed, Kipp hopped up, and, after circling in the manner of dogs and wolves, he lay down with a big lupine sigh, his muzzle stretched across my chest.

"If you start to dream about it again," Kipp said, "I'll take care of it for you."

My best friend and bonded symbiont could and had entered the part of my mind where dreams were created. Kipp could manipulate the outcome just as easily as he could enter the mind of a human or another symbiont and insert notions. But, I thought, it was time for me to move beyond my grief and loss over having left Harrow behind...he in his time, while I returned to mine.

"No, thanks, Kipp," I finally managed to say. "I don't need to hide out anymore."

The sounds from outside entered the room through the windows that I'd left slightly ajar. Crickets and what sounded like a chorus of bull frogs were singing in rhythm. I looked over to the window where I'd left the shutter open; there was a group of fireflies, flashing their tail lights as they sought to attract others of their kind.

"I like them," Kipp said, smiling in his thoughts. "They seem happy and, well, business-like."

"Me, too," I replied, yawning.

I'm not sure when I fell asleep, but I know my last thought was of the fireflies.

CHAPTER 2

"Do you think he'll show up?" I asked.

Kipp and I had slept in and, after a light breakfast, journeyed outside to do some serious work. The yard, which was narrow and deep, was cluttered with debris. Narrow trunked dogwoods crowded in amongst dark, looming oaks, and all were in need of light pruning; dead branches, lost in a previous storm, littered the ground. I glanced at the azaleas Kipp and I had planted, with a sentimental nod to the white one he'd put at the place where I'd buried my dear Tula's blanket. Kipp may have become my new partner, but Tula had been the first and would always be special. In Kipp's wonderful way, he understood that he didn't take her place but rather made one of his own.

I'd dragged a small stepladder to one tree that had been mercilessly ravaged by an unforgiving wind; several limbs were twisted and dead, although the tree itself had survived. With a small handsaw, I braced myself and began work. As each branch fell, Kipp would grab it in his jaws and drag it to the front of the yard where it could be picked up later. At one point, my human neighbor stuck his head over a bushy hedge and shouted out a hello to me.

"That's some dog you've got there!" he said with a

laugh. "How'd you train him to do that?"

As I created some lame excuse, I considered how amazed the man would be if he knew the reality of his neighbors. At some point, and I knew not when, Kipp and I would be reassigned and be compelled to move to another colony. There was only so long I could remain in a place without obvious aging and my existence playing human still be plausible. All symbionts knew this and understood, but it was still unwelcomed, at least for me. I liked my house and enjoyed living in the piedmont of North Carolina. The beach was in one direction, the mountains in the other; the climate was pleasant, and I especially enjoyed hiking in Duke Forest. And then there was my friendship with Philo and my evolving relationship with Fitzhugh to be considered.

Kipp's head went up and a moment later I recognized the thoughts of Philo. He must have just driven up and would be stalking around to the rear of my property at any moment. It was nice to recognize the familiar thoughts of Juno, an elderly lupine who served with him on the Technicorps governing board. Philo rounded the corner, head down, stalking with a long legged gait, dressed in his weekend garb of worn out jeans with one knee torn out and a NC State t-shirt that had seen better days. Knowing him as I did, I realized he preferred this to the suit he wore in his relatively new position as head of the Twelve.

"Can I help?" he asked. At my nod, he picked up some large clippers and began hacking savagely at some of the lower limbs with more energy than seemed necessary to complete the job. His shoulders were bunched with tension, his face turned away from me.

Juno lacked Kipp's youth and energy and didn't make an offer to assist; instead, she carefully folded her rear legs and, after rocking a little, finally eased down into the thick grass. Nagging arthritis was obvious in her stiff-legged gait and rigid neck movements.

We worked in relative silence for a while, only occasionally interrupting the quiet with a comment or observation about the yard, nature, or some stray story. As was appropriate behavior in contemporary symbiont society, neither Juno nor Philo intruded telepathically into our thoughts, even though they had the skills to do so. Kipp and I were a bit of an anomaly in that I allowed him complete access to my mind at all times, mimicking what was natural for us as a species before we over-civilized ourselves.

"Are you gonna feed me or what?" Philo finally asked, stopping to wipe his face with a frayed bandana that he produced from his pants pocket.

Kipp hovered over Juno, wishing he had hands that he could use to help her stand, but she managed quite nicely without his chivalrous assist and slowly made her way to the back door of my house. I followed and Philo made up the caboose of our symbiont train. The kitchen was a bit of a disaster; dishes from the night before were stacked in the sink. A basket of clean clothes from the dryer – unfolded and wadded into a mass—sat upon my kitchen table, which was an old dinette set rescued from a dusty, unvisited stall at an antique store. Shrugging, I removed the basket and gestured for Philo to sit.

"Kind of a mess around here," he said, making note of the obvious. He didn't have to be a telepath to read the thoughts I was having; my facial expression did the work that defied all use of verbal language.

"I'm having trouble getting back into the flow of things after my last time shift," I finally remarked, feeling too old to be evasive and too tired to play games.

Philo waited for me, patient and expectant. He was my most abrasive friend, the one who could deliver a thorough dressing down when I needed it most. We were as quarreling siblings, ones that would fight over a dropped cookie but then take on the world with our backs pressed together in solidarity. He was married, as I had been, and there was not a spark of romantic interest between us. He was like my big, nagging brother, and I loved him dearly.

"I've waited for you to talk about it," he began, his dark

eyes meeting mine. "I think you need to, Petra. Sitting on this is affecting your attitude," he said.

I looked first at Kipp, who returned my stare with his brilliant eyes; the dark fur surrounding them made me think of exotic, exaggerated eyeliner–sort of a Sophia Loren type of seductively slanted gaze but in a masculine, lupine face. Then I shifted to Juno who lay in a patch of sunlight that flowed through the back window to puddle like liquid gold on the kitchen floor. She thumped her tail in support and love. Yes, I thought, if I couldn't let go here, then it just wouldn't happen. And I wasn't so dense that I didn't realize that Philo was correct and my baggage would influence all I needed to do from here on out. I allowed myself to drift down into the opposing chair; tilting my head slightly, I met Philo's dark eyes.

"Go ahead," I said, offering an invitation.

His eyes opened wider. Although we symbionts shared thoughts in our telepathic way, there was typically no invasive inquiry or exploration. We'd evolved to think such a vulgar and unnecessary behavior. Only Kipp and I had the sort of openness that left no questions as to the heart and soul of the other. Philo bowed his head, and it was just a second later that I felt his tentative entry into my thoughts and memories. There was surprise as he struck the place where I kept my pain over Harrow, and I heard him sigh softly.

"Oh, Petra," he said, his voice low and quiet in my kitchen which was softly illuminated by the nagging sun. Reaching out, his hand sought mine across the table, its warmth capturing my flesh.

I was rather pleased that I didn't cry and managed a crooked, tremulous smile in response. Juno thumped her tail again and somehow that made me feel stronger. Aged lupine that she was, she'd been through her own episodes of love lost.

"Kipp knows, of course, and I somehow spilled the beans to Fitzhugh in an unguarded moment," I shared, twisting my mouth at the memory. My eyes rolled up as I recalled that moment. "He was actually quite sweet and supportive."

Fitzhugh, the keeper of our history as a species, had once funneled all his disapproval and agitation at me. In honesty, I must confess when I was younger, I was a reckless traveler, too cocky for my own good. Perhaps my own self-satisfaction at having matured came much too early, considering the emotional connections made during my last time shift. But oddly, Fitzhugh had become an ally of mine, working behind the scenes to support me and Kipp. And much to my dismay, when I was not travelling with Kipp, working with Fitzhugh had become my routine assignment. Living in the dark basement of Technicorps translating old manuscripts was not my dream job, but if I wanted to pay the water bill, I'd do what I was told. In the end, old Fitzhugh had grown on me.

"Grilled cheese," Philo suggested abruptly, "would be nice if you don't mind the bother." His head twisted as he surveyed the kitchen again, his lips compressing with some unexpressed emotion. "And iced tea, please."

He'd managed to shift gears; understanding my heart and mind, he knew I wouldn't want to continue to discuss the past. With a laugh of relief, I stood and began working on sandwiches for us all. Kipp and Juno, especially, enjoyed a gooey cheese sandwich toasted to perfection. As I cooked, Philo briefed me on some of the gossip at Technicorps.

"Suzanne fell for a guy who'd recently relocated here from a colony in Wales," Philo said as he picked up a potato chip to examine for imperfections before popping it into his mouth. "I thought they were going to get married, but then he started seeing someone else. Poor Suzanne's heart is broken, and she lacks that wonderful creative energy she normally puts into her work." He glanced at me. "Do you think I should force the issue and make her take some time off?"

"You aren't doing that for me, so no," I replied, trying to stare a hole through him.

Kipp rolled over on his back, satiated after his third

grilled cheese. With a yawn that exposed all of his teeth, he closed his eyes. I knew he didn't want to get pulled into my whine-fest over Philo's plan for us to become mentor-teachers.

"Well, we all know how tough you are, Petra," Philo remarked, lifting one dark eyebrow. Leaning forward, he pushed his plate out of the way and leaned his elbows on the table top that was marred by a past hot pot burn. The table predictably shifted due to uneven legs; leaning down, I replaced a folded up playing card under one foot and happily the table regained its balance. "We, and I mean all symbionts, need your help. We're in danger of losing the very skill sets that make us who we are." His voice was earnest. "Look at me…I can't travel and have never bonded as have you and Kipp. When we find someone who genetically can match up with another willing party, we must try. And the only reason I'm pushing you and Kipp is due to the age of this particular pair. You were older when you and Tula made your first time shift."

"Okay, Philo, I get it," I finally said, holding up my hands in mock surrender. "I understand the issues and will do my best." What other answer could I give? It did fall, in all cultures, for those of experience to bring along the young as meaningful members of the species.

"What on earth is taking you so long with that document?"

Fitzhugh's voice rang out unexpectedly loud in the echoing silence of the library. He, like all of us, had a home and eventually would leave as night fell, but I always had the impression he did so grudgingly. The dark green walls were an anomaly in a building that was exceedingly sterile with grayish walls and chrome furniture. Thankfully, Fitzhugh's antique desk from England brought its warm, organic presence to the room. The stacks were full of old manuscripts, some in various degrees of decline, hence the project to scan them, decipher the contents and share knowledge gained with others of our kind. Despite the ventilation in the room, which was adequate, there was a musty smell of decay thrown off by the myriad of papers contained in fragile binders. The welcomed fragrance of bergamot wafted beneath my nose as Fitzhugh carefully set an antique tea service on the table where I worked. Smiling, I happily turned off the bright light I was using. My eyes felt slightly hot and gritty after spending hours staring at a document written in an obscure French dialect.

"Where's Peter?" I asked, wondering where Fitzhugh's assistant–and my future apprentice–was hiding. It was well known the young symbiont did not care for the tedium of library and research work.

"Philo has given him reading to do and sent him and Elani to a room on the third floor. I pulled stories of time shifts for their perusal. Some were successful and by the book, you might say. Others were unmitigated disasters." Fitzhugh smiled at me.

"Are any of mine in the latter group?" I asked, watching as he poured the tea with a steady hand. Knowing my preferences by now, he added a generous dollop of local honey to the steaming brew.

"That is a secret I won't reveal," he replied, raising his thick eyebrows.

Fitzhugh and I had somehow, inexplicably, come to this place of comfort with one another. He was rigid, uncompromising, while I'd been known to cut more than one corner. But I'd found he had several surprisingly soft spots in his character. One of those came careening through the library as if conjured by my thoughts, crashing into a table leg before stopping to shake her head vigorously and zoom off in another direction. Lily, the little cat Kipp and I had found abandoned, was now Fitzhugh's treasured companion. He doted on the cat with an energy that almost seemed silly. And then there was his story of when he'd travelled–yes, old Fitzhugh had once taken on the perils of time shifts–and fallen in love with a human woman. All in all, I'd become very fond of him, despite the fact I'd once regarded him as meeting all the established criteria of a fussy old coot.

"Well, he has a way to go to prepare a pot of Earl Grey to rival yours," I said, tipping the edge of the fragile tea cup in salute towards the old historian.

He nodded in appreciation, his dark eyes almost lost in the folds of his eyelids. His hair, worn long, was almost completely white with only a few stubborn strands of silver threading through it. Fitzhugh still maintained a straight posture which only slumped on the occasion of extreme fatigue.

"Kipp and I are driving into Durham to pick up a pair of running shoes, and I thought we'd grab lunch. Wanna go?" I blurted out the invitation before I could stop myself.

His eyes opened wide as he stared at me; the expression on his face was comical. It must have been many years since he'd been asked out on a date.

"Why, yes," he finally replied, a smile creeping across his creased face. It was rare he was invited to join other symbionts' reindeer games due to his taciturn–and often unpleasant—manner.

I mentally summoned Kipp to wrap up his endeavors in the classroom where he was working with the young lupines. Not only did he teach ethics, but he also taught them how to read and comprehend English. At home, Kipp was currently plowing through Shelby Foote's enormously detailed Civil War trilogy. I was impressed that only occasionally would he have to ask me the meaning of a word or to explain the context of use.

With Fitzhugh in tow, I met Kipp, his plumed tail waving in the breeze, in the parking lot. Off to the west, the sky was darkening slightly, and predictions had been made for late summer storms that evening. A mild wind was beginning to kick up, dispersing the heat of the day. But it was not even noon, and I thought we'd be okay for an outside dining experience. With Kipp at my side, I was consigned to friendly establishments with tables in a courtyard or nestled up to the sidewalk.

My car was tiny, old and rarely used, since I preferred to walk to work. Kipp hopped in the back, insisting I roll down the window so he could hang his head, dog-like, out the aperture and angle it into the breeze. I slammed the door after Fitzhugh folded himself into the copilot seat, and we took off, my being careful to not accelerate in my usual carefree manner. At least I didn't drive like Philo, who was legendary for a style of driving that left his passengers with whiplash and bad memories.

We spoke little on the trip; occasionally, I would catch Kipp meeting my eyes in the rear-view mirror as he would toss a humorous thought my way. Kipp's ability to communicate telepathically with me unbeknownst to other symbionts had come in quite handy on more than one occasion. Kipp's other unusual talents–like thought blocking and the ability to insert thoughts into the mind of another symbiont or human–were only known to a select few in the collective. To date, the only ones in our group who knew his secrets were Philo, Juno, Fitzhugh and me. We'd thought his ability to enter and manipulate dreams was unique to him, but I'd found I shared this skill and suspected others could, too, if they only made the attempt. At some point when we felt confident enough to share with other symbionts, that information would be made public. But, as we well know, despite our collective wish as a species to do good, there are those among us who are corrupt and filled with avarice and greed. Notions that could change the trajectory of our species needed to be handled with care.

After picking up my shoes, I drove to a small café that served some of my favorite Middle Eastern fare, and we selected a small table on the patio where Kipp could lie unobtrusively. I was a vegetarian by choice but often had to eat meat and other things I don't like to recall in order to survive in harsh times. The stiff corn planks from the early American colony we visited during a time shift still left a bad taste in my mouth. And there was the rancid boiled fish stew that was just shy of qualifying as spoiled…I forced my mind elsewhere.

The waiter brought me a salad topped with feta cheese

and a side of hummus dip and pita bread. I'd ordered a plate of chicken kabobs–without the stick and minus vegetables–which I presented to a delighted Kipp. Fitzhugh ordered the kabobs, too, and we ate in silence, our thoughts curiously unoccupied for the moment. Kipp, curious, sniffed of the humus only to wrinkle his nose in disdain.

"Who is Philo gonna get to replace Peter if he really follows through with this nonsense of him becoming a traveler?" I asked.

Fitzhugh shrugged his shoulders and stared out across the street. The sidewalks were crowded; lunchtime brought people hurrying during their brief window of freedom to get business done or grab a bite to eat. A young couple breezed past, their fingers entwined in a love connection; the backpacks on their backs were full of school paraphernalia, their minds filled with hopes and dreams of a bright future. In contrast to their cheerful optimism, the darkening clouds from the west were pushing our way, and I realized we needed to wrap up our party soon.

"He hasn't said," the old symbiont replied. Cocking his head, he offered, "I know you are skeptical of Peter, and believe me, I understand that. But Petra, he has shown a lot of maturity, I think. You realize that much of the problem I have with his lack of motivation is that he hates the job in the library. It is tedious and boring to him due to his youth. He wants to experience life, not read about it."

His words rang true with me. I looked down at Kipp, who dropped his lower jaw in his manner of smiling. The thoughts of my partner drifted upward. Had it not been so with me, also? My earlier years were defined by notions that were rambunctious, to say the least. And even though I bridled at being made to work in the research section with Fitzhugh, I handled it better now than if I'd been, say, one hundred years of age.

"Let's go," I said, standing abruptly. "Those clouds are moving on in, and I want to get Kipp home before the deluge. You know what wet dog smells like," I added, just to provoke my partner.

"Ha, ha," he replied, giving me a rather powerful nip on the back of my leg. "And I know where you live and when you sleep," he replied, the tone of his thoughts darkly ominous.

CHAPTER 3

"I want you and Kipp to start spending time with Peter and Elani," Philo said, sitting across from me from behind his desk, which was cluttered with papers, folders, unopened mail and pens scattered like toothpicks tossed from an upended container.

"Why do you have so many pens?" I asked, truly curious, daring a peek into the mind of an office supply hoarder.

He frowned and began to gather them together as if he was herding cats. After a few seconds, he plopped them loudly into a coffee mug that I could only hope was empty of liquid. Summer had passed, and September was drawing to an uneventful close.

Philo went on to explain that the Twelve wanted me and Kipp to take small trips with Peter and Elani, removing them from the collective. The tutoring of novices was usually conducted in such a manner. Even with our policy of not interfering with the thoughts of other symbionts, being in the midst of so many busy symbiont minds posed a challenge to achieve focus and discipline. Peter and Elani needed to develop the ability to be completely in tune with one another despite all outside interference.

"They are on their way up here for us to talk. We've rented a large SUV and have reservations for you on the coast in Roanoke," he said. "When you get back, we'll arrange another excursion, this time to Chattanooga."

"Separate rooms, I hope," I said, raising my eyebrows.

Philo's face assumed that patient expression he wore when he knew I was being deliberately obtuse. Kipp curtailed our game by stepping in and posing the practical question.

"Why Chattanooga?" Kipp asked, curious but not confrontational.

"Peter, like you, Petra, has an interest in the American Civil War, and there are two battlefields there. We just thought it would make for a good setting for walking, exploring, and allowing them time to mature." He paused before adding again and unnecessarily, "They are on their way up here now."

At that moment, there was a polite tap on the door. At Philo's gruff reply, the door slowly opened to reveal Peter and Elani, both of whom I'd not seen for quite some time. Peter, in the guise of promising traveler, looked different somehow. Freed from the confines of the dark library, he seemed much more relaxed and actually exuded a gentle self confidence—not cocky, but a pleasant level of self assuredness. He wasn't as tall as Philo but was somewhere over average, with a slender build. Peter's dark hair was thick with a forelock that begged taming like that of a fractious pony. It occurred to me, as it had on my last leaving party, that he was an attractive young man. I hoped he'd put plans for a family, anytime soon, behind him for the time being. He was just under fifty years of age–a baby, really–and I could only suppose he finally told his domineering mother that he planned on following his heart and another direction.

Elani, on the other hand, was a totally feminine lupine, beautiful to the extreme, with thick gray fur interrupted by blonde long hairs interwoven throughout to give her a shimmering, almost ethereal appearance. She carried her head high and walked with delicate steps that were wolf-like in their soft and careful placement. I knew her to be bright, since she had been Kipp's stellar pupil in English class, but there was the nagging issue of her undying attraction for my partner. I could feel his tension as she entered the room, but it was something he'd have to manage.

"Petra," Peter said, walking forward to greet me with a formal handshake that seemed kind of funny, considering we knew each other from the library. I stood, however, and allowed him his display of courtesy, knowing he wanted to project a picture of maturity.

I think, looking back, that moment, carefully crafted by Philo, was important. Peter and I needed to reset our relationship as well as did Kipp and Elani. I was no longer a fellow researcher, stealing comical glances at Peter behind Fitzhugh's back when the old symbiont would utter some silly nonsense based upon an unbending and subjective set of rules. And Kipp was not the English teacher facing an eager class of fresh-faced lupines. We had, the four of us, become collaborators and team members. Peter and Elani would have to trust us completely as would we they.

Elani, for her part, moved forward tentatively, touching noses with Kipp, who stood upon her approach. With only a fleeting eye contact having been made, the two lupines circled, trampling an imaginary bed of sticks and leaves, before thumping down on the industrial carpet flooring, a polite distance between the two.

Kipp, unheard by the others, addressed me. "Petra, this is pretty uncomfortable." He rolled his expressive eyes slightly in their sockets. "I did have a talk with Elani and set the notion that we are professional collaborators and nothing else." He looked at her from the corners of his eyes. "I'm not sure she's okay yet."

"Well, she still thinks you are as cute as a button, so there's work still to be done." I couldn't help but gently tease him, given his anxiety.

I wrapped up a few business issues, and at week's end, we were ready to go. The weather remained nice as we entered October. The trees were still clad in green with only a lover's promise of beautiful things to come. Peter, to maximize efficiency, picked us up at my house; I sat in the front with him and suggested the original route that Kipp and I had taken to try and capture the feel of the area that once comprised Land's Point Colony. Philo suggested that as a starting place since Kipp and I had such strong associations to the location where we engaged in our first fact finding trip as a duo. Peter proved to be a surprisingly skillful driver and moved the vehicle along at a brisk pace, occasionally letting the speedometer edge up past the speed limit before catching himself. Looking over at me, he grinned.

"I tend to have a heavy foot," he said, laughing. "Usually someone fusses at me to slow down; I'm glad you haven't."

"Well, not yet," I replied, returning the smile. "Can I ask you something?" At his nod, I continued. "I thought your mother wouldn't give approval for you to become a traveler. How did you manage this?"

He was staring at the road ahead as a slight flush stained his neck. After a long pause, he glanced over at me; the expression in his dark eyes was intense and unreadable. "I told her and all my family that it was my life and I would make my own choices." He shrugged and turned his attention back to the road. "I don't think any of them were very happy."

I had no reply for his words and decided to gaze out the window at the scenery. It was seldom I got to the coast and always enjoyed the thrill of seeing the ocean…powerful, seemingly endless, and filled with dark unknowns. There was an ominous bank of scudding, anxious clouds gathering on the horizon, but I thought we could make it to the motel where we had reservations before the weather broke. Philo booked a couple of rooms at a place as near to the original site of the old colony as possible.

We arrived as the first raindrops started to patter on the windshield; I waited outside in the car with Kipp and Elani while Peter raced to the lobby. Of course, Philo found a place where pets were welcomed. For a moment, it seemed kind of furtive, like something a couple of kids might do to sneak away for a tryst. The window of the lobby had a slight, dewy mist on it; Peter, as he hunched over the desk to sign the register, appeared faded and slightly unreal. I shook my head to rid myself of the image and glanced over my shoulder to see Kipp staring back at me, his face unreadable. His mind, however, was active and audible just for my ears.

"What on earth are you doing?" he asked, his amber eyes opening wider.

I gave a start, embarrassed at having been caught thinking of such silliness. It quite frankly reminded me of my honeymoon with my husband and our first stop at a slightly run-down little hotel on the outskirts of Ashville. As I had waited in the car, excitement washed over me as I stared down at the plain gold band on my left hand. Being married was a big step for a contented loner, and the prospect of a future and family lay ahead. Closing my eyes, I shut away the memories. That part of my life was long distant and only served as a preamble to that which would follow and my dedication to traveling, my bond first with Tula and now Kipp. I shook my head at Kipp, unable to coherently give voice telepathically to all that came to me in a sudden rush of loosely connected and cascading thoughts. But in the wonderful manner of Kipp, he just understood and reached out with his mind to give me the love I needed. Then he closed an eye, winking at me, so that Elani could not see. Yes, it was our secret.

The wind was beginning to pick up, and I could only hope this patch of bad weather would blow through tonight. The idea of being stuck at a motel for a couple of days with Peter made me uneasy. I really didn't know him…and as that notion struck me, I realized that was the entire focus of this trip. All four of us had to move beyond polite boundaries; it had been so with me and Tula as we were taught the rules of the road, so to speak.

"Let's order pizza," I suggested as he jumped back in the car while trying to dodge the large rain drops banging on the hood of the vehicle, "and play Monopoly."

"You brought a Monopoly set?" Peter asked, trying not to laugh.

"Yes, a vintage one with the original tokens, thank you very much. And I want the top hat," I said, laying claim.

Three hours later, the remnants of two large cheese pizzas were cooling in the box and Kipp was just about to put hotels on Boardwalk and Park Place, courtesy of my humanoid fingers. Kipp's nose was useful for pushing his token, but he could neither handle money nor place a house or hotel on property. His audacious cannon had pretty much blown the rest of us to bits. Peter's hapless shoe managed a small landholding on Baltic and Mediterranean, while Elani's ship steamed its way to control the four railroads, much like J.P. Morgan in his attempt to control the world. My top hat had acquired next to nothing, and I had twenty-three dollars left with all properties mortgaged. We were huddled on the floor to accommodate the lupines and three hours of a bent posture left me sore with a completely numb butt. With a sigh, I stood and arched my back, trying to get my spinal column realigned.

"I surrender," I said, holding up my hands. "It's obvious Kipp has won this round."

Kipp looked up at me, his eyes bright, plumed tail wagging in a question mark over his back. He was not, by nature, excessively competitive, and I realized his joy at having won was diminished by the fact he had to beat me to do it. There was a loving aspect to it that warmed my heart. Peter began to carefully pick up the money, assembling it into neat stacks of matching denominations. I got the sense he wanted to ask something but was hesitating for some reason. Elani, however, with the sensibility of a well-matched lupine, framed the issue for them both.

"Tell us what to expect tomorrow, Petra," she requested, her soft brown eyes taking on a pretty glow of excitement.

The allure she might have for a male of the species was clearly apparent.

The motel was quiet, with only the distant sound of someone's television tuned to a movie. The rain had passed, and all that lingered was the dripping of residual water from the gutters as it gurgled out into the parking lot. A heavy layer of clouds blacked out stars and moon, leaving the landscape in utter darkness, except for the harsh neon sign that advertised the motel. I felt comfortable and relaxed in my room, even with the foreign presence of Peter and Elani.

"I'm learning as we go, Elani," I finally admitted with more honesty than she might have wished for. "The best thing to do, from my way of thinking, is to teach you the way I was taught."

Later, after we'd gone to bed, Kipp was still and his thoughts were quiet that night, as if he knew I did not need distractions. He rested his massive head across my chest and heaved that deep, shuddering sigh of a big dog. "I wonder if Peter and Elani sleep like us, close together, their thoughts tangled to the point of complete connectedness?" Kipp raised his head for a second, looking at me. "I'm not sure how we help them learn, Petra."

I rubbed the soft furry top knot on his head as I considered his words. In my thoughts, I urged him to turn off his busy mind, for a while, and let sleep overtake him, which it did. I lay awake, for some time after. When Kipp began to dream, I followed his dreams from start to finish, sharing in his excitement as he chased a fleeing rabbit across a thick field of tall grass. He never caught the rabbit but the pleasure in surrendering to the primal side of his nature was evident. As a civilized lupine, he kept the primitive urges under wraps.

The next morning after a light breakfast, we set out for the general area where Land's Point Colony had once stood. The area was relatively clear now, not actually at the water's edge, but close enough that if the wind was right, you could smell the salt air and feel the sting on your face from an ocean breeze. Once, centuries ago, old growth forests had covered the area; many trees twisted and fell through generations of hurricanes and gale force winds blowing in off the Atlantic. After Peter parked the SUV, the four of us walked to the area where Kipp and I had braved our first time shift to investigate a historical mystery. Kipp proceeded to a grassy knoll and raised his head, sniffing at the air. His eyes closed with the memories that seemed to haunt the landscape.

"It's almost as if the imprints of those people are here," he finally remarked. "They are vague shadows, something that moves with the wind…almost like ghosts."

It was at that moment I had a visceral understanding of why Philo had chosen this particular place for Peter and Elani's first lesson. Kipp and I had such a strong connection to the landscape and aura that we would naturally lead our apprentice team in a time shift. I, too, could sense the apparitions that Kipp described. Odd, I'd never really paid attention to such things until that moment.

Peter glanced at me, and I wondered what he was thinking. My relationship with Kipp had caused me to question the fact that we telepaths blocked ourselves so as to not intrude on each other's private thoughts; that behavior had evolved out of a need for civility with one another. Did Peter see a reasonably attractive female–one old enough to be his mother—with dark hair, hazel eyes, and a chaotic pattern of freckles splashed across a prominent nose? Harrow had liked my nose and the imperfection it gave to my face; a conventional beauty I was not by any means. Did Peter trust Kipp and me to be competent teachers? I wasn't sure I trusted myself. Unconsciously, my fingers reached for the dainty strand of pearls that were hidden beneath my collar.

"You know you can do this," Kipp said to me in our manner of private dialog as we stood on that quiet, deserted piece of land. Kipp would forever be my main cheerleader and tireless promoter.

I turned into the breeze and felt my hair flutter gently

around my face; although we were not on the beach and the sea was at a distance to be unseen, I could taste the salt in the air as it rested on my lips. Inhaling, I fancied I could smell the rich organic odor of the ocean with all its teeming life and death. Yes, Kipp was right. I needed to trust myself. Rolling my shoulders slightly, I stretched my neck which had acquired a decided crick after the rigors of the Monopoly tournament. Sitting on the motel room floor for hours hunched over a game board had not improved my posture or my humor.

"Kipp and I will guide you," I began, squaring my shoulders. "I want you to telepathically connect with us and simply follow us with your mind, just as you followed us from the car to this place," I said, pointing at the grass. "Kipp has a very powerful aura and will be like a searchlight in the dark."

"Is that how you did your first time shift?" Elani asked. Her thick tail was caught in the wind like a kite about to take flight. The air ruffled her dense, gray-blonde coat backwards, revealing silver tipped fur that captured the light like little sparks of fire. I liked the fact she was confident and eager but not cocky.

"Yes, just like this," I replied, reaching forward to give her a friendly caress on her head. She had a funny little point on the top of her noggin like an ordinary hound might have. Kipp's head, in contrast, was rounded in a soft, curving arc. Bending my knees, I sat on the grass, thankful that despite the early hour, the surface was relatively dry. We had not bothered with vintage clothing since our goal was to make a time shift and return almost immediately.

Relaxing, I decided to lie back in the grass, and Kipp nudged forward, putting his head across my chest. We usually assumed such a posture when preparing to journey. Peter, after gazing at us for a moment, copied our stance; Elani curled up close to him, her muzzle stretched up on his shoulder. I watched as his hand drifted up to touch her fur, his fingers tunneling into her pelt in a gentle caress. Yes, their bond was palpable and distinct.

Kipp and I began to concentrate on the Land's Point Colony…the time, place, topography, culture of the day and anything at all that would guide us. With Kipp's superior talents, I let him reach out a helping paw, so to speak, to Peter and Elani, given their youth and inexperience. The moment was exciting, despite the fact I'd done this many, many times before. It was as if we backed off a diving board into a black void, our bodies jack-knifing with grace and power as we folded ourselves into the distant past.

A time shift leaves one slightly disoriented for a moment, and this experience was no exception. And one could never predict the manner of landing. Mine were usually gentle, and I would open my eyes to find myself sitting or lying in a relatively comfortable position. But my last one had been rough, and this one was, too. I was lying on my left arm and had somehow twisted my shoulder and arm upon landing. As I sat up, the pain almost made me nauseous.

"Petra, are you okay?" Kipp's anxious thoughts pushed the pain from my head for a moment. His big, wet nose touched my cheek before beginning a tentative exploration of my shoulder.

My vision cleared, and I was gratified to see Peter and Elani, about two yards away from us, sitting in a patch of overgrown weeds, blinking their eyes in confusion. Peter looked up at me, and after a moment struggling for recognition, a huge grin split his face.

"This is neat!" he exclaimed, before I shushed him to keep his voice low. We had no idea if people were in close proximity.

"Petra's hurt," Kipp announced, more focused on me than anything else.

Peter, with his youth and energy, jumped to his feet and approached, reaching down a hand to assist me to my feet. Days like that made me feel older than my actual years.

"Just landed hard," I said gruffly, not caring for the attention. Privately, I thought I might have to make a little urgent care visit when we returned to modern times. My rebellious left wrist didn't seem to want to cooperate with the nagging instructions from my brain.

At my urging, Peter and Elani walked a short distance to evaluate our surroundings. We were, as Kipp and I had been before, in the midst of an ancient woods, surrounded by a dark, thick forest that would sadly disappear with the advancement of civilization. Many of the trees were down, torn up by the roots when Nature had a tantrum, and the rotting vegetation on the ground led to a fertile and active growth of young trees, shrubs and wild undergrowth. The goal was not to search out any human habitation but just to make this trip and return home successfully.

"Can you pick up human thoughts?" I asked Kipp, knowing that I didn't.

"No, not yet," he replied.

"Well, good. We don't want to run into anyone," I mumbled with relief.

Peter and Elani returned; his face was flushed with excitement. Elani's head was up as she used her superior nose to canvass the territory, taking in all that she could. Vaguely I recalled my first time shift; indeed, it was one of the most memorable experiences of my life. I was glad that this had gone well. History told of bad first time shifts that left a novice pair unwilling to try again.

"I think we need to get back," Kipp remarked, sniffing delicately at my wrist. "I can smell blood and fluid pooling under the skin, and you need to get this checked," he added.

I lay back, willing to let my better half give me orders and boss me completely. What is the good of a symbiotic partner if you don't allow him to tell you what to do some of the time? Kipp stretched his muzzle on my breastbone, twisting his head slightly so his eyes met mine. As always, a surge of love and trust flowed between us, and I felt my eyes begin to water with emotion. A short distance away, Peter and Elani copied our posture, and it was as if we were backing out of a parking spot as we reversed what we had just accomplished.

Our first time shift–Kipp and I as teachers and Peter and Elani as novices–was complete.

CHAPTER 4

"So how did this happen?" Fitzhugh asked, gazing down his long nose at the aircast splint on my left wrist.

"Hard landing," I muttered, not meeting his eyes.

"Maybe you are getting to old for this nonsense," he remarked, pouring me a cup of Earl Grey.

The tea service, like Fitzhugh, was antique and deceptively fragile. The cups were fine china, eggshell thin to the point of translucency. I'd always feared I would drop one and watch, horrified, as it smashed into a thousand pieces. My relationship with Fitzhugh had aged like a fine wine, mellowing over the years. Once he had targeted me for unending harassment, maintaining a posture of disapproval for pretty much anything I did. But finally it clicked with him that I was a serious symbiont; perhaps my relationship with Kipp had matured me. Yes, as I thought on it, the responsibility of taking on Kipp as my partner was a sobering experience. He was a unique being, innocent and untrained when I met him, and it was placed in my hands the responsibility to mold him in an ethical manner while preserving his natural talents. I'd not wanted the job, but Kipp attached himself to me and would not partner with any other.

"I had a hard landing once," Fitzhugh commented with a sigh as he sat back in his chair. After blowing gently on the rim of the tea cup, he gingerly took a sip. The steam was rising off the brew like fog off of a chilled lake caught in the unexpected glow of a morning sun. "It was during a trip to ancient Troy, and somehow Lydea and I ended up in a trash pit outside of the city along with the refuse and other unmentionable things." Closing his eyes, he shook his head. "I still shudder to think of it."

I had to laugh. At that moment, Lily the Terrible decided to make her feline presence known and jumped up in my lap, uninvited in the way that cats behave. She was a little tiger striped beauty with an utterly beguiling feminine face. As I scratched her chin, she gazed up at me, blinking her eyes as she delivered a silent kitty kiss. Before the welcomed tea break, I'd been working on a manuscript translation. Although my primary focus was to work with Peter and Elani, there was a planned brief pause following our return from the coast. All in all, the first time shift for the novice pair had been successful, and they passed the most critical test in that they chose to go on and make another attempt.

"What is your next excursion?" Fitzhugh asked.

As I looked over at him, I recognized, with mild surprise, the nature of my current relationship with the old symbiont. It seemed odd that I would feel tenderness and grudging affection for the grumpy old symbiont who typically held all at arm's length. Despite his rigid view of symbiont ethics and life in general, he quietly held more than a few secrets involving Kipp and me and had become a valued advisor.

"Philo wants us to go to the Chattanooga area and spend a few days." I made a face. "Both Peter and I have an interest in the American Civil War, so he thought we could check out the Chickamauga battlefield as well as Lookout Mountain." I sighed and carefully set down the teacup, making certain the amber contents didn't slop over onto the table top. "We will try another time shift, maybe to that period, but for no other purpose than to make the trip and back."

"Peter is showing great maturity," Fitzhugh replied, his dark eyes showing evidence of fatigue.

It had not been that long since he suffered a mild heart attack, and I had to exert self control to not hover and become bossy with him. He was too old and stubborn to permit such a thing, but any reasonable being would recognize he'd had a long day and it was time to rest. Knowing he was not reading my thoughts, I stood and stretched, wincing slightly as the movement put pressure on my sprained wrist.

"I'm tired and think I want to call it a day," I announced, feeling pleased with my cleverness.

"No you're not," he replied, his mouth turning down in a frown. "You just believe I need to take it easy, being the fragile old fossil that I am."

As I sat there inhaling the scent of the musty documents that crowded the stacks while considering my next move, the door opened and in walked Peter. It struck me again what a fine looking young fellow he was, as well as the fact he was easily young enough to be my son or even grandson. The latter thought made me shake my head in wonder and disbelief. On that particular day, he was wearing a stylish turtleneck sweater beneath a tweed jacket; the texture of the tweed was tantalizing, and I forced myself to not reach out for a sample touch. The combo made him look urbane and suave, and his dark hair, which had the tendency to fall carelessly across his forehead, had been tamed for the moment and was brushed clear of his eyes.

"I thought I'd barge in and grab some tea…that is, if you don't mind," Peter said, looking at Fitzhugh.

"Not at all," the old symbiont replied, nodding his head. "Would you make a fresh pot?" he asked, pointing at the now cold tea service.

Peter laughed, somewhat good naturedly I thought, considering his past grumblings over toting and fetching at the command of Fitzhugh. Carefully lifting the tray, he disappeared to the small kitchen in the rear. A moment later, the door to the library opened again, and Kipp appeared, looking relaxed despite his day of working with the young lupines. He walked over to greet Lily, who boxed his nose with sheathed claws. He was her surrogate mother, and even though she'd not lived with us for some time, she never forgot him and was most happy when curled between his forelegs, her feline arms stretched around his massive neck. Kipp circled and lay on the floor; Lily immediately staked out a place on his back, resting at the base of his neck along his curving spine, her wedge of a face peeking out from between his large ears. Kipp looked at me and sighed softly as he blinked his eyes. He didn't even need to send me any thoughts at all.

Peter returned with the tea service, having added an extra cup for himself. I noticed he thoughtfully refilled the little honey pot, knowing that was a particular vice of mine. He offered for me to pour, a talent I'd never mastered despite having to attempt it so many times over my lifetime. I shook my head, politely declining. We sat, the four of us and Lily, enjoying the stillness. Apparently, a storm had kicked up outside, and we could hear the rumbling of thunder as well as the occasional crack of lightening that seemed to send a tremor through the building. I glanced at Kipp and knew he had the same thought as did I we had walked to work that morning and would have to hang around until the storm passed or beg a ride.

"I can drive you and Kipp home," Peter offered, his face innocent, eyebrows raised on a smooth forehead.

I gave a start, wondering, just for a moment, if he had been able to somehow read my thoughts without my knowing he had done so. But I knew that only Kipp could manage such a feat, and if Peter was that evolved, perhaps he needed to fast track to another line of work. I glanced at Kipp who gave an imperceptible shake of his head. No, it seemed Peter was just being thoughtful. Telling Peter that I appreciated his gesture, I ignored the glance from Fitzhugh which was provocative, to say the least, and delicately sipped at my tea. We filled the time with pleasant chit chat and sharing our brief time shift with a curious Fitzhugh, who had not yet received the formal, documented report that he would add to the collective history of our species.

"I think the main objective, Peter, is to not be afraid of making some mistakes at first," Fitzhugh said, leaning forward to turn off a bright light that illuminated my work space. It was much more pleasant to chat in the dimness of the room.

I nearly fell out of my chair to hear such words come out of the old symbiont's mouth. From my recollection, every mistake I'd ever made was highlighted in large red letters just as if my elementary school teacher graded a poor paper with a big "F" and sent it home to a disapproving parent. After Fitzhugh had spent years on my back about one thing or the other, he was giving Peter a generous, unequivocal pass. Well, I knew he'd mellowed over the years, ending most recently with his comment that if he was younger and still in the market for a companion, he would try to court me! I tried to not shake my head at that amazing recollection.

Fitzhugh was apparently in a fine mood, because he offered to share some of my colossal blunders with Peter, just to help the young one gain confidence that certainly he wouldn't do anything that stupid! At one point, I rolled my eyes and was caught by Fitzhugh in mid-roll. He smiled broadly, a rare event.

"I think Kipp and I are ready, Peter," I said, standing, eager to get him away from Fitzhugh before any more of my secrets were spilled. While he took the tea service to the back to rinse out the cups, I stared a hole through Fitzhugh.

"Thanks for helping me to look even more incompetent than before," I hissed, keeping my voice low.

"You know I was just kidding," he replied, trying not to laugh.

I glanced at Kipp, who had rolled onto his back, his mouth dropped open in the well known lupine laugh. Yes, all were having a gay old time.

Peter returned and, with the courtesy of an old gentleman, offered me his elbow. I was a little surprised at the antique display of gentility but nodded and hooked my arm in his. It did seem a little strange that Peter and I would walk thus, arm in arm. Kipp hopped up and trotted after us, his mind curiously shielded from mine. Whatever was going on in his big noggin was privy only to him.

"You can keep your precious secrets," I growled at him in my thoughts.

"Uh hum," he replied smugly.

Since Peter and Elani had bonded, they resided together just as did Kipp and I. Peter had an apartment somewhere in Chapel Hill, one that allowed pets. He brought the car around so that the rest of us wouldn't have to get wet; Kipp and Elani hopped in the back while I took the seat next to Peter. My house was a couple of miles away, and it only took us a few minutes, considering the speed limits. Peter had been to my house at my leaving party before we departed for Whitechapel, so directions were not needed. With care, he pulled close to the curb.

"Wait," he said, stopping me as I reached to open the door. "I've wanted to talk to you."

Oops, I thought. Perhaps I should have looked for another ride home. My mind darted to Kipp, but he was still closed to me except to project the image of a large question mark. Funny guy, I thought.

"I want to tell you how I arrived at my decision of wanting to travel," Peter said.

The rain began to fall again in earnest. Not really in the mood to get soaked and also not wishing to be totally rude and dismissive of Peter, I relaxed. This wasn't so bad, sitting in the darkness of the car with the hypnotic sound of raindrops pinging as they struck the metal of the vehicle. The seats in the back of the small car had been laid flat; Kipp and Elani were stretched out, and I could hear their soft breathing, the warmth tickling the back of my neck as the lupines exhaled.

"My maternal grandfather was a noted traveler," Peter

began. "He specialized in ancient Egypt and was proficient in facts and details about more than one dynasty." He took a deep breath as he stared out the softly fogged windshield. "One time, he and his symbiont did not return." Peter half turned towards me, his brown eyes soft but guarded and unreadable. "The episode devastated my mother, which is the main reason she doesn't want me to travel. She never got over his disappearance and has worried the same would happen to me." Sighing, he added, "She pretty much told me if I chose this path that I would go it alone." Peter was a young man, and this was his first definitive break from his nuclear family. That sort of thing was hard for symbionts, as well as humans.

"Tell me more about your amazing grandfather," I requested, settling myself more comfortably in the bucket seat. The query was not made out of sheer politeness; I was genuinely interested. After all, I was a historian and the pursuit of information was my profession.

Peter continued to ramble on for an hour, sharing some of his grandfather's exploits. Once he began, I recognized the man from our recorded history, and he had, indeed, added much to our species. He had been a bold and intrepid traveler and once even served as an adviser to a pharaoh–Sneferu, from the fourth dynasty—no easy task for an outsider.

"Peter, I was sent to a prehistoric tundra where I lived with a primitive tribe for a couple of years. My symbiont, Tula, was killed defending me." Kipp crawled forward and stuck his cool, wet nose on the back of my neck; his tongue darted out to touch my skin, a little reminder that he wasn't going anywhere. In reply, I reached back to gently massage beneath his chin where the hairs had lost their silky feel and felt like the bristles on an old man's face.

"Kipp appeared and became a part of my life, so much so, I almost don't remember times before he arrived." I curved my hand so that I could scratch Kipp's head and felt him turn into the caress. Whereever he'd been hiding, telepathically speaking, he returned with a vengeance and all his thoughts, love, and connectedness returned in a rush like surging flood waters.

"You can play life safe and still face tragedy, loss, and disappointment. Or, you can use your God given talents and benefit yourself, your species, and hopefully humanity." There, I'd preached about all I could on that particular night. But as Peter drove off, his taillights winking in the darkness, I felt some measure of satisfaction.

"Good speech," Kipp said, pushing his head under my hand so I'd scratch his ears.

"Yeah, I thought so," I replied, opening the front door.

Kipp ran ahead to the kitchen, almost dancing as he waited for dinner, which was served later than usual. While he bolted down his food, I poured a bowl of Cheerios, too tired and unmotivated to fix anything more substantial.

"Why've you been so distant?" I finally asked, giving voice to what had bothered me all day.

He finished his food, and after sniffing carefully at the bowl to make certain he'd missed nothing, he circled once and lay down on the floor. Almost delicately, he began to lick his paws. "I haven't meant to be distant," he finally replied. Kipp turned his amber eyes up at me. "It's just the proximity to Elani that's a concern. She has accepted my rejection of her, uh, attentions, but it's hurt her heart." Kipp's eyes rounded. "I wouldn't hurt a kid like that for anything, Petra. It makes me feel bad."

I didn't know whether to laugh or cry at my thoughtful friend's dilemma. So, instead, I sat next to him on the floor, my legs crossed so that I sat with my elbows on my knees. "Kipp, you are so gentle and kind that I know you let her down easily. But it's always disappointing to be rejected."

"Has it happened to you?" Kipp lifted his head up and opened his eyes wider.

"Oh, yeah, and it still burns a little down deep."

That night, we both slept well. Kipp snuggled close, his head across my chest, my fingers tangled mindlessly in his fur. Outside, the storm increased in intensity; the winds moaned as they wove through the trees, causing the north side of my house to creak in protest. The thunder rumbled, causing a pretty little antique tray of amber glass to dance on the dresser top. But in my house, with Kipp by my side, I was safe, warm and loved. And that was more than enough.

CHAPTER 5

A cabin in the vicinity of Gatlinburg was made available to us as well as reservations for two hotel rooms in Chattanooga. Of course, a drive to Chattanooga from the North Carolina piedmont could easily be accomplished in a day, but I felt no need to hurry. After the late evening chat with Peter in the snug security of his car while the falling rain pooled like liquid mercury on the hood, I was convinced that ample bonding time for us four, as a team, was probably not a bad idea. The fact that Peter and Elani's first time shift had gone smoothly was a positive and indicated promise for their future adventures. Philo, as usual, would take care of all my business while I was gone. He had done this for years and probably knew my account information and bills better than did I. Having bid him, dear Juno and crusty Fitzhugh good bye, I waited at home for Peter.

With a last walk through my house, I checked the dryer since I was notorious for forgetting to retrieve that last load only to have to deal later with a hopelessly wrinkled mass. My typical solution was to spin it again, watching anxiously while hoping a few extra minutes would do the trick. Thankfully, the dryer was empty, and my sink was clear of dirty dishes. Kipp padded softly behind me, his stealth remarkable considering his bulk. His toenails, however, clicked on the worn wooden floors, a soothing tonic to my soul.

"It'll be okay, Petra. As much as I've worried about so much time spent with Elani, she is acting very mature." Kipp nuzzled my hand. I wondered if he was comforting me or was I, him?

I smiled mentally and projected a funny picture in my mind that Kipp immediately sought out. He did the same, and we played our telepathic mind game of silly tag, back and forth, using up the time until Peter arrived. Pausing, I glanced out my back window, the one in my kitchen, and marveled at the rapid change of the autumn leaves that year. The sun shone through the canopy of oaks, which had turned butter yellow; to the left was a lonely, perfectly shaped maple that seemed as if it was on fire, with blazes of brilliant orange red color overwhelming all the other trees. Just then, there was a mental tingle in the back of my mind, and I knew Peter was close by, probably pulling up at the curb.

With my duffle in one hand, I ushered Kipp out the front door. A surge of cool air hit both of us; I was grateful I'd packed a warmer jacket since it would be even colder in the mountains. I'd suggested, since Technicorps was insisting we travel, that we take a scenic route across North Carolina to Cherokee before picking up 441 that crossed over the peaks into the Great Smokey Mountains Park. It would be a lovely drive, and I was grateful we didn't have to compete with all the other nature lovers for a place to stay. The cabin, owned by Technicorps, was available and waiting. Taking my seat next to Peter, I smiled as he pulled out into the street. He was wearing a thick sweatshirt and a fleece vest, looking the part of an adventurer in search of a holiday.

"We can take turns driving," I offered, not wanting him to think I was just along for my wonderful company or scintillating wit.

"Oh, I don't mind," he answered. "This SUV is sweet,

compared to my small car. I kind of feel like I'm driving a tank."

"I'm interested in learning how to drive," Kipp announced from the rear, sticking his nose between us. It was typical of Kipp to think that there were no boundaries to his abilities. Privately I thought he might have trouble managing the steering wheel and floor pedals simultaneously, but that was just me.

Elani joined him, gazing between the two front seats at the oncoming traffic and quickly moving scenery. I noticed she was crowded in pretty close to my buddy, her silver and blonde shimmering fur brushing his, and he carefully made a little distance. At the same time, he sent me a message of worry, as he really didn't want to hurt her feelings.

To divert the lupines, I engaged them in a common symbiont mind game, where I conceived of a stray thought and then invited them to try and find it in my mind. Soon, I had the mental image of Elani racing, her body beautiful and sleek, alongside a magnificent Kipp, his muscles rippling in the sunlight, as they chased my little mind rabbit, like a pair of sight hounds coursing after prey. Mentally I took them over green, lush hillsides dotted with trees, down into shallow valleys where tall grass covered the meadow flats, and even angling through dense thickets of twisting vines and high wild shrubs.

After a couple of minutes, Peter laughed, and when I gave him a mental nod, he knew he was invited to join the festivities. He made believe he was a Pegasus-like creature and began to fly after the fleeing rabbit, causing Kipp and Elani to sprout wings, too, not to be outdone by a fanciful Peter. Their fluttering activity in my head finally made me dizzy, and I begged them to stop, as I surrendered the mind rabbit to a triumphant and surprisingly persistent Elani.

It was a postcard perfect day for a drive, and of course the North Carolina mountains at that time of year were magnificent. The spring and summer had sequenced with just enough rain and an absence of blast furnace heat so that the leaves would be especially vivid and long lasting. We'd made our way to highway 411, and after a brief pause in Cherokee for a pit stop and a snack, we entered the Great Smokey Mountains National Park. Kipp and Elani, with their color discriminating vision, uttered lupine ooohs and aaahs from the back seat, shifting from side to side of the SUV to catch a particularly scenic view. Kipp had his big head stuck out the window behind me while Elani was mimicking him on the other side of the car, their jowls fluttering in the wind. Peter continued to insist upon driving, so I shrugged my shoulders, sat back, and enjoyed the view. At the rest area at Newfound Gap, we pulled over and walked to the edge of a concrete and stone barrier. A mild breeze was causing the brightly colored leaves to shift, creating a washed, fluid blur of color, much like a finely painted watercolor that was oddly animated; the sky was that deep color of dark turquoise that seemed improbable in nature. I inhaled deeply and felt the cool air sting slightly as I filled my lungs. From across the rest area, Kipp turned and gazed at me, his tail wagging slightly. We'd picked an area where there were no people gathered as so to not draw attention to the large lupines who were decidedly off leash. Kipp was wearing his collar, as was Elani, but he hated the feel of it and even more despised the leather tether of bondage.

"There will be places where dogs are not allowed," I remarked to Peter. "We'll just see how far we can buffalo people." With all due respect to humans who depended upon their wonderful service dogs, symbionts simply had to be connected to their partners constantly. The team at Technicorps had written letters for both Peter and me explaining that Kipp and Elani were the property of Technicorps and had to be at our sides at all times as a critical component for a research project. It might fly in some areas, maybe not in others. And it was not far from the truth. As a group we were working on the clock, so to speak.

As we crossed over the state line into Tennessee and

began a gradual descent into a valley, we decided to take a small detour and make the vigorous hike to Chimney Tops, with the realization that Kipp and Elani could not make the final, almost vertical, approach to the summit. After parking the SUV, I paused to change into my hiking shoes and pulled out a lightweight pullover. It was pleasant weather, cool but not really cold, but we would get hot with the exertion of the long walk. We figured that the lupines could stretch their legs and the chances of being challenged by any authority wondering why we had dogs on the trail would be minimal. At most, we would face some humans wearing puzzled expressions and perhaps a tattle tale or two might report us at the nearest station, probably Sugarland. Well, it wasn't punishable by incarceration, I thought to myself, and the worst would be a stern talking to and maybe a shaken finger in my face by a park official. I'd blink my eyes, feign ignorance and plead forgiveness.

"If it says no dogs allowed, well, that doesn't apply to me and Elani anyway, since we aren't dogs," Kipp remarked in his clever way.

"We'll run that up the flagpole and see how it flies," I replied, ruffling his top knot, enjoying the feel of his warm fur against my cool fingers.

I was gratified to see that despite the fine fall weather, it was a little early in the morning and the parking area was relatively free of cars. So, after making certain I had Kipp's leash, we took off. The trail was almost 4 miles one way, so it was not long before we were warmed up. Kipp and Elani darted ahead, playing tag like young lupines do, reveling in their health and energy. When they heard humans approaching, they quickly returned to our sides, enduring the leash, and we would all act serious and manage to pass the oncoming humans with a sober expression and a curt nod that brokered no discussion. At one point, I glanced at Peter and wondered what had brought him to this place. He was definitely growing on me and had potential and more than a little likeability that he had successfully camouflaged in the dark confines of the Technicorps library. He caught my eyes and returned the stare.

"What?" he asked, a smile tugging at the corners of his mouth.

"I decided that I like you," I replied honestly.

He let his head drop forward for a moment, not sure how to respond. After a long pause, he laughed. "I like you, too," he said.

Up ahead, Kipp had managed to find a wonderful stick that was the perfect length and diameter for play and began to tease an increasingly frustrated Elani with the prize. As they played tug of war, I marveled over how easily lupines–as well as humanoid symbionts–blended into society.

"Have you ever been found out?" Peter asked.

His question made me wonder if he'd been reading my thoughts, but I'd have known if he had. Contemporary symbionts really couldn't manage that sort of thing without a clumsiness that was almost painful and definitely obvious. Kipp could, but then he was special.

"Yes, once," I replied. Unconsciously, my hand drifted up to the pearl necklace–my treasured gift from Harrow–which was concealed beneath my garment. For some reason, I didn't want to lie to Peter. On the other hand, I had no wish to unburden my soul. He was more sensitive that I'd have given him credit, and he had the good sense to not prod. Instead he chose a safer question.

"Fitzhugh says you've done stuff in the past that I shouldn't copy," he finally said, his cheeks reddened from either exertion or embarrassment, or both.

"Well, he should know," I replied, my voice gruff. "He keeps a tally sheet."

We walked another mile before either of us spoke again. Kipp finally gave up the valuable stick to Elani, showing the gentlemanly side of his nature. He'd returned to my side and kept nuzzling my hand, demanding I caress his upright ears. He was being remarkably quiet in terms of his thoughts merging with mine, and I realized he was giving me time to get to know Peter without his, Kipp's, interference.

"How do you keep from making horrible mistakes?" Peter asked. "We're supposed to go back in time, engage humans, explore issues and mysteries and leave no footprint when we leave." He reached out and gently touched my arm to stop my progress. "I don't know how to do that, Petra. And I don't want to end up on Fitzhugh's wall of shame."

Kipp's head went up; there was a party of humans approaching. Telepathically, I suggested he and Elani beat it into the brush. In a flash, both lupines disappeared, and Peter and I resumed our walk.

"Peter, you're going to make mistakes; both you and Elani will make bad choices." I sighed. "Even with my experience, I still make them." I paused to glance up at the leaves of a towering oak, narrowing my eyes against the filtered light. The sun was angling through the canopy and back lit the leaves that were the rosy-yellow color of a ripe, succulent peach. "You will engage with humans and find your feelings entangled with theirs before you know it. Without meaning to, you become part of their society and family." Of course, I knew intimately of what I spoke.

We made the remainder of our ascent in relative silence, with Kipp and Elani darting in and out of view. When we got to the last part of the trail, Kipp viewed the vertical climb to the summit; tilting his head, he tried to figure someway he could make that climb but recognized the impossibility of such a task. I had never been to the summit of Chimney Tops and had always wanted to do so; my companion, Kipp, generously urged me onwards. With Peter's assisting hand, I lurched over the last bump and was able to gaze out into the magnificent overlook that stretched across the Great Smokey Mountains. Taking a moment, I sat upon a rock so that I might soak in the beauty of nature. Off in the distance, a waterway glistened in the sun as it snaked its way through the hills and valleys until I could no longer follow its sinuous trail. The wind was more brisk in the absence of trees, and I pulled my jacket a little closer. Closing my eyes, I tilted my head back; the distinctive scent of wood smoke caught in the back of my throat. Most likely that fragrance was from someone's fireplace, where I could imagine a group of revelers sitting around the flames, laughing and enjoying mugs of hot apple cider.

"What's it like?" Kipp asked.

I felt a stab of guilt since I never left him behind in such a manner. Lowering every part of my mind that might be a barrier, I invited him to see the world through my view. He eagerly searched my memories as well as current impressions. For a moment, I had an odd sensation as if Kipp was behind my eyes, his lined up with mine to share my visions.

"Beautiful!" he finally exclaimed.

I didn't want to leave him below for much longer, so at my urging, Peter reluctantly left his perch and led the way, again holding out a hand assist as needed. Kipp and Elani looked up at us, dancing in place in their excitement to move on.

"How's it going, Kipp?" I asked, meaning his cautious relationship with the young female lupine, as I watched her leap at Peter's chest in a moment of affection and playfulness.

"I think she's decided that we can be friends, which is a good thing," he replied. With a rough head butt that almost caused my leg to collapse, he barked softly and darted ahead, challenging me to keep up with him.

Jogging on the rough trail was not easy, but I took off in hot pursuit of my friend who stayed a tantalizing few steps ahead, even stopping to bark at me again in a provocative, teasing manner. Peter apparently was in good shape, because he and Elani chased after us, jogging along at an easy pace, laughing from time to time at Kipp's craziness. We passed several hikers who stared at us in surprise as two humanoids and two big dogs raced down the trail. We were hot and breathless by the time we got to the SUV.

"You held your own pretty well," I remarked, smiling at Peter as I tried to get my breath.

He ducked his head and the dark sweep of hair carelessly fell across his eyes, almost concealing the expression. Elani pushed next to him, and the connection that had developed between the two sparked. For a moment, I wished they could share the unique bond such as the one Kipp and I had, but that was improbable; Kipp's nature made our connection special, even for symbionts.

"I used to run track," he said. "Hated cross country but did okay on sprints," he added.

We felt we had tempted fate with Kipp and Elani, so with that thought in mind, we loaded up in the SUV and continued towards Gatlinburg. The cabin rested in a remote area where the presence of the lupines would not be an issue. There was a kitchen, so we wouldn't be pressed to find outdoor cafes that would allow Kipp and Elani to crowd onto the cold, hard pavement. After a quick stop at a grocery store, we continued along, using the GPS system in the SUV. Part of me missed a plain old fold up paper map, but those days seemed lost with flashy contemporary aids.

"You were born in the early 1600's," Peter remarked, his comment coming out of left field.

"Yes, 1604," I replied.

"You've lived through amazing times," he said, simply. "Computers, space travel, the digital age…"

"The discovery of fire, the wheel…uh, pestilence, plague…" I replied wryly.

The GPS, which Peter had named "Lucy", barked out a turn ahead with its mechanical, feminine voice, and Peter dutifully complied. We took a right and found ourselves on a narrow trail that almost didn't allow the vehicle; thick, overgrown hedges brushed against the sides of the vehicle and slapped the windshield. But in a moment, the woods opened up, and we were in a small clearing; in the center of the clearing was a rustic cabin of dark timbers that were aged and scarred from years of weather exposure. After Peter pulled the SUV to a stop, I jumped out and opened the back hatch so that Kipp and Elani could explore. Without hesitation, they charged around the rear of the building, circling it before I removed the first bag from the vehicle.

"I smell something odd," Kipp said, pulling his lips back from his teeth in a bizarre grimace.

"Me, too," Elani said, her dark eyes rounding a little as she pushed a little closer to Kipp.

I looked around; there were definitely no humans or we would pick up their thoughts. But the area was dense with wildlife. "There are raccoons, opossum, bears, deer and all sorts of critters around here. I'd be cautious that bears lurk thinking that people will feed them or maybe they can scavenge the trash." Looking down at Kipp, my voice became stern. "Be careful of them, Kipp. They're dangerous."

"Okay, mom," he replied saucily. With his plumed tail waving over his ruddy back, he sauntered off again, Elani close behind. I heard him mutter, "Like I never saw a bear before."

"Slacker," I called after him. No, he couldn't help unpack the car, but he didn't have to be so arrogant about it. Peter and I managed, however, to get everything inside in less than five minutes. I didn't like to cook, and it turned out that Peter did, so I was content to putter around the cabin before joining Kipp and Elani outside.

The cabin was old and decidedly worn, and dust clung to most of the high surfaces. With my interest in antiques, I took time to walk through, enjoying the little pieces that would have been treasured in an estate sale or lingered on the shelf of some off-the-beaten-path store. There was an unattractive sofa that looked like it dated to the 70's, when wagon wheel wood ornamentation was fashionable; faded plaid material covered sagging seat cushions. I was frankly horrified and simultaneously pleased that the wagon wheel was no longer in use in furniture design. A large, round braided rug covered some of the wood plank flooring that had seen better days. It was late afternoon and would be dark soon. If the previous days were any measure, it would be cold and feel damp, despite the low humidity;

fortunately, the cabin had electric heat, and also there was a stack of wood out front for the stone fireplace. Well, I did know how to manage a fire. Having been born in 1604, I possessed a few skill sets, some of which had become extinct in the modern age. I walked to the stack, which was on the end of the long front porch, and picked out a few smaller pieces. There was some fatwood in a battered metal bucket angled near the fireplace. Kipp and Elani finally returned from their wilderness expedition and tried to help, grabbing smaller sticks in their jaws and running to and from the fireplace, bringing kindling to me. Finally, Elani wandered to the kitchen where both Kipp and I could feel the waves of happiness and contentment radiating from her and Peter.

"They are bonding nicely," Kipp observed, assuming his pose of Egyptian sphinx, tucking his legs beneath him as he huddled on the braided rug; he watched me laboring to get the fire to catch. "Do you remember those first nights in that cave when we met?" At my nod, he continued. "I'd never been around a fire pit before and thought it was the most wonderful feeling I'd ever experienced. I was used to being cold and often wet."

I took a seat next to him, my legs crossed in a modified yoga pose; leaning over, I captured him in my arms. He pushed back against me, and we sat that way as we watched the tiny flames grow and begin to chew into the dry wood. I could have drifted off into sleep, sitting there on the floor, my head cushioned upon Kipp's soft flank, but dinner was almost ready, and we were both hungry.

CHAPTER 6

—◆—

"This cabin has been here about 150 years," I remarked. "It's been used for past time shifts due to its longevity and history." At Peter's expression I added, "There have been long periods when it was vacant for one reason or another." The cabin had been the property of a symbiont pair who lived there in the latter part of the past century. It pretty much had been empty on and off since that time, the exception being the occasional Technicorps visitors.

We played Scrabble while sitting on the floor on the large rug that nestled close to the radiating warmth of the fireplace. Of course, I'd brought that game on purpose, thinking it would help expand Elani's English language skills, and I was pleased to discover she had already developed a vocabulary that might rival the ordinary human's. We decided to play in teams since there was no way the lupines could maneuver the little wooden tiles, and, in the end, Peter and Elani won more sets than did Kipp and I.

"Your fault," Kipp said, his amber eyes wearing an accusatory expression as he glared at me. "You can't just make up words to fit the space and available letters," he added. With a shrug of his massive shoulders, he stood and stretched fore and aft, groaning slightly as he did so. Yes, we'd all become a little stiff with our bodies stationary for too long. With a yawn and a congratulatory salute to the victors, Kipp and I stumbled off to our little room in the rear of the cabin. The rooms were all small—especially the bedrooms—since anything spacious would have been considered a waste of labor and space. Outside, the wind was blowing briskly, whistling through the trees, and finding a few chinks in the fragile armor of the cabin while doing so. I shivered and pulled my hoodie a little closer. Kipp was better armed than I for such changes in the temperature. I slept with Kipp's head on my chest in our customary position, which was good, since the cabin was not insulated, and the windows were loosely mounted, to say the least.

The following morning, the windows in our room were wet with condensation, as the cold outside struggled against the warmth inside. In the yard, a lacy crust of frost coated the SUV as well as the grass, a silent testament to the overnight chill; the shallow dips and hollows carved into the earth were lightly dusted with white and would remain so until the sun burned away the frigid, crystalline layer. There was a down comforter on the bed, and I was reluctant to stir from my cocoon. Finally, the fragrance of food cooking threaded its way down the shotgun hallway, and Kipp, with his nose in the air, hopped from the bed and trotted down the linking corridor, his toenails ticking loudly in the narrow confines. I grimaced as my bare feet hit the wide planks and quickly donned my tennis shoes. With the laces untied and my shoes flopping loosely about my feet, I scuffed my way into the kitchen, another small room; Peter looked around from where he stood at the stove. Kipp and Elani both sat at his feet, trying not to drool. He was pan frying some chicken in olive oil for the lupines. Although I didn't eat meat, I did enjoy eggs and cheese and allowed myself to be treated like a queen as Peter sautéed some vegetables and fixed us both cheese and vegetable omelets.

"How come you haven't been scooped up yet?" I asked

before I could stay my hasty and occasionally clumsy tongue. Peter's face flushed red as he dropped his gaze towards his plate.

"Gee, Petra. Try and learn some tact," Kipp said, pausing in his chewing of chicken to chastise me.

"I'm sorry," I said hastily, reaching across the table to gently touch Peter's forearm. "You are just a really nice guy...talented, smart, good looking and a terrific cook." I almost shocked myself as I named off the young symbiont's attributes. He'd not seemed particularly magnificent until that moment.

Peter finally looked up at me with a toss of his head that shook his long bangs to the side. His hair reminded me of the style in the 60's and early 70's when boys would wear their hair in their eyes and manage a cocky swing of the head when visibility was a must. "Thanks, Petra. I know you meant it kindly, so no harm, no foul." He pushed his plate away and took a sip of coffee, which he seemed to prefer to Fitzhugh's ever present Earl Grey tea. "I let my parents, especially my mother, control my destiny too long. I've had some females who were interested in who they thought I should be, but unfortunately none of that would include traveling. And I've wanted to do this since I was a child."

Smiling, I reached over to the coffee pot to warm up my almost empty mug. I knew the dilemma, since I'd done both and understood the two could not be mixed. Odd, I'd never been tempted to go back to a more conventional life of partnership, marriage and parenting. Well, that is, until I met William Harrow. Yes, marriage with him would have been fascinating, and I knew there was ample and abundant love. But there would be no children–an impossibility between two different species—and I would outlive him by centuries. And then that nagging issue of telepathy always gave my kind an unfair advantage over humans, since we could quite literally out-think them at all times. That in itself was enough to turn me away, for him, if not for me. My hand touched the pearls which were hidden beneath the soft, worn fabric of my sweatshirt. I could feel the nubby texture as I caressed them, almost like worry beads.

Kipp, following me in his constant way, stood and walked over to put his head in my lap. With practiced fingers, I gently stroked the top of his head and the large, upright ears. He was so much a part of me that I knew I could recognize him by just the unique feel of his fur against my fingertips. Turning his head, his eyes met mine, and I felt him touch my mind in a soft caress, the mark of a friend who could heal me when none other could.

"Will Peter and I share the kind of closeness that you and Petra have?" Elani asked, tilting her pretty head to one side. She stood and walked over to Peter, placing her head on his knee; his hand drifted up, automatically, to stroke her neck.

"Yes," Kipp answered. "It comes with time and patience. When you put yourself in the hands of your partner and trust that one with your life and well-being, you will find what you seek. Each time you time shift, it gets nearer."

Peter cleared his throat and seemed a little uncomfortable with the general tone of the conversation, which had descended to deep levels of intimacy; he rose to clear the table. I had no partiality to washing dishes and was completely comfortable sitting back and letting him keep busy. Actually, I understood. We had another time shift planned for that day, and he was nervous. Cooking and clearing away the debris was part of his way of coping.

"So what's on for today?" he finally asked. His dark eyes were guarded, as if he knew he appeared vulnerable and had no wish to do so.

"Well, we will make a shift and go back, uh, to roughly 1950 and then return. Our main focus will be on accuracy." I sipped my now cool coffee and made a face at the horrible taste. "And this time, instead of following Kipp and me, we will follow you."

Peter glanced at Elani, who again drew close so that he could caress her soft head. She was massive, as were all lupines, but she definitely was all girl and projected her feminine aura just as Kipp did his masculine side. The blonde tips of the hairs on her coat looked as if they were ignited, flashing fire, despite the low lighting in the room. She looked up at him with her deep brown eyes.

"We're ready, Peter. You know we are." She lolled her tongue out in the familiar lupine version of a smile.

Just because I was a creature of habit, I returned to my room, made up the bed and completed a quick survey to make certain I'd left nothing strewn around carelessly. One never knew if one would return successfully, and I hated to leave a mess behind for someone else to clean. Just as I did at home, I took a quick walk through of the kitchen to wordlessly inspect Peter's kitchen. He was so superior to me in that aspect of life that I wisely kept my mouth shut and offered no commentary. Back in the small living area, Peter and Elani were seated, cross legged on the worn, round braided rug where we'd played Scrabble the night before; the fire had died overnight, with only a few glowing embers winking at us from the ash pile. Kipp waited for me, his tail wagging like a flag, excited and ready. I took my place next to him, and he lay down, placing his head in my lap.

At my direction, Peter and Elani began to concentrate on the year 1950, which was an arbitrary choice but not too distant in the past that our clothing would be completely inappropriate. True, I would not be wearing a dress and heels–I was wearing my pearls, however—but I didn't think my fashion errors would draw untoward attention in the event we encountered any humans. With their permission, we marginally entered into the experience of Peter and Elani. I felt myself smile as I shared their joy and excitement at the rushing sensation which, by now, was old hat to me but still new, like a bright, shiny coin, to them. As they fell into the dark vortex of time, Kipp and I followed, happy to ride the time continuum wake and let someone else take the lead for once.

Time travel is never exact, and somehow we ended up about fifty yards from the cabin in the midst of a driving rain storm. Peter looked up at me, mud covered from where he and Elani had landed in a ditch. The expression of total chagrin was priceless, and I had to laugh, along with Kipp. I was quickly becoming soaked by a cold, wet rain but at least was not plastered with mud.

Holding out my arms, I said rather loudly to be heard over the rainfall, "Sometimes you land hard, Peter!"

He quickly rediscovered his good nature and laughed in response. All four of us felt a need to hurry, considering the weather, and made haste to the cabin, which we hoped would be empty. As we drew closer, we collectively threw out our telepathic nets and were gratified to sense that no one was present. Our time shift had taken us from bright daylight to darkest night, and we trudged along, struggling to see past the pelting rain, waiting for an idle lightening flash to illuminate the distance ahead. Fortunately, Kipp and Elani had the superior vision of lupines and guided our progress. I felt pretty lucky to only fall once, managing to soar spread eagled, until I hit the ground with a resounding thump. Kipp darted to my side, his anxious muzzle poking in the back of my neck. After I caught my breath, I allowed Peter to help me up.

"Sometimes you land hard, Petra," he wise cracked, trying not to smile but failing.

By the time we reached the cabin, which was shrouded in darkness, we were drenched. Cautiously, we made our way up the neglected drive, where the branches of large shrubs and overgrown trees threatened to close the pathway. It seemed nothing much had changed over the years. Another flash of lightening forked across the sky; overhead, the tree limbs snapped back and forth, driven into a fury by an angry wind.

"Kipp?" I asked, wanting to make certain we wouldn't walk in on a person who might be armed with a shotgun on the other side of the door.

He stood for a minute, his ears flattened by the rain. Once, he looked up at me and wagged his tail; I realized he was enjoying our soggy adventure. But he agreed—no unwanted visitors ahead, and we moved to the porch, which creaked with loose boards underfoot. It was odd how we'd left this cabin just a few minutes ago only to return and find the structure similar but with enough changes to draw our attention. For example, the front porch lacked the rusted metal glider and, instead, featured a couple of worn wooden rocking chairs. At the far end, a swing gently moved to and fro, the chains creaking from the rafter overhead where it was tethered. Peter looked at me and the reality of what we were doing seemed to finally have sunk in. Eager to see inside, he tried the door, which was locked. Persistence paid off, however, and he finally found a window in the rear that was open a crack, and he managed to jimmy it up and climb inside. Within a minute, he had the front door open, and the three of us rushed inside as the wind began to blow harder, sideways, engulfing us with rain spray beneath the relative shelter of the porch.

Inside, the differences between what we'd left and what we encountered was even more profound. A tattered camelback sofa, stuffed with feathers and with decorative button ticking, sat angled near the rock fireplace. There was little else in the room with the exception of a square oak table with legs that ended in wicked claws fiercely clutching little glass balls that rested delicately on the scarred floor. I walked to the kitchen to find there were no modern appliances; an old fashioned pump for water was secured to a heavy board that ran alongside a chipped cast iron sink. Above the sink a calendar hung from a nail; the date was 1950, and various local hardware stores as well as a five and dime were advertised on the pages. Peter followed me, and I turned to smile at his expression of wonder.

"I guess we really did it," he finally uttered. Elani, at his side, looked up at him, her tail wagging so furiously that her entire rear end shimmied.

"Well, this calendar could have been hanging here for a number of years, so we can't be certain, but we'll take it as a good omen. I know from the history of this cabin, that a symbiont pair lived here for many years, but they died a long time ago. Technicorps just held on to the property thinking it would make a good getaway when needed." I sighed and looked around. "We could just as easily have gone back to meet the couple that lived here, but such travel is ill advised."

Peter looked at me quizzically, but my attention was diverted as Kipp tilted his head slightly before turning towards the door. Elani did the same as her coat dripped water on the bare wood planks.

"A vehicle is coming up the drive," Kipp announced just before the glare of headlights reflected through the front window onto the wall.

"Let's beat it!" I said, not wanting the drama of getting caught and having to explain our presence. No doubt the local sheriff made rounds of abandoned properties to make certain vagrants were not present. Without an ID or anything else, Peter and I would definitely be classified as potential trouble and would be hauled off.

The four of us went to the small rear bedroom and began our preparations, as Peter and I sat on the floor, our partners close by. One would think that the pressure of feeling hurried might have impeded our work, but it really didn't at all. Peter, showing a focus and leadership quality that was amazing for one so young, led the way. Kipp only had to soar in once on our trip forward in time to help Peter and Elani make as accurate a return as was possible. I don't think I could have done any better. We checked the time, since I'd left my watch behind, and we arrived only five minutes after we'd departed. And instead of landing in the living room, we were inexplicably in the kitchen. I looked over at Peter, who was crusted in mud, his hair plastered down in wet spikes on his forehead. Elani looked just about as rough, her pretty gray and blonde tipped fur was splotched with large patches of brown mud with the consistency of pudding. She and Kipp both reeked of wet dog, and although I tried to nab that thought and hide it from Kipp, he latched onto it with vigor.

"Well, I didn't mention that you stink, too," he said,

flaring his nostrils slightly. "You should have taken a bath last night but fell asleep. You didn't brush your teeth this morning and your breath smells like a dirty sock." He was glaring at me now.

"Sorry," I muttered, not knowing what else to say.

"And I have to sleep with you, too," Kipp went on, not finished yet.

"Really sorry," I said, managing to stand despite the crick in my back. Was I getting too old for the rambunctious nature of time shifts, I wondered? Maybe it was a game for youth. With my right hand, I rubbed my left wrist which was still sore despite the fact I'd long ago abandoned the air cast. Kipp saw the gesture and reminded himself that he couldn't be angry at me for long; he loved me despite my multitude of flaws.

"Is your wrist okay?" he asked, standing to come over and inspect it with his black nose. With the delicate touch of a fluttering hummingbird, he grazed my wrist, leaving little damp marks where his nose touched my flesh. It tickled, and I involuntarily giggled.

"I think I'll make it, Stinky," I replied with a smile.

Peter left to take a shower and change clothes. While he was busy, I took thick towels and vigorously rubbed down the lupines, using damp wash cloths to remove the dirt and debris from Elani. I wasn't coated in mud but was a wet mess, so I grabbed a shower after Peter finished. Feeling refreshed and smelling of Irish Spring soap, I suggested we go in search of laundry facilities, since the cabin lacked such an amenity. We hopped in the SUV and drove into Gatlinburg where there was a laundromat next to a grocery store. It was cool enough for Kipp and Elani to stay in the vehicle, so while our clothes and towels washed, Peter and I made a quick trip through the store. At the deli counter, I found some smoked gouda cheese and thought Kipp might be fascinated with a different taste, since he was a notorious cheese hog. Feeling decadent, I picked up a box of Little Debbie Swiss Cake Rolls as well as some strawberry Pop Tarts. Somehow, anything in a box just had to be good since convenience and portability were two of my favorite qualities in any food item. With laundry neatly folded in a basket and a couple of bags of groceries securely stowed, we drove back to the cabin. It was drawing close to twilight, and the glare of the oncoming headlights kept causing me to duck my head and peek out covertly, waiting until the coast was clear again. I guess it was good Peter was driving.

Once home, I decided it was my turn in the kitchen and displayed my skill at making grilled cheese sandwiches. Elani had never had such a treat, and I tried not to laugh as she began to chew the hot, chewy mess. She, trying to be delicate, was forced to open her mouth wide with each mouthful, since the cheese stuck everywhere in gooey abandon. Kipp sampled the gouda and his eyes rounded at the new taste of an old favorite...cheese. However, we all were exhausted since we'd made a time shift that day, and it was true for our kind that such was inherently tiring. So, after I took my turn cleaning the kitchen, Kipp and I trailed off to the rear bedroom. Since I'd already showered, nothing was left but to disrobe and collapse upon the worn mattress that was so soft I felt as if I might sink through the center onto the floor below. Kipp was softly snoring by the time I got into a comfortable position.

CHAPTER 7

"**P**etra, wake up!" The urgent voice of Peter disturbed the soothing dream I was having about walking along the sandy stretch of Kill Devil Hills, Kipp racing ahead to tag a ball I'd thrown for him. The salt spray was so strong in the wind, that I could actually taste it lingering softly on my lips in my dream. Reluctantly, I opened one eye and stared at him, outlined in the semidarkness of the room. Elani stood at his side, her posture rigid and tense.

"You have a phone call," Peter added, thrusting out his cell phone.

Cell phones, although considered indispensible items for humans, were in relatively infrequent use among symbionts. Maybe it was a sign of the times that some of the youngsters, like Peter, would carry one. To be honest, telepaths really didn't have a need for cell phones which, when used to create distance between beings as well as avoid emotions by the use of texting, just didn't further us as a species. And the lupines couldn't manage them in any case. Propping myself up on an elbow, I paused to glance down and was relieved to see that I was wearing an intact t-shirt and a pair of sweat pants. There was the happy realization that I'd not gone to bed commando that night.

No good phone calls come after midnight, and this was

no exception. Philo's voice barreled out into the darkness. In his usual blunt fashion, he told me that Fitzhugh had another heart attack and was at Duke Hospital in intensive care. The first one had been mild; this one seemed to be of greater severity.

I sat up, anxious, distressed; automatically, I held out my arms and Kipp nestled into me, his pointed nose pressing against the juncture where neck meets shoulder. Of course, we would start for home immediately and postpone the next time shift. It only took us about ten minutes to get dressed, packed and be on the road, Peter driving with his usual ruthless intensity, returning the way we'd come. There was nothing to be said, and I forced myself to relax and put the worst-case scenario from my mind. Before we left Gatlinburg, I asked Peter to stop at a convenience store, startling the sleepy clerk whose head was nodding on the counter, so I could buy large travel cups of black coffee. Peter nodded his thanks and off we went, swallowed by the cold darkness. Kipp remained unusually guarded, shielding his thoughts from me. I realized he was worried and not willing to share those anxious musings so as to not increase my distress. Elani felt like a raw nerve, although I didn't probe her thoughts; however, her stress filled the tight confines of the SUV like an overinflated balloon about to burst. At some point, I let down my window a tad, enjoying the bracing feel of the cold air that grew more frigid as we ascended into the mountain range that stretched from Tennessee to North Carolina. Kipp stuck his nose against the back of my neck and sighed deeply, the hot breath from his lungs feeling like a blast furnace on my chilled flesh.

I don't think Peter and I spoke ten words for that entire drive home, except for my occasional entreaty to let me drive so that he could rest. Resolutely, he shook his head no and kept up the pace. I watched as the speedometer needle hovered at eighty and beyond as we raced home. What if Fitzhugh didn't make it, I wondered? Kipp must have been tuned in to my thoughts because his next question was one for philosophers and not for mere travelers such as me.

"If someone dies, what happens if you go back in time and prevent the event from happening?" Kipp asked.

Turning my head, I looked at Peter, who dared to glance away from the road to meet my gaze. There I was, supposed to be a mentor, wondering how to correctly answer such a deeply philosophical and ethical question. Thanks, Kipp, I said silently to myself.

"You're welcome," he murmured, rather sarcastically it seemed.

"We are taught it's wrong to tamper with the progression of history. So, going back in time to prevent an accident, for example, from happening in which a life is lost would be dangerous."

"Why?" Elani asked. She shoved her head up between the seats and was jammed in tight next to Kipp. I could imagine his discomfiture at her physical proximity as her soft, gray blonde coat brushed against his ruddy shoulder.

"When a timeline is disturbed, there is a risk that the next generation will be changed," I answered. "If a child is kept from dying in a car crash," I continued, thinking of my baby George, "then that person can grow to maturity, have offspring, and influence future generations that would not have been born." I shook my head and gazed out my window at the dark, shapeless countryside where farms nestled, their lights piercing the night as the early risers met their day. "It is just something we can't do, no matter how tempting."

"So, if you had the ability to prevent what happened to Fitzhugh from taking place, you wouldn't?" Peter asked.

I felt myself swallow hard and shook my head again. It was a slippery slope for my kind, the constant lure to tamper with history as well as the future. The ones who'd tried it had become outcasts, usually abandoned by a more principled symbiont partner who would not agree to such an abomination of our cultural dictates.

Peter spied another convenience store, and after a quick pit stop and another large cup of coffee, he swung behind the wheel again. "It keeps me from thinking too much," he said as a manner of explanation of his dogged insistence that he drive. I was relieved it was not due to any perceived need to protect me or care for me.

"And why would you care if he was being nice to you, just because?" Kipp asked, his thoughts resonating in my mind alone. "I've heard Philo say it, as well as Fitzhugh…you don't have to be independent and act as if you need no one," Kipp continued. "And you know you need me, so to pretend otherwise is ridiculous."

I chose to ignore Kipp and returned my attention to the road. The yellow and white lines became hypnotic, and I found myself killing time by counting road signs and occasionally looking above through the large, curving windshield to see if I could identify any constellations. As we finally approached Durham, I sighed in relief. There had been no more phone calls so I could only hope old Fitzhugh was holding his own. While Fitzhugh was well past a millennium of age, he had the appearance of a human man in his late seventies or early eighties. Tall and a little stooped, he carried his years well and had been notoriously healthy up until the first heart attack.

The intersection of humans and symbionts for health care purposes was avoided when possible, but sometimes admissions to hospitals were required. We may look human but our genetic makeup is different and that means our physiology is unique to our species. One of our Technicorps symbiont doctors was on staff at Duke, and he always served as the attending or a consultant and surreptitiously guided all that occurred.

Daylight had broken, and the eastern horizon appeared flat and expectant as coral colored clouds that were thin and narrow took up position, backlit by a bright orange sun; the clouds looked like wisps of fragile, voile fabric pasted on an artificial sky, like something an ambitious child might have created as an art project for an overly zealous teacher. Our solitary journey home was finally interrupted as we hit the early morning traffic, with lines of stop and go cars whose occupants chafed in agitation at the slowdown brought on by a minor fender bender. Many of the people were no doubt on their way to punch a clock at Duke Hospital. I could easily imagine the raised eyebrow of a nursing supervisor as the employee gave the all too frequent reason for excessive tardiness.

We finally arrived, and Peter pulled up at the front entrance. I looked over my shoulder at Kipp, my eyes meeting his in the dim interior of the SUV. We were not parted, ever, and the idea I'd have to leave him behind was toxic to me. But there was simply no feasible way to get him in the hospital, and I didn't have time or presence of mind to try and create some clever game by which he could pass muster.

"Go," he said, nodding at the door with his pointed muzzle. "I'll be with you," he said, blinking his eyes once. Yes, he could easily follow me telepathically and see the world through my eyes.

"I'll let you know what's going on," I said to him, knowing he could relay all to Peter and Elani more accurately than if they tried to follow my thoughts amidst the cacophony of churning human minds roiling with emotions contained in that one large building.

I exited the vehicle and within a few seconds felt the blast of warm air as the automatic doors to the hospital entrance silently opened and closed. Without appearing as if I needed help since I didn't want to be told it was too early to go to the intensive care unit, I determinedly marched past the reception desk, purposely not making eye contact with the harried clerk who was fielding questions about the location of one-day surgery and registrations for colonoscopies. I'd made this trip before and knew my way around. When the elevators opened, I searched for the waiting room that stabled the exhausted and stressed families who were perpetually waiting for news of some kind. Philo was there, and I could already tweak loose the familiar patterns of his thoughts and feel happiness when he recognized my mind greeting his. A few seconds later, he met me in the hallway, pulling me against his chest so hard that I was left slightly breathless.

"The cardiologist just came out and said that Fitzhugh is stable, but he's going to need prolonged rest after this one," Philo said. Linking his hand with mine, our fingers interlaced, he led me to his corner of the waiting room where he'd left a book sitting in his chair, marking his place. I took a deep breath and looked around the room. Across from me sat a young woman whose face wore a tear-stained expression of distress. For an instant, I allowed myself access to her thoughts and immediately pulled free as if I'd stepped in quicksand.

"You have to keep your wall up," Philo said. "It's almost intolerable sitting here amidst all this pain and worry."

Oddly, I felt Kipp on the scene, via remote, and he nodded his head mentally as if he agreed with Philo. With the knowledge my boundaries might have been weakened due to my own anxiety, Kipp took up position in my head and effectively prevented any more forays into the thoughts of the surrounding humans.

"Thanks, Kipp," I muttered quietly.

"I knew Fitzhugh was under some personal stress, and I should have helped him more," Philo said, leaning forward to rest his elbows on his knees. Gently, I placed my hand on his back, feeling the tension between his shoulder blades; his shirt was slightly damp from sweat born of worry. "You know that Juno was living with a symbiont couple who were recently relocated to a colony in Sweden. Juno, at Fitzhugh's invitation, went to live with him. However, his landlord went ballistic, said he'd violated his lease and was going to evict him." Philo turned to me and raised an eyebrow. "The landlord had some college kids that could pay more money and probably was looking for a reason to kick Fitzhugh out." He sighed. "It could have been argued in court, but Fitzhugh didn't have the heart or fight in him to challenge the landlord."

"Where's Juno?" I asked.

"At home with Claire," he answered.

"Fitzhugh is going to have to deal with finding a new home for him and Juno as well as moving all his things.

When I went over to get Juno to take her to my house, I noticed he really has almost no belongings. I think his entire investment is in the Technicorps library, and he's not bothered to acquire a lot of stuff."

I thought briefly of my own house which was slightly overrun with objects that belonged to the past existences of countless, unnamed humans. Maybe as I got older, like Fitzhugh, I would have a simpler existence.

"No, you'll always have a bunch of junk around," Kipp chimed in from his listening post in the SUV. "Just like that little china creamer with the broken handle that you glued back on. It's a damaged piece that no one else wanted until you came along."

I huffed silently, annoyed at Kipp for making the wrong assessment, something totally unlike him. It wasn't that I needed to rescue the damaged goods in the world; rather, I just happened to look at things and imagine them before age and wear took the luster and left an article languishing in a dusty corner, overlooked by people who were deceived by another pretty, perfect face. Did that sum up my psyche and make me seem artificially complex, or was I just a hopeless romantic?

Philo, during my mental tug of war with Kipp, disappeared and returned with coffee. Visiting hours were about to begin, and I gulped my coffee–which tasted as if it had been sitting all night, until it morphed into a thick, unpalatable mass—unwilling to leave the half-consumed cup to cool while I visited my old friend. Yes, it seemed odd even to me to admit he was a friend. A nurse stuck her head out and nodded; Philo nudged my arm, and I joined the others who politely waited their turn. The nurse showed me to Fitzhugh's room; I wiped sweaty palms on my jeans before entering.

He was fortunate to have a room with a decent view and even luckier to be positioned where the window allowed the morning sun to splash across the equipment cluttered area, illuminating his bed and him as if he were some type of angelic being. For a moment, the rays of the sun were tangled in his wispy hair, giving even more of an illusion of a heavenly aura about him.

"Snap out of it," Kipp growled, kicking me mentally in the butt.

Fitzhugh's eyes opened as I entered the room, and I really couldn't have imagined a broader smile on his wrinkled face if I'd tried. No, there was no mistaking that he was happy to see me. The bland room, with walls the color of old, dried putty, smelled faintly of some type of disinfectant solution.

"So, you bothered to come back, did you?" he began, after controlling the smile and replacing it with a frown. "I guess you were worried I might die, and you'd be stuck with having to take over the library," he added, drawing his brows together in a frown.

"Oh, shut up your grumbling," I said, leaning over to kiss his cheek; his dry skin felt a little like thin parchment beneath my lips. The look of pleased surprise on his face at the caress was enough to cheer me. Feeling a little embarrassed at my impulsive show of affection, I made busy straightening his cover and settling his pillow under his head.

"I suppose you were overdoing it as usual," I remarked, raising one dark eyebrow in what I hoped to be a stare of intimidation leveled at him.

He merely laughed in reply and looked away. There was a prolonged period of silence between us as I pondered on what to say next, if anything.

"Philo says there is some problem with your landlord," I finally said after careful consideration.

"Yes," Fitzhugh replied. "I must look for new, uh, digs, when I get out of this place," he said with a frown and a gesture of his arms to indicate the hospital room that he despised. I knew he just wanted to be back in his library. "Philo has said I can't live in my office," he added, huffing slightly through pursed lips.

"Why don't you come and stay with Kipp and me?" I asked before I realized that the words had tumbled out of my mouth. In the back of my head, a huge, emphatic question mark formed itself, courtesy of Kipp.

Fitzhugh's dark eyes, which had looked weary and lacking their usual sharp, inquisitive expression, snapped to attention as he turned his head to look at me. Using both hands, he pushed himself up in the bed and settled his shoulders against the bunched up wad of pillows I'd erected for comfort.

"Are you serious?" he asked before I could retract my hasty offer.

But as I thought about the matter, why not, I wondered? I loved Juno, and she would be a quiet, unobtrusive shadowy figure, adding her stability and comfort to my home. Fitzhugh, although not unobtrusive, would probably spend most of his time at the library anyway and just use my house for a sleep over.

"Lily, too?" he said, his voice quieter than before, as if he was afraid to push the limits of my generosity.

I widened my eyes and stared at him, unblinking. Lily the Terrible would be delighted to be home again, since she'd be close to her beloved Kipp. The words dried up in my mouth like dust as I nodded my head.

He turned away and gazed at the far wall. There was a dry erase board that listed the name of his nurse and patient care assistant. An annoying smiley face was drawn next to the name of the hospital, in case he forgot that critical fact. The name of his doctor was carefully written, just a little larger than the names of the others and offset so as to stand out. After a full minute, he looked at me again.

"Thank you, Petra. I'm grateful and will, of course, look for another place as soon as I'm up to full speed again." His hands clutched at the thin, cotton blanket that stretched from his toes to his chin. "I don't have many things, and we can just put it all in storage."

"We'll work that out later," I said, standing. The nurse named Mitzi hovered in the doorway, her hand on her hip as she waited for me to conclude my summit. I could tell she was in a hurry and in no mood for me to stand around yakking. Plus, Philo wanted to visit Fitzhugh, too. With a little wave of my hand, I left that room which seemed to echo with memories of past successes as well as tragedies. I was happy Fitzhugh was not in the latter category.

I stopped briefly to tell Philo of my invitation and was immediately irritated at his gaping, open mouthed response of astonishment. Why would that be so hard to believe, I wondered? Did everyone find me to be an unchanging stick in the mud? Knowing I'd left Peter with the two lupines confined in the cramped interior of the SUV for much too long, I hurried back outside and spied them waiting just beyond the patient pick up zone. Peter gunned the motor slightly and glided to my location, the vehicle's motor softly purring. Despite the cheery sun, it was cold outside, my breath creating a little fog as I exhaled, so I quickly jumped in the SUV, appreciative of the fact that Ford manufactured really good car heaters.

"So, you invited Fitzhugh, Juno and Lily to move in with us?" Kipp asked, prodding the back of my neck with his big nose. His breath was warm and wet, and I felt a little trickle of moisture roll down my flesh to disappear beneath the collar of my sweatshirt.

"Yes, and I have no idea how we will all cram into my house, but we'll figure it out somehow," I replied, trying to keep the spirit of optimism alive and kicking. "We'll transform the study into a spare room." Reaching back with my hand, I curled my fingers beneath Kipp's neck and allowed myself to enjoy the texture of his thick fur. For a moment, my fingers burrowed deep before beginning a gentle combing of his pelt.

"I'm fine with it," he remarked, huffing slightly. "You tend to spend too much time alone anyway; Fitzhugh will be there to kick your backside and keep you on your toes."

That wasn't really what I'd had in mind but realized an offer was an offer, so I drifted off into a self-imposed trance of relaxation as Peter maneuvered the vehicle amongst traffic on the way to my house. Within a half an hour, he was handing me my duffle, since I drew the line at allowing him to carry it inside for me.

"If you're free, maybe you could help me and Philo figure out what needs moving over here and what I need to store?" I smiled at the young man who seemed relaxed now that we knew Fitzhugh would live to see another day.

"Sure," he nodded. Without a word of complaint about all the driving and the fact our expedition which would have strengthened his bond to Elani had been disrupted, he got back into the SUV and disappeared down my street, taking the turn towards Technicorps.

Kipp and I stood on the front porch for a moment, gazing out at our little world. With a well practiced gesture, Kipp stuck his big head under my hand, asking for an ear rub and a scratch in that difficult to reach place between his ears. The character of our household would change, but maybe that was a good thing, I reasoned. Kipp just listened to me think. He was right in that I was much too comfortable in my predictable ways. Things were about to be disrupted, and in a big way.

CHAPTER 8

"What on earth are you eating for breakfast?" Fitzhugh asked, as he strolled into my kitchen, his worn leather house shoes making a loud, dragging noise on the wooden flooring. Leaning over my shoulder, he stared at the two objects resting on a paper napkin that was unfolded and spread on the surface of the dinette table. "What is that?"

"These are Pop Tarts which rank alongside the best breakfast foods ever made," I replied saucily. "They are fortified with vitamins and minerals," I added, pointing at the back of the box which listed all the attributes of the beloved tart. Just to prove my point, I broke off a corner and delicately nibbled on it while I sipped my coffee.

He mumbled something not meant for my ears, and had I been an undisciplined telepath, I might have eavesdropped in order to start a fight. Kipp looked up at me, smiling in his lupine way. He and Juno were resting in a diffuse patch of light that spread like an open fan across the kitchen floor. They had already eaten and were satiated, along with Lily, who was stretched out between Kipp's massive paws. He'd been grooming her with his tongue, and she was still damp, her fur spiky and drying in chaotic waves reminiscent of when human women used Dippity Do and hair pins to create pin curls.

Actually, other than the few times when Fitzhugh acted as if he thought he was my mother, we settled in quite effortlessly. Of course, I was at work all day and would come home to find him resting with Juno at his feet, often asleep in his chair with a book splayed open across his lap.

Between Philo, Peter and me, we managed to relocate my heavy desk into my bedroom, leaving only a couple of small bookcases in what had been a study. On one bright, cool day, Philo borrowed a friend's truck, and we moved Fitzhugh's bed, a desk and his favorite chair, which was an old, battered Lazy Boy with a no-nonsense metal frame that made it weigh more than Gibraltar. As the three of us struggled to get the chair around a tight corner, I muttered a vicious oath as my knuckles were scrapped raw on a door frame.

"Watch that mouth," Kipp ordered, his tail wagging with support. "No opposable thumbs," he added, "Or I'd help."

"Where've I heard that before?" I grumbled. Philo and Peter only laughed, and we finally managed to shove the old chair past the doorway and set it up by the window where Fitzhugh could read if he wished. The rest of his sparse belongings were placed in storage until he found a permanent home.

"Why'd you agree to this if you're gonna complain all the time?" Kipp asked, folding his rear haunches up under his body as he tilted his head towards me.

I decided to plop down into the recliner; despite the cool weather, I was hot, my face beaded in sweat. With one hand, I pushed back my hair which had escaped from a braid. Looking up, I saw that Philo and Peter were both waiting for me to answer Kipp, since it was obvious he was challenging me with that amber colored stare of his.

"I really don't know," I began, taking a deep breath. Gazing at the floor, I saw a cavalcade of dust bunnies in retreat, disturbed from their slumber by our activities. A good housekeeper I was not. "It just seemed the right thing to do at the time," I grumbled, using my toe to squash one of the dust balls.

"I know why," Philo commented. "You feel affection for Fitzhugh despite all claims to the contrary. You care about him."

I shrugged my shoulders dismissively, ignoring Peter's laugh. The three of us got back to work and within the hour had the room ready for occupancy. Kipp even managed to drag a small, round woolen accent rug from the front room so that Juno would have a cushy place to rest her arthritic bones.

That was then, and I guess, in retrospect, we managed the transition with relatively few bumps. I was accustomed to living solo, just me and my symbiont. Having a house full of other beings was an adjustment. Per Philo, as soon as Fitzhugh was able to come back to work and had regained his usual level of vigor, Peter, Elani, Kipp and I would continue with our collective business of learning and teaching.

"Do you want me to fix you something?" I asked awkwardly, looking up at Fitzhugh.

"I'm having raisin bran, which is much better than that piece of fake pastry you are eating," he replied.

I'd noticed he had a favorite cereal bowl, one I'd found at a junk shop. It was an old piece of vintage blue Fiesta ware with a tiny chip off the base but still a pretty token from a past time. Kipp, as usual, was hovering in my mind. Lately, he was given to projecting a large question mark that floated like an overinflated balloon in the occipital region of my brain. It was annoying, and I formed the picture of a large pin which I stuck in the balloon to deflate it. In response, he projected a large exclamation point. Kipp and I were overdue a serious conversation.

"When will the new library assistant actually start work?" Fitzhugh asked, after he'd swallowed his first spoonful of cereal.

I rose and put on the kettle, thinking he'd like a pot of Earl Grey. We'd brought his tea service from his home, careful to not damage the delicate china pieces. Lily rose and began to do figure eights between my legs, depositing cat hair freely on my sweatpants as I danced in unsuccessful avoidance.

"Well, she's been involved in orientation and human resources stuff, so I haven't met her but hear she is doing okay so far," I replied. "She's older than Peter and less likely to chase adventure. And the gossip is that she's obsessive compulsive to the point of tedium and that helps with library work." After I said it, I turned to look at him, realizing how rude I'd sounded.

"Yes, you're quite right," he said. "And one of the reasons you do such a poor job is that you lack that quality."

Bam! Yes, he'd scored another direct hit. But I knew by now that such remarks were a part of how he showed his affection. I raised an eyebrow at him, while managing to remain silent. Leaving him to his cereal, I went to my room, Kipp trotting after me, to get ready. Fitzhugh was on medical leave, but I was not. With the usual care given to my wardrobe, I pulled on a pair of jeans and a sweatshirt. It was cool outside but nice walking weather, nonetheless, so after donning a jacket, I stuck my head in the kitchen to say goodbye.

Juno, although not on medical leave, had been deployed to stay with Fitzhugh until he could work again. She was still resting contentedly in her little patch of sun; her fur seemed a little faded and lacking the typically cautious, meticulous grooming seen in lupines. I told myself that I would give her a good brushing when I got home. Fitzhugh lingered at the battered kitchen table, leaning forward as he stared at something in the local paper. Many people had gone to the internet for news or watched the television, but Fitzhugh still liked to read as did I. He was wearing delicate half glasses that I'd not seen before. Impulsively, I walked in and leaned forward to give him a little kiss on the cheek.

"Bye, honey," I said, smiling. "See you this afternoon after work," I continued, trying to sound like a happy member of a stereotypical family, like June Cleaver telling

Ward goodbye–and check on the Beaver and Wally while you're at it.

"Okay, sweetheart," he rejoined, shocking me to my core. He grinned broadly, something rarely seen. Juno looked up and smiled, her tail thumping hard on the wooden floor. Fitzhugh had beaten me at my own game! But in any case, I needed to go. Kipp ran ahead, wagging his tail, impatient to feel the cool air on his face and body. He almost knocked me down as we exited through the front door.

"Trying to get out before Lily figures out I'm leaving and wants to follow me," he said, panting with the effort.

We started along the sidewalk, beginning the two mile trek to Technicorps. The weather forecast predicted rain later in the week, but for now it was lovely. November was right around the corner; the colors of October were fading. The air was thick with the fragrance of dying leaves, and my feet made a whooshing sound as they pushed through the leaves that had already fallen to the earth below, dotting the sidewalk in the carefree pattern of nature. Kipp saw a squirrel dart across our path no more than three yards ahead; he made a false move just to watch the squirrel dart away in alarm and scamper up a tree. From a low branch, it paused and turned to noisily scold us as we wandered past.

"Sometimes, I just like to mess with their little heads," Kipp confessed, his eyes bright as he glanced up at me.

"How do you think Fitzhugh is doing?" I asked, wanting Kipp's opinion which would be unvarnished. "You've been doing this annoying thing lately of sending me question marks rather than thoughts." Narrowing my eyes, I stared at him.

He sauntered ahead, and if I wasn't mistaken, he assumed a little swagger to his walk. Deliberately, he blocked his thoughts from mine and sent back, instead, a series of punctuation marks, all bobbing like helium balloons, careening around in my brain until I almost felt dizzy.

"Kipp, stop that!" I shouted mentally. "You're gonna give me a headache."

He turned and quickly returned to my side, his shoulders slumped in contrition. "I'm sorry, Petra. I was just trying to be funny."

I knew he never intentionally tried to aggravate me; there was too much love and the most he would do was to push the limits of playfulness. Reaching down, I ruffled the fur on the top of his head and scratched the underside of his chin. Nothing unpleasant ever lingered between us for more than a second. Bonded symbionts couldn't manage that sort of thing because of the nature of our connections.

"In answer to your question," Kipp continued, "I think Fitzhugh is doing well. I wondered how it would go, since he's a loner like you, but he seems comfortable and well adjusted. For a while, I saw something unusual, almost like a color around his chest area, but that seems to be fading."

"What did you see?" I asked, curious, since I'd never heard him speak thus previously.

He tilted his head and gazed upward, as if he was trying to accurately capture the memory. The air was crisp and dry as we walked along; a brisk northerly wind disturbed the fallen leaves, herding the fallen soldiers into little groupings caught up, helplessly, against the concrete curbs. Ahead, a wind devil spun up, the leaves scratching against one another as they whirled into a mini funnel that charged down the street before veering off across a vacant lot to die a natural death.

"As I looked at Fitzhugh," Kipp explained, "it was as if there was a watercolor-like washing of red and orange on his chest where his heart would be." He looked at me again. "Do you think I created that in my mind?"

Kipp's talents were like ancient and valuable treasures, revealed to an unsuspecting world at unpredictable intervals. I took nothing he told me lightly, since many things had proven to signal untapped skill sets lost to the rest of our kind. Could we see pain and illness in waves of color?

"Have you seen it before?" I asked.

He paused before nodding his head. "Yes, I saw it in

Claire when she was grieving over Silas." Kipp's eyes became slightly unfocused. "She became blue-gray, as if all her flesh lost the usual color."

The thought of Claire and Silas brought me, selfishly, I suppose, back to my own pain. It was during the search for Philo and Claire's son, Silas, that Kipp and I went back in time to Victorian England. Fate would have it I met a human man who fell in love with me and for whom I felt love in return. My hand reached for the dainty pearl necklace I wore almost constantly. Had the tiny pearls gained the famous luster because of being in contact with my flesh, or was it that when I looked at them I thought of Harrow and they became beautiful?

"I see a little color in you, now," Kipp said, his words soft and gentle in the back of my mind. "When you've looked like this before, I think you were sad."

With an effort, I pushed the lingering thoughts behind me and deliberately hastened my pace. Today, I was supposed to meet Fitzhugh's new assistant and try, with Peter's help, to get her oriented to her job at Technicorps. No one believed Fitzhugh would be out for long, but it would be nice to have a competent person at the wheel so that he would feel less of a burden. Kipp, caught up in the spirit of my new focus, began to play a game with me where he deposited a word from the title of a famous novel, and I was supposed to guess the remainder of the title. I was doing pretty good but objected strenuously to his using "The" as one of the words, leaving me to guess the remainder. It was patently unfair and not in the spirit of true sport.

When we arrived at Technicorps, Kipp peeled off to the learning lab where his class of young lupines waited. After ducking my head in Philo's office to give him a quick update on Fitzhugh, I jogged down the staircase to the basement, enjoying the feeling it gave me to rev up my heart rate a little. I'd not run since Fitzhugh came to live with me and realized I needed to get on a normal schedule again. Pushing open the door to the library, I inhaled deeply, hoping to catch a little of the familiar fragrance of bergamot, but instead caught a whiff of coffee, strong and darkly mellow, floating from the back kitchenette. Well, I thought, it was silly to expect things to be unchanged. Chiding myself for my own rigidity, I called out a cheery hello and started through the stacks to the back office. Halfway there, I almost literally ran into a female, about my height, wearing a dark, tailored suit, unexpected pantyhose and severe black pumps on her small, disgustingly dainty feet. It was mildly shocking to see such formality at Technicorps, where an easygoing atmosphere prevailed. Only when Philo was promoted did he begin to occasionally wear a tie, although that accessory was typically discarded by mid-morning, thrown carelessly over the back of a chair.

"Hello," the female said in greeting, brown eyes staring at me from behind a pair of tortoiseshell glasses.

If I'd had to guess, I would think she was roughly half my age and quite pretty beneath the glasses that were too heavy for her oval face. Her thick brown hair was pulled back and contained in a severe knot at the nape of her neck. I was rather in awe, since I'd never been successful in taming my hair with any style or contraption. She shifted a sheaf of papers from one arm to the other and stuck out her right hand.

"I'm Margaret Shelton," she said, smiling. "You must be Petra."

"Guilty, so I hope you've heard only wonderful things about me," I replied, taking her hand.

We did the female shake, not too wimpy but also not too heavy to the point of seeming as if we were about to arm wrestle. She invited me back to share coffee in the kitchen, and I followed along, already missing Fitzhugh and his proper, antique tea service but trying to be open to new people and new ways. Change was always difficult for me– an odd admission for a symbiont to make.

"So, I'm excited to meet Fitzhugh," she began, pushing a mug of black coffee towards me. I noticed she took hers with cream and a teaspoon of sugar…exactly a flat, level teaspoon, not a grain more or less.

"Well, I think he should be back by the end of the month, so you'll not have long to wait," I replied, taking a sip of the coffee which beat any espresso I'd ever had in terms of blackness and strength. My heart skipped a beat or two as the caffeine surged into my system.

As we sat and chatted, I learned she came from a collective outside of Atlanta, which explained her soft accent and the occasionally dropped "r" to a degree. Usually, we stayed in one place long enough to pick up customs and mannerisms before moving on. Kind of like a dog picks up fleas, I thought, the picture unflattering in my mind.

"This is a plum position," she went on to remark. "Fitzhugh will probably retire soon, and I hope I can move into his job permanently."

I felt my back go up in alarm, and my lips pursed in disapproval. Why would she make such an assumption about Fitzhugh? She must have seen the unguarded expression on my face because she leaned forward and gently touched my forearm.

"Philo told me, when he hired me, that this would be a position with advancement. So I naturally assumed," she said, allowing the sentence to drift off, unfinished.

I took another sip of coffee which suddenly became bitter in my mouth. Kipp, from his vantage point four floors above me, was still in the back of my head, and I acknowledged his alarm at what I was being told. If there was some plan to retire Fitzhugh, they might as well go ahead and shoot him and put him out of his misery. The library was his life and what kept him vigorous. He was one of those symbionts, like many humans, who needed to work, and idleness and lack of purpose would destroy him.

With effort, I managed to discuss the workings of the library with Margaret, who was not at fault in her wish for a better life and a job advancement. My issue was with Philo, and I'd be making a visit to his office again, later on that afternoon.

"I'll meet you there after we finish for the day and before we go home," Kipp said.

I could almost imagine him nodding his head firmly, the ruff of auburn fur circling his neck bristling with outrage. There was no stronger advocate than Kipp, who'd gone to my defense more times than I could recall. But for now, I needed to pay attention to the matter at hand. As it were, I had several ongoing translation projects and Margaret needed to be up to speed. She had a PhD in library science and obviously qualified but was still the new kid on the block

CHAPTER 9

"So, what did you plan to do with Fitzhugh?" I asked, barely managing to keep the fury from my tone. I cared not for fighting with Philo, but he'd brought on this chain of events, and he was the only one who could address the issue.

Philo and I had the closeness that forged trust but also allowed for combativeness when needed. We would forgive one another the occasional over-the-top lapses with memories of good times spent and shared love over many years. But I'd found, since he'd taken command at Technicorps, that my natural dislike of authority was coloring my ability to deal with him in a reasonable manner.

"Yes, I'm glad you realize that," Kipp pointed out helpfully. "You don't like people telling you what to do." He was stretched out on his side, enjoying the soft pile of the carpeted surface on the floor in Philo's office.

I sighed deeply and uncrossed my legs. Turning my head, I looked out the window which overlooked the garden; the sky was growing dark with a storm threatening on the horizon. Great, I thought, and I chose to walk to work today. It was obvious I missed the revised weather forecast.

"Since I'm absolutely certain you and Kipp are having

your usual exchange of thoughts without being courteous enough to loop me in, perhaps you'll tell me what's going on, Petra." Philo rose and came to sit on the side of his desk after pushing aside a tower of paper that threatened to topple over the edge and onto the floor. "And, yes, I could listen in but choose not to do so."

I rolled my eyes at Kipp, who stuck his tongue out at me in response. He was at my feet, his head twisted up so that his eyes were locked with mine. "Kipp says I'm stubborn and that I don't like authority." I finally muttered.

"Gee, let me write that one down in case I forget," Philo said, his tone flat with sarcasm. After deliberately changing his attitude, he added, with a softer voice, "I know you care about Fitzhugh and that the two of you have grown close." He ignored the blaze that ignited in my eyes. "You need to trust me that I would never do anything to harm him."

"So, why does Margaret think she will be promoted?" I asked.

"Because the position calls for that. Actually, it was no different for Peter, but he would have had to go back to school to acquire the necessary degrees, which Margaret already possesses."

I muttered some response, not exactly happy but also not terribly distressed. Philo would not tell me a lie, so perhaps I'd not understood the situation. Kipp stretched over and nipped my foot, making me catch my breath as I felt his incisor nick my left big toe through the thin fabric of the running shoes I wore. He was getting a little too free with the teeth lately.

"Need a ride home?" Philo asked. It was clear he wanted to get ahead of the storm.

I declined, wanting to be alone. However, fate had another plan. Kipp and I finished the first mile towards home, when a sudden wind hit my back with an intensity that felt as if it would push me to the ground. Kipp turned and gave a defiant bark at the storm which was literally upon us. I could see the tree tops bent from the force of the winds, and roughly three blocks behind us, the rain began to fall in a sudden and dense downpour. Shrugging my shoulders, I smiled at Kipp, who never minded the weather. There was no way to outrun it, or so I thought. A moment later, a familiar vehicle approached—it was Peter and Elani. He didn't even ask as he threw open the passenger side door. I ushered Kipp into the back, where Elani literally pranced as she touched noses gently with him. She'd missed her friend…that much was evident from her behavior. Since we'd returned, I'd been occupied with Fitzhugh and the library while Kipp returned to his work. Our lessons with Peter and Elani were on hold until further notice.

"Thanks," I said, almost wincing as the rain pummeled the vehicle, which rocked slightly against the wind. "We would have been soaked."

Peter drove slowly, since the water was rapidly pooling on the road. As we passed a convenience store, I recalled Fitzhugh's request for milk, since he seemed to have developed a craving for boxed cereal. I ran in, timing my exit and entry with the waning intensity of rainfall, and managed to hop back inside the vehicle without introducing a mini deluge. As we rode along, I told Peter about my chat with Philo.

"Oh, yeah, that assistant job was always meant to be an eventual replacement. But I was told that there was no time frame on it, and it would only be when Fitzhugh made the decision to quit and just act as an advisor." He looked over at me. Peter was wearing his dark rimmed glasses, and somehow they made him appear much older than his fifty-or-so years.

"I left a crock pot full of vegetable soup simmering this morning, Peter. Why don't you and Elani join us tonight?" I smiled. "It's Friday, and since I don't have to get up early tomorrow, Fitzhugh has challenged me to a Monopoly game. It will be him and Juno against me and Kipp. You and Elani can balance us out."

I wasn't quite sure why the youngster had nothing to do on a Friday night but join us older folks for Monopoly, but

I also had no desire to examine the fact I had no social life of my own. But in any case, the six of us found ourselves hovering around a low coffee table, Fitzhugh leaning in from his perch in my favorite wing chair. The dirty bowls from dinner rested in the kitchen sink, and the remainder of a jumbo box of Little Debbie oatmeal cakes sat forlornly on a vacant foot stool. I once again used my jaunty top hat but, even with Kipp's advice and consent, failed to gather any steam. It was Fitzhugh and Juno, the elder statesmen, who managed to use the little iron to flatten us all into submission.

"Tea, anyone?" Fitzhugh asked, raising his eyebrows at me. I recognized the signal and knew he wanted me to prepare and deliver a pot. Well, a little tea this late in the evening would probably do no harm since we were all too wired to sleep anyway.

While I was busy preparing the brew, Fitzhugh and Kipp searched for a movie on TCM and were pleased to find "The Ten Commandments". I was mildly horrified, since any movie that required intermissions so patrons could run to the bathroom was too long, in my humble opinion. But, as I remarked, there was no work in the morning, and I didn't really care if the rest of them wanted to watch it.

I think it was when Charlton Heston was sent out of Egypt by Yul Brynner that I fell asleep on the floor, my head resting on Kipp's warm and sturdy shoulder. Fitzhugh had stretched out on the sofa, and Peter and Elani were, like Kipp and me, enjoying the floor and a blanket. Lily managed to squirm her way next to my left ear and wedged herself in between Kipp and me. Actually, she served as a very nice cat hat, bringing warmth and soothing to my shoulder and neck. To my amazement, I awoke early the next morning to find everyone dozing, just as I'd left them the previous evening. The television was still on and halfway through "My Man Godfrey", one of my favorite comedies. Kipp stirred with me and raised his head to look around the room, simultaneously amused and pleased.

"This was a good time," he remarked with satisfaction.

I yawned in agreement before groaning at my body's response to the hard mattress upon which it had rested. In symbiont years, I was not even middle aged, not really, but my body creaked and protested like that of one of greatly advanced years. It was clear my usual routine had been disrupted, and my daily runs would begin again, that morning.

"It's a pretty day, so let's go see George," Kipp suggested. He stood and was stretching to and fro. "Believe it or not, but I'm a little stiff, too. I think I've grown soft with sleeping on your nice bed at night. Before that, I was accustomed to the hard ground."

"Don't blame your decline on me, my lad," I whispered into his upright ear before kissing the side of his furry face.

Soundlessly, I crept into the kitchen to begin a pot of coffee and then padded back to my room at the rear of the house. As I gazed into the mirror in my bathroom, I noticed a large, bright red crease where my face had been mashed into a hard chair pillow at some point when I abandoned Kipp's soft fur. With the thought a hot shower would loosen up my muscles, I hopped in, while Kipp reclined on the rug on the tile floor.

"Keep the water running, I'm next," he called out, thinking what a fine wit had he.

I found my sweats and dressed in preparation for a run later that morning. I was a pretty speedy dresser and, other than some sunscreen slathered on my face, did little to prepare for the day. Even my hair lay in a tangle down my back in the same mussed braid I'd worn the previous day. By the time I walked to the kitchen, Peter had stirred and sat with his sleepy face at the dinette table; his eyes opened wider when the coffee timer sounded, and the smell of fresh brew filled the room. Elani darted over to greet me, her moist nose nuzzling my hand.

"I need to get back in my routine," I commented, as he raised an eyebrow at my garb. Pouring him and me both cups of coffee, I set the mugs on the table and located the little creamer pitcher as well as some sugar for him.

"Believe it or not, I don't know when I've had so much fun," Peter said.

I guess it could have been a commentary on his lack of an outlet. But I agreed; it had been pleasant. At that moment, Juno came creaking in, her body stiff and a little wobbly. She shook off any assistance as I opened the back door for her to go into the yard. Kipp and Elani went with her, silent guardians on either side. Standing on the porch, I noticed the cool, damp freshness from the night's previous storm. A few small limbs had fallen, littering the grass which was brown and withered with the onset of winter. A group of geese flew overhead, their V-shaped formation filling the sky for a moment before they disappeared, honking noisily. The sun was low on the eastern horizon, projecting a soft, pastel glow in the sky. Leaving the lupines to wander around the yard, I returned to Peter. From the living room, I could hear Fitzhugh's soft snoring as he lapsed into another stage of sleep.

"I'll help with that mess," Peter said, gesturing at the kitchen counter where the dirty bowls and plates from the night before remained.

"Thanks," I replied with a smile. "And I'm glad to let you."

Kipp trotted energetically at my side. The road we took to visit baby George was not the one most traveled, but it was filled with memories nonetheless. As we ran along, I recalled that William Harrow had fancied he might marry me and have children. Little did he know that I had been married, once, a long time ago and was the mother to a dear baby named George. By the time I left Harrow, he knew there was something inexplicable but thought I merely was an errant time traveler transported by a mechanical device of some unknown nature. I wonder what his reaction would have been if he'd understood I was of a different species, despite my deceptively familiar appearance. Would he have still loved me?

"Yes, he would," Kipp replied confidently.

"How would you know that?" I asked, while carefully navigating a particular stretch of pavement which was notoriously bruised and posed all types of hazards for unsuspecting runners.

"I just go by his temperament," Kipp replied. "He was a broad-minded man, very much so for the times in which he lived."

I sighed, content with the answer. Kipp might only be sputtering comforting nonsense, but it helped my feelings to nurse the notion that I would have been loved, no matter what. I guess humans feel the same way. All sentient beings harbor secret rooms in their inner selves and wonder, from time to time, if others knew what was held there, would they still be loveable. Symbionts had created secret rooms voluntarily although Kipp and I violated those boundaries on a daily basis.

"That's my point," Kipp said, "I know all your faults, and I still love you."

"Thanks, buddy," I said, giving him a mock salute before reaching up to adjust my baseball cap.

We'd left Peter washing dishes, since he insisted, with Fitzhugh lurking nearby enjoying a pot of Earl Grey and a strawberry Pop Tart. Peter assured me he would work on breakfast and make certain Fitzhugh had some fresh fruit and oatmeal to finish off the pastry.

"We used to be alone," I said, watching the man who approached us with a large mastiff on a leash. Out of courtesy, since I saw him eyeing us in return, Kipp and I crossed the road; the man had no wish to struggle with his dog who would demand a friendly and professional canine inspection of the equally massive Kipp. "And now our house seems full of others," I concluded. We passed the man and his companion and crossed back to resume our path.

"Do you mind?" Kipp asked.

"Not too much." As I answered, I realized I spoke the truth. Maybe I wasn't the loner I claimed myself to be.

The tall grass in the field we passed had collapsed into a

damp, matted mess; I missed the times when it stood proudly, rippling as would an ocean wave propelled by nagging winds. The trees had been stripped naked, except for the few stubborn leaves that just insisted on clinging to the branches despite nature's death edict. A couple of trees were still cloaked in a large number of withered, brown leaves; I'd been told this was the signal of a dying tree, but I didn't know if that was true or just country legend.

It felt good to be back in my routine, and as I ran, I felt the familiar pleasure sink in after I'd gone the first couple of miles. My legs felt strong and solid as my feet hit the payment with soft, little thuds. Kipp was so close to me that his fur brushed my leg as we ran in synch, our pacing identical despite the fact he could outrun me in speed as well as endurance. Our minds were in perfect symbiosis, too, and I felt the total completeness of my kind.

We approached the cemetery and passed under the arching entrance that silently welcomed us as visitors. I was glad George was here, out in the country, where it was quiet and lonely. Graveyards should be lonely, I thought, occupied by the spirits of the departed and courted only by the occasional living visitor. His resting place was near the crest of the hill; I often would stretch out in the grass, staring up at the sky, just lying next to him. The ground was rather damp, despite the cold temperatures, so I chose, instead, to let my hand rest on his granite marker before prowling about. Maybe there was something odd about me, but I'd always been fascinated by old cemeteries. In past times, people would devise creative and poetic inscriptions to mark their sentiments of their loved ones. Kipp ambled after me, pausing to read them, too, and would call me, excited, when he'd find one of interest.

"Mattie Jo, beloved wife and daughter; I'll see you again in Heaven," Kipp read. He sat at that grave, his thoughts mired in contemplation. We'd talked of spiritual matters many times, and he usually had endless queries, a testament to his bright mind.

"If most humans and symbionts, too, believe in a creator,

how do you explain those who don't?" he asked.

"I don't have an answer for that, Kipp." I crossed over to another very old headstone, the inscription almost unreadable after years of exposure to the elements. It was sad that the heartfelt last words were lost in time.

"Maybe some people need demonstrable proof of a creator and an afterlife. Belief in both of those is a matter of faith, and there is nothing you can hold in your hands—or paws–and use your five senses to indicate the reality of it."

I'd been raised to believe in a higher power, a creator, and found that to be a comforting belief. Kipp, coming from a primitive era with little exposure to such since he lost his mother so early, was working on his own beliefs. I knew, from our discussions, he had the most solid moral core of any symbiont I'd known, and definitely believed in right and wrong. He also believed in creation and a creator but from there, he was still working to figure it all out.

"Humans have a lot of names for God," he remarked. "Do you think it matters?"

"It does matter to many people, Kipp. And I can't tell you what to think. All I know is that our beliefs are a guidebook on how to treat one another with compassion. If there is judgment, I think it will be based upon that."

What better place to muse about ethereal matters than in a graveyard? All of the current residents had already left earth and crossed to the world of that which was unseen and not of the flesh. Kipp walked a step ahead of me and paused; his body became stiff, his hair rising in a strip from his neck to his tail. One of his forelegs bent up, almost like a pointer who was signaling a bird hidden in a darkening thicket.

"I just felt something I've never felt before," he said. "In that row of headstones, there is the sense of humans who are still here; I can almost read their thoughts, but they are jumbled and chaotic."

I walked closer to the plain, white markers, which were on the backside of the sloping hill and recognized the line signaled the graves of unknown Civil War soldiers. The sight was not an uncommon one in older cemeteries and had always been sad to me. In past times, a mother, perhaps, may have received the message that her son fell somewhere, his body to never be brought home.

Kipp was clearly anxious but after a moment of settling his thoughts, he moved slowly closer to the line. He paused once, and his body stiffened again.

"Something or someone just moved through my body," he said. "I can almost smell him but not quite."

"I think you are detecting apparitions–ghosts–of men who died in battle." This new Kipp development would be something to share with Fitzhugh. "How does it feel to you?"

"Sad, frightening, unstable…" Kipp began to reel off the words. "There's not enough of it to indicate all of these men are still present," he said, his nose following the long double line. Just a few…" his thoughts trailed off again. "One in particular stands out to me. I think he was very young, no more than a boy." Kipp turned to me, his eyes rounded with emotion. "He wants to go home, Petra. He misses his mother."

"Let's go, Kipp." I knew he was getting lost in the odd experience, and it was taking an emotional toll.

Retracing our steps, we rounded the hilltop, and, as we left, I once again touched the granite headstone of George's resting place with my hand in a mute goodbye, and, after a brief warm up, we began to jog again, our steps slow at first, but picking up with time. I think we were both ready to get home and leave that sad place.

CHAPTER 10

To say that Fitzhugh was curious would have been an understatement. He knew that there were instances of such phenomena experienced by Kipp in our recorded history, but the documentation of those moments was rare.

"It's probably due to Kipp's superior telepathic skills that are more developed than are ours," he remarked. "Kipp, at some point, I'd like to interview you and record this."

Kipp nodded his head. He and Juno, with Lily in the mix, were lying in front of the fireplace. That winter threatened to be cold, and the *Farmer's Almanac* prediction was remarkably accurate. We'd already had one thin snowfall that coated the land like a threadbare wool blanket as well as a few icy mornings that caused me to gauge my comings and goings with more care than was common. Outside, a brisk wind howled as it skirted along the sides of the house, causing the storm door to rattle restlessly in its frame.

"We are supposed to go with Peter to Chickamauga," I said. "I'm wondering if we should cancel that trip." Restless, I tossed the magazine I'd been idly thumbing without actually reading to the floor.

"Why? Because of me?" Kipp asked. Lily managed to climb on his back and had her feline arms stretched on either side of his neck, while her head rested on top of his, her little face wedged between his large, upright ears.

"Well, duh, yes," I replied, sticking out my tongue at him. "There's no need to have you subjected to such an experience. Remember, we were in a small cemetery, and Chickamauga will be filled with disturbances far beyond what you felt here."

Fitzhugh listened to us bicker back and forth, his chair angled so that he could enjoy the warmth from the fire. He did not weigh in with an opinion but occasionally would close his eyes in thought.

"What do you think?" I finally asked him.

"I think it is Kipp's decision," he replied. "I trust him to pull back from anything unpleasant or intolerable."

I began to mutter that I trusted him, too. Irritated at all of them, except maybe Juno and, oddly enough, Lily–who was usually a predictable source of chaos—I rose and went to the kitchen to fix a pot of tea. The sound of Fitzhugh's worn scuffs scrubbing against the wood floors echoed softly in the hallway before he entered the room. Wordlessly, he crossed and unexpectedly came to stand behind me.

"I know how to do it," I said, feeling grumpy without knowing why.

"I know you do, Petra." His voice was gentle and filled with an unusual level of approval. Unexpectedly, his hands found my shoulders, which he squeezed. "Thank you for making tea," he added.

Despite his not giving voice to the obvious, I realized he understood the depth of my love for Kipp and the resulting protectiveness with which I regarded my bonded partner. I didn't like to see Kipp hurt in any fashion, even in the pursuit of knowledge. Maybe that's a flaw in humans as well as symbionts. Growth, after all, comes from pain, and we are enhanced as result of the experience.

"I want a Christmas tree," Kipp declared, his nose pressed against the frosty passenger side window of my car. We were riding along the familiar route home after having been to the market. Although it was only afternoon, winter darkness had fallen, and the day was dismal and frigid, the air damp and filled with unexpected promise. Although the holiday was still two weeks hence, several houses we passed prominently displayed trees in their front windows. The tree lights formed a soft blur of color through windows made damp and foggy through condensation and gave the appearance of cozy, festive warmth in contrast to the bleak conditions outside.

My husband and I had been married in a church and enjoyed observing Christmas for the spiritual nature of the day as well as its secular beauty. Since Kipp had been with me, we really hadn't marked the day in any special manner. In my attic, in some dark, cobweb-coated corner, there was a large box of decorations. They would be, by now, considered vintage in nature. Armed with a flashlight, since I knew the box was in an unlit area, I pulled down the creaking, metal stairway, and began my ascent. Kipp hovered anxiously at the base, along with Fitzhugh, who had his arms crossed at his chest. He'd wanted to accompany me but I firmly declined. All I needed was for the old symbiont to have a heart attack in my attic. I hadn't been up there in years, and I mean years. Against a far wall was George's crib. I'd not had the heart to dispose of it after his death. Kipp followed my thoughts and felt my hard swallow as I pushed on.

"I'm sorry," he began, feeling my pain.

"It's okay, Kipp. Just old memories..." I replied, stiffening my shoulders. The box of decorations was in front of me, and I managed to lift it without too much struggle. Maneuvering it down the staircase was not easy, but I backed out, using the stairs to brace and catch the box as it thumped gently down the cross steps until it was safely in the hallway.

"Let me see one!" Kipp demanded, prancing excitedly across the floor, his toenails clicking against the wood.

I opened the box and after rummaging in some tissue paper, found a lovely red sphere, a perfect glass globe that caught the light in the hallway. Holding it up, I enjoyed seeing the glow of excitement and pleasure in Kipp's eyes. A short time later, Kipp, Fitzhugh and I took off in my small car to a tree lot I'd seen when I went to the market. The timing was right to have a live tree so that it wouldn't linger too long and become dry. I'd found an old tree stand in the bottom of the box from the attic that was well used and heavy as a cast iron tub, unlike the flimsy modern ones.

Kipp hopped out to help me search, while Fitzhugh stayed in the car with the motor running so that he could enjoy the manufactured heat. I let Kipp select the tree, after giving him size parameters. No, we did not need that eight-foot monster that cost as much as five pairs of running shoes. Finally, he found a pretty, nicely formed little fir that was maybe five feet tall. I could manage it, which was critical, since Kipp couldn't help. After money changed hands and the salesman tied it to the roof of my car, we returned home. As we drove up, I could see Juno and Lily peering out, their noses pressed against the large, center window in the front room. Yes, this had all the hallmarks of enjoyment, and the lupines were acting like small children, almost clapping their paws with excitement.

After a vigorous debate between Fitzhugh and Kipp as to the proper height and trajectory for maximum window display, I managed to get the tree settled on a low table and secured the base of the tree into the holder. I'd had concerns about the wiring of the lights in the box which, like the ornaments, were vintage items. So I'd stopped by the home improvement store and picked up a pack of multicolor LEDs which looked pretty and soft on the display.

Fitzhugh prepared a pot of hot cocoa and found a Christmas movie on TCM. Actually, it was one of my favorites, "White Christmas". Kipp barked and chased me around the room as I tried to emulate Vera Ellen's dancing, failing miserably in my efforts; Fitzhugh had the good sense to not pretend to be Danny Kaye. At some point, Lily had enough of Kipp's howling and Juno's high-pitched, enthusiastic choruses and managed a slinking crawl through the house to hide away in the back of the closet in my bedroom. So that's what it took to get rid of the little monster, I thought with satisfaction—whirl frenetically around the room while stringing Christmas lights.

Fitzhugh sat close by and handed me the ornaments, one by one, with care as if he was holding irreplaceable treasures. Kipp and Juno argued over where each ornament should go and debated over which was the loveliest. Kipp found a favorite of mine lurking at the bottom of the box. It was a mercury glass—almost translucent—silver globe with glitter that had been applied in the design of a snowflake. His eyes crossed as he tried to inspect it too closely.

"That's the prettiest thing I've ever seen," he stated matter-of-factly. "Why can't I see a real snowflake?"

We had a robust discussion on things not seen, and I treated him to a series of snowflakes made of paper I cut with a pair of kitchen scissors. With string and tape, I hung the fake flakes from the door frames so that they would sway gently with the slightest breath of air. After we'd finished–and the day was growing darker as evening arrived–the four of us dashed outside, braving the temperature, to look at our pretty front window.

"We have the best tree on the street," Kipp said, nodding his head with satisfaction.

"It's not a competition," I replied, ruffling his fur while silently agreeing. Yes, our little tree with its old glass ornaments stood out amongst so many others with a modern twist of plastic decorations or large silky bows. A frigid breeze hit the back of my neck, and I herded the others back indoors.

"And it will be your job," I said to Kipp, "to keep Lily from climbing the tree and breaking the ornaments." She'd been driven off earlier by my dancing, but I spied her little triangular face staring at the tree, captivated, her eyes almost crossed with delight, from across the room where she skulked—thinking she was invisible—beneath my wing chair.

"I'm on it, chief," Kipp replied. He would, in his way, try to implant a thought into Lily's feline brain that the tree was off limits. A minute later his head turned and lifted, as he cocked it to one side like a big dog fascinated by a squeaky toy. "Philo's coming," he announced, darting over to the front door, tail wagging.

Philo didn't bother to knock, since he could clearly see all the festivities in the front room. As he entered, a current of cold air followed him, causing the flames in the fireplace to dance in the updraft that made a little whoosh of fire up the chimney; the paper snowflakes twisted and turned on their string tethers. I took his coat; his lips, which felt like ice cubes, brushed my cheek.

"Get by the fire, and I'll get you some hot cocoa," I ordered.

He and the others were discussing the merits of holiday celebrations, including trees, when I came back. Not only did I bring cocoa, but also there was a plate of cookies. No, they were not homemade but were those that one sees at the holiday…a large, pretty tin full of different kind of cookies allegedly from Belgium. Kipp, not unexpectedly, was engaged in an opposing view and paused momentarily to sample a butter cookie.

"I just don't see the reason to spend so much time and money to decorate a house for what is, essentially, a religious day," Philo was saying. "If you want to honor the day, do it quietly."

"But don't you think all of the festivities, the decorations, the shopping for a gift for someone…those things help build the energy for the day, and make it even more special?" Kipp asked. "Combining the secular beauty with the meaning of the day just builds the excitement," he concluded. My Kipp loved a good debate.

"Well, I guess it's a personal choice," Philo concluded diplomatically. "And your tree is particularly lovely," he added graciously.

His last comment seemed to mollify Kipp, who was getting a bit huffy. After all, he'd helped with the tree selection as well as the decoration and had a significant emotional investment in the final product.

Philo, with his mug of cocoa in hand, sat with us as we gathered around the fire. Juno and Kipp settled on the floor as close as possible to the flames without actually risking the danger of being ignited. Lily pushed in between them and curled up, her head resting on Kipp's right front paw. I knew it wouldn't take long for Fitzhugh to give voice what had been on his mind, and it came quickly.

"So how is Margaret Shelton coming along in my library?" he asked, avoiding eye contact with Philo as he delicately took a sip of his chocolate. With a napkin, Fitzhugh dabbed at his mustache to remove any clinging droplets. "Has she managed not to muck it up too badly?"

The reference to the library being his was not made without thought. Fitzhugh had put a large portion of his life into the collections held there and, in many ways, the stories were like his family, children which needed nurturing and care.

"She seems to be adjusting," Philo answered. "Of course, when you return, she will take less of a leadership role and will assist you," he added carefully.

I knew Philo very well, and he wouldn't say things just to soothe someone's angst or create cheer. If he told Fitzhugh his position was secure, then it was. Obviously, Fitzhugh knew the same of Philo because he dropped the subject and relaxed in his chair.

Christmas arrived, and although I had not done so for many years since my house had been empty save for Tula, who did not observe holidays, I'd gone shopping, thinking it would be fun to have presents under the tree for all the creatures who happened to be stirring under my roof. So early that morning, before Fitzhugh or Juno awakened, I tried to slip from bed without disturbing Kipp. Of course, that endeavor was a miserable failure as it was a physical and telepathic impossibility.

"Where are you going?" he asked, putting his paw on my shoulder to push me back down against the mattress.

"None of your beeswax," I answered. "Close your mind and don't pry," I added.

I felt his mind leave mine; since this was an unusual occurrence, I took note of the novel feeling. Odd, I felt empty and alone without his constant presence in the back of my head, offering a running commentary on events as well as the assurance of his love and constancy. Mildly anxious, I almost called for him to come back but managed to control the outburst and continued on my way, tippy toeing down the narrow hallway from my room to the living room. Fitzhugh's door was closed, and I carefully stepped over the one squeaky floorboard that I knew like a stubborn key stuck on a piano.

Entering the living room, I was content to note that some stubborn embers still glowed in the fireplace. Igniting a roaring fire would take little effort, so, before I did anything else, I added a couple of small pieces of wood from my stack and used the iron poker to stir the embers. A soft meow startled me; I turned to see Lily curled up in my favorite chair, her mouth yawning wide open, eyes blinking sleepily at me. She'd obviously spent the night enjoying the fireplace. Crossing over, I gave her a little pat on the head, watching her twist her head as I scratched under her chin. The sound of purring almost filled the room; her soft fur radiated the warmth of the fireplace to my cold fingers.

There was a small hall closet at the front door entrance; I opened the door and pushed aside some coats to pull out several wrapped boxes. These I carefully placed beneath the tree, feeling an excited burst of delight at being able to have a surprise waiting for my little family. That done, I was in the kitchen preparing coffee when Fitzhugh trudged in, his old plaid flannel robe cinched around his narrow waist; his hair stood erect in an untidy shock like the comb on a rooster. Juno trailed after him, her tail wagging. Bending down, I gave her a kiss on top of her old noggin before opening the back door. Kipp zoomed in at that moment, and both lupines disappeared out the back door to take their morning constitutional.

I think Fitzhugh and I had lived together too long at that moment, because the morning was filled with queries as to the quality of sleep, was one feeling rested, and questions about general health and well being. Bored with the inane chit chat, I hurried him to get his coffee; Kipp and Juno had returned, so I herded them all into the living room with a childish glee.

I actually don't think Juno had ever received a Christmas present, and I knew Kipp hadn't. They acted like kids, looking at me and then looking at their boxes as if to ask permission to just rip into the containers. I had to help, since furry paws weren't made for such, but the looks on their faces were priceless. For Juno, I'd ordered a fleece dog jacket with her name embroidered on the collar area.

"I know this weather is tough on you, so I thought this might help," I said, hoping she liked it. I'd debated over the color for weeks before deciding upon a nice turquoise blue with a brown contrast trim. Pink seemed too little girlie for the aged Juno.

"Oh, Petra! It's beautiful," she said, her dark eyes turning to me. "Thank you so much."

Kipp, ever the gentleman, waited for her before we opened his box. I knew he would not wear a jacket, so I'd gone another route.

"What is this?" he asked, looking at the box which held a flat, silvery object.

"I got you a Kindle," I replied. "You like to read and turning pages is a problem, so you can download books on this and use this stylus to progress the pages." Since I lacked a home computer, I'd given it to Peter to set up an account and begin to download books. There was already a sizeable history collection available. "You can adjust the font as you get older and need bigger type," I said, laughing. Also, I'd ordered a nifty cover from a company in England that made one that looked and felt like an actual bound book. I'd chosen "The Hound of the Baskervilles" cover and also had Peter download the entire Sherlock Holmes library, knowing Kipp would enjoy having his brain challenged by a good mystery.

He hopped over the discarded wrapping paper and jumped up to put his massive paws on my shoulders, as I struggled to keep my balance. The next thing I knew, I got a sloppy, wet, lupine kiss all over my right cheek.

"Gee, a thank you would have been enough," I said, trying to dry my face with the sleeve of my robe.

Lily was next, and in her impatience, she managed to snag my right forefinger with her claw as she grabbed the catnip mouse from my hand. The last we saw of her, she was low crawling, slinking along the baseboards, mouse in her jaws, before she disappeared down the dark hallway to the rear of the house.

"And not a word of thanks," I muttered. "What an ingrate."

Fitzhugh waited patiently, smiling as I put a box in his lap. I crossed over to my wing chair, now vacated by Lily, sat and curled my feet beneath me. The old symbiont raised his eyebrows and stared at me for a moment.

"I didn't get you anything," he said.

"I know," I answered. "But I wanted you to have something I found that had you written all over it."

He almost seemed like he was trying to preserve the paper, considering the care with which he removed and creased it as if he might reuse it later. Kipp became impatient and was almost dancing up and down as he eyed Fitzhugh's slow fingers. Finally, the box was revealed as Fitzhugh pried open the top. I could tell from the look on his face that he was pleased.

"It is an Irish sweater," he said, holding it up.

I'd picked a tweedy looking cardigan, brown with flecks of navy and olive, with leather patches on the elbows. It seemed perfect for a librarian, and I thought he could use it when he resumed work.

"Is this my return to work sweater?" he asked, as if he was reading my thoughts even though I knew he was not inside my head.

"Yes," I answered simply. Philo had told him that he was to be at Technicorps on the first work day after New Year's

Day. "You have about another week to loaf around and then you will be earning an honest living again," I added, smiling at him.

He nodded his head. Standing, he removed his robe and pushed his arms through the sleeves of the sweater. "A perfect fit," he announced, turning so that we might view him in his magnificence.

CHAPTER 11

"**P**eggy has done a wonderful job of organizing things while I've been gone," Fitzhugh remarked as he settled in my small car. Somehow, he, Juno, Kipp and I all managed to squeeze in and ride the short distance home. I'd cranked the heater up to full blast and was gratified to hear it roar in response. There was a dusting of ice on the road, lingering from the previous night, and I slowed down as I felt the rear wheels slide a little in some left-over slush. Kipp, who thought he was my copilot despite no license or experience, poked his cold nose up against my neck. It was a mild chastisement.

I admit it was totally childish on my part, but I felt a little hurt…just a tiny bee sting of something that didn't quite feel like jealousy…but I was confident it was a feeling lacking in nobility. After all, I'd been there, too, working with her, so it wasn't as if she had come in and conquered the library on her own. And even Peter had been reassigned to help her become adjusted to Technicorps and the filing systems we used.

"I was thinking, if you don't mind, Petra, we might have her over for dinner one night?" Fitzhugh asked. He was wearing the cardigan I'd given him beneath his heavy coat, a favorite despite the frayed collar and a torn pocket. I don't think he'd missed wearing the sweater one day since he opened the box.

"Yeah, whatever you want to do," I responded in a lackluster way.

Fitzhugh glanced over at me, but I doggedly focused on the road in front of me. I think I was afraid if he saw the expression on my face that he might recognize what a child I was being and how silly I was to feel I was left out of this new, special relationship. After all, I'd worked for years to get to a place of mutual respect and unexpected affection, and it'd only taken Peggy, an upstart, about four minutes. Looking in the rearview mirror, I caught Kipp's eyes staring back at mine.

"What is wrong?" he asked, tilting his head to the side. He knew only I could hear him when he spoke thus to me and felt emboldened to push the issue. "You sound like you are jealous of Peggy, or something."

I pretended to ignore him and acted as if my sole concentration was required to negotiate the slippery road which really wasn't that bad. With a twist of the knob, I turned off the loudly slapping windshield wipers, since the glass was long since clear. Looking up, I saw Kipp's eyes still looking at me. Well, great, I thought. I couldn't even wallow in self pity or have a private moment and just get away with it by lying and brushing it aside. I had a persistent symbiont prying into my brain, and there was nowhere I could tuck those thoughts and feelings away from his nagging enquiries.

"I guess it was nice feeling special," I said lamely in response to Kipp.

"And you still are special," he answered. "Peggy will never have the kind of closeness you have with Fitzhugh. But aren't you glad he likes her? Would you rather he detest her and that would somehow make you more important while he was miserable?"

Well, darn it. There was just no lying to a symbiont. Maybe I did need to return to London, marry Harrow and disappear.

"No, you don't need to do that," Kipp replied. "Anyway, you like sweat pants and being a slob, and you'd have to dress up all the time in those fancy long skirts. And you can't pour a decent cup of tea for the life of you."

"It would be nice to have Peggy over for dinner, Fitzhugh," I said aloud, responding to the old symbiont's enquiry, after having made the decision to act like a well-adjusted adult for a change. "I've only seen her at work, and she probably has few friends in the area." Glancing at him I smiled across the small expanse that separated us in the car. "Just pick a day, and I'll make vegetarian chili, since it's so cold out."

He smiled back and began to prattle on about a new project they had tackled together. He seemed to forget that I'd been in the library, too, working all day. I tried not to grit my teeth and glanced at Kipp again in the mirror.

"We need to get on with our job, Petra," he said. "Fitzhugh is okay, and it's time we resume our work with Peter and Elani. Once you get some distance from this, you'll feel better."

I wasn't sure where he got his degree in counseling, but he was right. I needed to return to my purpose in life.

"Philo," I began, after having taken a seat in his office, "I need to move ahead with Peter and Elani. It's time, and Fitzhugh is doing great, medically speaking."

"How's it going, you guys all living together?" Philo asked. Reaching up, he removed the reading glasses that were a relatively new adornment and massaged the bridge of his nose with a thumb and forefinger. He was aging, in the slow manner of our kind, as was I. Kipp, who knew of my plans to meet with Philo, was downstairs in the learning lab with the juvenile lupines. I'd started my day in the library with the usual pile of translations. It was much too easy to get comfortable there, even though I grumbled at the tedium of the work.

"Surprisingly well," I responded. Glancing down, I saw a big mud clod that had inexplicably been attached to the toe of my right boot all morning. From the back of my head, I heard Kipp giggle; he'd known about my nasty boot but said nothing, thinking it was amusing. He was right in that I was not fussy enough to survive on Harrow's elegant arm at some high brow soiree. "In fact, he can stay as long as he likes," I added. "Juno is a dear, and Fitzhugh reads a lot or just putters around. He's not critical of my sloppy housekeeping and actually cooks on occasion."

Philo's dark eyebrows scooted up almost out of sight on his high forehead. It was clear he was surprised at my passive surrender at having lost my privacy. "I think your Whitechapel trip changed you in more ways than you might have counted," he said. At my look of surprise, he remarked, "I can't imagine you would have been this resigned in the past to having three new, uh, bodies, invade your space."

Well, there was probably some truth in what he said. I'd lived in Harrow's home for months and came to enjoy his companionship as well as that of Mac and the household staff. And then there were the boys at the school who tugged at my heartstrings with their winsome and mischievous ways.

"But I agree; it's time for you and Kipp to return to your job of tutoring Peter and Elani. I'll make the necessary reservations in Chattanooga, and you can leave by the end of the week, if that's okay."

A few days later, I was standing at the front door of my house waiting for Peter to arrive. It remained harshly cold outside–that kind of cold weather that makes one's skin hurt—since we were only in the third week of January; the glass storm door was covered with frost as I stood with my nose almost pressed against it. Peggy had volunteered to pick up Fitzhugh and Juno each morning since he didn't drive, but it was still early for her arrival. In some ways, I was grateful to her and hoped she might continue this practice when spring arrived. It was time for me to begin walking to work with Kipp as I'd done before the arrival of Fitzhugh. I heard soft steps behind me and turned. Fitzhugh was dressed for the day, Irish sweater in place and neatly buttoned.

"Be careful," he said, avoiding eye contact with me.

"I will," I replied, avoiding eye contact with him. Tenderness between the two of us was a fleeting thing, tenuous and unpredictable.

Thankfully Peter arrived, and I was in the SUV, Kipp safely in the back with Elani, in less than two minutes. Peter was warmly dressed even to the point of a knit hat covering his dark hair, which still managed to curl loosely around his ears and neck.

"We're going a different route," he said. "There was snow last night in the Smokies, and I'm sure the roads are a mess or even closed."

I admit it was pleasant to be on the road again with him. Kipp appeared to be more relaxed with Elani as I listened in at their playful banter from the back of the SUV. There was no need to rush, and Peter didn't drive with his normal excessive acceleration. He, as usual, insisted upon driving, so I stared out the window and enjoyed the scenery. Since it was mid January, the landscape was dry and withered; a gray starkness hovered over the physical world in vivid contrast to a cloudless blue sky above.

"I hope Peggy is enjoying working in the library more than I did," Peter remarked, darting a glance at me from beneath his dark forelock of hair.

"Seems to," I replied, keeping my tone neutral. I didn't really think Peter was trying to gossip but decided to take the high road nonetheless.

"I've been wondering about something related to time shifts," Peter said, managing to change the conversation nicely. "Why don't we actively look for other symbionts or colonies when we travel back in time?"

"We're not actually prohibited, but it's not advisable for the very reasons we don't reveal ourselves to humans. Our species can't take a chance on altering history, and it would be hazardous to go back and inadvertently let things slip about the future to our own kind. And the mere dynamics are mind boggling...sort of like trying to figure out when time started or where outer space stops. Let's say I travel back to the time when I was ten years old and encounter myself and my family of origin." I looked over at Peter who diligently kept his eyes on the road. "You can see where that would be unwise. I have met other symbionts during time trips, and it is always tricky. We typically can "ping" one another from a distance and probably need to keep our contacts brief if they occur at all."

It had been considered indisputable fact that symbionts lacked the ability to travel into the future. Our existence was linear, and we could only return to the date of departure plus the amount of time actually gone. With skill and experience, I could come fairly close to hitting that mark within a few days or a week. That sort of precision was an asset and the mark of the efforts of a disciplined team. Kipp's achievement of having progressed in the timeline when he joined with me to travel was, in itself, remarkable. To date, no researcher at Technicorps had been able to explain that little anomaly. Kipp effortlessly avoided their attempts to define his existence.

Lookout Mountain was located to the south and west of Chattanooga; Chickamauga stretched over the rolling landscape just a little farther west. Peter bypassed the city since our accommodations were on the outskirts of the town proper. We located the hotel where we had reservations and stowed our meager gear.

"What game have you brought?" Elani asked, her tail wagging slightly with excitement.

"Clue," I answered, laughing. "You'll like this one."

We decided to drive through the park to get a sense of the topography and general layout and return on the following day for a time shift exercise. Since we were still at the point of Peter and Elani just learning to make the coordinated shift, we really had no particular destination and wouldn't remain for any measurable time. But as Peter slowly drove through the park, he began to plan our most ambitious journey, if we could convince the Twelve to issue an approval.

"I'd like to visit the time in history when the *General* was stolen," Peter announced.

"That's pretty specific," I replied, raising my eyebrows. With effort, I stopped myself from making any other negative remarks.

He glanced at me, and I knew he was trying to figure out the best way to convince me of his wish. Elani and Kipp crowded together and poked their heads between the seats so that all four of us were jammed in the front of the SUV.

"I figured it would be low risk," Peter began. "There was no fighting in Atlanta at that point in history; the actual combat wouldn't take place until later. We could travel south after we leave here and visit the *General* which is housed in a museum in Marietta. I thought that experience would help ground us and tie us to it."

"Go on," I said. So far he was thinking logically about the trip.

"Then we could ride on down to Atlanta and find the general location where the train station, or Car Shed as it was called, would have been. This will further give us an attachment point. My thought was that we would time shift to 1862 Atlanta, ride on the *General* to its stopping point where it was hijacked and witness the event. Then we could return home."

Considering some of the things I'd done, this one seemed to have a mild risk element involved. There was no actual warfare in the area, although there were troops–both formal and informal militia groups—and there was no loss of life during the actual theft of the *General*. Our main issue would be to get the timing down, and we would only hit the correct date through sheer luck and the influence of Kipp's superior talents. At best, we'd be a few days off, but that was typical. For a timing exercise, it would prove to be a good test.

"We'll run it by the Twelve," I answered. "They will either approve it or not."

We completed a drive through Chickamauga and decided to return the next day, if the weather held. In less than an hour, we were at our hotel with bags full of food we'd ordered. We gathered in my room, where there was a small table with a couple of chairs. I had a Greek salad while the others ate hamburgers. After Kipp finished his third large burger, he sighed and stretched out on the floor.

"I'm good," he announced with satisfaction. "Glad they left the onions off; they taste good but give me indigestion." He saw me eyeing his unfinished portion of French fries. "Help yourself." I got down on the floor next to him and shared fries drenched in ketchup while Peter chatted about the *General* and events of the time.

"The South was at a disadvantage, strategically. It was limited by the number of main railroad lines moving into and within the region. There was only one trunk line running from Chattanooga to Atlanta, and both of those cities were important rail centers. So, in order to move goods, troops, ammunition, anything, that main line—the Western & Atlantic Railroad or the W&ARR, as it was called–was critical. The North realized the strategic importance of disrupting the railroad services and even more so recognized that those lines utilized a large number of wooden bridges to cross rivers and other natural barriers. Any spy or soldier found burning a bridge to disrupt the rail lines was executed, sometimes on the spot.

"James Andrews, the leader of the raiders, was a mystery man. He'd been smuggling goods into the South and developed contacts who trusted him. However, he took information gained back to the Federals for their use in the war effort. So, he cleverly played both sides of the fence."

I had long been interested in the Civil War and had made many time shifts to that period and met various people whose names resonated in history. Of course, having been born in 1604, I was alive during the war but didn't live in the States at that time and didn't experience any of it firsthand.

"Andrews wanted to steal the *General*, take it north to Chattanooga on that critical trunk line, burning bridges behind him as he went. None of it transpired as planned, mostly due to the stubbornness of the conductor of the *General*, Bill Fuller."

Peter continued on for a while with the enthusiasm of a young fanatic who was consumed with obtaining knowledge about a specific event. I leaned back on Kipp and enjoyed listening to Peter as well as allowing Kipp and Elani to process the information. After all, Kipp and Elani would have to agree to this time shift, too. It was not purely Peter's call.

"Peter, if I remember correctly, wasn't it raining constantly during that whole episode?" I asked, my voice couched in innocence.

"Yes," he replied, his face screwed up over the strangeness of my query.

"Well, then, we'll have to contend with the smell of wet dog the whole time," I replied, digging Kipp in the ribs with my elbow. Kipp, growling playfully, grabbed my braid in his mouth and threatened to pull me across the floor by my hair until I begged for mercy.

"I'm ready for Clue, if you are," Peter announced, a slight frown on his face. His thoughts of the *General* were serious, and my lightheartedness was obviously not appreciated. "That is, if you two are finished messing around."

We spread the board out on the floor. I claimed my favorite character, Professor Plum; Kipp gleefully chose Mr. Green, liking the sinister aspect of his persona. He even tried to act out the part by pulling his lips back to display his teeth while squinting his eyes half-closed before assuming his Sphinx pose, thoughts shuttered and guarded. Peter, after careful consideration, became Colonel Mustard, and Elani, rather deliberately I thought, became Miss Scarlet. When playing any game with Kipp, he had to be on an honor system since he could peek at any of our thoughts and then evaporate like an early morning mist without our having known he'd been privy to any private musings. At one point when he was kicking all our butts, I stared at him, accusation written on my face.

"And, Kipp, how is it you seem to be so spot on with all of your accusations?"

"I'm just good, very good," he answered, smiling, his tongue lolling out.

"Does he cheat?" Peter asked, frustrated.

"He claims not to," I replied. "But how would you know?"

After we finished, I turned on the television, and we were fairly surprised to see an old John Wayne movie that was set during the Civil War, "Rio Lobo". Kipp almost danced in place with excitement since he had become a huge fan of westerns.

"You know," he said, "I think I'd like to time shift back and watch one of these old westerns being filmed."

"Yeah, you could get signed on as an extra," I remarked, poking a little fun at my buddy.

It wasn't long before Kipp had Peter and Elani rolling with laughter as he did his best impression of John Wayne walking with his short-stepped leaning walk across the room. Elani, with her infatuation of Kipp, had found a new, endearing side to his character–he could be silly and playful. I didn't think that revelation would help in his efforts to distance her emotionally from him. After Peter and Elani had retired to their room, Kipp and I climbed into bed. He assumed his usual place at my side, his muzzle stretched across my chest.

"I have to admit, this mentor gig is not as bad as I'd thought," Kipp remarked. "Maybe this should be our new focus going forward."

I listened to him prattle on, not in agreement, but willing to listen to his point of view. He was probably more of a natural teacher than was I. Kipp had the patience needed to work with the young lupines, staying late, adapting his style of instruction to their learning needs. I feared I lacked his best qualities–in fact, I know I did and still do–and wasn't sure I shared his enthusiasm for becoming a full-time mentor. He obviously noted my thoughts were straying and pressed his jaw against my breastbone.

"But if you don't want to, Petra, we'll do whatever makes you happy," he said, turning his massive, auburn head so that his eyes stared into mine. The warmth from his furry pelt was radiating through the thin sheet; I put my hand up on his head, scratching between his ears.

"I'm not sure what I want, Kipp," I replied honestly. "Except, of course, to keep my bond with you."

"That's how I feel, too," he said, his body heaving with a huge, lupine sigh. "As long as we're together, life is good."

To be loved completely is a wonderful thing. I'm not sure, in retrospect, if it's common or rare, or if we just fail to recognize it when it hits us in the face. I tried to think of others who had loved me completely, without question. There had been a few in the past and were some in the present. I knew Philo was in that group, as well as an improbable Fitzhugh. He'd never say it, of course, but it was there, lurking like a drifting, pale wisp of fog hovering hesitantly over a sandy marsh. And, my human love interest, Harrow, was able to stretch his imagination and accept the impossible, so great was his love for me. But none paralleled Kipp. Our complete attachment that followed the natural inclines of our species had taught me the true meaning of connectedness and trust. Without meaning to, I began to quietly cry.

Kipp pushed his head forward and began to gently bathe my face, cleaning away my tears with his raspy tongue. Sometimes words–or thoughts–were not needed, and that was one of those times.

CHAPTER 12

There is something about a graveyard in the winter–when the wind is harsh, the tree limbs bare, and the landscape rolls in empty waves–that echoes the loneliness of lost souls. A heavy, lingering frost from the previous night promised to leave the grass stiff and crisp, an unwelcome mat of entry. From the top limbs of a massive oak, a solitary crow cawed loudly, the sound echoing across the empty fields.

Due to the frigid cold, our small party had been the only one to visit the battlefield so far that day. We planned to stop as far away from the visitors' center as possible, so that Kipp and Elani could leave the heated confines of the SUV and explore with us. Dogs weren't allowed to roam freely on the fields, so we'd have to work around that unreasonable restriction.

"Why do humans build monuments?" Elani asked, as we passed the 35th Indiana marker.

Well, that was a good question, I thought. It had been done for a long time, if Stonehenge was any measure. And speaking of Stonehenge, there had been a symbiont visit to that particular piece of history but the outcome had been unsatisfactory. Hmm, I thought, before Kipp interrupted me.

"No way," Kipp began, cutting my hopeful musings short. "I've lived in primitive times and have no wish to go that far back in history again. Human sacrifices and stuff like that…uh uh."

"People need to memorialize other people and events. Human beings seem to need heroes for inspiration," Peter remarked, taking up the mantle of explanation. He drove the SUV slowly until we finally came to an area that seemed as good a choice as any. There was a barren hillside, sparse of trees, where a herd of whitetail deer clustered. The sun was beginning to burn off the frost, and a soft, translucent gray mist rose above the grassy knoll. The deer raised their heads in unison, ears forward and alert; after a long pause, they ambled off, unhurried, making their way to the dense woods to the rear of the park before melting out of view.

We'd reached Viniard Field. Per the brochure, there was a skirmish on September 19th, 1863 that marked one of the bloodiest battles of the conflict. The Hans C. Heg monument, a large pyramid of cannon balls, caught my attention. This would be a good place to stop and attempt a time shift. Peter pulled the SUV to a halt, and, after checking around, we let Kipp and Elani free. They were grateful to be able to stretch their legs; a small wind was blowing and Kipp's dense pelt of fur was brushed back, making him look larger than in reality. I pulled my parka closer and noticed that even Peter took care to dress warmly; there were times I envied the lupines' natural attributes. Kipp's thoughts, however, became disturbed and anxious, in contrast to those of Elani, which were balanced and calm. Going to his side, I ran my hand down his back, smoothing his erect fur.

"What is it?" I asked, since his thoughts were too confused for me to pluck out one train to follow.

"You remember that sense I got in the cemetery back home?" As I nodded, he continued. "I'm getting it again, here and now." He turned slightly into the wind, his profile lost to me for a moment.

Peter and Elani were understandably curious, and I took a moment to describe what Kipp had experienced when we walked along the row of unknown soldiers' tombstones on that day we visited George's resting place. I knew they wanted more, but it was not my place to encourage their eavesdropping on Kipp's tangled web of thoughts. But after a moment, he seemed to have pushed down his anxiety and nodded his head. Tentatively we all entered into his thoughts, and I almost recoiled in horror and more than a little fear when I experienced what seemed to be a human figure walking towards us, his hands outstretched. As he drew closer, I could clearly see the visage of a boy—at most a young teenager—with a face that had been hit by gunfire and mangled almost beyond recognition. The place where his mouth should have been opened, and a gaping hole emerged; from that black hole in ghostly flesh, a shriek of despair sounded, echoing in my head. To this day, I've never been able to shake the way I felt in response to that sound.

Peter and Elani were disturbed, too, and Peter reached out for my arm as I staggered towards a park bench, almost unable to stand any longer. Kipp turned to look at me, his expression one of pain and sorrow. Peter sat next to me and, after a moment's pause, put his arm around my shoulder, pulling me into him; a second later, both Elani and Kipp huddled close, and the four of us managed a symbiont group hug. Ahead, as we looked across the field, a covey of mourning doves flushed from the grass, their wings beating the air with a musical thumping sound that disturbed the stillness of the park. I welcomed the noise, anything that would keep me from hearing the reverberations of the specter's cry in my head.

"I'm sorry," Kipp began, "I tried to tell you…"

I leaned forward, pulling him against my chest. Burying my face in the fur on his neck, I inhaled and caught the scent of his wildness, that part of the lupine branch of the family tree that was different from the humanoid. Kipp had the instincts of a wild beast with the senses to match any creature alive. Elani did too, but carried hers in a much more ladylike package than did the massive Kipp.

"Fitzhugh assigned me to compile research once on a phenomenon such as we just encountered." Peter looked away from me as he watched the thin mist hovering over the grass fragment into wispy bits of nothing before surrendering to the rising sun, which had emerged from its hiding place behind the morning clouds. "I found instances where symbionts encountered inexplicable experiences surrounding battlefields or places of mass casualties, such as the eruption of Krakatoa." He glanced at Kipp, who was staring at a copse of trees that stood as silent guardians over the field. It was January, and before much longer the crocuses and daffodils would poke their stubborn heads through the hard soil to dot the landscape with vivid dashes of violet blue and yellow. This patch of earth, where so much death and pain had occurred, would erupt into a place of natural beauty, as it was meant to be in the eyes of God before man declared war upon one another. Peter reached over to gently stroke Kipp's head.

"Thank you, Kipp. I know that was hard on you, holding on to the moment so we could experience it so vividly." Peter sighed. "I'm glad our kind has avoided war and keeps our silliness to the boardrooms of Technicorps."

"Well, I'm not too sure that we've managed to contain our own foibles," I replied. "I've run into more than one of us who have been totally corrupted and fell into the pit of evil." Peter looked at me, curious for more, but I chose to stop there. He didn't need to know about Fitzhugh's nephew; nor did he require knowledge about at least two leaders of our collective who were self–serving and would have used Kipp and me to further their own political interests. If I'd learned anything from my 400 years, it was the need to try and keep some degree of humility.

Elani took the lead and stood, shaking herself hard. In the early morning sun, particles of dust and all the microscopic bits and pieces of the world around us flew into the air, surrounding her with a little halo. She touched noses with

Kipp before turning to stare at first me, then Peter.

"We need to get on with the business that brought us here," she remarked, obviously ready to get to work.

"It's your call," I invited, thinking it was time for her to make a leadership decision. In the world of symbiont pairings, it was an equal partnership and neither humanoid nor lupine had dominion over the other.

Elani raised her head and oddly appeared as if she was testing the air for the scent of some wayward creature. With a funny little roll of her neck, she seemed to dispel the nagging tension between her shoulder blades. Overhead, a small flock of goldfinches, early for the season, flew in formation overhead, their yellow bodies making a bright splash of color against the blue sky.

"Let's go back seventy-five years," Elani finally suggested. "The battlefield was turned over to the National Park Service in 1933. The monuments should be in place, and I think we'll arrive and see the cannonball monument to Heg just as we do right now."

We all agreed; it really mattered little, anyway, where we went, as long as we made a successful jump. This would be our last practice run, and after this we would approach the Twelve and outline a more serious journey that would have specific destination targets to test our skills.

The Viniard Field remained empty of other visitors. The cold weather, which had discouraged idle travelers, would break as the sun stubbornly rose higher in the sky to bring a modicum of warmth to the barren fields. Standing, I walked over to a patch of dead grass and sat, my knees crossed. Kipp followed and lay next to me, his head across my knees. Peter and Elani copied us, and at my nod, they knew to take the lead, and we would follow.

It is impossible to really describe the feeling of a time shift. If one can combine exhilaration, anxiety, excitement, anticipation and lace it with a tiny dose of fear, then that is the best collection of words that come to mind. After an unfortunate spate of hard landings, it was gratifying and more than pleasant to open my eyes and discover I was still seated, my legs crossed, Kipp's massive head stretched across my knees. It was unusual to arrive in almost an identical position to that of the launch, and I met Kipp's self-satisfied expression with one of my own. Yes, that was pretty darn good, I thought, as he closed one eye in a wink of approval.

Peter and Elani were close by but seemed a little discombobulated. Peter was standing with his back to us, while Elani was sitting, turned towards us; her face wore the momentary confusion associated with having found oneself displaced by some seventy-five years, if our journey was accurate. Happily, I located the pyramid of cannon balls some fifty yards distant and knew we were, at least, in the general vicinity. The landscape had the topographical differences one might expect. Some trees were no longer present; others had grown from the small saplings in sight to enormous oaks in the modern-day park.

Not too far away, we spied a truck containing a couple of men who were puttering along an unpaved road–we'd driven our SUV along that same road which was now paved–their vehicle belching puffs of exhaust as it slowly rolled to a stop. The battered truck seemed to fit the profile of those manufactured in the mid thirties. My assumption was that we'd hit our planned target, and Elani's time shift had been successful. One of the men raised his head, and I saw him nudge the driver with a poke on his arm. The driver shoved the truck in gear, the noise loud and raspy in the quiet of the field. I stood and walked next to Peter.

"Are you okay?" I asked, putting my hand on his shoulder.

"Yeah, just a little dizzy," he replied with a wan smile.

"We have company," I said, pointing out the obvious.

The truck ground to a stop with brakes that squealed loudly enough to frighten off any lingering wildlife that might have been lurking nearby. Squinting slightly, I gazed up at the sun. It hovered directly overhead and thus indicated midday.

The men swung down from the truck and walked

towards us; their appearance was that of workmen, both wearing worn overalls. From their collars, I could see the frayed red necklines that hinted at long johns, something that once was a fashionable necessity but had been lost in the modern age. Rather sad, I thoughts, since long underwear was an inherently practical garment. The air surrounding us was cold, the field was void of anything remotely green, so it seemed we made a lateral shift, arriving in the same season from which we departed. All of that was good and spoke to Peter and Elani's precision.

"Can we help you folks?" the driver drawled, pulling his hat from his head in deference to me. His hair, which was wispy, barely covered the top of his head; his cheeks were chapped and reddened from the cold and wind that had no natural barriers in the largely open field.

"We were out walking and got lost," Peter said, smiling guilelessly. Yes, lying quickly and adeptly was a skill needed by any proficient traveler. With his brown eyes and mop of hair, Peter looked like little more than a kid, innocent and kind of helpless. He blinked his eyes a couple of times to hit home what a youngster he was.

Trying not to smirk, I surveyed our surroundings. Chickamauga was one of four military parks authorized following the Civil War; Chickamauga was the first and the largest. I'd been to Gettysburg, but it had been many years ago. Chickamauga was dedicated in 1895 and actually, the War Department had control over the military parks until the National Park Service took over in 1933.

"Sir, may I ask you a question?" Peter asked, continuing with his guileless manner.

"Sure, son," the older of the two answered.

"What year is it?"

The two men glanced at one another before the older man spat in the dirt, wiping his mouth with the back of his hand. He chewed tobacco and undoubtedly was nursing a chaw in his cheek pouch. The sweet, fragrant tang of the tobacco juice filled the frigid air.

"It's 1940," the man answered. "And son, you and your

lady friend probably need to stay away from the spirits and find your way home."

I knew he meant liquor and explained to Kipp and Elani, much to their delight, that the men thought Peter and I had been out drinking moonshine or something along those lines. Why else would an oddly dressed woman and a young man be walking in circles, accompanied by two really big dogs on the grounds of a military park in the middle of the winter? Alcohol seemed to be the most reasonable explanation.

"Yes, sir!" Peter responded. Grabbing me by the hand, he began to pull me towards the rear of the park, hoping that the men would go about their business and forget us.

We didn't look back but heard the truck roar into action as the driver forced it into first gear, the gears grinding in protest. In less than five minutes, we'd reached a barrier of trees and disappeared from view; Peter sank down, breathing hard, somehow combining laughter with his gasping attempts to get control over his lungs. After he managed to calm himself and get centered, we effortlessly made the time shift forward to the present day with Elani leading and were gratified to find our vehicle sitting where we'd left it, unscathed, with the exception of a light coating of frost. We wouldn't find out until later that we were two days off our mark; fortunately, the management of the park had not become concerned over the parked SUV and had it towed. Our luck held in that there were no people in view who would stare, mouths gaping open at the sudden appearance of two humanoids and two enormous lupines. Peter fished the key to the SUV from his pocket; as he did so, he raised one dark eyebrow at me.

"So, are you all in agreement that we drive down to Marietta and then on to Atlanta?" he asked, addressing me as well as the lupines. "In the event the Twelve approve our shift to see the *General*, we will have been to the locations involved, and that will help with the accuracy."

It was a fact that accuracy in time shifts increased with experience. As a mature traveler, I could research a location, study topography maps, focus on a period of time, and pretty much nail it to within a few days or so of my target. Any aids or assists to a novice pair were acceptable and, in any case, given Peter's fascination with the *General*, he'd probably enjoy visiting the museum where she was housed.

"I don't think we can get the lupines into the exhibit," I began cautiously.

Peter's face fell; he'd not considered that issue. Elani pushed her head next to his and licked his face with enthusiasm.

"It's not a problem, Peter," she said. "Kipp and I can hang out in the car, and you and Petra can fill our minds with the images."

Her offer was a mark of her inherent kindness and generosity. No one ever enjoyed being left behind, but she knew how important it was to Peter, whose face took on the excited glow of a teenager about to drive his first car or go to the prom with the homecoming queen.

We left the park behind us, with all its tragic memories; Kipp had purposefully blocked any more, uh, other worldly experiences that would be unsettling, and after returning to the hotel to check out, we dashed through a drive through to grab a bag of biscuits and hit the road again, finding Interstate 75 south which would take us to Kennesaw, Georgia and on to Atlanta.

"We'll take 85 back, and it'll be a straight shot home," Peter said, trying to talk while eating his steak biscuit.

I took a sip of coffee and turned to watch, with some amusement, Kipp and Elani decide who would get the last chicken biscuit. Finally, I acted as Solomon and divided it in half, giving Elani the larger piece since I knew that action would feed Kipp's chivalrous and generous soul. The sky above had turned overcast and rain threatened. As we headed south, I hoped the temperatures, which had hovered around freezing, would climb. Atlanta, despite being a southern city, was notorious for some rather spectacular ice storms that caused massive gridlock. With that unpleasant thought hovering annoyingly in the back of my brain, I used Peter's cell phone to call Philo. After a few moments, his secretary put him on.

"What's up?" he asked.

"First off, how's my little boy?" I asked, trying to be humorous as I enquired about Fitzhugh.

"He's doing well and is getting along quite spectacularly with Peggy," he added. I thought that latter insertion was unnecessary. Kipp, following my selfish thoughts, poked me in the back of my head with his pointed nose so hard that I almost dropped Peter's cell phone.

"We're driving down to Kennesaw, Georgia and then on to Atlanta. Can you have your secretary book us a hotel where we can take Kipp and Elani? Maybe somewhere on I-85 just north of Atlanta?

"Can do," he replied. "How did the time shift go?"

"Very good; accurate, safe, predictable," I said, adding the three descriptive words that managers in the world of symbionts loved to hear, in case he didn't believe me.

After telling me he was busy and would have his secretary text Peter the accommodations, he hung up. Neither he nor I enjoyed phone conversations; it just didn't work very well considering our telepathic connections. After reassuring myself that Peter wanted to continue to drive, I settled in my seat and closed my eyes. In the rear, Elani and Kipp were playing another telepathic mind game with one another; I shut them out, and before I knew it, I fell asleep, comfortable with the warm air from the heater blowing against my face and neck.

CHAPTER 13

The original *General* was painted dark green with orange accents, and the number was 39," Peter said as he pointed at the contemporary *General* that loomed in front of us. It was housed in a large, open room; the massive engine was black, with red accents, the cab interior painted green. On the front of the engine, a gold number 3 stood out. Peter pursed his lips as he considered that the current *General* was, perhaps, not exact in every detail. It still looked pretty good to me, no matter what.

I thought Peter would faint dead away when he first spied the *General*, at rest in all her splendor. The museum, a Smithsonian affiliated project, was small but well managed. He requested I take some pictures of him as he posed at different angles with a much too serious expression on his young face. I admit the engine was structurally beautiful and physically intimidating. It didn't take much imagination to picture it steaming along, smoke belching from the smokestack to curve in a trailing arc across an unblemished sky. Instinctively, I realized the experience of being this close to the engine would provide Peter with the grounding he needed—me, too. There was really no way to sneak the lupines inside, so they rested in the SUV while we shot images their way. The weather was cool, so the

interior of the SUV was pleasant to the heavily coated
lupines.

"I'm gonna get to ride on a train!" Kipp's thoughts
merged with mine with the excitement of a young child.
Kipp seemed to momentarily forget he'd made train trips
previously, but the notion of being pulled by a famous
locomotive propelled his energy.

"Let's find the Car Shed location next," Peter said.

He continued to insist upon driving, and I'd long since
given up that argument along with any lingering residual
guilt. I leaned forward and found a pretty solid oldies
station on the FM dial. A Karen Carpenter song, fueled by
her beautiful, mellow voice, drifted through the car. Before
I knew it, Kipp was singing in his thoughts, "Just like me,
they long to be, close to you…" Standing, he stepped to my
headrest and pressed his wet nose against the back of my
neck and gave me a little lick to boot. The next thing I
knew, he was whining that he didn't understand the lyrics
to "Flashlight". Well, who did, I wondered? As we
approached Atlanta, the traffic associated with a large city
suddenly overwhelmed us, and Peter was forced to slow his
pace. I saw him grimace and twist his head from side to
side to work out the tension in his neck. I'd set the GPS and
eventually, with patience, we arrived on Wall Street, and
made our way to the general location of the old train station
between Prior and Central Avenues. Peter managed to pull
to the curb, flashers on. Elani insisted that her feet must
touch the ground, so I hopped out and let her jump down
from the SUV. After a moment of staring around the
vicinity, she dipped her head down to the ground, snuffling,
as if she could divine the scents from one hundred and
fifty-some odd years in the past. Kipp leapt out and stood
beside her, the bright afternoon sun reflecting off his
burnished coat. After shaking himself hard, he climbed
back in, followed by Elani.

"I think I have it!" she exclaimed excitedly. "My eyes
were closed, and as I took a deep breath, I felt as if I
connected to the buildings that once sat here. There were

vague impressions of people, long since gone, as well as the feelings of horror when the city was burned." She glanced at me, confusion on her pretty face. "Is that possible or did I insert my own impressions?"

Well, that was a good question, and there was really no good answer. I'd had a similar experience when my concentration was complete and uninterrupted by other things. Kipp, too, had felt the impressions on time left by past people, forces and events. Oddly, Peter, the one with the least experience, seemed to have an answer.

"I've read of that phenomenon in past time shift recordings," he said, as he watched the traffic carefully so that he could pull out. The GPS was set to help us wind our way to I-85, and he tried to talk while the GPS bleated out directions. "I think, Elani, it means you are extraordinarily sensitive and will be a great traveler." Peter glanced at me, his dark eyes troubled. "I've not had anything remotely happen like that, Petra. Do you think I'm doomed?"

I knew that there was a wide range of skills and capabilities within members of our species and assured Peter of that. "If anything, Peter, you will learn from Elani, and it may imprint upon you to a degree. As she experiences it, you can, too, as long as she permits you the access to her mind." I knew she would, or else I wouldn't have mentioned it to him.

All of us were tired–even the inexhaustible Kipp– at that point in our journey. After spending a night in a hotel just off the interstate in north Georgia, we managed to arrive home by late morning the next day. Our timing was such that we arrived on Saturday, which meant that Peter dropped me and Kipp off at my house before going on to his apartment. The front door was locked, so I dug out my key, but before I could turn it in the lock, the door flew back to reveal a smiling Fitzhugh. Just behind him stood Juno, her tail wagging so furiously that her entire hind end was shimmying like an exotic dancer in motion.

"Petra!" Fitzhugh exclaimed before stopping himself. I realized any verbal exchange would be limited, and he merely reached out and clapped me on the shoulder. "Glad you're home," he finally said. "The house was oddly empty without you here."

That was as close as I'd come to hearing that I'd been missed, but I embraced the remarks. Throwing down my duffle, I startled him with a quick hug.

"I've got things to tell you," I said, wanting to set up a mystery to keep him hanging. When his eyebrows raised in response, I added, "Strange events that seemed unusual and unexpected."

Predictably, he disappeared to brew a pot of tea while I dumped the dirty clothes from my duffle into the washing machine. I'd never been one for careful sorting and tossed everything into one load, filled the soap dispenser and turned the knob. There was a lot to be said for modern conveniences. Having lived when one went to the creek with a scrub board and a cake of lye soap–as well as times when bi-yearly ablutions were the norm—the electric washer was immensely preferable.

Kipp, after touching noses with a delighted Juno, followed her to the rug in front of the fireplace, which was roaring, and, after circling, he lay down with her. She nestled close, her grizzled muzzle stretched across his back.

Fitzhugh brought his lovely antique service in on a tray, with a tiny little pitcher of cream as well as my honey pot crowded next to a tin of English biscuits. I made a space on the low coffee table, and after I allowed Fitzhugh to pour, I grabbed my wing chair and tucked my feet up under me.

"Kipp, help me with this," I requested. "We had a couple of interesting, uh, moments. Kipp experienced the first, which he shared with us." I nodded at my partner.

"We were on the battlefield, and I saw a young man who'd been killed in battle. He walked towards me, and I could see him as clearly as I see you; I could even hear his cry and knew the content of his thoughts." Kipp shuddered slightly. We didn't speak while he gathered himself. A log in the fireplace broke, and a shower of sparks flew up the chimney, caught in the updraft. The room was quiet, save for the sound of the fire and the soft ticking of the mantle clock.

"Kipp let us experience it through him," I said, taking up the story. "The sound of the boy's scream was clear, completely audible, with the feelings associated. Then, we got to Atlanta and found the historical vicinity of the Car Shed. Elani was able to connect to impressions of the past, people who lived there as well as the general flow of the times."

Fitzhugh closed his eyes as he relaxed in his chair. His chin dipped down so that his beard spread like a bib across his chest. For a second I wondered if he was asleep, but then he opened his dark eyes to gaze at me.

"There are archives, of which I have a vague memory, that catalog both types of phenomena. The first is rare while the second seems to be something that only certain symbionts have an ability to do. It would appear Elani has that ability, and it will definitely be a boon to her and Peter." He cradled the tea cup in his hands, enjoying the warmth radiating through the thin porcelain shell.

"Peter wants to visit the time when the *General* was stolen and witness that event," I said, waiting for his reaction. I knew his response might give a clue as to the one of the Twelve.

Fitzhugh sat for a moment, his lips slightly pursed, before he reached out for the teapot to pour another cup. I shook my head to indicate I was fine and took a pass.

"You know, there have been many trips to that period, but none to that specific event simply because there was no question about the accuracy of the facts. The only reason one might go would be for curiosity, the sort of thing done on one's vacation. As he and Elani are in a learning mode, I think there's a good chance it will be approved."

My species has several characteristics that separate us from humans. We are telepaths; we can bond with our lupine brothers and sisters and travel through time. Kipp, who possesses more of our natural instincts, can manipulate thoughts and dreams as well as enter into another symbiont's mind and not be detectable. We are also very long lived, physically quite hardy and have very slow metabolisms, which means we can endure deprivation better than humans. But we do get fatigued, and even I had to admit the recent frequency of time shifts had caught up with me, and I was, well, just tired. So I spent most of the remainder of the weekend in bed, dozing or reading, usually with Kipp cuddled up next to me, his large body acting like a heater. My house was relatively snug, but my bedroom in the rear of the house tended to stay cooler due to an annoyingly persistent north wind. But by the time Monday arrived, I was ready to return to Technicorps and get back to work. I'd let Peter and Elani take the initiative of approaching the Twelve and not worry myself with all the bother. Over an early morning breakfast that Monday, I hesitantly broached a subject with Fitzhugh, hoping he would not misinterpret my intent. Yes, as with humans, even telepaths can get it miserably wrong.

"Do you think Peggy will mind continuing to pick you up for work most days, unless I'm taking my car?" I asked, crumbling a piece of toast on my plate. Fitzhugh, who worried about my eating things like Pop Tarts, had poached eggs and presented them to me on whole grain toast. I'd taken care of the lupines while he worked; lifting my head, I peeked out the window into my back yard. Kipp and Juno were wandering through the cold-stiffened grass, dipping their heads down to sniff at the earth and allow their senses to comprehend more about the natural world than could I. Kipp's body stiffened as he came upon a particularly intriguing patch of grass. Then followed his sense of disgust as he realized some errant canine had thoughtlessly used Kipp's beloved yard as a personal toilet. I tried not to laugh as he glared at me through the window.

"I'm glad you brought it up," Fitzhugh replied. "I know you like to use the time to and from work to walk or run and trundling me back and forth is disruptive to your routine. Peggy offered to keep driving me, unless it's a bad weather day and you choose to take the car." He paused to take a sip of the coffee which was still steaming in the cup. Unexpectedly he added, "I don't want to burden your lifestyle, Petra. Maybe it's time I start looking around for a new situation since my health seems stable?" He left the question hanging.

Kipp and I never–or at least rarely–misunderstand one another since we keep our minds completely open at all times. Words alone can be interpreted in many ways, the intent of the message left to the receiver to discern. Humans had always and will always struggle with that fact. Contemporary symbionts use polite rules of order and found such enmeshment as practiced by Kipp and me to be vulgar. With that in mind, I looked at Fitzhugh, my hazel eyes locked for an instant with his dark ones.

"Fitzhugh, I've enjoyed your being here. And," I said, with a slight laugh, "unless things change, and we get to the point we can't abide one another, you and Juno may continue to live here." The pronouncement surprised me more than it did him, I think. Oddly, the two of them felt like family and I knew Kipp loved Juno intensely. "Lily, too, of course."

Fitzhugh's withered cheeks reddened slightly as he was uncomfortable with expressions of endearment. But as he dipped his head, I caught a flash of a smile, which he had managed to subdue by the time he raised his head again.

"Okay," he answered meekly, as he took another sip of coffee. "Peggy will be here soon, so I need to get ready."

Since he cooked, I would clean and managed to get the dishes washed and put away in record time. Kipp and Juno came in and kept me company, dropping down to an out of the way spot on the wooden floor. The cold weather was making Juno more stiff than usual but she still insisted on puttering around outside with Kipp. She was wearing the jaunty little jacket I'd given her at Christmas and looked fetching with the collar turned up in a rakish manner. I think in some ways, she modeled the lupine mother Kipp had lost when a young pup.

I heard a car pull up out front and in less than thirty

seconds, Fitzhugh and Juno were off with Peggy, her nice, spotlessly clean SUV rolling along safely like an armored tank. My battered little car sat in the driveway looking forlorn and abandoned. It was old, had paint missing and more than one ding in the side panels, but it still ran and that was enough for me. Kipp and I began our own journey, and it felt good to be back in a solid routine. I could tell Kipp enjoyed it, too.

"More car rides, and I was gonna get fat," he remarked. He walked politely at my side so as to not draw the attention of well-meaning police officers who would remind us there was a leash law. His collar and leash were in my backpack and could be quickly put into play if needed. As we got farther from the congested street, he drifted away, his nose busy searching for compelling scents.

"I pulled up a couple of books on the *General* and the Great Locomotive Chase on my Kindle," Kipp began, before noticing my raised eyebrows. "Or rather, I got Peter to download the books to my Kindle. I've been reading about the events, and I think it would make for an interesting trip as well as an exciting one. With the pre-work we've done visiting the location and the actual locomotive, I think it could be relatively safe. Get in, observe, get out," he added.

We tossed the notion around as we walked the two miles; I had clothes with me for changing later, since I planned on jogging home that evening. The frigid cold showed no signs of abating; Kipp's fur was standing on end in a natural response to the cold; he looked like a big, puffy, red fur ball. By the time we got to Technicorps, my nose was running, and my face literally hurt from the cold. Kipp twisted his head and looked at me.

"Maybe we should ask Peggy if we can ride in her nice car, too?" he asked, trying to get a rise out of me.

"If you can't take the cold, sweetums, then feel free." I stretched and yawned. "I guess I'm just tougher than you."

Kipp replied to the latter by leaning in and giving me a

rather significant nip on the calf of my left leg; I was certain there would be a bruise. In any case, I limped on down to the library while Kipp went to meet Juno and the class of juvenile lupines that they instructed.

"Why are you hobbling?" Fitzhugh asked, as I walked in.

"Kipp bit me."

"Oh, okay," he answered, as if I'd said nothing of importance. "On a more significant note," he began, "I took a little peek at the archives and so far find nothing to indicate there has been a time shift to chronicle the abduction of the *General*." Fitzhugh stared at me over his reading glasses. "That doesn't guarantee an approval, of course, but it does help if one is not completely duplicating a past trip."

Peggy walked up and greeted me politely before beginning to outline my work load for the day. Fitzhugh stood next to her like a proud papa, watching his baby girl speak or walk for the first time. Honestly, it sort of irritated me. I'd been in the library long before Peggy, and I really didn't need her telling me what to do. Fitzhugh was another matter since he couldn't help but be bossy.

"Take it easy," Kipp said, his voice resonating in my mind from his perch several floors above me. "She's just trying to do her job. Take a deep breath, count to, uh, five, since ten takes too long, and let it go."

"Whatever you say, Dr. Kipp," I replied sarcastically. But I took his advice as well as my sheaf of papers and went to my desk. Or at least I thought I was going to my desk. "Okay, where's my desk?" I asked. It had been in a comfortable nook where there was a small collection of upholstered chairs for reading as well as gathering.

"I moved it to the back where it would be out of the way," Peggy replied, her expression neutral.

"I'm on my way," Kipp echoed in my head, sensing a Petra meltdown.

"You moved my desk without speaking to me?" I said, trying to keep my tone level. But it was difficult. "I was out on a job, on a time shift, and you moved my desk that has been here for years without the courtesy of speaking to me, right?"

The more I spoke, the angrier I got. I was not necessarily given to rages of temperament, but I could get hot, just like the next symbiont. And this particular moment was a little complex. Fitzhugh could have intervened and told her to not move my desk, but he had just stood there, like a silly love-struck teenager, and let her do whatever she wanted with a pat on the head, despite how it made me feel. The door to the library opened softly, and in a second Kipp was at my side, staring up at me with concern.

"I didn't think it was a big deal, Petra. I really didn't think it would bother you, but it obviously does," Peggy began, her pretty face beginning to flush. She could have backed down, apologized at that moment and salvaged the situation. But she, unfortunately, didn't. "After all, Petra, you just work here. Fitzhugh is in charge, and I am next in charge, so we make the decisions about where subordinates work and what they do." Peggy put her hands on her hips once she decided to go the aggressive, dominant route.

I stared at Fitzhugh and immediately noticed that his face had taken on a gray pallor; he looked absolutely stricken. At that moment, I knew he realized how shabbily I'd been treated and his immense regret and horror over the situation. He'd been so caught up in liking Peggy that he'd taken me for granted. My worry over his health humbled me in a flash, because I knew he had deep affection for me and wouldn't have deliberately injured me. Even symbionts could be thoughtless at times with those whom they loved.

"It's okay," I said, forcing a smile. "You're right, Peggy. I'm in and out a lot, anyway. And my desk is always cluttered and disrupts the seating area." I managed a laugh. "Actually, I've always been worried someone would mess with my manuscripts since they were so close to the front of the library. A little privacy is a good thing."

Fitzhugh was frowning at me at that point, but I was relieved to see he was no longer gray. Kipp pushed up next to my leg, the one he'd nipped, and folded his haunches so that he was seated, his head in the right location for a good scratch between the ears. I almost could hear him utter a sigh of relief.

"I'm gonna get to work if you'll point me in the right direction," I said, a little too brightly, feeling a silly, artificial grin overtake my face.

Following Peggy, I almost skipped through the stacks until we located my desk which was in a dimly lit, far corner of the library. I wondered if I would need to bring a Swiffer to keep ahead of the cobwebs that would accumulate in the dungeon to which I'd been relegated. Peggy looked as if she would hover a moment, but I politely shooed her away, saying I was late getting started and had a pile of translations waiting on me.

"She really didn't mean harm to you," Kipp said, after Peggy had left.

"Did you do one of your stealth runs into her brain?" I asked. "You know that's not really ethical unless it is an emergency-type situation," I grumbled, as I tried to find a pen that would write. My favorite pen, the one with the chewed end, seemed to be missing in action. Another notch in Peggy's belt, I thought irritably.

"This was an emergency, since it compromises your relationship with Fitzhugh," he said. "Peggy was only thinking of the aesthetics of the library and thought, since you are absent a great deal, that it wouldn't matter to you."

"Well," I muttered, "I guess it helps to know it wasn't on purpose."

Fitzhugh suddenly appeared, his footsteps quiet and unexpected. I looked up and smiled, a rolled-up sheaf of papers in my hand.

"Trying to get my head wrapped around this stuff again," I began, my voice superficially cheerful as I tried to suppress an inappropriate giggle.

"Oh, Petra, put that stuff down and talk with me," Fitzhugh replied. He looked better but still held an air of fragility. "The bottom line is that moving your desk was thoughtless and rude, and had I been thinking about your feelings, it wouldn't have happened. I am truly sorry." He paused and looked around. "And this is entirely unsuitable, because I'm now missing a chair that I can sit in when I consult with you or…" He drew the last sentence out in a dramatic pause. "Just visit," he concluded. "I plan on correcting the oversight."

I sat on the edge of my desk and beckoned him to sit in my chair. After a moment's hesitation, he did so. Fitzhugh was wearing the Irish sweater I'd given him; the knotted tie at his throat was slightly askew. Feeling bold, I leaned forward to straighten it and brushed a stray cat hair from one Lily feline from his collar. Kipp, seeing things were calmer, winked at me and trotted off, since he had a classroom full of youngsters waiting on him.

"I was angry, but I'm really not any longer," I said, hoping he'd hear my sincerity. "It's just a desk, and the location does not matter. You're here, and I need to be more flexible."

When I say I'm over something, I mean it, and I was gratified when we both arrived home that night that neither one of us mentioned the desk issue again. However, when I got to work the next morning, my desk was back in its old spot, with my stack of papers right where I'd left them the previous day.

CHAPTER 14

"So, Peter wants to make his first, uh, serious trip to experience the Great Locomotive Chase?" Philo asked, after I'd given him a brief outline. "He's not made the formal request yet," he added.

"No, but he will. He's still fine tuning his application since he wants it to be perfect. It may take him a year," I added, yawning without bothering to politely cover my mouth. I was sitting across from Philo, wishing there was not a desk there between us. The physical barrier felt odd and had only come about since his promotion.

"And why are you telling me this prematurely?" Philo asked, his heavy eyebrows rising in query. I noticed more and more gray flecking in the hairs. He looked tired, I thought, noticing dark smudges beneath his eyes.

"Well, you're the boss, so I want to advocate for Peter." I tried to keep my voice neutral, my affect one of uninvolved innocence.

"On another matter, Peggy Shelton approached me about a transfer," Philo said, his dark eyes meeting mine. "She seems to think there is conflict in the library and would be better served in another location." Philo carefully moved a stack of papers from one side of the desk to the other. When he sat back in his desk chair, I heard it squeak in protest and almost offered to find him some WD40 before I saw the look on his face. He was not amused.

"I don't think she should leave," I replied after a moment's thought. "She is qualified and Fitzhugh likes her. It's rare he finds someone he enjoys."

"The issue is with Fitzhugh; he seems to be cold towards her, and you know how he is when he gets harsh," Philo said.

"I'll talk with him, and in the meantime why don't you see if you can convince her to stay." I startled myself in that I was sincere at that moment. Here was the chance to get rid of Peggy, and oddly I didn't want to see her go. Fitzhugh liked her, and she was talented. The problem was me, and it boiled down to an ugly emotion–jealousy.

That evening, Fitzhugh and I sat across my small dinette table from one another after having finished some vegetarian chili that had been simmering in the crock pot all day. There is nothing better in cold weather than hot soup or chili, to my way of thinking. Kipp and Juno were full from their chicken and rice and both lay on the kitchen floor; Kipp seemed to be waiting for me to go ahead and do what needed to be done. Lily, after finished off the scraps in Juno's bowl, crawled between the two lupines and had fallen asleep on her back, her four paws stuck up in the air like a dead raccoon stuck on the side of the road.

"Fitzhugh, Philo told me that Peggy wants to leave," I began. His bent head tilted up as he glanced at me. "I think that would be a huge mistake."

"You do?" he asked, his voice soft.

Outside, the wind was picking up and began that eerie howl that it acquires in the winter when there is no foliage to help brake its progression. There was humidity in the air, and the forecasters predicted snow and ice. The world was dark and full of anticipation.

"Yes," I replied, my voice gaining more force. "I fear that maybe your attitude has been influenced by my feelings," I said. It was getting harder to go on with him staring at me.

"And what are those, might I ask?" he said, tilting his gray head.

"This is hard…." I stammered. Kipp was looking up at me, prodding me like a red hot poker in the back of my brain.

"Go on," Fitzhugh urged.

"I've been jealous," I finally said. Gosh, that felt good to get it off my soul. Even as bad and even silly as it sounded, it was a relief to say the words.

Fitzhugh started to smile but caught himself and ducked his head while he regained his composure. I sat there, my lips trembling, as I crumbled a piece of cornbread to tiny shreds while waiting.

"It's been a long time since I've had an attractive female express jealousy towards me, so I am gratified," he said, nodding his head. "I knew you were uncomfortable, Petra, so I encouraged Peggy to leave. But I think the source of the problem is me, and the fact I've not bothered to see how all these disruptions have affected you. For example, the desk thing was done without any thought as to how you might feel about it."

"Do you think we can start over again?" I asked. "I would hate to see a qualified and very nice person leave due to my insecurity." Dipping my head, I finally managed to peek up and meet his eyes. "I know you like her, too, and would prefer she stay."

I was relieved the situation did eventually resolve itself, and I was able to return to the library and regain my focus. Peter and Elani completed and presented their application for a more complicated time shift to the Twelve, and it was accepted. The next thing I knew, the four of us were dispatched to Suzanne's work room for her to plan a wardrobe for Peter and me.

Remembering the stories I'd heard about Suzanne, I tried to keep my banter light. It was easy to tell that she was still somewhat listless, a hangover of sorts from her depression at her lost love. A pretty woman, with dark hair and flashing eyes, Suzanne had the air of a bohemian, but on that day, she seemed deflated. Her usual bright red lipstick had faded, and she'd drawn one cat eye line crooked so that one eye looked smaller than the other, almost as if she had a pirate's squint. However, she did hold out a cup of coffee when I walked in, knowing my tastes. Peter shook his head at her offer.

"1862...right?" she began. Looking over at me, she smiled. "Crinolines, Petra, your favorite."

"Ugh," I replied, looking down at Kipp and Elani who had found a spot from which to watch in amusement. Kipp always got by with a collar designed like a money belt to carry extra currency. I figured Suzanne would concoct something similar for Elani.

"This period is a challenge, in a fashion sense," Suzanne began. "Women's clothes contained a lot of fabric. The amount of fabric in one formal dress could contain twenty yards of material." She paused and added, "Your bustle bank is of no use since a bustle is a few years away."

Thoughts of the bustle evoked fond memories. It was a clever design constructed to carry concealed currency and had been used more than once. And then there were my leather boots designed by Suzanne. I almost sighed. Elani looked at Kipp and smiled as only a lupine can. I knew, without reading her thoughts, what was on her mind–she was glad to be a lupine and not of my sort.

"Almost all women wore corsets, crinolines and very full skirts." Suzanne put down her coffee cup and pulled out a well-worn book with pictures of fashions over decades. She, as did everyone at Technicorps, had access to computers but still liked the feel of a tabbed and familiar book in her hand. "You've shifted to the 1860s during various points in the American Civil War, so you know the drill," Suzanne remarked.

I felt a grimace assemble on my face. I liked the comfort of jeans, sweatshirts, sweatpants, hoodies and the like. We were going to have to make some quick compromises, or I might just stay home. Indeed, I'd made several trips during the war era and dressed appropriately for the times but just felt a stubborn resolve come over me in a wave of rebellion.

"I'm not wearing a corset or a crinoline," I began, putting down my cup of coffee. Cutting my eyes over to Kipp, I was gratified to see him nod his support. "We're not going to be there very long, and I just refuse to be cramped into something where I can't breathe." I shrugged my shoulders. "And who's gonna know anyway unless they peek up my skirt?"

Suzanne sat down in her swivel chair and began to rock slightly, closing her eyes as she contemplated my dilemma. I was not her most difficult client but probably ranked up in the top tier.

"Why don't you go as a man?" Elani asked, tilting her head at me. "It would be a disguise, and since you are assuming a different character, what would be the problem?"

For a second, I thought she was trying to be funny, before I realized she was serious. I glanced at Peter, who raised his eyebrows and shrugged his shoulders. Suzanne's eyes flew open in horror, since her mind had gone in the direction of full, hooped skirts and bonnets festooned with lace. But after the shock wore off, she smiled. At her core, Suzanne loved a design challenge.

"Why not?" she said, lifting her shoulders with a delicate shrug of surprising indifference.

Men's fashions were simpler and required much less physical bondage–since the despised corset was eliminated–and there was no reason why she couldn't dress me as she did Peter. After all, we predicted a quick in and out and would have very few interactions. We could keep my hair contained, my, uh, natural endowments under tight control, and I could wear a hat pulled down low so that much of my face was not visible.

It was not long before she'd sketched out the basics. Peter and I would both wear full length trousers, a frock coat, waistcoat and a white shirt with a stiff, upright collar. She lined the top part of my waistcoat with a compression fabric, much like a sports bra, that would keep me contained. Extreme stove pipe type hats were popular, but Peter and I both turned down that idea and he opted for the bowler, which was coming into fashion. Mine was a slouch hat with a larger brim that dipped down in front, to conceal my face.

Why had I not thought of this earlier, I wondered? So much simpler than all the falderal associated with women's fashions, application of makeup and the like.

"I'm not sure William Harrow would have appreciated me as much if had been dressed like this," I remarked, as I looked at my reflection in the mirror of Suzanne's work room. I'd carefully tucked the dainty pearl necklace so that it was hidden beneath the stiff collar of the shirt. With deliberation, I tried to loop the wide tie until I had it secured, using an antique stick pin Suzanne supplied.

"He would have loved you if you arrived in a potato sack," Kipp replied as he gazed at me critically. "It's hard for me to think of you as a guy like me, so put on the hat and let's see how you look."

I wound my hair into a rope and tucked it on top of my head before settling the slouch hat, pulling the brim a little lower in front. Suzanne had constructed the body of the hat to accommodate my hair, which I planned on pinning in place. I did a little promenade back and forth and was in the middle of my cat-walk turn when Suzanne arrived.

"Looks pretty good, but I think your booty looks a little too big," she opined, looking at my posterior with eyes half closed. "I think I'll do something to the cut of the trousers to help diminish that feature."

"Great, thanks," I replied, my voice dull.

"I told you to lay off the ice cream," Kipp said, trying to not laugh. "And you might consider running an extra mile or so." The door to the work room opened, and Philo entered, accompanied by Fitzhugh. I raised my eyebrows at Suzanne, wondering what was up.

"I asked them to come by since this is a little more unusual, and I wanted plenty of critical review," she said, as she circled around me, using a piece of tailor's chalk to mark a couple of places for alterations.

"I think you'll pass," Fitzhugh said, nodding. "It will

make travelling easier, less stressful, without the encumbrance of so much fabric."

"Yes, I think so, too," Philo added. "If you were staying for any length of time, I'd say no, but since this is a quick test for Peter and Elani, and you and Kipp are along as shotgun, it seems reasonable to do so in comfort and ease."

"All I have to do is supply them both with clean undergarments, a fresh shirt or two, perhaps, and they will be good to go," Suzanne commented, standing back and tilting her head from side to side as she stared at my too-large backside. "But I've got to do something to contain this," she said, gesturing with her hands.

I rolled my eyes as Philo tried not to laugh. Fitzhugh felt no such constraints and erupted into a fit of laughter. I'd never seen him in state of such utter enjoyment.

"I'm glad everyone is enjoying my big caboose," I muttered as I stared at a far wall.

"I'm working on making it appear smaller," Suzanne said, answering in a literal way while managing to completely miss the sarcastic nuance of my statement.

In the end, Peter and I were nicely dressed and would carry a couple of changes of undergarments and clean shirts in backpacks that could be reversed to appear as a travelling valise. I'd used such a conveyance in the past, but mine had become pretty tattered from all the hard travel. The new one would function in the same manner, but the reverse fabric was a neutral wool tweed that was less flashy than the materials used in my previous carpetbag. To conceal our funds, Suzanne duplicated the money collar that Kipp wore, making one for Elani, while Peter wore a money belt. Suzanne created some wide suspenders for me that helped to conceal my feminine attributes, and on the underside of the back of the braces was a cleverly concealed slip for currency. At my final fitting, I fingered the gold stick pin at my throat; a tiny ruby gem winked back at me, its facets caught in the light.

"Is this real or a reproduction?" I asked, removing it from my tie to better examine it.

"Real, so don't lose it, please," Suzanne answered firmly. She was happy because she'd managed, through the use of exercise-type compression fabric, to subdue my female curves and with the frock coat, which hung to my knees, I'd pass. My biggest challenge would be to contain my hair up under the hat.

"Did men ever wear their hair really long?" I asked. "Why couldn't I just put it in a ponytail and let it hang?"

"You don't want to draw attention, and no, they usually didn't." She sighed and sat down in her work chair, which squeaked as she rocked back. "Peter is growing some whiskers to fit the style of the day, so you'll be his baby face brother. I can try to come up with a wig, and we could do that, since you don't want a buzz cut."

I poo-pooed the idea of a wig, not liking the thought that my fake hair risked become awkwardly dislodged during the midst of a sensitive moment. That, if it happened, would be more difficult to explain away than my long hair. My voice was not high but neither was it very low in tone. I'd just let Peter handle the dialog.

The timing was set for us to leave on April 9, since the actual train event took place on April 12. That would give us the flexibility of a couple of days in case the target was missed, and it probably would be. The chance of us hitting an exact date, even with the amazing Kipp, was pretty low. The plan was for us to engage a couple of hotel rooms and hide out, as unobtrusively as possible, until time to board the *General* as paying passengers. I'd already argued over the issue with the lupines, since there was probably no way the conductor, William Fuller, would allow dogs to ride in a passenger car.

"We might end up in the boxcar," I said.

"I think if we pay enough and are content with the boxcar, we can persuade him." Peter was sitting at my desk in the library. I'd pushed aside my manuscripts, and we were enjoying cups of coffee. "The trains were pretty full and sometimes people rode in the boxcars as well as on top of the passenger cars."

"Why not just travel to Big Shanty and observe the train abduction from there? Then you don't have to worry about it!" Fitzhugh posed emphatically, as if he had closed the matter. He'd claimed his favorite chair while sipping the hot coffee, a rarity for him, since afternoon was definitely tea time in his book.

"Peter wants to ride the train," I explained, noting Fitzhugh's raised eyebrows. "And so do I. It will be a rare chance to experience that particular event." I felt a need to give my novice friend a little cover.

"There is always the unexpected when time shifting," Fitzhugh remarked with a nod. "Such things help to create the adaptability needed."

A time shift was always preceded by a leaving party. On April 8, Philo, his wife Claire, Suzanne, Peggy and, unexpectedly, Peter's mother, whom I'd not met, arrived. Fitzhugh helped me prepare a pan of vegetable lasagna, French bread and salad; he showed an unusual talent and baked a chocolate cake, too. The lupines, who lacked the digestive issues with chocolate as did canines, helped to finish the entire cake.

I was subjected to the usual leaving party roast; since Peter had no history, he was left relatively unscathed, as were Kipp and Elani. When Philo revealed one previously untold story about me, I excused myself and retired to the kitchen so that my reddened face could return to its pre-humiliation color. I was surprised to see Peter's mother had followed me, and lingered, hesitantly, in the doorway.

"I wanted to speak with you privately, if you don't mind," she said, her voice soft so that we would not be overheard.

"Philo embellished that story," I remarked defensively, certain she was horrified her dear son was travelling to parts unknown with a scoundrel such as me.

Peter's mother was a delicately built female, barely reaching five feet in height. She was pretty, and I could easily see where Peter got his good looks. I indicated a chair at the table, and she joined me.

"Peter told me that you are aware of my reluctance over his, uh, vocation," she began. Her eyes were brown, like Peter's, and I noticed they began to water with emotion as she folded and unfolded her hands in her lap. "But I have come to realize this is important to him, and if I try to stand in his way, he'll resent me." Evelyn, as she was called, tilted her head to the side and smiled, her lips slightly tremulous. "He's such a good son," she added. "I need you to promise me you'll bring him back safely," Evelyn said, as she took a deep breath and squared her shoulders.

Kipp was in my thoughts, and I heard and felt his alarm at such a request, which was unreasonable and forced me into a promise I could not make.

"Evelyn, I know of your history with your father and understand why this is so difficult. All I can promise is that Kipp and I will do everything possible to bring both Peter and Elani back successfully. But I can't guarantee that will happen, since travelling is unpredictable, as you know."

She nodded her head and stared at a point on the wall just over my right shoulder. After a moment, she sighed and managed a weak smile. "That's good enough," she said. "I'd have known you were not being truthful if you had promised me the impossible."

I had been prepared to not like her, based on Peter's conflicted feelings about her domineering attitude. But after understanding her heart and journey, I found that I sympathized with her worry and pain. It said a lot that she managed to make herself come to Peter's leaving party. Leaning forward, I held out my hands and she placed hers in mine; her slender fingers with their gracefully tapered tips were surprisingly cold. I squeezed her hands gently, pressing my warmth against her chilled flesh.

"Let's go back and see what else Philo can come up with," I said, smiling.

"Was that story true?" she asked, a frown on her face.

"Not a bit of it," I lied.

CHAPTER 15

Peter retired to the guest bathroom to dress, while I did the same in the privacy of my bedroom. Kipp padded after me, his feet silent on the worn floors, watching with his critical eye as I pulled on the layers of clothing. It was still more than my typical t-shirt and sweat pants but, nevertheless, a great advancement from the dreaded crinoline and corset. Kipp drew his lips back from his teeth and grimaced as I buckled his collar around his massive neck.

"I hate this thing," he whined.

"Oh, come on, you get off lightly. Look at what I have to do," I said, as I fumbled with the dark blue necktie. It took me several attempts to get it the way I wanted before I added the stick pin. Turning, I checked out my appearance in the full length mirror and felt some satisfaction that my rear end was cleverly concealed. Everyone would be happy, I thought dismally.

Fitzhugh made arrangements to spend the night with Philo and Claire, taking Juno and Lily with him. We could not risk any telepathic distractions and travelling was best done in a quiet environment. If it had just been me and Kipp, it wouldn't have mattered, but Peter and Elani were a little nervous.

It was time, and Kipp and I made the walk to the living room; Peter had arrived ahead of me and closed the plantation shutters so we would not be visible. I looked over at the fireplace and thought, a little too late, that I should have had the chimney cleaned since April had arrived.

"You'll take care of that when you get back," Kipp said, confidently.

Peter looked much more the part than did I. He'd grown, as Suzanne promised, a carefully groomed mustache and goatee, both of which aged him nicely. The coat, which hung past his knees, made him appear taller and accentuated his rangy frame. Stretched across his vest was a gold chain, something I didn't recall having been issued by Suzanne.

"What's that?" I asked, pointing at the adornment.

Smiling, he pulled a large, gold watch from a little pocket on the front of the dark gray vest he wore. After hesitating, he held it out for me to cradle in my hands; with care, I pushed the stem and watched the front cover swing open. It was a lovely piece with delicately engraved initials in an ornate script on the interior.

"My mother gave it to me to take," Peter said, his voice soft. "It was her father's–my grandfather's–and she wanted me to carry it on this time shift." After a moment, he added, "She made me promise I'd bring it back safely."

Of course, that was her code language for wanting Peter to come home in one piece. In any case, it was a fine gesture, one that indicated her trust and belief in her son. Kipp's eyes opened wide as he stared at the piece.

"Uh, oh," he said to me. "I hope nothing bad happens to that watch, or she'll be mad at us…particularly you."

"It's wonderful," I said to Peter, ignoring Kipp, who tilted his head at me. "It was very supportive of your mom," I added, pausing a moment to glare at Kipp.

The four of us sat cross legged on the floor, breathing deeply and evenly, before I lay back so that Kipp could nestle next to me, his head across my chest. After watching us, Peter and Elani copied our movements, and shortly thereafter there was silence in the room with the exception of deep breathing. My thoughts darted to Lily, and I was grateful Philo had allowed her to stay one night at his house. All we needed was Lily racing through the house, jumping on Kipp and biting his ears while he tried to concentrate.

We decided, since Elani felt she had captured the aura of the area and the time, she would lead, with careful monitoring by Kipp. He was confident he could change our trajectory if needed. With that in mind, we collectively focused on 1862 Atlanta and felt the rushing sensation as if we were hurtling though space, our bodies accelerating to almost impossible speeds. And in the blink of an eye, we were there.

I heard a groan; Peter was to my left, he and Elani, and we seemed to be in an alleyway behind a large, two storey red brick building. The only illumination came from a silver sliver of the moon above and a few scattered oil lanterns propped on tables in front of the rear windows of the building. Automatically, I reached out for Kipp, and he was at my side, steady and calm as always. He'd already turned on his telepathic radar and was busy canvassing the area.

"Are you okay?" I asked Peter. Wordlessly, he nodded, but was rubbing his head. He'd sat up too quickly and banged his forehead on a wooden crate that sat at a precarious angle on a piece of siding. Elani's eyes were bright, her head up, tail wagging.

"As soon as you can stand, let's check it out," I said, taking a moment to work the kinks out of my back and my left leg. Somehow I'd managed to land as if I were doing a seated "herkie", my leg angled back behind me. Yeah, that was gonna be sore by tomorrow. Whatever tomorrow was…?

Peter actually got to his feet before I did and leaned down to give me a hand. Yes, the left knee was a little sore, but it seemed to work okay, so I played the part of the brave symbiont and walked in a circle, squatted a couple of times and did a cat-walk turn, stopping once to pose, my chin up, to the soft laughter of Peter, who couldn't help but grin.

"Back to normal," I declared cheerfully.

Kipp, meantime, stretched fore and aft before shaking himself hard, as if he was clearing his head as well as resetting his body. He gazed up at me, wagging his tail to signal he was unharmed.

"I feel like I've been dragged by my collar down the aisle of a Greyhound bus," Peter grumbled, rubbing his head. "It hasn't felt this rough before," he added, staring at me accusatorily, as if I'd held back some mystical secret to the fountain of youth or something along those lines.

"We haven't gone this far back in time before," I said. "The longer the journey, the worse it feels."

I knew Kipp hated the bondage of the leash as did Elani, but we were forced to play the part of gentlemen who observed the niceties. My buddy ducked his head slightly as I clipped on the leather lead. Elani took it in stride, her head up, fur bristling with excitement and enthusiasm.

"Youngster," Kipp said to me, shaking his head at her positive attitude.

We spent a few minutes unloading our back packs, reversing them, and repacking our meager belongings in what seemed to be conventional carrying bags. Peter posed while I checked his attire, straightening his tie which was askew. He did the same for me, taking care to not overly inspect my chest or behind.

The four of us walked to the end of the alley and paused to get our bearings. We knew that the conductor for the *General*, Bill Fuller, had a room at the Washington Hall hotel on Lloyd Street. Thinking it might be a hoot to stay where he resided, we asked a passerby, who seemed more than a little intoxicated, for directions and managed to find our way through the gas-lit streets to the correct location. We didn't mind walking a little, since it cleared our heads. The packed dirt roads held puddles of moisture, and the high humidity was cloying. Fortunately, the temperature was pleasantly cool, and I was grateful we'd not arrived in the midst of a stereotypical blast-furnace-hot Georgia summer.

I'd made countless journeys back and forth but arriving at my destination never lost that sense of novelty. My own birth, in 1604, had occurred on the European continent. Unlike humans, symbionts did not have ethnic or cultural affiliations. My formative years, before I was allowed to bond and travel, were spent moving around so that the locals would not become suspicious of the family and those with whom we travelled. In some ways, we were considered tribal, much like gypsies, and the locals despised us out of fear and misunderstanding. The idea of symbiont collectives had evolved in the modern age and provided more security and guidance than in old times. Our culture, like that of humans, was constantly evolving.

We kept walking and in a few minutes found ourselves standing at the front of Washington Hall, another two storey red brick building. Peter took the lead since he didn't have to conceal his, uh, essence, as did I, and boldly walked in through the large, double doors which were decorated by etched glass panels; chin up, he projected a mild air of arrogance. As we approached the front desk, Peter stared around the lobby as if he was slightly displeased but would make do with the less than superior accommodations.

"May I help you sirs?" the desk man asked. He looked bored, sleepy and more than ready to go home. He stared down at Kipp and Elani, both of whom sat politely.

There was a faint smell of lemon beeswax in the room, so at some point the wooden surfaces had been polished, although a fine layer of dust was collecting on exposed areas. It would have been impossible, considering the dirt roads, horses, wagons and other conveyances passing by, to keep the area free of dust. The lobby was neat, sparsely furnished, and empty of any guests, which made me think it was either very late or very early…one or the other. From the walls as well as overhead, the light from oil lanterns flickered, casting shadows that danced with the air flow. The minimal furnishings probably indicated the owner of the hotel didn't want people loitering in his facility having meet and greets. We'd seen a few people on our way to the hotel, but I was suspicious that most of them were up to no good. Men were stumbling out of saloons, followed by women who wore brightly colored dresses and makeup applied with too heavy a hand to be the mark of good taste. Yes, I think I had their number. I could have used my telepathy, but some things are just evident and really require no additional clarification.

"We are in Atlanta on business and need two rooms," Peter said, trying to sound officious by dropping his voice a little. "Our dogs," he said, gesturing to the lupines, who looked both bored and innocent, "travel with us and are very well behaved. Of course, we will pay extra for the bother." His voice held such a dismissive tone that I half expected him to flick a piece of nonexistent lint from his lapel.

I did peek inside the mind of the clerk and realized that the hotel policy didn't address the dogs. But the clerk, an opportunistic soul, saw an effortless way to enhance his income. I guess I couldn't fault his entrepreneurial spirit since times could be hard. The man listed a figure, which was excessive, with the notion he'd pocket the extra. Peter, without complaint, handed over the currency, and the clerk called for a young boy to lead us to the second floor where we had rooms located side by side. Kipp had suggested I use the name "Samuel" as my travelling name, so Peter and I became the Keaton brothers. The boy took a moment to show us the water closet and an adjoining room with a large, cast iron hip bath with copper reservoirs for water which could be heated.

The lad preceded us and carefully lit the interior lamps which cast soft, wavering illumination in the rooms, which were small but clean. Mine overlooked the alley while Peter's had a front view of Lloyd Street. Peter and Elani followed me into my room and shut the door, lest the boy, who'd been given a coin, hovered to eavesdrop.

"When I signed the register, I noticed the date is April 10, 1862," Peter said, barely containing his excitement. Reaching down, he ruffled Elani's ears. "She did an amazing job of accuracy," he bragged.

I had to admit, for a novice, she was very good. My first time shift was nowhere near as accurate, and it had taken me a few years to improve. Kipp cast some subtle influence, I suspected, but there was no need to take away from Elani's success. He was too much of a gentleman to admit it and even concealed that part of his mind from me when I asked. Kipp was wagging his tail before he leaned over and gave her a little nose bump of congratulations.

"So, we have a little time to kill before we meet the train," I said.

Outside, a few people walked past, their voices disruptive to the early morning quiet of the street. I knew that Atlanta, in some ways, was still much like a frontier town, loud and boisterous with magistrates handing out citations left and right as the lawful element tried to build a genteel city. Large homes with ivy wrapped supportive columns fringed the streets, while saloons and houses of ill repute stretched down other byways. Despite her occasionally cultivated appearance, Atlanta was a raw nerve waiting for something to happen.

"I'd wish you'd have brought Clue," Elani said, laughing in her lupine way.

After Peter and Elani retired, I undressed and donned the man's nightshirt that Suzanne had constructed in what she obviously thought was a clever touch. I sank into the too soft bed, feeling my back descend through the stuffing until it came to a rest on something hard and unyielding. Kipp hopped up and managed to circle without falling over before he lay down suddenly, his jaw thumping my chest.

"What are we gonna do tomorrow?" he asked, twisting his big head slightly to gaze at me.

"I'd thought we'd hire a buggy and sightsee, but you know, Kipp, I think I want to sleep."

He lifted his head in alarm and began to inspect me, his nostrils flaring as he took in my scent, as if he was searching me for an undeclared infirmity. It was uncharacteristic for me to not be curious to the point of total irrationality.

"I'm okay, Kipp. It's just we've had three time shifts in fairly close proximity to one another, and it's taxing on me. I'm not a youngster like you guys." I scratched his chin in what I hoped was a convincing manner.

"I don't mind sleeping," he said, nestling closer to me. "Maybe we'll dream together."

I did dream, but the experience wasn't pleasant, and I awoke, finally, sweating, my heart pounding. Kipp was alert next to me, his profile a dark silhouette in the unlit room. He'd let me be, knowing I didn't want him to interfere with my nocturnal musing. In my dream state, Peter and I got separated, and as I searched frantically, I kept encountering females who looked like his mother, Evelyn, who were silent but shaking their heads sadly at my failure. At some point, Philo and Fitzhugh joined the party, and I knew I'd disappointed everyone who had once cared about me.

"I wasn't in your dream," Kipp pointed out. "And I will never be disappointed in you," he added. "Except, maybe, when you tell me I stink when I get wet. That hurts my feelings."

"I won't say it again," I promised.

Peter and Elani did venture out the next morning to canvass the neighborhood and brought Kipp and me food. Kipp bolted his down with the eagerness of a starving wolf while I picked at mine delicately. Honestly, I was enjoying just holing up for a day, wearing my nightshirt, listening to the rain patter outside. Our journey was going to be a damp one; I already knew that tidy fact from my brief review of history.

"I am still trying to understand why we symbionts have some of the rules that govern us," Elani remarked as she delicately licked her paw. "Like today, I thought I picked up a very vague ping of another of us, somewhere in this city."

We were gathered on a wool blanket spread across the floor of my room, lazing around, while the rain continued to fall. The sound of the rain acted as a soporific, and I began to yawn. The plan was to be at the train depot, or Car Shed, at 3:30 am. That would give us thirty minutes to obtain passage and deal with the issue of the lupines. How the conductor, William Fuller–who was notoriously rigid— would manage that wrinkle was unpredictable.

"Elani, our society has evolved, and our species has changed. You can see it in Kipp, who has skills and talents that surpass the rest of us. But even from the time I was born in 1604 to now, we have increasingly seen the need to develop structure and ethics so that we don't harm humans or do anything to change history. That's one reason we try to avoid our own kind when traveling, although it's not exactly forbidden. You could run into a corrupt symbiont who plows through your mind trying to figure out how to benefit from altering what's meant to be."

Her massive jaw dropped down in a pant. It wasn't hot, but the thick humidity made the air seem close and sticky. "Have you had that happen?" she asked.

"Yes," I replied, thinking of my distasteful encounter with Fitzhugh's nephew, John Gold, as well as that nasty piece of work, Andrea Collins. "You make me think of Kipp, Elani, in that you are innocent and have trouble conceiving of evil in others." I leaned over and scratched her head, my fingers finding the funny little point on her head, concealed by the thick gray-blonde fur. "Stay that way, okay?" I asked, smiling.

"So you've known others of our kind who are, uh, bad?" she asked. Her eyes were dark and depthless, unlike Kipp's bright amber ones that seemed backlit with an inner fire.

"Oh, yes," I answered. "But fortunately, there have been very few."

Peter stayed quiet through all these exchanges, but I knew he was absorbing everything that passed. He was the youngest of the group in terms of years, and he lacked some of Elani's natural talents. I knew he felt a little insecure, but that was to be expected until he got more experience behind him. Already I'd seen maturity in him just from the time shifts we'd made that were successful. At some point, he and Elani would go off on their own. I almost wondered if he was listening in to my thoughts, because a moment later he asked an interesting question.

"Do symbionts ever work in teams?" he asked as he gazed out the window at the rain which was falling in a fine mist outside. The natural imperfections in the window glass caused the scene to be slightly distorted, with the blurred and fuzzy aspect of a soft watercolor painting.

"You mean, like the four of us?" I asked.

"Yes."

"Well, I don't think so. This is done in the spirit of training, but I've not heard of team time shifting for the purposes of our actual work." I smiled at him. "But, as I said, we are a constantly evolving species." It was an interesting notion and could have a useful application. Maybe it would be something to pose to the Twelve.

"He seems nervous," Kipp pointed out, his voice quiet in the back of my brain.

"Yes, but he'll settle down," I replied with a confidence I didn't feel. How was I to know how he would perform when placed under pressure? Symbionts had to think and adapt in an instant, and we took pride in the fact we could lie with a talent unsurpassed by any human in existence. We made deception into a fluid, flowing art of subterfuge.

Kipp helped us all to relax by introducing a complex mind game as only a brilliant Kipp could do. He somehow laid out the Clue game board in his mind and we, after choosing our characters–I was Professor Plum, naturally– began to play telepathically. It was almost as much fun as the physical board game, except I missed the tactile pleasure of the tiny little rope and candlestick props that I could cradle in the palm of my hand.

After a modest meal in the late afternoon, Peter dashed

down to the front desk to ask the clerk on duty to have us awakened at 2:30 am. We'd need time to dress and walk to the Car Shed and wanted plenty of adjustment room if needed. The *General* would leave Atlanta for Marietta at precisely 4am.

CHAPTER 16

<hr>

"**D**arn it," I said, in frustration, as I tried to get my tie straight. There was a mirror of poor quality hanging on the wall, its borders contained in a narrow, slightly warped wooden frame. Leaning forward, I frowned at my wavy reflection. I'd managed to get my hair secured on top of my head and pulled the slouch hat firmly down, its brim tipping forward. Since I had no plans to remove my hat, the chances I'd be seen as rude and ill-mannered were high, but I'd have to take that chance. Peter could over-compensate and act even more genteel to divert attention from his sullen brother, Sam. Finally, Kipp gave me his nod of approval that I would pass muster.

"If I haven't said it before, let me say again that I am thankful to be lupine. No showers, no layers of clothing, don't have to eat with a fork and knife…all kinds of things." His jaw dropped as he began to pant with excitement. Kipp was definitely eager to get on with our business. "So the usual rules apply?" he asked, tilting his head towards me.

"What do you mean?" I replied, stopping my self-examination to sit on the side of the too soft bed.

"If Peter or Elani get into trouble due to their youth and inexperience, I still need to follow all the standard rules of what I can and can't do." His eyes were bright and caught the minimal glow from the lantern in the dimly lit room. "Right?"

"Kipp, you know I can't answer that question," I replied, feeling mildly frustrated. "That is like asking a human if he sees a crime being committed, will he commit one, too, to stop a crime. It falls to ethics but also to judgment."

There was a light tap on my door which, after my soft invitation, swung inward. Peter, with his mustache and goatee neatly combed into submission, stood in the doorway, Elani at his side. He was holding his valise, which indicated he was ready to go.

"Come with me," he said.

I blew out the light in the lamp and followed him, closing the door quietly so as to not disturb other guests. Peter walked ahead on the slightly worn wool runner, which was patterned in faded colors of brown, red and green, leading me and Kipp to his room. It was dark, with only the solitary front window outlined on the wall, illuminated by exterior, ambient lighting. I joined him at the window; a couple of minutes later, a tall, slender man exited the front of the hotel and turned left to walk down Lloyd Street. He was visible in the soft halo of light cast by the gas lamps that fringed the street at evenly spaced intervals.

"William Fuller," Peter intoned. He tried to keep his voice low and even but the almost tremulous quality of excitement was there, nonetheless.

As we stood there watching his passage, I became aware of a novel fragrance, somewhere between sweet and spicy; my nose wrinkled in curiosity. The odor was coming from Peter's direction, and I turned to stare at him. "What's that smell?" I asked.

He shifted uncomfortably and kept looking out the window, pretending to ignore me for a moment. Finally, he sighed and answered. "It's pomade." Cocking his head to the side he glanced at me. "I bought some pomade while I was out and put it on my mustache and goatee to help keep them from curling up in the damp weather." His chin lifted as he stared at me as if he dared me to make a comment. Feeling noble, I kept my replies internal and tried to ignore Kipp who was giggling in the back of my brain. Looking down, I caught a glimpse of Elani happily wagging her tail in support of her man, which was natural.

"Well, let's go," I said, understanding his emotion over having seen William Fuller as well as the need to segue from the pomade confession. It was one thing to read about a historical figure and quite another experience to actually meet that person in the flesh. We descended the staircase to the lobby, nodding our heads at the same surly clerk who had registered us upon our arrival.

"Y'all feel free to visit again and bring those nice doggies, too," he said, sneering. Yes, he was hoping we'd do just that so he could charge another personal premium for the visit. Peter managed to murmur something pleasant as we passed.

Atlanta was a busy town with a lot of commerce, so people from different backgrounds merged there. Therefore, we weren't going overboard to copy the soft native Southern drawl. I'd lived in North Carolina for some time, but I worked in situations with humans and symbionts of different backgrounds; consequently, my manner of speech was not particularly distinctive. I knew several languages and had the adaptability of my species to assume the local dialects with speed and accuracy. However, I was happy to be surly Sam and just ignore people or glower at them. We left the Washington House; outside, a fine drizzle continued to fall, turning the street into a cloying mess of unpleasant red mud.

"Another good reason to not wear skirts," I remarked, pointing down. "I can't imagine trying to keep my skirts hiked up over this stuff."

Kipp agreed as he and Elani tried to take delicate steps. We managed to find a sidewalk that was paved with river rock and thus escaped most of the mud.

"Not a word about wet dogs," Kipp cautioned me.

"I promised," I replied with a smile.

We encountered a few people; most of those on foot had obviously left saloons and were wobbling their way home or to other destinations. The mist, combined with the yellow halos of light radiating from the gas lamps, created a surreal appearance. It almost looked like a chalk drawing, one that had become wet and was beginning to fade into nothingness. In a few minutes, we passed what was seemed to be a city park, a new addition to a growing city. It only took a few more minutes to arrive at the train station, or Car Shed as it was locally called.

I've seen a few places where the energy of humans was concentrated, but the Car Shed would go down in my memory book as exceptional. It was easily the largest building we'd seen, and although I not studied the architectural specifications for municipal buildings in Atlanta, I suspected nothing else rivaled the station. Constructed of red brick, there were two enormous arching entries on either end of the rectangular structure. As we entered, the echoing sounds of metal clanging, steam hissing, and men shouting almost caused the lupines' sensitive ears to ache from the booming, intensified noise. The four of us crowded closer together. We passed a row of men hawking food, everything from fresh fruit to hunks of cheese and fresh bread, thickly sliced. Two young girls labored over churns as they worked to produce buttermilk, about as close to the cow as possible.

"We didn't eat," Kipp remarked, his eyes large and rather sad as he stared at me.

I wasn't sure how he could manage that hollow-eyed appearance and almost asked him to turn to the side so I could check if his ribs were visible. This was the same Kipp who consumed three whole chickens and a plate of mashed potatoes the previous night.

"Remember," I said, raising my eyebrows, "we can be deprived of food for a long time and not suffer any ill effects."

"Yes, but I've done that on plenty of occasions, and let me state for the record, it's no fun," Kipp replied. He lifted his lips from his teeth in a lopsided grimace that looked intimidating to the unknowing humans nearby.

Peter approached a few of the vendors and purchased cheese and bread, and because I had what might be thought of as a hankering for buttermilk, he bought me a glassful. It was tart, lumpy and everything buttermilk should be. Kipp, always curious, took a whiff and turned it down after rolling his eyes in disgust. Well, I guess buttermilk is one of those things that you either love or hate.

We walked to a far corner of the Car Shed and let the lupines snack on cheese and bread, which Peter shared. I confess I was too nervous to have any appetite at all. There was a large clock in the center of the station that indicated it was 3:40 am. The time had arrived for us to determine if we could manage to convince Bill Fuller to allow us passage on his precious train, lupines and all.

Peter brushed the bread crumbs from his coat and took the lead, walking a step ahead of me, while I kept my chin down. Up ahead, we spied the *General* in all her splendor, noting the subtle differences between the original and the version that rested in a tidy, well-kept museum in the distant future. The brass fittings had been polished to a high shine, indicating the pride and perfectionism of her crew. On the sandbox of the boiler, the number 39 was inscribed, correct as per historical records. The tender, which was painted in dark green stripes, displayed the company initials–W&ARR–boldly painted in gold paint. The man we knew from photographs to be Bill Fuller swung down from the locomotive, adjusting his hat as his feet touched the ground. He was a well built man, tall for those days, with a serious face decorated by a mustache and wispy chin whiskers. Fuller pulled his gold watch from the little pocket on his vest and checked the time against the large station clock. He didn't have to speak to project a completely no-nonsense attitude. People were beginning to gather, so before we got lost in the crowd, Peter approached him.

"Sir, I understand you are the conductor," Peter began. He stuck out his hand as a courtesy, and after a moment,

Fuller shook his hand, as his unblinking blue eyes stared at Peter. "I am Peter Keaton and this is my brother, Sam," he said, gesturing at me. "We are traveling to Dalton to meet a man about purchasing some land." He looked up at the *General* and his face slightly flushed. "We need to purchase tickets to ride on your magnificent *General*, sir," he concluded politely.

Fuller, who thought of the engine as a prized possession that he loved more than he could love another human being, caught the look of admiration on Peter's face and smiled. He enjoyed any instance when a rider could appreciate the perfection and beauty of the *General*.

"Why of course, sirs," he replied. "You'll need to go to the ticket counter," he said, pointing at a location close by.

"We have a little problem," Peter responded, tilting his head forward. "We travel with our beloved pets, you see, and can't leave them behind." He laughed a little self-consciously. "You know how attached people can get to their dogs."

It was clear Fuller had never experienced such an attachment and that he thought a couple of grown men dragging around two large dogs were pretty ridiculous. I was monitoring his thoughts, and he wasn't suspicious; he just thought we were silly.

"I realize we can't crowd our pets on the passenger car, but we'd be more than happy to purchase passage and can sit comfortably in a box car so as to not incommode your other passengers," Peter concluded, his expression earnest. He quietly asked me, telepathically, how was he doing? I gave him a thumbs-up in return, psychically speaking.

Fuller gave us another look over; people had travelled in the box cars before as well as troops riding on top of the cars. But gentlemen usually didn't want to sit in a dirty box car that was used for storing and transporting who knows what. But passage was passage and a ticket was a ticket. So he nodded, and we went to stand in line to purchase our passages to Dalton.

Kipp and Elani were almost jumping up and down with

excitement, and after Fuller punched our tickets, he showed us to the first box car that sat behind the tender. There were a total of three box cars, followed by the mail and baggage car, and two passenger cars. It took a little running leap, but Kipp managed to scramble up first, followed by Elani. Peter managed to heft himself into the empty box car and lent down a hand to help haul me up. The box cars were empty and would be taken to Chattanooga to be filled with cargo. Fuller walked by and stuck his head inside.

"I'll partially close the door so you won't get coated in soot," he said, nodding. There was some stray hay from broken bales scattered on the wooden floor; we'd just sit and relax while the countryside passed by like frames unwinding in a motion picture reel. Marietta was twenty miles away, while Big Shanty–later named Kennesaw–was twenty-eight.

The train whistle sounded, steam driven with a sound not ever duplicated by any other artificial mechanism; with a jerk and a squeal of the wheels on the metal rails, the train began to move north. Kipp lay down close to the open door and gazed out. I joined him, sitting with my knees crossed, my arm around Kipp's neck as I pulled him into my chest. The skyline of Atlanta began to fade away as recognizable businesses, such as the *Daily Intelligencer* newspaper and the M. Geuterbruck Tobacco Company, dropped off into the darkness. The rain continued to fall softly, and the cooling mist drifted into the interior of the boxcar, helping to mitigate the effect of the ash and cinders from the *General's* smokestack.

I looked up at Peter, and he grinned in return. Yes, the first time shift where one really melted into history was exiting, and to date, all had gone well. The train was rocking from side to side with a gentle motion, the wheels clacking on the metal tracks below. It seemed we had only gone a short distance when the train began to slow.

"Vinings," Peter said. "We stop for wood and water." He had carefully stored all details about the numerous stops in his brain.

After we left Atlanta, the countryside was curtained in darkness, with only the rare sighting of a household where a farmer, perhaps, was stirring, ready to tackle another day of labor. A single oil lantern would be visible in a windowsill of a remote dwelling, backlighting the aperture with a soft, golden glow. Occasionally, we would hear the lonely lowing of a cow punctuated by the bright sound of a rooster crowing. It seemed lonely and rather poignant. The smell of damp, fertile farm land circulated through the open door of the car. The war had not hit Georgia yet, but it would. William Tecumseh Sherman would bring his army and burn a path through the state wide enough to ensure that recovery and retreat would be impossible.

"He believed in total war," Peter said, explaining the concept to Kipp and Elani, who followed my thoughts. "If the populace was made to suffer and lessen their support of the military, he felt it would bring the war to an end sooner."

"Our species has never engaged in war," Elani commented. Peter was seated to my right as she tucked in next to him, her head stretched across his legs. "I don't understand it all sometimes."

"Humans fight for certain things. I guess we don't have or create some of the same issues," I replied as way of a feeble reply.

"Why don't they ever learn?" she asked, persistent. "War seems to be a constant for their kind."

"I can't answer that," I said. Kipp nestled closer, if that was possible, and closed his eyes, dozing for little cat naps as the rocking of the train threatened to soothe us all to sleep as if we were babes cradled by our mothers.

Our little group of travelers fell quiet; Peter amused himself by plucking stray thoughts from the passengers. I had no objection, since he was still relatively new at this and practicing his telepathy was time well spent. Elani joined him, their thoughts merging in and out in a playfully polite dance. It was my hope that one day they could drop some of the contemporary formalities and dig deeper at our essence, as had Kipp and I…but that would take time and trust.

The trip north revealed an engineering feat to be admired. The journey through North Georgia was a steady, unnoticeable incline, and the rails had been laid in such a fashion to deal with rocky terrain, rivers, and one particularly large barrier, Chetoogeta Mountain. Eventually, a tunnel was constructed, and the area became known as Tunnel Hill, which was probably easier to pronounce. I knew it was my imagination, since there was no way I could really feel an incline that subtle, but it did seem as if we were going up rather than down. The train began to slow; from our itinerary, we knew that we must be approaching Marietta station. The rhythmic sound of the box car wheels clacking on the rails softened as we drew to a stop. Peter decided to stand at the door of the car and watch as new passengers came on board, including Andrews' Raiders, the group destined to abduct the train.

"Petra, I just saw him enter the passenger coach," Peter hissed, whipping around to stare at me. "James Andrews!" He began to shake his head. "I can't believe it!" For an instance, his energy seemed much like that of a youngster and not an adult.

I grinned at Kipp. Peter had seen pictures of the man and recognized him on sight. Even with my legacy of many trips, I felt a definite spark of excitement when I met Doc Holliday and Wyatt Earp, so I understood the emotion. I guess the question is whether or not historical figures will be as expected or has the telling of their stories done them an injustice?

Peter began to tick off the names, based on his familiarity with the faces, since he had studied them all extensively before the trip. I had not done his degree of research but knew enough to recall that it ended badly for many of the raiders after they were captured, following the unsuccessful conclusion of the train abduction.

After the brief stop to allow people to disembark as well as board, the train eased off again. Jeff Cain, the engineer, handled the throttle with experience and managed to avoid the neck jarring jerk that was common. I knew, in later years, there was some discussion of whether or not the crew of the *General* was actually suspicious of so many men boarding at once. Just because I am a curious cuss, I briefly touched Bill Fuller's mind, as well as that of Anthony Murphy, the W&ARR supervisor who was riding that day. Honestly, I will say that their minds only wondered why so many able-bodied men were apparently traveling in a northward direction. There were certainly no alarm bells ringing, despite later claims to the contrary.

The *General* continued her journey; the next stop was Big Shanty, the location that would one day become Kennesaw. The train would halt so that the crew and passengers could have breakfast at the Lacy Hotel. There was little else in Big Shanty other than the hotel, a few houses scattered in a haphazard pattern, and muddy roads that crisscrossed one another. Directly across the tracks was Camp McDonald, which was a training post for the 4th Brigade of the Georgia Volunteers, also called Phillip's Division.

It was like catnip, being in such proximity to the raiders, and all of us were compelled, out of curiosity, to probe into the minds of the train abductors. Some were quite young, and although their self talk was meant to nurture bravery, there was intense anxiety amongst some of the men. I admired their courage to attempt something so hazardous. They knew, all of them, if they were caught burning a bridge, they would be hanged on the spot. And it was a long way back to the safety of the federal troops. Even their journey to get to this point had been physically arduous and filled with great risk.

The engine began to slow again as Big Shanty came into view on the far side of a lazy, graceful curve in the tracks. As the train ground to a halt, I went to the open door and looked out; the Lacy Hotel, a white, two story wooden building adorned with green shutters to interrupt the plainness, stood across the rail siding. The roads were muddy, with deep ruts carved into the dirt by the constant passage of wagons and horses. It was still raining, but only falling as a light, cascading mist at that time. Turning, I crossed to the other side of the boxcar where that door was slightly ajar. Rows of white tents were laid out in a field; I could see camp fires lit and men walking amongst the tents, their voices low, as if they maintained a hush deliberately because of the early time of day.

"Camp McDonald," Kipp said, staring at the field.

"I guess this is where we get off," I said, looking at Peter, as he watched the other passengers, who began to leave the train in an orderly but hurried fashion. Twenty minutes were allotted for breakfast, and, no doubt, Bill Fuller was watching the passage of time with his gold watch.

Peter hopped from the car to land lightly in a patch of trampled grass and stopped himself from giving me an assist, since I was supposed to be his brother, Sam. Kipp and Elani followed, and the four of us trudged across the muddy way towards the hotel. For the most part, our trip was over, and we had accomplished our goal. After witnessing the raiders elope with the *General*, we would take rooms at the hotel and sometime later that evening, time shift home. Simple enough…or so it seemed.

CHAPTER 17

Kipp wanted to take a little fun run at the bunched up knot of ducks, ones that were rather famous locally as being part and parcel of the community. There was a small pond near the hotel, and Mrs. Lacey, as legend had it, was very protective of her plump ducks which benefited from left over biscuits that were left uneaten at breakfast. Kipp looked at me, eyes bright, tail wagging, and looked a little deflated when I shook my head no.

"I thought I was supposed to be in character," Kipp whined. "Any self respecting canine would rush the ducks," he said dipping his head and giving them one last intimidating stare. The ducks responded by quacking loudly and swimming as fast as possible, their little paddleboat legs churning, to the far end of the shallow, muddy pond. Changing the subject, Kipp looked up at me and asked, "Do you think you can get me a bowl of real southern grits? I've always wanted to try grits." I assured him that was a distinct possibility. After all, we were in no hurry. We would remain here after the engine was abducted until we chose to time shift home.

Peter and I slowed to allow the other passengers to go ahead. Surreptitiously, we turned and watched as the team of Andrews' men began to leave the train, mixing for a moment with other passengers so as to be unobtrusive. All of a sudden, Peter gave a start and reached out to clutch my forearm.

"Petra, I've lost my grandfather's watch!" he exclaimed, forgetting to call me Sam. "I'll be right back," he said, trotting quickly towards the train.

"Peter, wait," I called, but he ignored me. I remembered the promise he'd made his mother and knew he had to try and find the precious article. Since the line had just started to enter the hotel, he had a few minutes; Elani, after glancing at Kipp, ran after Peter.

Kipp and I stopped, letting people continue to brush past us. Peter was walking quickly, his eyes focused down on the ground as he stopped to examine ragged islands of rain soaked grass. He paused at the boxcar in which we'd ridden; craning his neck, he stood on tiptoes and looked inside. The next thing I knew, he vaulted up and disappeared into the box car.

"Peter, no!" I shouted at him in my head so loud it made Kipp flatten his ears in response. "Get out of there right now!"

Elani stood at the entrance to the box car and was about to jump inside, too, but at that moment, three of the raiders walked down the beaten pathway on the near side of the tracks and pushed between her and the entrance to the car.

"Peter, jump out the other door!" I shouted, feeling about as impotent as I've ever been in my life. Kipp started to move quickly, as did I.

"Petra, they are blocking my exit out either side!" Peter's voice came to me with an urgency that broke my heart.

As Kipp and I watched, the three men jumped into the box car and closed the door. Elani began to bark in frustration; standing up on her back legs, she tried, in vain, to scrabble at the heavy door with her front paws. The next moment, the engine gave a loud whoosh as the steam was released, and the big driving wheels began to turn. I looked at Kipp in horror–the train was moving, Peter was trapped inside the box car with the raiders, and there was nothing I could do to stop what had begun in motion. The raiders had unhooked the passenger cars and the mail car, leaving the engine to pull the empty box cars.

The door to the Lacy hotel was flung open, and Bill Fuller, followed by the engineer, Jefferson Cain, and the W&ARR supervisor, Anthony Murphy, ran out on the porch. A second later, the fireman, Andrew Anderson, joined them still clutching a fork, with a cloth napkin fluttering from where he'd carefully stuck it into the collar of his shirt. After the reality of what was happening sank in, Murphy, thinking quickly, barked out an order to a local man to ride his horse to Marietta, where the closest operational telegraph office could be found. The men clearly didn't know why the train was stolen and even speculated it might be Confederate deserters, but in any case, the action was nefarious and a violation of the law.

Bill Fuller, without hesitation, began to run along the railroad tracks, chasing the rapidly disappearing *General*. Kipp and I both entered his thoughts and were amazed by his single-minded sense of purpose. I think there is no doubt, if he had been able, that he would have run all the way to Chattanooga if needed. There was a seething fury in the man over the audacity of someone absconding with his train. For certain, he had a highly developed sense of responsibility. After a moment, Murphy and Cain, the latter of whom was in poor health, began to run after Fuller. Elani joined us, distraught and breathless.

"I tried to get him out," she said. I knew if lupines could cry, she would have a furry face covered in tears.

"It's not your fault," I snapped firmly, knowing she needed to get control and focus. Then, with no further discussion, I ordered, "Let's go."

We began to run, the three of us, chasing after the train men, who quickly found that the burden of running across a surface of soil that had been turned into a sticky mud by the softly falling rain was even more of a challenge than expected. I ran regularly, so a jog of a few miles was easily within my capabilities; Kipp and Elani could go for miles without pause. In less than a minute, I caught up to the men. Murphy glanced at me in surprise, his cheeks red from the exertion of the dash.

"My brother was on that train," I said, keeping my breathing even.

Fuller looked back at me, a scowl on his face, but said nothing and kept moving. I realized he was agitated already, and the appearance of an interloper who was not a member of the crew didn't make him happy. But he didn't waste time or breath by speaking, and the four of us—and Kipp and Elani—kept running. The rain made the run treacherous, and it took our full concentration to not trip and fall. The *General* drew ahead quickly until the sounds of its chugging became lost in the heavily wooded landscape that acted like a muffler in the wilderness.

After a couple of miles of steady jogging, we came up upon Moon's station. We stopped, breathing deeply; Jeff Cain leaned forward, hands on thin knees as he had a coughing fit. There was a work crew at the station, men assembled to do track repair. Fuller approached the supervisor, a man named Jackson Bond, to see if he could find him a horse. Bill Fuller's determination was unchanged, and he planned on chasing down the train by horse, if possible.

"Bond, somebody has taken the *General*," Fuller said, trying to not gasp while speaking. Although in good shape, the run along the tracks in the mud and rain had been taxing. His neat attire was mud splattered, his slouch hat askew.

Murphy arched his back and tilted his head back for a moment, letting the rain fall onto his ruddy face. Bond, the supervisor of the work crew, glanced at the Irishman, who nodded an affirmation of the incredulous assertion as their eyes met. Poor Jefferson Cain leaned up against a shed wall, his thin chest heaving with exertion, his face gray and drawn.

"Well, they stopped here, and there were about fifteen men we saw, although there could have been more in the box cars. They took our tools and a load of ties, saying they needed them for urgent repairs up along the line," Bond said as he spat out a stream of tobacco juice, wiping his face with a stained kerchief produced from a back pocket.

"What do we do?" Elani asked me, her damp nose touching the back of my hand.

"We let history evolve, untouched, but we must keep moving so that when this plays out, we can be reunited with Peter," I said. It was evident that without his symbiont, Peter would be lost in time, much as had happened to me before the miracle of Kipp; Elani, likewise, couldn't return home. There was no question that we would not leave this place until Elani was joined with Peter. Kipp, understanding her anxiety, approached her and nuzzled her comfortingly. We were all a sodden mess at that point.

"We got this here pole car," Bond was saying, addressing Murphy since he was in the chain of authority for the Western & Atlantic Railroad. Pole cars preceded hand cars in the evolutionary chain and consisted of a large, flat plank of wood on wheels that was propelled by men pushing against the ground with long poles. Kipp looked at the contraption and then at me.

"I may just run," he said, his eyes rounding.

The crew carried the pole car to the tracks and began settling it on the rails. I looked around the immediate vicinity. There was little at the station…just a rail siding, a wobbly looking shed with a distinct lean to it, and a road curving off into the woods that had been turned to red mud by the constant rain. Looking up, I saw a small break in the cloud cover. It was possible that the rain was tapering off for a while. Bond looked over at me, curious at the presence of a stranger. Then he glanced at the two lupines, who always drew attention due to their size and unusual appearance.

"Sam Keaton," I said, trying to keep my voice low. "My brother is on that train."

"Petra," Kipp said, interrupting my conversation, "Fuller is beginning to waver at having us along." He'd obviously been monitoring the conductor's thoughts. "He thinks we'll hold him back, and we're not part of the railroad. He wants to leave us here."

Well, I believe in ethical conduct and all that jazz, but there are times when one just has to break the rules for a greater cause. This was one of those times.

"Kipp, I want you to go into his thoughts and insert the notion that he wants us along. And make sure it sticks," I said, glancing at my friend, my eyes narrowed. Elani looked up at me and tilted her head to the side. Reaching down, I ruffled her ears. "Sometimes, Elani, you have to do the right thing, and the right thing might not necessarily follow the book," I said. "We'll find Peter, and that's a promise."

The pole car was crowded, and the addition of me and two lupines didn't help matters, but since Kipp had left a very strong suggestion in the back of Fuller's brain, he told the others to make room as we squeezed on board the platform. Bond and one of his men jumped on, too. Instead of using the poles, Bond and the workman sat on the front edge of the platform and used their legs and feet to propel it. In a relatively short time, we actually began to pick up quite a nice bit of speed; I looked at Kipp and realized he was enjoying the thrill of the ride.

"I might have to figure out some way to get you on a roller coaster," I said, winking at him. His tongue lolled out in response. Elani stayed quiet, her worry palpable to us.

We were passing through dense, rocky terrain at times, and I marveled at how efficient the engineers had been in terms of laying out this path. In those days, construction was done the hard way. The trees, which had been cut back from the track, set up a thick barrier at the edge of old forests. Huge long-leafed pine trees, dark and intimidating, intermixed with oaks, beech and poplars. Since it was early April, the new growth was bright green, only slightly darkened by the rain which had drenched the foliage. Thankfully, the rainfall, which had abated, remained on a momentary break; I crouched down on the pole car, trying to keep my balance as it rocked from side to side. Elaini lay flat while Kipp stood, splaying his feet out, his head pointed into the wind.

"Whoa," Murphy called out. The men immediately stopped their propulsion, letting their feet scrape along the ground like Fred Flintstone braking his Stone Age car. Murphy, his handsome face dark with exertion and stress, glanced back at Cain and Fuller. "They've put cross ties across the track."

The raiders not only had thrown ties on the track to slow down pursuers but also had cut the telegraph line. The pole car ground to a halt, and Fuller, Murphy and Bond jumped off and began to pull the ties to the side. Thinking I needed to make an appearance, I started to hop off the car but was stopped by a glance by Murphy, who was a tall man with dark eyes and brown hair worn unfashionably long for the day.

"I think your name is Samantha, not Sam," he said, smiling slightly. "And my poor dead father would roll in his grave if I were to let you try to lift these ties." His voice carried the lilting cadence of his Irish birth.

The other men stopped to stare at me; I could feel my face flush bright red. It must have been intuition on Murphy's part, since the others had not picked up on my disguise. Of course, Fuller had been so single-minded in his pursuit that he'd not have noticed if I'd disrobed and stood naked. And Cain was struggling, with his poor health, to just stay in the game. I smiled at Murphy and decided the disguise was at an end. While they continued to work, I removed my hat, unpinned my hair and quickly braided it, tying off the end with a piece of torn handkerchief. Murphy walked to me and tipped his rain flattened hat, smiling.

"How did you know?" I asked, looking up at him.

He smiled again, and tapped his finger at the side of his head. Wordlessly, he indicated he was just smart and perceptive. Actually, in an odd way, the fact I was female helped in the pursuit. The men were less likely to leave me abandoned in the wilderness and would feel obliged to help me find my brother. Yes, chivalry was alive and well on the tracks of the W&ARR.

The work of clearing the cross ties was not easy, since the raiders had piled at least twenty on the tracks, and it took sheer manpower to clear the way. The men hopped back on the swaying pole car, and Bond and his man used their legs and feet to push off. This time, Fuller and Murphy took a couple of the long poles and began to assist. It became clear that this was no simple abduction of the train, perhaps the act of deserters. And the pursuing men began to play with the notion that maybe the unknown gang ahead of us had more serious plans that included burning bridges. Just stealing a train would not cripple the movement of goods and troops; destroying bridges definitely would do so.

"You remind me of my wife, Adelia," Murphy said unexpectedly. "She has the same quiet ways about her, and there was something about the manner in which you carry yourself that told me you are not a man."

At the mention of his wife, I peeked into his mind and felt a wave of sentimental notions as well as his love for his bride. Looking at him, I appreciated she'd been drawn to his strength of character as well as his handsome face and robust build. He was wet and muddy like the rest of us, but he still held a dignity that was not touched by the weather or the adverse events.

"I'm glad that's over," Kipp said, sighing. "It was only a matter of time and now you don't have to try so hard to play a part. You can be yourself, uh, sort of."

"So do you and your brother always travel with your dogs?" Murphy asked.

He was curious and polite; Fuller scowled at him, not interested in my private life or that of my brother. It's not that Fuller was unpleasant; he was just single-mindedly focused on the job at hand. I harbored no ill will towards him for not showing interest in the new and unexpected fact of my femininity.

"Yes, we are very attached," I said. "This is Kipp, and that is Elani."

Murphy nodded and tried to keep a sociable conversation going as he dug the long pole into the mud and dirt by the side of the track to push us along. The pole car was small, and we were pretty jammed in together.

"I had a dog when I was a lad," Murphy said. "A terrier that helped herd the sheep. A smarter dog I've never seen. He'd snap at me when my mother made me comb the brambles from his rough coat. Never the one for the grooming was he."

Kipp rolled his eyes and looked at me, trying to get me to laugh. I knew he wanted to show off and act goofy, so I shook my head at him and tried to frown as I pursed my lips.

"Oh, come on," Kipp said. "You could have me do tricks, and it'll really impress him. He just thinks his dog was special. I could count, bark out the lyrics to a song...uh, any number of things."

I realized he was trying to lighten the mood for Elani's sake. She was worried and consumed with anxiety. Her face was pointed north, her ears swiveling constantly as if she was trying to hear the sound of the *General*. Peter's essence had been pinging, but the sensation was lessening due to the fact the *General* was lengthening its distance from us with every passing second. A few more minutes passed, and I saw a clearing ahead with another station, Ackworth, where several people clustered under a wooden shelter that extended out from a small station house. The pole car slid, shaking, to a halt; Fuller and Murphy jumped off and began explaining what had happened as well as gathering information.

"The *General* stopped, and a couple of men got off while the engineer took care of the engine," an old man said. His eyes narrowed as he turned to point north following the track. The man skillfully moved a wad of chewing tobacco from one cheek pouch to the other before speaking again. "They said they was on a special dispatch mission and in a hurry," he added. "Not much to say and not very sociable neither."

Fuller and Murphy began to canvass the few people present, gathering assistance as well as procuring a couple of old shotguns that looked as if they'd seen better days. The word spread quickly that a nefarious operation was in play, and excitement built in waves over the people present. Two volunteers, after grabbing their guns, jumped on board the extremely crowded pole car. They looked at me in amazement before staring at Kipp and Elani.

"This is Mr. Stokely and Mr. Rainey," Murphy said, introducing them to me. No matter the situation, it seemed he needed to be mannerly and inclusive of his uninvited guests. "Gentlemen, this is Miss Samantha Keaton. Her brother has been kidnapped and is on board the *General*."

The men tried to not stare at my attire that was an odd choice for a lady in 1860's Georgia and managed to nod their heads politely. The two enormous lupines seemed to be more of an unexpected event than was I. The lupines and I tried to limit the square footage we occupied; I sat, my knees tucked under me with Kipp on one side and Elani on the other, my arms anchoring them as I pulled the lupines close to me. Elani, poor soul, was miserable over the loss of Peter, and I realized she was blaming herself but, of course, didn't pry deeply into her thoughts.

"It's not your fault," I said, kissing the top of her head, feeling the rub of wet, matted fur scrape against my chin. "We'll find him," I added emphatically, generating a positive emotion within myself that my words were not just an empty promise.

The little pole car rumbled dependably along the tracks and passed the Allatoona station. Another man, a fellow named Smith, joined the crew, and we wedged together tighter than ever. The rain started again, a fine mist, but just enough to make us more uncomfortable. I was glad to be rid of my drenched hat, the sodden brim of which kept dipping over my eyes. Having taken it off some miles back, I tucked it into my waistband, thinking I might need it later. We topped a hill, and the Etowah station was visible at the bottom of a steep grade. The men became excited because there was a working steam engine, the *Yonah*, at that station. From our vantage point, I could see smoke coming from its stack, meaning it had a boiler full of steam, as it sat, almost as if it anticipated our arrival.

The men pushing the car lifted their legs, and the others, our speed building with momentum, dropped their poles, which would not be needed for propulsion. We started down the grade, faster and faster. Kipp stood, bracing himself, his face in the wind. The temptation was too great for him to not enjoy this free fall, just as if he were hanging his head out of my car window.

"Wheeeee!" he cried, hoping beyond hope that we'd go faster.

At that moment, the men up front spied a break in the rail line, and their alarmed thoughts banged inside my head as if they'd hit me with a mallet. But it was too late to stop or do anything other than prepare. The next thing I knew, all of us, eight men, one humanoid symbiont and two lupines– waterlogged and sodden through and through—were airborne, our bodies twisting in the air as we were flung from the relative safety of the pole car into a muddy ditch. Kipp and Elani fared best since their instincts helped them to adapt midair, twisting adroitly to land on their feet. I landed on the far side of the ditch and came to a rolling stop, my face down in a wad of wet grass. Kipp immediately bounded over to me, followed by Elani.

"Petra, are you okay?" he asked, worried, as he hovered over my prone body.

That was one of those times when I really wondered if I was entirely too old to be traveling. My body felt as if someone had run over it with a Mack truck and everything hurt simultaneously. But, after a quick inventory, I realized I was unharmed. Murphy, who also took a similarly bad roll, clambered to his feet and came over to reach down and assist me to stand, his hand on my elbow.

"Miss Sam, are you unharmed?" he asked, his face creased with concern.

I nodded my head, unable to speak. The hit had knocked

me breathless, and it would take me a few minutes to recover. As I tried to take a few deep breaths, the men pulled the little pole car up and placed it on the other sides of the broken tracks; we continued our glide down the hill, across the bridge, and coasted to a gentle stop in the Etowah station. The pursuit would now take on a different flavor since our party had the option of a steam engine, the *Yonah*, and would no longer be bound by the slow and dangerous pole car.

"We'll be able to catch him now," Kipp said confidently.

Yes, unless the arc of history had changed, the party with whom I travelled eventually would catch the *General*. But our journey would prove to be long and complicated.

CHAPTER 18

◆

The *Yonah* was an older engine than the *General* but of the same 4-4-0 gauge. She had been removed from service from the Western and Atlantic Railroad previously and put into use transporting coal and iron for a privately owned mining company. She lacked the beauty and flash of the *General* but was, nonetheless, an iron horse, and she could run.

As the pole car rolled into the Etowah station, the *Yonah* was resting on the turntable. The men jumped off the pole car, and I followed. I knew I'd have to be insistent or Fuller would leave me behind at the first convenient moment. Kipp could execute another persuasive mind invasion as he'd done previously on the resolute conductor, if needed. The initial suggestion was made before he found out I was a female, and his doubts as to the appropriateness of my being present had grown since that jaw dropping revelation.

I looked down at Kipp. He stared back and began to wag his tail. I think it was his eternal optimism that fueled his energy; there was no doubt in his mind that we would find Peter. The ride on the pole car had helped dry his fur although mud and dirt was clinging to his undercarriage. Poor Elani was forlorn looking, her ears drooping with misery. It was then Kipp took things in hand with inspirational energy.

"Listen, Elani. You have to change your attitude. Things happen in this business. In case you didn't get the memo, this is a dangerous line of work. You need to man up, get your game face on, and help focus on Peter. We will find him, and we won't stop until we do."

I'm not sure where Kipp was acquiring his impressive store of slang expressions and fashionable phrases, but I considered that we might want to limit our exposure to popular culture at the house. I recalled his uttering things such as "Talk to the paw", "I've got your backand more recently, "Do you feel me?". Yes, time to read more and watch less television.

"Kipp, be prepared to plant another suggestion if the men decide to leave us behind," I said, cutting into his kick butt speech to Elani. "And you might want to read about a man named George Patton," I added.

"Sure, boss," he replied. "And who is George Patton?" Kipp asked, looking up at me.

"A very tough man, a general in World War 2," I replied. "He gave a lot of motivational speeches, some of which his troops regretted receiving. I met him once," I added, off-handedly.

Meanwhile, the men were maneuvering the *Yonah* onto the turntable, connecting the tender as well as a flat car. Murphy realized they needed to take repair items due to the nagging notion that the fugitives on the *General* would probably continue to damage the tracks up ahead of us. Some of our party left us at that point, and only Fuller, Murphy and Cain boarded the new train. There were some scattered Confederate soldiers loitering near the siding, who appeared to have nothing pressing, and they jumped aboard too, gathering on the open flat car that was hitched to the tender.

I ran towards the *Yonah* and put my hand on the railing to climb aboard, planning to sit on the front of the tender. Fuller stared at me, the notions of Kipp's implanted ideas having faded in the excitement of the chase. But oddly, Kipp had no need to intervene. Murphy stepped to the edge of the engine and held his hand out to me.

"You've earned the right to be here," he said.

Monitoring his thoughts, I knew he admired my courage and tenacity; for a man of his times, he appreciated strong women. Murphy's thoughts drifted to his mother, who'd raised a large family in the midst of poverty and survived the move to a new country and an uncertain destiny. Kipp and Elani, after getting a little running start, hopped on board just as the engine began to roll forward. We picked up speed quickly and soon were going at what I later figured to be close to sixty miles an hour, the countryside passing in a faded blur of color. Sometimes we would see cleared pastures with cattle grazing on green hillsides and small homesteads plopped down in the midst of nowhere; north Georgia was made up of such versus the larger estates and plantations that might be found farther south. The encroaching forests were thick and at times looming, despite the fact they'd been trimmed back to accommodate the rail line.

Fuller climbed to the front of the train, clinging to the side rails, so that he could signal of obstructions where the raiders threw ties onto the tracks or even pulled up rails. Cain, who was fatigued from the stress of the day, sat at the front of the tender with me, his face pale and crumpled. He was only in his thirties but looked older, his frame thin, his face deeply lined. At one point, he managed a tremulous smile. Kipp was lying close to his feet, and the man reached down to gently pat Kipp's head.

"I had a big dog when I was a little boy," Cain said. "Once, a black bear came after me in the woods, and Big Mike took off after that old bear and chased him up a tree." He smiled at the memory. "We'll get to the *General* and find your brother, Miss Sam," he added softly, before ducking his eyes.

I moved forward into the cab of the *Yonah* and stood next to Murphy, who was controlling the throttle of the engine.

Kipp followed, leaving Elani to stay with Cain, who was gently finger combing her wet fur.

"So, Mr. Murphy, how did you get involved in the train business?" I asked. Symbionts are naturally curious, and I was no exception. Kipp managed to rear up, putting his front paws in the cab window so he could crane his neck and stick his head out into the wind. We managed to stay out of the way of one of the soldiers who was acting as fireman stoking the firebox, which, I might add, was very hard work. The man's face was beaded with sweat caused by the blistering heat from the firebox as well as the exertion of stoking. He was a hardworking young man but not very clean; in the confines of the cab, his body odor was oppressive. Kipp looked at me and blinked his eyes.

"Don't say it, Kipp," I warned him from the obvious.

"My father moved our family here from Ireland when I was a young lad," Murphy said, smiling. "He was in search of a better life, not willing to scrabble in the hard dirt for little to nothing." Murphy's handsome face was wistful. "I remember the look on his face when we were hungry despite the fact he'd worked an eighteen hour day." Murphy looked at me and shrugged his shoulders. "I went on to become a machinist's apprentice and managed to work my way up to become an engineer." He leaned forward a little. "And I'll tell you honestly, Miss Sam, that despite the fact I may have been promoted past that job, I always liked doing this best," he said, nodding at the throttle. We rode along for another minute or so before he turned to me again.

"Do you mind telling me, Miss Sam, why you are dressed like a gentleman and not like a lady?" He tried not to smile but failed. "I'm not trying to be impertinent or nothing like that."

Symbionts lie with a practiced ease that is a necessary skill set for survival. When we do so, we have no attack of conscience, thinking that we're wrong to be deceptive. Well, I still felt nagging guilt over having to lie to Harrow, but in the end I told him as much as I could and not sound utterly unbelievable to his loving ears. Yes, I wore the pearls he'd given me beneath my masculine shirt with its stiff collar. Deception is just part of what we must do to blend effortlessly in the human society. Kipp turned to stare at me, curious as to what I would hatch. Even Elani's bedraggled head went up.

"My brother and I hail from North Carolina," I began. "We lost our family home due to bad debt," I added, trying to look sad. It never hurt to try and get some compassion and pity going. "We managed to scrape up some money and came south with the plan of buying land in Georgia, hoping to try our hand at cattle."

"Do you know anything about cattle?" Murphy asked, tilting his head to the side.

"Yes, our father raised cattle, and we grew up helping him," I lied.

"But why Georgia?"

"Land prices here are much cheaper than in North Carolina. Ever since the last governor was elected, the price of land has escalated dramatically," I said, making the story bigger as I talked. "Some people think it has to do with graft in his cabinet, but I don't know about that."

"So why are you dressed as a gent?" Murphy persisted.

"Mr. Murphy, have you ever had to ride for long distances on a train while wearing a hoop skirt?" I asked, opening my eyes wide and trying to look my most honest. "And, in any case, we thought it would be easier to do business if we were two brothers and not a brother and a sister." I didn't explain the last comment, and he didn't ask. In fact, he seemed happy with the hoop skirt remark.

"Yeah, his wife has complained about the skirt thing, too," Kipp said, from his vantage point across the cab. "He's had to hear her whine about the difficulties of getting on and off a train while you have something that is shaped like the Liberty Bell hanging off your butt. And then there is the finding a seat that will accommodate the sheer yardage."

Liberty Bell? I really wondered where Kipp was getting his ideas.

"I read and watch television…that's where," Kipp answered sharply, in response to my thinly veiled criticism. "You might try and do the same. You know you can broaden your horizons with just a little effort," he added, sniffing dismissively.

Murphy focused less on me and more on the cues from Fuller, who motioned a couple of times that we needed to stop and remove more ties from the tracks. The errant soldiers who'd hopped on board came in handy and jumped from the rear trailing flat car to help dislodge the heavy ties and load them onto the flat car. After all, the ties were W&ARR property, and Murphy was not going to let them sit forlornly off to the side of the tracks in a patch of overgrown weeds. We passed by two more stations, Rogers and Cass, pausing long enough to get information about the raiders and the *General*. It was necessary to top off our water supply and add additional wood to the tender, since the men had no way of knowing how long the *Yonah* would be in hot pursuit. I did know–in vague generalities— but didn't have the precise information of Peter, who had studied the event extensively.

"See, I tell you that you need to read more, and you just blow me off," Kipp said, yawning.

"Well, what do you know, Mr. Wizard?" I asked, tired of his running commentary on my too-numerous-to-count shortcomings.

"Well, Miss Smarty Pants, I know that we are about to arrive in Kingston and will change engines and leave on the *William R. Smith*," he replied.

That was more than I knew, which was almost nothing. In retrospect, I realized that I should have prepared more extensively for this trip. There were many books about the Great Locomotive Chase, but I'd contented myself with allowing Peter to do the research while I'd watched the Disney movie starring handsome Fess Parker and the equally gorgeous Jeffrey Hunter.

Thankfully, there was another break in the rain, and as we breezed along at the high rate of speed that rather surprised me for the times, my clothes, which were flapping in the wind, dried, as did my hair. I rejoined Jeff Cain on the tender and braided my hair, which had come loose in frizzy, wet strands giving me the appearance of a raggedy stray cat. Kipp remained in the engine cab with Murphy, his big head still stuck out the window. I was glad to see the talk Kipp had given to Elani seemed to help, and she seemed brighter and projected an optimism that had been lacking. Cain's finger combing of her, along with the wind, had dried her coat and she looked halfway normal again. The tender was swaying from side to side on the tracks, and the clacking of the wheels could have nudged me to sleep if the situation had been different. We were in a heavily wooded part of the state and saw fewer cleared fields from our perspective on the *Yonah*. As we drew close to Kingston, Fuller returned to the cab from his precarious perch on the front of the engine. He was frowning and appeared agitated, as he removed his hat and ran his hands through his hair in frustration.

"The line is jammed," he said, raising his voice slightly to be heard over the sounds of the locomotive.

I stayed aboard the *Yonah* with the lupines while the men hopped down and began telling their story to all who gathered. At some point, Murphy ran in one direction, towards the locomotive *New York*, while Fuller darted towards the *William R. Smith*. I followed both men's thoughts and realized they had failed to communicate in the most basic way, and both of them were planning on proceeding with different locomotives.

"Well, you read about this stuff," I said. "Which train do we take?"

"Just too lazy to prepare," Kipp said, shaking his head. "We need to be on the *William R. Smith*, as I think I mentioned." The Kindle had obviously come in handy, and I had no good reply to his scathing assessment of my lack of knowledge.

The lupines followed me as we left the *Yonah* and made our way across the siding to the *William R. Smith*. Fuller was in discussion with the engineer, Wiley Harbin. Cain and Fuller were explaining, in clipped, hurried tones what had happened, and without hesitation, Harbin disconnected the passenger coach, leaving the locomotive with only a tender and a baggage car. I trotted over to the engine and definitely made a sorry–and unexpectedly shocking—sight to the new player, Harbin. He was a youthful man, perhaps in his mid thirties, with a face sunburned from days of toil outside. Harbin stared at me, too startled to not gaze in a rude manner; my clothes were mud splattered, and my coat, so lovingly tailored by Suzanne, had a long tear on the right side and my tie was askew. Looking down, I noted with dismay that the pretty antique stickpin was gone. I'd probably left it in the ditch when we went airborne during the pole car adventure. Suzanne would hold me accountable for that loss, I thought, my face twisting in a grimace.

"She's with us," Fuller growled. But he obviously was confused as to why he continued to allow me to tag along like a happy puppy. All I could be was thankful that Kipp's planted mental suggestion seemed to have the half-life of uranium and was still potent.

I took my place on the tender, along with Kipp and Elani, and felt a slight jerk as the *William R. Smith* began to move forward. Craning my neck, I looked for Murphy and saw him racing after us along the siding; at the last minute he jumped, grabbed the railing and pulled himself into the cab.

"You sorry son of a…" Murphy's words drifted off as he turned to see me. "Uh, you could have waited, Fuller."

The Irishman was furious but managed admirably to control his temper, and after a few minutes, the high color along his cheekbones began to return to a normal hue. I knew what he didn't and that was Fuller harbored no intention to deliberately leave him, Murphy, behind. It was just that Fuller was so single-minded of purpose, he would have run over his own mother had she been tied to the railroad tracks by a dastardly Snidely Whiplash. Kipp enjoyed the cartoon reference and plumbed my tired brain for all images of Snidely, Dudley Doright and the like.

To make our journey northward more festive, we'd been joined at Kingston by a number of inebriated militia men who were drilling nearby. Or, at least, the working rumor was that they were practicing, but in their current state, one wondered to what end? When they heard of our pursuit of alleged traitors, spies or outright Northern soldiers, they crowded, whooping and hollering, into the baggage car. Kipp, after canvassing their thoughts, looked at me and frowned as only a lupine can.

"They are drunk," he said. "And they are carrying weapons," Kipp added, for good measure. "That can't be a good combination."

I heard a shout and then something that must have been an intoxicated rebel yell fueled by home brew. All I know is, the sound was loud enough and of a high enough pitch that it made both the lupines cringe. Oh, yes, the addition of the militia men was an excellent choice, I thought cynically.

The *William R. Smith* was not as fast a train as the *General*, and in retrospect, the *New York* would have proven a more sound choice, but it was too late to change iron horses. We continued onward—six railroad men, including Harbin's fireman and brakeman, a humanoid symbiont who was female dressed as a male, two muddy and matted lupines and a train full of drunk and armed militia men. It seemed to be a pretty average day on the W&ARR.

Fuller, taking up point again, carefully climbed along the running board of the moving engine so that he could warn of obstructions. Unfortunately, the locomotive rounded a curve at a high rate of speed and plowed into a huge pile of cross ties before the train could stop. The cowcatcher did its job and tossed the heavy ties into the air like matchsticks. Fuller took a moment to thank his lucky stars for an uncomfortably near miss by one of the heavy ties. At that point, the rain started again in earnest, and as I sat on the tender and watched the rain drip from the brim of my sodden hat, I almost became cross eyed as I tried to focus on the too-near globules of water. Kipp looked up at me and smiled, his jaw dropping down.

"This is great!" he exclaimed. "Everything a time shift should be."

"Is that true?" Elani asked, looking to me for corroboration.

I had the sense she was a little disappointed. The wonderful allure of the past and the romantic nature of the traveler was part of what drew our kind to the job. But here we sat, wet, anxious, hungry and unsettled. Elani's eyes met mine.

"If you recall, I once said sometimes you land hard." I smiled at her. "These trips can be just plain old hard work, sweetheart."

She wagged her tail at the endearment and turned her massive head to gaze out into the thick woods. Off to the right, a herd of white tailed deer flashed the warning sign of their flag-like tails and began to zig zag off into the forest. Both Elani and Kipp were superb hunters and could shift on their own when needed and food supplies were low. I felt their primal surge of natural instincts as they watched the deer in retreat.

Fuller shouted out another warning, his words finding their way back to us despite the rain and wind from the movement of the engine. Harbin pulled back on the throttle and the engine slid gracefully to a halt. The raiders had destroyed a large section of rail, and there would be no way to repair it. The bunch of drunken militia men, feeling the momentum of the train had slowed, piled out of the baggage car, cheering and cursing simultaneously. Their agitation grew as they realized they would not be players in the final pursuit and would be left out in the middle of nowhere with nothing to do.

Since the *William R. Smith* was of no further use, Fuller and Murphy decided they would begin to run again, and this decision propelled me into action. Leaping from the tender, followed by Kipp and Elani, I chased after them, easily catching up within the first minute. Jeff Cain, although resolute of heart, didn't possess the needed physical vigor and was left behind. Murphy smiled, amused by my dogged persistence. Fuller frowned; his common sense told him to be rid of me, but he still struggled against the thoughts Kipp had wedged in his brain. The rain intensified again, making the trip even more difficult with soaked woolen clothes that were made heavier and unpleasantly cumbersome by the water.

"Fuller knows that we will run into the *Texas*, which is travelling south on this line," Kipp said. "And he's banking on that fact, knowing the *Texas* is fully a match for the *General* in terms of speed and function. The two engines were manufactured in the same factory, have the same specs and are pretty much identical, except for their outward appearances."

"Thank you, Mr. Professor," I said sarcastically.

"Don't take it out on me that you failed to do your homework," Kipp replied airily, as he yawned, showing every tooth in his head. "Elani knows more about this period than do you."

His harshness stung but was accurate. I'd let my broken heartedness over Harrow and my new-found attachment to Fitzhugh cloud my judgment. Kipp, following the tenor of my thoughts, was immediately contrite.

"I'm sorry, Petra. That was unkind of me." He tried to nuzzle my hand as we ran along.

"It's okay, Kipp. You are right in everything you said," I said. After all, I was supposed to be a mature leader, and it was time I acted like it.

In a surprisingly short time, we heard the approach of the *Texas* as the loud chuffing sound of the steam engine reverberated in the air. Oddly, I could feel the vibrations it cast through its sheer weight in the ground beneath my feet. Fuller and Murphy began to swing their arms in attempt to slow and stop the *Texas*. Of course, all the W&ARR men knew one another, and the engineer of the *Texas* recognized both Fuller and Murphy from a distance. The engineer slowly reversed the engine and eased the locomotive to a halt.

"Pete, we need your help!" Fuller cried out.

We were, at that time, about two miles from the next station which was in Adairsville. With his knowledge of Fuller and Murphy, Peter Bracken, the engineer of the *Texas*, didn't question the credibility of their story. He looked at me, and a momentary expression of confusion crossed his pleasant features.

"Miss Samantha Keaton," Murphy said, again acting as if he were introducing me at a fancy cotillion. Fuller glanced my way, his eyes narrowed, and once again searched his brain for a good reason why he had not objected to my presence.

"Her brother was kidnapped by the scoundrels who stole the *General*. We fear for his safety and are assisting her in his recovery," Murphy explained concisely. The two and a half-mile run had brought out the deep, rich color in his flesh, and his face was a nice, glowing shade of pink. We were fortunate that despite the ongoing rain, the temperatures were tolerable, and we were neither hot nor freezing. But we were miserable.

Bracken showed the same discipline of the other railroad men I'd met, in that he was neatly dressed with carefully groomed facial hair and a precise nature. Kipp knew, from his studies, that both Murphy and Bracken hailed from the North. If I'd had the time and focus to plumb their minds, it would have been interesting to see how they viewed being transplanted Northerners in what was seen as an increasingly combative South as war threatened just outside of Chattanooga.

Without delay, we climbed on board and Bracken reversed the locomotive, which had the capability to run in reverse at close to its maximum rate of speed, only stopping when we got to Adairsville. Murphy remained in the cab while Fuller climbed to the rear of the tender where he could shout out warnings in case the track had been sabotaged. Bracken skillfully dropped the long line of freight cars to a vacant siding, while managing to never completely stop the momentum of the engine during the process, and the *Texas* continued northward, following the trail of the *General*. Murphy stayed in the cab with Bracken, while Kipp, Elani and I perched on the tender, trying to keep out from under foot. Elani looked up at me, her eyes huge in the pretty blonde-gray mask of her face. I will admit, flying backwards at close to 60 miles an hour at times while riding on the tender of the *Texas*, was one of the more exciting things I've done over a lifetime of adventure. It was both exhilarating and terrifying. Kipp kept his head poked up, the wind flattening his ears.

"At least, since we are moving in reverse, the smoke and cinders aren't hitting us in the face any more," Kipp remarked with a sigh, offering his optimistic assessment.

CHAPTER 19

A t the Calhoun station, we slowed up enough to pick up a couple of more helpers. An engineer for a rival company happened to be passing through and jumped on our train to take over for the fireman. In addition, another locomotive, the *Catoosa*, was pressed into service by the coercion of one Captain W.J. Whitsitt, who convinced the reluctant engineer at gunpoint that the *Catoosa* needed to join the pursuit. Kipp looked up at me, questioning the entire transaction, but I just shook my head. Passions ran high, I suppose. This time, there was a contingent of thankfully sober infantry who boarded the *Catoosa* and followed us to assist. We'd only traveled a couple of miles when Fuller's exclamation traveled back to us. He'd spied the *General*, which was stopped ahead, while its crew struggled to sabotage the rails. I never got a chance to speak with any of the Union soldiers who abducted the *General,* but I have to think their amazement at seeing the *Texas* appear in full speed reverse was profound. It must have thrown them off their game, because they quickly took off again, leaving a box car stranded on the tracks. We drew to a span of tracks where the spikes had been removed, but as Fuller carefully walked ahead of the engine, Bracken eased the *Texas* over the unsecured area.

I'll admit, I held my breath, thinking of what would happen if the *Texas* tumbled off, since we were on a rather steeply banked grade. History told me that we would make the span safely, but I reminded myself that history could have been changed in unexpected ways simply with the addition of four misplaced symbionts.

We finally got past the damage and rolled up to the abandoned box car. There was no siding upon which to leave it, so Bracken eased the tender up to the car, coupled with it, and off we went, pushing the box car, which was full of the raiders' items they had used to damage the rails and telegraph lines. There was also wood and brush that seemed to be destined for use in burning bridges, and we were yet to encounter the long, covered bridge that spanned the Oostanaula River. Bracken looked back at me and smiled; I knew without being intrusive that his good natured humor concerned my appearance. Murphy stared, too.

"We can make room, Miss Sam, in the cab, so that you can get out of this rain," he offered courteously.

What a nice man, I thought...kind, compassionate and dedicated to his work. I really liked him then and still have fond memories today.

"I'm okay, Mr. Murphy, but thank you very much." I smiled at him, because he was soaked, too. "I don't think the cab offers much protection, either."

The excitement grew, and Kipp, who enjoyed a ride in a car or, now, a locomotive, was standing, his feet braced widely for balance against the swaying of the tender, his plumed tail wagging. He began to bark, a full-throated sound that made Murphy stare at him and laugh. The landscape was hilly, strewn with large boulders, and it was impossible to view ahead for any stretch due to the curving nature of the tracks. Fuller continued to call out warnings from his precarious perch on the back of the boxcar we pushed, which would be relayed by the tender brakeman who shouted them to Bracken.

"Do you think the arc of history has been changed by our

presence?" Elani asked. She had been quiet but now seemed a little more optimistic since we'd boarded the *Texas*.

"Well, it's always changed a little, if only that these men have met us. Before, we wouldn't have been in the picture. We have no way of knowing what will happen with Peter having influenced the actions of the men on the *General*. All we can do is leave as little a path as possible, as if we are walking through the leaves on the forest floor while trying not to disturb them." I didn't mean to wax poetic, but that image was how I conceptualized our journey.

We passed through the tiny station at Resaca; our tender was still relatively well stocked, our boiler full. I knew little of steam engines, but Bracken and Murphy were calculating that since the *General* no longer had the opportunity to stop and refuel, it was only a matter of time before we would catch up to the fleeing raiders. Elani, following the conversations, looked up at me; her tail wagged, just for a couple of seconds, as her dark mood lifted.

The tracks evened out a little, following the bank of the Connasauga River. The men's excitement grew when we were able to spy the *General*, which had stopped at a wood and water station near Tilton. I went to the edge of the car, and as we rounded a curve, I could see the raiders running back and forth, trying desperately to get wood loaded on the waiting tender. In just a few seconds, the *General* set off again, a belch of black smoke from its smokestack drifted up to be lost in the dense, heavy clouds that were barely clearing the tree tops. We followed, steaming though Tilton without pausing.

The next town was Dalton, and that station was more complicated to navigate, as Murphy and Bracken were thinking. There was a switch that led to another line that headed in the wrong direction for the plans of the raiders; in addition, there was a passenger shed as well as a turntable, and all of these factors would slow both the speeding *General* as well as the *Texas*. We were, perhaps, a couple of miles behind the other train at that point. The *General* had cleared the station obstacles by the time we arrived, and Fuller ordered a pause so that a telegraph message could be sent to General Leadbetter in Chattanooga, before we resumed our pursuit, having loosened our burden by dumping the extra box car on a vacant siding.

The men's anxiety began to grow as we approached Tunnel Hill, where a 1,447 foot-long tunnel had been drilled through the base of the Chetoogeta Mountain. The rocky terrain was covered in a layer of moss made black from the constant rain; lichens, pale and scaly, formed a lacy dusting of color on some of the stones as they wound up the hill to become lost in deep crevasses. Because of the utter darkness in the tunnel, there would be no way to safely view the tracks ahead. Fuller, from his vantage point on the backside of the tender, would have no lantern and would be essentially blind. Our speed slowed to a crawl; I reached down to touch Kipp, my fingers finding his wet fur in the black void that surrounded us.

"At least we are out of the rain for a few minutes," he remarked cheerfully.

"Oh, Kipp," I cried. "I love you!"

"Back at you, kid," he replied.

We got to the end of the tunnel in safety, and Bracken opened the throttle as wide as it could go. The *Texas*, champing at the bit like a thoroughbred race horse, almost did a wheelie in her eagerness to run. The rain seemed to take pleasure in falling harder than ever, and I was forced to continually wipe the water from my eyes so I could see. Kipp and Elani had to shake themselves about every thirty seconds. Although their coats were relatively water proof, the constant deluge had soaked them down to the skin.

I knew that the *General* would stop when she ran out of fuel; it was a mechanical certainty. The raiders would scatter into the woods and hills; most of the fleeing men would ultimately be captured. I could only hope that Peter stayed by the train and was not removed forcibly by the raiders; also, there was concern that he might have high-tailed it on his own, thinking that he was subject to being captured by an angry mob of people. In any case, the journey would stop somewhere past Ringgold, and that was the next station some four miles after we passed Catoosa. As we roared through the small highlands village and its neatly kept station, I noticed a group of mounted soldiers in the distance moving off to the southwest. Kipp's head went up and his ears, despite being waterlogged, perked up. He felt a ping, as did I, but the image was blurry and neither one of us could tweak out a single thought.

"Is that Peter?" Elani asked.

For a moment, I thought she was going to jump from our speeding train, and despite having the remarkable agility of a lupine, she would have been badly injured since we were still moving at close to 50 miles per hour. I put my hand on her chest to settle her.

"I can't tell and neither can Kipp. It could be another resident symbiont, Elani. But if it is Peter, we'll come back here and track him down," I promised. "This train will stop in about four miles and then we'll find out."

We charged through the Ringgold station and on the far side spied the halted General, which clung to the incline of a grass covered hill. It's odd to think that a mechanical object can look tired, but the locomotive, indeed appeared worn out. It was rather amazing, per Murphy, that the engine was undamaged, with the exception of one burnt out brass fitting. The single box car, what little remained, had been cannibalized for the wood, and apparently the raiders had tried to set it on fire, but that wasn't successful due to the constant rain. As the *Texas* glided to a halt, I noticed people arriving from town, some on horseback, others in wagons. They had hunting dogs with them, held back on long leads; deep throated baying echoed on the lonely hillside. The town's folk had been alerted from the telegraph warnings sent at the earlier station and converged on the site with a festive attitude as if a square dance and picnic had been planned.

Elani didn't wait for a complete stop before she leapt

from the tender and charged up the muddy hillside to the *General*. Kipp followed close behind, and I was moving as fast as possible given the fact I lacked the four wheel drive capability of the lupines. The slick mud and tall, wet grass were a deterrent to speed and grace of movement. But even as I watched Elani stand on her hind legs and peer inside what was left of the box car, there were no thoughts of Peter, only those of the many humans who clustered nearby. She turned to look at me, hurt and confused.

"We should have made them stop back in Catoosa," she said, shaking her head.

Kipp bristled a little, thinking her condemnation was aimed at me. I didn't take it personally and understood she spoke from anxiety.

"Elani, it's time to focus and problem solve and not fixate on the impossible or missed opportunities," he said. "There would have been no way to make Bracken stop the train for us, and we couldn't jump off of a train moving at high rate of speed." Elani ducked her head in response to his harsh tone. "We will find Peter, and if we have to stay here one hundred years, we will find him."

"I'm sorry," she said, her thoughts plaintive and distraught. "I feel responsible as his partner."

"And that is exactly how you are supposed to feel," I said, putting my arms around her wet, bramble-tangled coat. "It shows you are bonded to him." Leaning over, I pressed my cheek against the top of her head. "And Kipp is right; we will stay until we find Peter. There is no other choice."

While groups of men armed with pistols and shotguns took off in various directions to quickly disappear into the surrounding woods, I approached Murphy, who was, with Fuller, inspecting the *General*. Both men were pleased over the condition of the locomotive, which had suffered being driven beyond her specifications and arrived little the worse for wear.

"Mr. Murphy, I've got to get back to Catoosa. I think my brother was let off the train at that station, and I must return there as quickly as possible." I stopped myself just shy of plucking at his sodden coat sleeve. Fuller ignored my plea and walked to the other side of the *General*.

"And why would you think that?" he asked, turning his soft, brown eyes on me.

"He's not here, and there would have been no reason for him to run off with the raiders and illogical for them to take him with them, since he'd be a burden. The last stop was Catoosa, and when we went through the station, my dogs acted strangely as if they caught his scent." Well, it was close to the truth.

Several of the townspeople from Ringgold who'd not joined in the pursuit were standing around gawking at the two locomotives. The poor *General's* smoke stack was devoid of smoke since she had no wood or water left to create steam; all she emitted was a pitiful little hiss, the last vestiges of moisture captured in her boiler. The *Texas* was still puffing out black smoke and looked ready to run another fifty miles.

"I need a wagon and horse," Murphy said, addressing one of the men whose attire was a notch finer than his peers. Murphy sized him up as, perhaps, a man of means with the ability to provide the needed assistance. "Miss Keaton needs transportation to Catoosa immediately," he added.

"I can pay well," I added, earnestly.

The well-dressed man stared at me in my drenched, torn and muddy menswear as he removed a damp cigar from the corner of his mouth. He started to ask how much I could pay but was cut off by Murphy.

"I'm sure any of our fine gentlemen will be happy to assist a lady in need," Murphy added, his skin flushing high along the angles of his face.

"And I'm certain that is true, Mr. Murphy, but I still have means to pay for the service," I said again, more firmly this time.

The cigar smoker was caught in a bind, wanting to meet the expectations of a gentleman but also not desirous of having to drive an oddly dressed stranger and two big dogs the four miles in the rain to Catoosa.

"I can handle a horse and wagon," I offered. "If you could make it available to me, I will drive myself to the station and leave the wagon there for you to retrieve."

Kipp looked at me from the corners of his eyes. Even Elani got a little rigid in her posture.

"Are you sure?" Kipp asked.

"You forget, sweetheart, I was born in 1604. I've handled many horses pulling carts, wagons, and can ride side saddle, English or Western." I tried to sound confident, although it had been a while. "Don't you remember Tombstone?"

The man still had not responded, so I remarked in an offhanded way, "Or I can purchase a horse and wagon and not inconvenience anyone at all."

The cigar man, a fellow named Robertson, stalked towards town. It was clear he had no interest in taking me, nor was he happy at having to leave all the action involved in chasing down the raiders. When we got clear of Murphy, Robertson turned towards me, his pale eyes staring at me as if I were some type of loathsome fungus. Yes, my choice of attire was biting me in the butt.

"I was about my business when all this happened," he grunted.

"Mr. Robertson, if you can direct me to someone who will rent me a horse and cart, I am willing to pay twice the going price."

Avarice won the day, and I was checking the last harness strap as Kipp and Elani hopped up into the back of the two-wheel cart. It actually was fairly sturdy and there was ample room for the two lupines. The horse was much more than just a swaybacked nag and seemed up to the task of a quick pace to Catoosa. I felt familiar thoughts behind me and turned to see Murphy slogging through the mud. He removed his waterlogged hat and looked up at the skies, which were dark with the storminess of the day. The rain, thankfully, had stopped for the time being.

"I think it's all about to clear and make for a lovely day," Murphy said, smiling at me. "A wonderful day for a cart ride," he added.

I felt my heart jump up in my throat and at the same time acknowledged Kipp's notions. If Murphy went with us, the arc of history was changing and could lead to unintended events. But I felt the steely resolve of the Irishman and wasn't sure I could prevent him short of trying to surreptitiously leave while his back was turned.

"Let him come," Kipp said. "He gives you legitimacy, and we might get farther with him along."

The minute Kipp said it, I knew he was correct. My attire was drawing more attention than my quest, and each time I'd have to go through another explanation and deal with disapproving and disbelieving men, just as I had Mr. Robertson in Ringgold. Unless Murphy was killed or his actions caused someone else to die, there was little chance of history changing in any significant manner.

I appreciated the fact Murphy trusted my checking of the cart and horse because he didn't go behind me to make certain all the straps and buckles were secure. After lending a gentle hand to my elbow to assist me into the cart, he swung up next to me, gave the horse a nudge forward and off we went, trotting down the road as best we could, given the ruts carved out from too much rain in too short a time. Kipp stuck his head up between us, his jaws opening in a pant.

"Nice dog," Murphy said. "He seems very intelligent."

"Oh, he's smart all right." I put my arm around Kipp and pulled him closer.

Murphy drove in silence for a few minutes, speaking only to make a commentary about the railroad tracks we were following south as the road snaked along, following the sinuous path of the tracks. He pointed at a well constructed trestle, and his pride in the engineering was evident.

"So, Mr. Murphy, have you always lived in the South since coming to America?" I asked, knowing he did not. It just seemed polite to be conversant.

"Oh no, Miss Sam. My dad settled in Pennsylvania. It was beautiful there, with rolling green countryside," he replied. "Of course, my parents had no time for idle mouths to feed so when I came of age, I struck off on my own."

"Do you miss living up North?" I persisted. It must be conflicted for this man to live in the South with a war brewing.

"Well, the heat here in the summer is not always pleasant," Murphy replied, laughing. "But this is my wife's home, and it would cause her great distress to leave." He gave a mild correction to the horse which had a determined tendency to drift to the right. "I think Robertson sold you a horse that's blind in his left eye. Anyway, I was promoted to engineer and then later became a foreman, which is my current position, so I'd be hard pressed to leave the W&ARR."

He was a good, decent man. And as it was with humans, he had a sense of me reminding me of his wife, and that fact subconsciously drove his compassion towards me. In his thoughts, he'd hate for his dear wife to be out here, alone, on these roads, trying to make her way in a two-wheeled cart drawn by a half-blind horse. Kipp yawned, his massive mouth opening wide, showing all his teeth in their ivory, gleaming glory. Leaning over, he gave me a lick on the side of my face, wiping away some of the residual rain of the day.

"I'd wager he'd give anyone trying to interfere with you a bit of a fight," Murphy said, nodding at Kipp, who wagged his tail.

Yes, I thought. He would.

CHAPTER 20

The four miles to Catoosa took longer than on a day when the hot, Southern sun would have baked the road to the hardness of concrete pavement. The dirt roads were still sloppy, exceedingly so in places, making the travel difficult at times. To the left side of us, towering long-leafed pine trees seemed deflated, their needles sagging with the weight of accumulated rain water. And on the right, there was a cleared expanse of land leading to the train track that had taken us to Ringgold. The tall grass, which normally waved in ripples in the wind like the flutter of waves on the ocean's surface, was beaten flat. Murphy's prediction was correct, however, and the rain seemed to have stopped. Although the sky was still heavily overcast, I could see the hazy outline of the sun, which was hiding behind the clouds, making the gray turn to a soft, hazy yellow in places. The horse's hooves made a soft thudding sound against the wet earth rather than a sharp clip clop against a compacted surface. Lifting my head, I could smell wood smoke from a residence hidden behind the veil of pine trees, suggesting life existed just beyond the scope of my view. Murphy kept up a pleasant banter, no doubt thinking his discourse necessary while accompanying a lady. Since I was new to Georgia, he pointed out topographical points of note as well as distinctive characteristics of the region.

"And what do you think about the war?" I asked, thinking it was odd to not bring up the elephant in the room.

"Well, quite honestly, it makes me sick to consider it. As I mentioned, I'm from Pennsylvania, lived in New Jersey...I still have friends and family up North. But I married a precious Southern woman and my allegiance is to her. But I pray daily that some way can be found to avert all the bloodshed and come to a peaceful solution. I get the impression that Mr. Lincoln is a good man, and I think he would have chosen another path if he'd found one open to him."

Indeed, I thought that, too. Lincoln was one of the most fascinating men in American history. I liked the fact that he recognized his weaknesses and had a basic humility of character. When he became commander in chief of the army and war loomed, he haunted the Library of Congress to study history and battle tactics used in past conflicts to better prepare to counsel his generals. The war would prove to be the costliest in the history of the nation. Slavery, an abomination, could not be permitted to survive.

"And tell me, Miss Sam, where did you and your brother find such handsome dogs?" Murphy asked. It was clear he felt it indelicate to discuss such things as war, blood and guts with a lady.

"Well, they are Chinese red crested mastiffs," I replied, smiling to myself at the old fabrication I'd used in the past. "A pretty rare breed...very intelligent and the most loyal of dogs."

Kipp, happy with my description of him as intelligent and loyal, pointed his nose to the sky and barked. Elani copied him with a sharp yip or two.

"Hey, Petra, we are just coming up on Catoosa," Kipp said. "I pick up a lot of human thoughts." He concentrated for a moment. "But I don't get any pinging from Peter."

I could feel Elani's anxiety grow and reached out with

my mind to comfort her. "I told you, Elani, we will find him," I said, turning on the hard, wooden bench seat to look at her. "I promise you."

Our cart crested a hill, and the horse's head went up with excitement. He understood that approaching a town probably meant food, water and rest. The beast's pace hastened a little as we sailed down the muddy slope. As we approached habitation, I looked down at my clothes, which were mud splattered, covered in grass stains, torn and still damp. My dark hair hung in a plait over my shoulder but was mussed and tangled; Murphy didn't look much better. Our dash through the mud was a contributing factor to our current appearances. But the tumble off the pole car into the ditch had been a defining moment.

Murphy pulled the horse to a gentle stop in front of the small train station, which was little more than a rectangular wooden building constructed of wide pine planks set horizontally and a shelter under which to stand in case of inclement weather. Hopping off the cart, he went to the building where he, as an employee of the W&ARR, was well recognized.

"It's good he came with us," Kipp commented. "You look so bedraggled, that we'd probably end up in the clink."

"In the clink?" I asked. "Where on earth do you get these phrases?"

"It was a James Cagney movie," he replied, with a derisive snort. "You fell asleep on the couch while I watched TCM."

"In any case, you're correct in that Murphy lends us credibility," I responded, trying to not look at Kipp for fear of laughing.

We waited anxiously in the cart. Murphy stuck his head around the corner and nodded in what he hoped was a reassuring manner. A few seconds later, he rejoined us.

"Your brother was here," Murphy said smiling. It was obvious he was happy to give us promising news. "Apparently, the men put him off the train at this station."

He took a deep breath. "Unfortunately, one of the telegraphs Fuller sent got through to here, and the locals were suspicious of your brother, thinking he was part of the gang and party to a larger conspiracy." Murphy took a kerchief from his pocket and wiped his face, which was damp from the humidity as well as exertion. "A contingency of soldiers were heading towards Rome, and they took him into custody and planned on escorting him there for further examination."

I felt my heart sink and couldn't bear to look at Elani. Her stricken thoughts banged inside my brain like a pair of cymbals.

"We'll find him," Kipp said, his thoughts full of optimism. "The good news is that he was here, he is safe, alive and we just need to keep on his trail."

It was after one o'clock in the afternoon when the *General* ground to a halt a couple of miles north of Ringgold, Georgia. It had taken me another hour to secure transport south to Catoosa, another hour to make the journey, slowed by the muddy, rutted roads. Now it was after three o'clock in the afternoon. I felt pressed to leave immediately but was cautioned by Kipp.

"I understand the urgency, but let's think about this logically, Petra. By the time we get to Rome, he may have been moved somewhere else. You look like a drowned swamp rat and won't be able to convince anyone of anything." Kipp pushed his head up next to mine and licked my face.

"So what do you propose?" I asked, feeling deflated.

"We need to get accommodations for the night. We need to eat, get cleaned up and somehow get some new clothing for you to wear. There's plenty of money, and we can buy a cart and horse to continue; we'll need supplies for a long trip." Kipp tossed his head. "Murphy obviously has to go back to Ringgold."

It took some convincing of Murphy that he could return to his life and destiny, which did not include accompanying our odd trio all over the state of Georgia. We were fortunate, however, in that he was personal friends with the couple who owned the only hotel in town. Murphy, in his genial way, explained my situation to the wide-eyed Hoskins couple. The wife, who was much older than me–or so she thought–took me under her compassionate wing. It was not long before I had a hot bath, scrubbed my hair clean and managed to get the accumulated dirt of the day off my body. The woman also had a local youth who worked in the hotel to take Kipp and Elani out back and use pitchers of hot water to get them clean. The boy, who fortunately was a dog lover, took a curry comb and worked the tangles out of their coats. In retrospect, Kipp was right in that we needed to be fully prepared for the next leg of our adventure, and beginning with clean bodies and full stomachs changed our attitudes. The kind proprietress supplied me with a nightgown before bringing one of her own dresses, which was old and well used, but clean. I gently turned away the offer of a crinoline and merely washed out my own underwear and would go partially commando, in terms of hoops and corset. Kipp and Elani, clean and brushed–and dry, for the most part, thanks to the heat from the wood burning stove in the kitchen—looked up from their bowls which were filled with chicken and mashed potatoes. I thought Kipp was going to eat his bowl, too. I'd joined them on the back porch of the house, enjoying the sudden breeze that seemed to push any lingering humidity towards the south.

"I've come to the conclusion that potatoes, cooked in any manner, are a wonderful thing!" he opined. "Oh, my, this is good."

"You are a potato hog," I observed. I'd finished my own dinner of potatoes, fried okra, fresh tomatoes and snap beans. There was also a piece of cornbread on the side.

Murphy had explained my situation, but I requested Mr. Hoskins to try and procure a buggy, preferably one with a top, for me to continue my journey. He, like Murphy, didn't care for the thought I'd be travelling alone in the countryside, but in the end, he had to bend to my will.

Pointing to the lupines, I indicated there was ample protection riding shotgun for the trip.

We slept well that night in a four poster bed that I don't think was usually reserved for guests. In fact, Kipp, after doing a little off the cuff investigative work, told me that the room and the bed had belonged to the couple's daughter, who died during childbirth. I felt humbled and a little ashamed that I misled those kind, gentle people who gave me such a special room in which to sleep. I lay in the center of the soft mattress, with Kipp on one side, his head across my chest, and Elani snuggled in on the other. I gently caressed her head until she drifted off to sleep. At some point during the night, she awoke me with the disturbing qualities of her tormented dreams about Peter. I opened my eyes in the darkness of the room and looked up at the ceiling, which was lost in the void. The window aperture was black, too, since there was no ambient lighting outside and there was a new moon hidden in the darkness of the sky. Kipp stirred briefly, his jaw rubbing against my chest.

"Her dreams woke me, too," he said. "Should I take care of it for her and make them go away?"

Scratching his head, I considered his offer. Was it moral to let someone hurt when you had the ability to remove the painful stimulus? Or did all beings, human and symbiont, need to experience pain in order to grow?

"Let her be," I finally replied, sighing. "She needs to work it out."

Kipp and I fell back into an uneasy sleep and awoke before dawn the next morning. The smell of bacon frying and bread baking filled the small hotel, which might have been more properly thought of as a boarding house with a fairly stable clientele.

Our hostess left a pitcher of water and a stack of clean towels in the room, so I scrubbed my face vigorously and used the towel to burnish my skin to a rosy glow. Today would be taxing, and I needed to have my best game in place. The dress she'd given me buttoned up the back, so it took a while, with me cursing softly, but I finally managed to get most of them secured, or at least so I hoped. It was still early, but we drifted down to the main sitting room, eager to be on our way, since the trip to Rome would be long.

Mrs. Hoskins appeared and called to Kipp and Elani, who were forced to eat on the back porch again. Ordinarily, I might have tried to connive a way to keep them with me, but Kipp warned me off. The situation was fragile, and the Hoskins were being extraordinarily generous to us. In addition, the lupines were busy with plates piled high with home fried potatoes, scrambled eggs and bacon, so there were no complaints from my friends. I was the earliest riser in the hotel, so Mrs. Hoskins invited me to sit with her in the kitchen as she worked. My offer to help was shrugged away, as she set a plate of food in front of me.

"My husband has gone to get the horse and buggy, but I must tell you we're worried about this plan of yours. People around here are decent, but there have been evil-doers since the time of the first sin, and a woman traveling alone in the country is not a good idea."

As she talked, I looked around the kitchen. The early morning sun was beginning to break through the line of long, narrow windows stretching along one wall; the old fashioned glass was filled with ripples and imperfections that distorted the light, casting intriguing patterns on the table top and floor. A bruised wooden table was pushed against a wall covered in a faded floral wallpaper; on its top rested rows of what appeared to be jams and jellies that Mrs. Hoskins had "put up". I felt my mouth water at the thought of homemade jam. As if she read my mind, Mrs. Hoskins selected a jar and brought it to the table.

"Try some of that on a biscuit, child," she said.

As I savored the sweet plum jam on the crumbling biscuit that was dripping with butter and other good things, I reflected upon the nature of my journey. True, it was probably about a forty mile trip over rough country roads in a buggy, but there was no way around it. Sometimes, you just make a decision and realize you don't have the choice to not succeed. We could not, would not, fail. If the horse was in good condition, I thought we could make it in three days, maybe four if the roads were bad.

Mrs. Hoskins packed some food for us, along with canisters of fresh well water for me, while we waited on her husband to return. This was one of many times I was thankful we always took an overly abundant amount of currency with us. I'd collected my assets, which had been hidden in the now discarded suspenders. And there was still money in the collars that Kipp and Elani wore, so we'd be good for some time.

I'd just finished eating when I heard the scrape of feet on the back porch and a friendly voice: it was Mr. Hoskins stopping to greet Kipp and Elani with a pat on the head and a rub down their furry backs. As he came inside, the lupines entered, too, but with consideration of our hostess. After a couple of tight, canine-like circles, they lay by the door, curled in unbelievably small furry wads of lupine fur. Mr. Hoskins came over to sit across from me at the table, nodding as his wife poured him a cup of coffee. I noticed she was using what was obviously her fine china–probably wedding china–for me. Her husband struggled to pick up the dainty coffee cup of eggshell thin porcelain with his large hands.

"Miss Sam, I have something else I must insist you take along," he said, nodding at me. "I have a double barrel shotgun that will help to scare off anyone who might try to get in your way," Mr. Hoskins said, nodding to a short barrel gun propped up against the wall by the door. His brow creased with the earnest nature of his entreaty. "I doubt you'd even have to fire it; just sticking it in a man's face is usually enough persuasion."

If Kipp possessed the physical ability to raise his eyebrows, he would have done so. I looked at him, amused at the expression on his face.

"Do you know how to shoot that thing?" he asked. I had the distinct impression he didn't want an affirmative answer.

"Yes, as a matter of fact, I do," I replied. I took the knowledge seriously, as should anyone who holds firepower in his or her hands.

It was time for us to move on, so I surreptitiously left extra currency to cover the cost of the gun as well as the many kindnesses of the couple. Mr. Hoskins followed me out and gave me an assist to the elbow as I climbed up into the carriage that had a half canopy which I welcomed, since the sky was still dark and filled with ominous, scudding clouds. At least I and the lupines would stay fairly dry, and we could sleep in the back of the carriage with the canopy over us. Taking the reins in my hands, I gently clucked the horse forward; I had the distinct impression he appreciated that I left the buggy whip in its notch, unused. Rome was roughly southwest, and I knew enough about the progress of the sun across the sky to find my way. Yes, there were definite advantages in having lived in times when there were no artificial assists.

"How long will it take us?" Elani asked. She, like Kipp, had her big head stuck next to me as they pressed forward against the bench seat upon which I sat.

"I think, if we don't run into issues, three days," I answered. "I don't want to press the horse too much, since we have no idea about his health and endurance."

The horse, although not young, seemed game enough and clopped along at a quick pace, his ears swiveling pertly front and back. We appeared to be a on a fairly well-travelled road, but I didn't encounter anyone until a couple of hours later, when an oxen drawn dray approached, driven by an old man who looked as if he was about to fall asleep at the wheel. The dray was filled with oaken barrels, and the man flicked a whip lightly over the backs of the oxen, which seemed bored with the entire business.

The man pulled his team to a halt as I eased my grateful horse to a stop, coming to rest under the expansive, low hanging branches of a large oak tree. Spring was still early, and the leaves were not fully bunched out, but they still gave some shade from the sun, which unexpectedly decided to make an appearance. Despite the mild temperature, the rays of sunlight began to evaporate the moisture left behind from days of constant rain, and a fine, translucent mist hovered low over the land.

"How do!" the man called out politely. "Where you be headed, young miss?"

I took the opportunity to leave the hard bench seat of the buggy and landed lightly on the ground, stretching my back as I did so. Kipp and Elani, too, hopped down and put their noses to the dirt as they began to scan the surrounding territory.

"Nice looking doggies," the man remarked pleasantly. He used the break to pull a pipe from his jacket pocket and a worn leather pouch, containing tobacco, from another. I watched, fascinated, at the ritual of cleaning and then packing the bowl. After he was satisfied, he lit the tobacco, drawing deeply; the sweet fragrance of the smoke wafted past me and drifted across an open meadow that was full of early spring flowers. I noted the bright yellow splash of Leopard's Bane interspersed with the soft, lavender blue of bluebells, one of my favorites.

"I'm headed to Rome," I answered him, looking up at the sky to measure my progress as well as direction.

"I might not want any lady folk of mine travelling alone for that distance," the man replied, frowning. Taking out a bandana, he pulled his hat from his head and wiped his face, which was covered with the sweat and grime of an honest, hard working man. "Ninety nine percent of all the people around here are God fearing Christians, but there is that one percent who're utter heathens." He nodded at me. "I carry a gun up under my seat for the second group."

"I appreciate your warning," I replied. "I plan on being careful." I'd been cautioned many times in my life to not play my hand prematurely. So the fact I was equally armed with a shotgun was not something to mention to this man, even though he was well-meaning. Reaching to the back of the buggy, I pulled out a canister of water and took a sip. Stretching out my arm, I offered some to the man, who smiled.

"Don't mind if I do," he replied as he hopped off the bench of the dray to approach, his legs stiff from having sat too long.

We stood there in companionable silence as Kipp and Elani bounded across the meadow, playfully chasing butterflies that they had no intention of harming. Overhead, a large red tailed hawk circled, casting a fleeting shadow across the new grass that was still damp at the roots from the recent and constant rain. Kipp's thoughts merged with mine; he was monitoring the man's thoughts, as was I, and knew him to be a harmless presence.

"I'm Toby Smith," the man said, finding his manners on that isolated patch of country road.

"Samantha Keaton," I replied, continuing my pretense. "My brother was mistakenly taken by some soldiers to Rome, and I must find him," I said, in response to Toby's unspoken query.

"Keep on this road going south; the road will take a slight zig zag to the west, and you will eventually get to Rome. If you don't lollygag, you should make it to Rome in a couple of days." With an assessing gaze at my horse he added, "I don't think you need to push that animal of yours too hard." Toby took another deep draw off his pipe and tipped the edge of his hat at me. "I wish you well, young miss." As he approached his dray, he turned and darted another glance at me. "And be careful of who you meet on this road."

I assured him I would do just that. His oxen grunted, their thick tails flicking flies from their broad rumps as they pulled against their harnesses; I waited for Kipp and Elani to return. We shared a small snack before climbing back into the buggy and nudging the horse forward. He was still game but lacked the enthusiasm he'd shown early that morning. I think he figured out we weren't going for some short, casual clip through the countryside.

The dirt road which was in reasonably good condition curved along the margins of heavily wooded hillsides before dipping down into broad meadows. The sun hovered, bright and warm, overhead. We passed a remote farmstead where I saw a farmer out in a field, manhandling a plow pulled by a dusty, thin mule. A young child, his hair bleached white by the sun, sat on the lip of a furrow, his bare feet tunneling down into the freshly turned dirt. The boy raised his head to watch my passage, throwing up a hand in a friendly wave, which I returned. Everything that lived in those hills seemed to be lean and driven towards survival. I stopped briefly in a couple of small hamlets to allow the horse to rest, cool down and have water. Kipp and Elani stayed alert, canvassing the thoughts of the humans we encountered to watch for any signs of evil intent.

We travelled on until darkness fell. I unhitched the horse and set him to rest and graze, knowing Kipp could persuade him to return if he wandered too far. Our camp was a cold one, and I'd decided to sleep in the back of the buggy since I lacked a sleeping pallet or much else. The ambient temperature was pleasant and mild, and the lupines would snuggle up against me, in any case. I was drifting off when I heard the horse give a loud snort of alarm. He didn't bolt but instead hovered close to us, since we had become his herd mates. Off in the tree line, I could barely make out a large dark shape that was causing the underbrush to tremble. There was a loud, wet, snuffling sound, and I felt the hair go up on the back of my neck. Kipp was standing in the buggy, his body rigid, as he stared into the darkness.

"A bear," he finally said. "A mother bear with two cubs," he added.

Mother bears were notoriously unstable, and I wanted her away from the camp. For a moment, I gave consideration to firing off a dummy round from the shotgun but realized the horse would probably run ten miles in response.

"Elani and I can handle this," Kipp said, never the one to lack self confidence. "We'll get up wind of her, and she'll think we are wolves. She should turn and head off up that hillside," he concluded.

"Make sure you get your trajectory correct so that she doesn't run this way and try to hop up here with me," I replied. Despite the fact I completely trusted Kipp, I had no trust at all in the mother bear. And, after all, how many bears had Kipp herded in his brief lifetime?

Elani, looking game and ready for a wildlife adventure, hopped down after him, and I watched their forms, slunk low to the ground like predatory wolves, running back and forth until the bear finally caught wind of them and wheeled, rushing her cubs to the deepening forest. Kipp sauntered back, cocky and happy, his tongue lolling almost to the ground. He paused to give the horse a reassuring mind suggestion that all was well before returning to me.

"Just call me The Bear Whisperer," he said as he circled and became comfortable, plopping his head on my chest. Elani mimicked him on the other side of me. Warmth and safety was not a problem on that night.

CHAPTER 21

Since I'd eaten so well the previous day, I wasn't particularly hungry and nibbled while Kipp and Elani feasted on cheese, dried beef and bread. They could have gone without and suffered no ill effects, but as Kipp liked to remind me, we never knew when the next meal might be available, so we might as well eat hearty when opportunity knocked.

The horse, grateful for his night of rest, rubbed his big head up and down against my chest as I tried to get the harness bit between his teeth. It finally took the bribe of an apple to get him to open his mouth. After settling the bit, I finished buckling the harnesses into place and backed him into position in front of the buggy.

"You really know how to do this stuff!" Kipp exclaimed, his eyes wide with wonder.

"You just think you know me," I said, winking at him. Turning, I smiled at Elani. Her heart was still aching over Peter, but I gave her a reassuring nod. "We're almost on our way."

The landscape was relatively unchanged from the previous day, and we met a few people going in the opposite direction. Invariably, we were greeted with a tipped hat and a muttered "Good day, ma'am." Just after midday, a couple of men on horseback passed us, nodding as they went by. Kipp's head, which was wedged on top of my left shoulder, pivoted as he watched the men progress northward. Of course, his thoughts were so constantly entangled with mine, that I felt his alarm and conducted my own survey of the men.

"They are going to turn around any minute," Kipp said. "They're arguing if we have anything of value and figure, at the very least, we have a horse and buggy they can sell."

I felt my heart begin to pound. I suppose it was time that our good fortune having met decent people had run out. Leaning forward, I reached under the seat, and my fingers felt the hard, cold metal of the shotgun. I really had no wish to harm anyone and my doing so would definitely change the arc of history. But even symbionts had the right to protect themselves.

"Let me and Elani try to deal with this first," Kipp said. His voice was firm and insistent in my head.

"Be careful," I replied.

The two men had turned and were trotting up behind me, their horses on either side of the buggy. I kept my eyes forward and purposefully ignored them, even though I could see them drawing close in my peripheral vision. My gaze was focused to a distant spot highlighted between the bobbing, upright ears of the horse. Despite my confidence in my abilities and those of the lupines, the moment grew tense with anticipation.

"Hold up there, missy," one of the men called out. He kicked his horse, urging it forward so that he could go ahead and grab the reins of my horse.

I heard a series of shouts as Kipp and Elani both leapt, as if spring loaded, knocking each of their targeted men off their horses, respectively, to fall hard to the unyielding ground. Once down, after the shock and amazement wore off, the men's hands automatically went to the waistbands of their pants where each of them had a long-barreled revolver shoved into their britches. However, their hands never touched the guns; Kipp and Elani took up position, teeth bared, growling in that truly intimidating deep throated style of a large dog or wolf. Both men froze, staring at the lupines who were just inches away from their faces. I pulled up my horse and climbed down, nabbing the shotgun from beneath the bench seat. With it cradled in my arms, I walked slowly towards the men, my thumb on the hammer to show them I meant business.

"Kipp, Elani, step back," I ordered. They both complied, getting clear of the scene. I stared at the men who still wore that silly look of amazement on their grimy faces. They were poor, from the look of their clothing, scavengers, perhaps. But my empathy stopped at humans who wished to do me or mine harm.

"Take it easy," Kipp said, looking at me, rolling his eyes.

"Oh, I'm not going to shoot them, Kipp. You know that. But I want to scare the absolute living stink out of them." I closed one eye at my partner.

Overhead the skies suddenly cleared as if all the angels in heaven wanted to view our little human drama. One could only hope that I would frighten the two men enough that they would rethink their current career choice of opportunistic scallywags, or else they would continue along their sociopathic journey of life. Yes, there was no doubt I was doing them a great favor. A breeze from the northwest stirred the leaves; we must have been near a body of water, because I could distinctly hear the bright sound of water tumbling over rocks in its rush to an uncertain destination.

"I want you both to take your guns and lay them on the ground." I frowned at the men. "And be careful, because if I just vaguely get the impression you're going to try and shoot me, I will let go with a barrel full for each of you."

The men hesitated for just a second; Kipp, as a motivator, growled and took a step towards them. With alacrity, the men carefully pulled the pistols out, barrels down, and laid them on the grass. I ordered the crestfallen duo to stand and begin walking in the opposite direction. With care, I picked up the guns and put them under the bench seat.

"Petra, they are saying really bad things about you,"

Elani said, her voice worried. "I'm not familiar with some of the words but understand the sentiment behind them…unfortunately."

I grinned at her in response. Bless her, she was still so young and naïve in so many ways…a gentle soul in a not-so-gentle world. Reaching forward, I scratched the top of her broad skull before sending her and Kipp to chase the men's horses to Timbuktu while I resumed our trip to Rome. After a few minutes, the lupines rejoined me, their tongues hanging with exertion.

"They won't see their horses again anytime soon," Kipp said, laughing. "We didn't scare them, just kind of trotted them along."

Fortunately, we ran into no more highwaymen, but we did warn those who we passed of the men we had left behind. I planned on surrendering the confiscated guns to the law or military, whichever I encountered first upon our arrival in Rome.

Twilight was falling; the wall of the western horizon was a curtain of dove gray shot through with unexpected blazes of fiery red and soft orange. The horse was tired but held his head a little higher; he could smell wood smoke, as could I. We climbed a small hill and over the rise we saw the outline of a sizeable town, which had to be Rome. We'd made it despite all odds. Raising my head to the sky, I gave silent thanks and set my resolve. Now we must find Peter.

The road on which we approached the town seemed to be the main thoroughfare, because with no preamble, we found ourselves moving past busy store fronts, speakeasies that were just beginning to recruit evening business, as well as people hurrying home, tired from a day of labor. As we passed an obvious saloon, the tinny sound of a poorly played piano assaulted my ears. Kipp leaned forward and licked my face.

"Why'd you do that?" I asked.

"Just because I love you."

"Back at you, my lad," I replied, smiling.

I pulled up my horse and called out to a man who was walking in front of what seemed to be a general merchandise store. He paused, and I inquired about a stable where I could rest my weary and very deserving horse. After he pointed the way, I asked about the military encampment, and he told me that a company of infantry were located on the south end of town in a place called Beauchamp's Meadow.

"How many of those can there be?" Kipp asked humorously.

I almost drove the horse on out to the camp but hated to push him any farther when we could easily walk. Following the directions given to me, we stumbled upon the stable nestled between two narrow store fronts. A lantern illuminated the entrance, its flickering light casting shadows along the raw split wood framing; the smell of pine sap from the relatively freshly cut boards—the odor sharp and elemental—filled the evening air. I hopped down, followed by Kipp and Elani, who both appreciated a good stretch, and went inside. An old man wearing stained dungarees and a shapeless work coat left a stall, pitchfork in hand, to greet me. Narrowing his eyes, he gazed at me; clearly he didn't have many women to approach him as did I. His beard, which fanned out across his chest, was flecked with gray and liberally stained with tobacco juice, which made two darkened trails on either side of his mouth.

"Ma'am," he said, tilting his head in greeting.

"I've had a long journey from Catoosa and need to stable my horse," I remarked. "I have goods in my buggy that need to be secured, and I will pay well to make sure nothing is taken from me."

The old man cleared his throat and widened his eyes. He really wasn't offended but puffed out his chest and acted injured by my suggestion anything would disappear while in his care. The stable was well kept even though it reeked of ripe manure, but it was, after all, a horse hotel, so some rich bouquet was to be expected. After he finished acting put off by my directness, he led the tired horse inside. The horse recognized a stopping place in the journey and almost hurried into a stall as soon as he was free of the harness. The stable man backed up my buggy against a far wall. Beckoning to him, I reached under the seat and showed him the shotgun and two pistols.

"I was given the shotgun by a well-meaning friend when I left Catoosa," I said. "The pistols were taken from two men who acted as highwaymen and tried to rob me."

The old man leaned up against the wheel of the buggy and stared at me. Reaching forward, he took one of the pistols and casually inspected it.

"You little bit of a gal disarmed two men?" he asked. His lips trembled as he tried not to laugh.

"Yes, with a little help from my friends," I replied, smiling. With a gesture of my hands, I included Kipp and Elani. "You may have the pistols, if you want them," I added. "I may need the shotgun but am not certain yet." There was no harm in sweetening the deal with this man, who nodded in satisfaction at the unexpected bonus.

After leaving the stable, we continued to move towards the south end of town. Many people were hurrying to get home, and I found it was easier to walk along the margin of the main road since the boarded sidewalks were crowded. Passing a dining hall, the fragrance of fresh baked bread almost knocked me to my knees. Looking down, I couldn't help but notice Kipp was salivating.

"It smells good, but I'm fine," he assured me. The lupines had eaten earlier that day, and I wasn't truly hungry.

Outside of the last halo of light cast by a swinging lantern suspended from a wooden post, the thoughts of many men in close quarters drifted to me. Symbionts didn't, as a rule, need a lot of direction since we could follow the scattered trails of human thought. From the ambient light from the town as well as the stars above–the clouds seemed to have finally broken for good–I could see the outlines of countless tents strung up in neat rows across a cleared field and stretching up a far hillock. The smell of pork frying in seasoned skillets and coffee simmering over hot fires filled the air, along with the sounds of soft laughter. There were pockets of men clustered, raising their voice in song, and the homesick strains of "Lorena", a song familiar to me, were audible. Somebody was playing a fiddle and doing so with remarkable skill.

"It's profound, somehow," Elani said. She walked at my left side, her dense coat brushing up against my rustling skirt; I'm not certain who drew more comfort from the closeness: Elani or me? "Many of these so-called men are just boys and have no idea what is ahead. Some are afraid but cover it with boastful talk." She looked up at me, her dark eyes filled with a sober expression. "Many of them will never go home again."

"This is what war is and what war does," I said. "Even wars fought for a valid cause are filled with the painful after effects."

A sentry noted our approach and stepped forward. He relaxed at seeing a woman and the grip on his rifle loosened somewhat. The gun, I noted, was an old musket style that was probably used for hunting game back home. This rough infantry was composed of men in mismatched clothing who brought their own goods from home knowing nothing of significance would be available for them. The man—no, boy—looked down at Kipp, who smiled back in what Kipp hoped to be a friendly, doggy manner. He waved his plumed tail for good advantage.

"May I help you, ma'am?" the boy asked, his tone and attitude polite. After a nano second, he tipped the end of his gray kepi. At least someone had distributed the cap of the day since the fellow was otherwise dressed in patched dungarees and a faded, flannel shirt that had seen too much work under a hot sun.

"I need to see whoever is in command," I replied, trying to sound very assertive. My take on the lad was that he was dutiful but not certain enough of himself to confront an aggressive female. I presented him with an anachronism that boggled his mind.

"And why would you need to see Colonel Duncan?" he asked.

"It is a personal matter," I replied, staring him down. Kipp was chomping at the bit and wanted to plant a suggestion in the back of the boy's brain, but I knew the youngster would eventually submit to my strength of will. After a few seconds, he turned, beckoning to me to follow him.

We wove past several tents that were illuminated from the inside by lanterns; the stretched white cloth almost glowed in the semi-darkness and formed little soft pops of light in even rows. As I walked, the men's heads turned to watch me, but they were honestly more amazed by Kipp and Elani, who followed me like tugboats escorting a barge. After a few minutes we arrived at a larger tent, one that had a long flap extended out under which several wooden chairs were clustered. Five men were seated there, all of whom stood as I approached.

"Colonel Duncan," the boy said with a tip of his hat, "This young lady needs to speak with you."

The colonel, a man of perhaps forty, was tall, well built with a strong face marred by a terrible scar than ran from his left temple down across his cheek, marring the symmetry of his lips and ending on the tip of his chin. It had only been providence and his reflexes that saved him from losing his left eye, too.

"He got that in Mexico, fighting in another war," Kipp said. He was obviously busy canvassing the man's thoughts and memories. I stopped myself from questioning his need to do a deeper dive than was necessary into the mind of a human.

"I am Samantha Keaton," I began, nodding as Duncan pressed his heels together and gave a little bow from the waist. The men, shifting about in discomfort since they weren't sure what to do with me, resumed their seats after a chair had been offered to me. "My brother, Peter, was abducted by a group of Union soldiers who stole the *General* from Big Shanty," I said, widening my eyes for effect. It was clear the word had spread by telegraph, and the men knew of the train abduction. "He was trying to retrieve our grandfather's gold watch which had been left on the train and ended up being taken against his will." I paused and smiled at the other men, hoping they would feel sympathy for me and my plight. "I have it on good authority that the Union men dropped him off in Catoosa, and a group of your soldiers, thinking he was an enemy, brought him here." I concluded my story triumphantly.

A porter arrived with a pot of fresh coffee, and one of the men, a fresh-faced lieutenant, offered me a hot cup of brew. It wasn't quite like having it in the cozy confines of the library with Fitzhugh, but coffee was coffee and I accepted with gratitude. Maybe the caffeine stimulant awakened my lazy telepathy, because I immediately became aware of something else: someone in the camp had Peter's watch because a wave of guilt wafted past me like the stench off of a stagnant pool of black water. I glanced at Kipp, who nodded his head in agreement. Colonel Duncan resumed his place and sat forward in his chair as he listened to my story. I noticed, as he wrinkled his forehead in concentration, the scarred part of his face puckered even more, distorting what once had been very nice, balanced features. He looked down at the lupines and smiled.

"Do you always travel with an entourage?" he asked.

"Yes," I replied. "And they came in quite handy, too." I was ready to tell a story as I shamelessly manipulated this man's sensibilities in order to find Peter. "I was on the road in an isolated area when two men approached me and were planning on stealing my horse and buggy. Kipp jumped on one, knocking him to the ground while Elani jumped on the other." I paused, wide-eyed and somewhat breathless. "Then, I held them at gun point while I took their guns, and we scared their horses off. The last I saw, they were walking towards Catoosa." I took a sip of my coffee. "My, this is good and fortifying after long days on the road with nothing hot to eat." Glancing at Duncan, I was happy to see his horrified expression.

Leaning forward, he beckoned to the lupines, who dutifully did their dog routine and approached him. He scratched ears and thumped sides with vigor. He liked dogs anyway but was very impressed by my guardians.

"What kind of dogs are these?" he asked.

"Chinese red crested mastiffs," I answered, trying to keep a straight face.

"Can't you come up with something new?" Kipp grumbled as Elani giggled.

The next thing I knew, Duncan was barking orders at some young man. Those two highwaymen who were walking, somewhere north of Rome, were about to find themselves in deep trouble if they were found.

"Lieutenant Forsyth was in charge of the detail that arrived from Catoosa, but I don't recall any prisoners," Duncan said, nodding at a fresh-faced youth sitting at the edge of the group. The minute he stood, I knew he was the guilty party and that he had Peter's watch hidden in his pocket. Kipp and Elani knew it, too, and it was with restraint that Elani didn't leap across the camp and give the man a serious chomp.

"We did have a prisoner, sir," Forsyth stuttered, his face red, "but released him to a company of men traveling to Atlanta."

"And why would you take such an action?" Duncan asked as I felt my heart drop. Peter wasn't here, which explained why Kipp, especially, had not gotten any pings on his symbiont radar. I'd thought it was just due to so many human minds clustered in one place as well as stress and fatigue. As the lieutenant muttered some inadequate reply, Duncan's face got redder, and beads of perspiration formed on Forsyth's forehead as he began to sweat. From the views of the other men, Duncan was not an unreasonable commander, but he was intolerant of many things, and he didn't care for Forsyth's free-wheeling decision making under the circumstances.

"So the man we think to be this lady's brother is on his way to Atlanta?" he asked.

"Yes, sir," Forsyth muttered, hoping the moment would end. His hand made its way to his neck, fumbling at his collar. He desperately wished he'd not fastened that top button that constricted his throat, but he'd hoped to impress Duncan with his precise attire.

It was dark now; from the woods that bordered the meadow crowded by men and horses, there was the scream of a wildcat, the sound of which made the hair stand up on my neck. A pattern of stars became visible in the sky overhead; I picked out Orion's belt, which was always an easy constellation to find. The moon, only a sliver of pale, glowing white, hovered in the blackness, while we waited for Duncan to make a decision.

"I feel bad that this has happened, Miss Keaton, and it falls on me to make it right," Duncan said, turning his ruined face towards me in the flickering half light of the campfire around which we sat. "I will send a detail to accompany you to Atlanta, and they will assist you in finding your brother. Also, I'll write a letter that explains this was a mistake and to release him to you." He smiled and the ruined lips stretched awkwardly, distorting his features even more. "A man will escort you to town and help you locate lodgings for the night."

The men rose, indicating the interview was at an end. I stood, too, beckoning for Elani and Kipp to follow me. However, Elani didn't move and was staring at Lieutenant Forsyth.

"He has Peter's grandfather's watch, and I'm not leaving without it," she said.

"I'm not sure how to get it back," I replied, wishing she'd let the issue drop.

"I do," Kipp said.

Kipp is a remarkably large lupine and projects intimidation with little to no effort. So when he approaches a human— hackles up, teeth exposed, low growl reverberating—it's a sight to see. He turned towards Forsyth and began such a walk. The young man looked alarmed, and his hand instinctively went towards his sidearm.

"Hold," Duncan said, ordering Forsyth to not pull his gun. "Miss Keaton, will you please call off your dog?" he asked.

"Kipp knows there is something wrong, probably smells something, for him to act like this," I stuttered, desperately trying to play along with my partner.

"So, Forsyth, what is it?" Duncan asked.

It took Forsyth a full minute, during which Kipp kept up his threatening display, to finally pull the gold watch from his pants pocket. I didn't even want to visit Duncan's thoughts at that point and realized Forsyth was in some serious trouble. As far as Duncan was concerned, Forsyth was no better than the highwaymen who'd attempted to rob me. Duncan, after inspecting the watch closely, handed it to me, bowing over my hand.

"Your brother's watch, ma'am."

As we walked to town, accompanied by a sergeant who looked as if he'd just graduated from knee pants, I looked at Kipp, frowning slightly. "You might warn me next time you plan some stunt like that," I reprimanded my buddy.

"We got the watch, so what are you whining about?" Kipp replied. He sauntered ahead, his large noggin tilted in a saucy manner. We'd reached the edge of Rome, and Kipp paused under a large lantern, where a flurry of moths darted back and forth, seeking the elusive light that drew them. Twisting his thick neck, he looked back at me and slowly closed one eye. Kipp was, at times, a handful.

CHAPTER 22

———◆———

A lthough I had absolutely no concern about traveling on my own with the two lupines for company, it was equally fine to ride along with a small squad of men. I'd not have to worry about highwaymen, and the men scouted ahead for potential issues. Fortunately, Duncan did not send along the disgraced Lieutenant Forsyth, since that man would probably hold a sizeable grudge against me and, even more so, Kipp. I'd retrieved my horse and buggy from the stable; the old stable worker was delighted to receive two pistols and one shotgun as a bonus. There was no need for me to carry those items since I'd have an armed entourage at my side.

"I'm glad to see you rid of those things," Kipp remarked, as he rolled his shoulders a little. "I'm still not sure you know how to handle them." Elani vigorously nodded her head in agreement. I admit that I was a little deflated over their mutual lack of confidence in me. True, I was no Annie Oakley, but I could aim a shotgun and pull the trigger if needed.

The distance to Atlanta was a little over fifty miles over roads that were left rutted and sloppy from the continuous rain. We were in luck, however, in that the rain remained in check for the present, as a bright sun hovered overhead.

Along the roadside, wildflowers bunched in chaotic abandon, covering the hills with unexpected flashes of blue, pink and yellow. Kipp and Elani, who shared my color discrimination vision, oohed and aahed as we drove along. The foliage on the trees seemed to thicken daily, and the lighter green of the oaks and poplars stood out from the deep, almost forbiddingly dark colors of the numerous, towering Georgia pines, which pushed up towards the sky with their impressively thick trunks; wild dogwoods, their white blooming flowers bobbing in the mild breeze, stubbornly competed for space amongst their larger cousins. A pleasant, garrulous young man sat next to me on the bench of the carriage, his horse tied to the back railing. Two men rode in front of us, and two trialed behind. Obviously, Duncan was trying to right a wrong.

"And how was it, ma'am, that your brother got himself kidnapped?" Lieutenant Andrews asked, cautious not to stare at me in what would have been considered ill-mannered behavior for the times.

We chatted amiably to get to know one another the first day out, and we were now into the middle segment of the trip. Andrews was barely twenty and a graduate from a military academy–not West Point–but a smaller, state run school. His family was solidly middle-class and owned a general store in Atlanta. He was happy to get an opportunity to see them, if only for a brief time. I knew, from reading Duncan's thoughts, that he liked the young man and gave him this assignment to facilitate a home visit. Although the boy's back was straight and his face wore a determined, dutiful expression, he was just another homesick lad.

"Tragic thing," Elani observed. "War tears families apart, and people who normally might not see themselves as combative become so out of need or conscription."

The wheel of the buggy hit a deep rut; with the road conditions being compromised, it was difficult not to. As the vehicle lurched sideways, Andrews fell against my shoulder, his arm brushing mine. Red faced, he apologized and moved away from me on the seat, gaining a polite distance. Kipp almost lost his footing and shoved his head up between us.

"Tell this amateur to watch himself or else I'll have to take matters into my own hands," he said. Baring his teeth, he showed a mouthful of ivory to the back of the unknowing young man's neck. I suppressed a giggle.

"I'm sure your family misses you," I said, gently probing Andrews.

"Oh, my mama sends me letters all the time," he laughed. "She worries if I have enough to eat and if my socks are dry and not full of holes." After a pause, he added, "She knits me new socks to wear; I've got more socks than any man in my company."

"I wonder if he lived through the war or if he died in a battle?" Elani queried.

"It would be something that could be researched," I responded. "But would you really want to know?"

I made it a practice to avoid investigating what happened to people I'd met during a time shift–with the exception of Harrow—unless the arc of their lives was already known to me. Even though we were not to become personally involved with humans, it was impossible to not have some level of attachment after a connection had been made. The bureaucrats who thought up such rules had never travelled and had no idea of what they spoke. Fitzhugh and I made a computer search of my beloved William Harrow following my return from the last time shift. Doing so had oddly comforted me; viewing a sepia toned photograph of his remarkable face reproduced on the screen brought a rush of memories as well as emotions. My hand reached for my neck, where the delicate strand of pearls pooled like quicksilver in the hollow of my throat.

"No, I guess not," Elani replied after she considered my query.

Although Elani remained subdued, I could tell she was feeling more optimistic that we could locate Peter. If he had been taken to Atlanta, he was most likely in the Fulton

County jail, which was located on the intersection of Fair and Fraser Streets per Mr. Professor, i. e., Kipp. Unless Peter was found to be a Union soldier in civilian clothes–a spy, worthy of hanging–he would be transported to a prison camp until evidence could be given to prove his innocence. The raiders wouldn't end up in Atlanta for a while, so the disposition of Peter would have to be managed without their corroborating statements that he was not a collaborator.

We approached another small settlement, and Andrews pulled up my horse so that the animals could rest. A pack of dogs, excited over strangers, surged out from under the wooden rafters of a raised porch, eager to show us who owned the town. However, one sniff of Kipp and Elani sent them reeling back to their hideout, where they glowered at the odd newcomers. Kipp winked at me.

"I guess they figured out who owns this," Kipp said, rolling his shoulder and lifting his head.

"You really need to learn some new slang," I suggested, arching my eyebrow.

There was a small eating establishment, but the owner took a firm stance and would not allow the lupines to enter, so I took my food and theirs and sat on the back porch, a place usually reserved for drifters. Andrews, who was horrified that I would do such a thing, brought his plate and sat with me.

"It's really okay," I told him, squinting my eyes against the bright sun; I lacked a hat and the modern convenience of polarized sun glasses. "I just didn't want to leave them alone out here," I explained, not caring how silly I might seem.

"Oh, I understand, ma'am," he replied, although he didn't. Andrews was just trying to be polite, and it wasn't a part of his makeup to tell me I was obviously a crazy woman. "I have a dog at home who sleeps on the floor next to my bed. Or at least he's supposed to. My mama won't allow him in the bed, but when she goes to sleep, he hops up anyway and lies on my feet. His name is Buddy," Andrews added.

"I like this guy," Kipp said. "He's a rule breaker…a renegade…my kind of human. You know those tags on pillows that say don't tear off upon penalty of law? I bet he'd pull 'em off and never look back!"

I tried to ignore Kipp, who seemed determined to make me break my concentration, as he and Elani finished off their bowls of what I might think of as mixed fare. The cook had piled chunks of meat in with butterbeans, cornbread, and fried okra. The latter was an interesting addition, and Kipp nosed it carefully before trying a piece, letting it rest on the back of his tongue to savor the full flavor.

"Oh, my gosh!" he exclaimed, as the piece of okra skidded down his throat. "Why have you kept this from me?" Kipp asked, referring to the fried okra. "Do you know how to cook this stuff?"

"Yes," I replied. "And I'll fix you some when we get home, if you just won't go on and on about it."

We finished the meal and resumed our journey. At our rate of our progress, we would reach Atlanta the following afternoon. Later that day, dark clouds unexpectedly began to bunch up on the western horizon. Despite my assumption that the rain was gone for the immediate future, it appeared we were in for a storm and no one was particularly interested in getting soaked. Fortunately, we were passing an isolated farm and noted the farmer was leading his team of mules in from the field he'd just finished plowing. Andrews guided the buggy over to the man, who paused to run a sweat stained bandanna over his dirt caked face. His dungarees were torn and rudely patched, but his face was open and pleasant. Years of hard work outside had left him with lined, leathery skin; the dust seemed to cake like fine powder in the furrows of his flesh.

Andrews politely asked if we might use the shelter of his barn for the night, and the man agreed, although he assured us he had no extra food or supplies for us. His thoughts reflected his embarrassment, but he was a poor man, barely scrabbling out a living for him and his family. A hoard of

small children, all barefoot and tow-headed, clambered out
on the front porch of a ramshackle cabin. At first, the
farmer told them to give us wide berth, but finally he gave
in to their curiosity, especially about Kipp and Elani.

As Andrews and his men were unsaddling the horses and
caring for the animals, one of the little girls was brave
enough to come over to where I was resting–at the
insistence of the gallant Andrews—on a pile of straw. The
barn was much larger than the cabin in which the family
lived. Despite its relative cleanliness, the barn interior
reeked of the smell of manure and sweaty animals; Kipp
wrinkled his nose.

"Whew!" he said, blinking his eyes. "Kinda close in
here."

"What kinda dog is that?" the little girl asked, pointing at
Elani, who was seated at my feet.

"She's a Chinese mastiff," I replied, shortening the name
since Kipp was obviously ready for something new. "Her
name is Elani." After a pause, I added, "You can touch her
if you want. She is very sweet and loves little girls to pat
her head."

The child opened her blue eyes wide and walked up to
Elani, holding out one small hand. With wonder, she
scratched Elani gently between her ears. "She's soft," the
girl said, giggling.

At that point her father walked in to see how we were
getting along. He stared at the girl who was oblivious to
him. After a moment, his expression softened. "Mary Alice
has always had a fondness for the beasts of the earth," he
said. "We had a dog that died last winter. She was real
attached to him." He cleared his throat and added, "My
wife just gave me the what for and told me I was rude to
not offer food to you people." His face flushed red.

Andrews quickly assured him that we had provisions,
since it was very obvious there was little to nothing to share
in this home. He did, however, state that we would
appreciate use of the well for fresh water.

Mary Alice grasped her father's strong hand as they were

called to supper. As they disappeared, a storm broke in earnest and rain began to pelt the roof of the barn. Over a long lifetime, I've slept in fine hotels and beautiful homes as well as on the dirt floors of caves. But that night, sleeping in fragrant hay while the rain beat on the tin roof of the barn, was one of the most memorable, in terms of comfort. The horses, in response to thunder, would whinny softly; occasionally, the mules would shift in their stalls, their heavy hooves thudding on the dirt. The men, with whom I travelled, fell into deep sleep, some snoring in rhythm with their breathing. Kipp and Elani were wedged on either side of me; their soft warmth and the rise and fall of their chests was reassuring. I knew I'd have to pluck straw from my hair the next day but didn't care. Sleep came as I drifted off into a dreamless state.

The harsh crowing of a rooster awoke me; I sat up suddenly, momentarily disoriented as to where I was since the reality of lying in a pile of hay seemed a little atypical. Kipp walked towards me, followed by Elani. Both had obviously been outside for their morning constitutional. Their paws were damp and colored with reddish dirt collected from the rain softened earth. I looked at them and giggled.

"What?" Kipp asked.

The moment reminded me of a funny detergent commercial, maybe from the 70's. A distressed woman, with an exaggerated southern accent, was touting the benefits of either Tide or Cheer. As she held up a white t-shirt in dismay, she exclaimed "Jeff just gets into our Georgia red clay." Somehow, Georgia came out sounding like JawJah and clay was spoken as if it consisted of two syllables.

"I think you got into some Georgia red clay," I responded, trying to mimic the woman in the ad.

The men were stirring in response to nature's alarm clock, which began to crow again for good measure in case we missed the first call. It was obvious the rooster felt we'd overstayed our welcome and needed to move on. We knew the farmer would be in momentarily to begin milking the cow. Since we'd over burdened the barn with our horses, Andrews and one of the men led them out and begin the process of saddling as well as getting the buggy ready. Two other men drew the short straw and were given the assignment to muck out the barn so we wouldn't create more of a burden on our host. And then another was about to work on breakfast when the farmer's wife approached. She'd made a pan full of biscuits, which were piping hot, the fragrance preceding her arrival. On an overturned barrel, she laid out a nice spread of biscuits, fresh butter, homemade apple butter, and slices of fried ham.

"Sorry this isn't more," she said before Andrews stopped her.

"Ma'am, we are so grateful for your kindness."

I fixed Kipp and Elani both a couple of ham biscuits complete with butter, while I nibbled on a biscuit with some of the apple butter. The man who was assigned breakfast duty prepared a pot of coffee while the others worked with the animals. Since Andrews had ordered me to not exert myself, I occupied my time by attempting to brush the straw and debris from the faded blue cotton of my dress. Then, with Kipp and Elani working as spotters, I pulled straw from my hair and did my best to rebraid it into some semblance of tidy order.

"Will we make it to Atlanta today?" I asked Andrews as he passed by, nodding at me.

"Yes, ma'am." He smiled. "Or at least we should, unless we run into problems. It will be late, however."

I could feel his excitement growing over the opportunity to go home for a day. The other men looked forward to a night in a relatively large town, where they could drink, carouse and generally be irresponsible for a few hours. Kipp looked at me and winked, while pretending to be astonished at the lascivious content of their collective thoughts. The storm from the previous night had cleared the air and all humidity had evaporated. Except for the compromised roads, the trip should be fairly pleasant with mild temperatures and clear skies. Our party was underway within thirty minutes. I looked back, once, over my shoulder, and saw little Mary Alice waving good bye. She really wasn't concerned about the humans but hated to see the "dogs" leave.

"She needs a puppy," Kipp remarked.

We kept up a steady pace, only stopping periodically to rest the horses. Andrews ordered the men to dismount and walk, too, for brief periods. Riding for hours was difficult on horse and man, so the men did not object to stretching their legs and relieving the pressure on their backsides. Just after midday, one of the men who road point cantered towards us, his face bright with sheen from sweat; his horse was breathing a little harder from exertion. Andrews signaled for the others to halt as the soldier pulled the horse to a stop.

"There was a bridge up ahead that crossed a creek," the soldier said. "But it ain't there no more. Must have been washed away by the storms."

"How bad is the water?" Andrews asked.

"Pretty swole up, sir."

Andrews sent the men in either direction of the creek to find a crossing place that looked safe. While we waited, he pulled the carriage underneath the spreading boughs of a large oak that sat at the edge of a grove of old growth trees. The wind had picked up and cooled my face as well as the back of my neck. Overhead, the leaves rustled as they were tossed by the active movement of the air; the tree limbs groaned as they scraped against one another.

"Mind if we do some scouting, too?" Kipp asked.

"Knock yourself out," I replied, knowing the lupines were tired of riding for so long. I watched as they bounded out of sight.

Andrews was seeing to his horse, which seemed to have picked up a pebble in its front right hoof. While he scraped at the object with his knife, I hopped down and walked for a short distance. The sun shone down on my upturned face; it was nice to feel the warmth after having been waterlogged since my arrival to this time. My freckles, I knew, would pop out with vigor, but I cared not. Harrow had liked those spots of imperfection in his world of exquisitely coiffed, beautiful women. My big nose, freckles, and impertinent attitude had been my selling points to a human man who was unconventional, to say the least.

In a short while, the men began to return; only one, a private named Jones, had found a possible crossing place. As I listened to him discuss the plan of an alternate route with Andrews, Kipp and Elani returned, their tongues hanging out.

"The water looks pretty fast, no matter where we looked," Kipp announced, pausing to shake, his burnished coat darkened with water from the creek. Obviously he'd tested the currents in the creek.

I hoped the crossing was favorable and knew Andrews wouldn't make an attempt unless he thought the horses could manage. Kipp and Elani found a place a short distance upstream where a large tree had fallen across the stream, creating a natural bridge. They both assured me they would be careful and were off in a flash. By the time we got to the proposed crossing spot, Kipp and Elani were waiting on the other side, their tails wagging. The sun stayed true overhead, its rays filtering down through the heavy canopy of leaves. One shaft of light outlined Kipp, who stood with his head up, eyes fixed on me.

Half of the men went first, letting their horses find secure footing on the creek bed. The water came to the animals' bellies, but the horses, seasoned campaigners, didn't seem to mind. Andrews decided to lighten the load in the buggy, to lessen the chance the wheels might become stuck in the creek sediment. So, he mounted his horse and snapped a lead on my horse, which was dutifully pulling the buggy.

I still, to this day, don't recall exactly what happened. I was traveling along quite nicely when the horse decided, literally in midstream, that he cared not for rushing water that tickled the underside of his tummy. He began to bob his dark head up and down, ears flattened to his head. I couldn't see his face, but could hear him snorting in fear. No matter what Andrews did, the horse would not budge. Kipp told me later that a large piece of debris from a tree hit the side of the buggy, causing it to suddenly tip. I was unprepared for such and, with a cry, toppled into the river. I am actually a competent swimmer but immediately realized that the force of the water combined with the weight of my dress, which became sodden and heavy, was hampering me, and I could not use my legs at all for propulsion since they became entangled in the fabric. Fear gripped me as I struggled to keep my head above the surging water; I bobbed downstream like a helpless top. The sounds of the men crying out to me reached my ears, in and out, as I would go underwater, only to resurface, coughing and sputtering. I knew they would try and reach me; the question was would I last long enough?

"I'm coming!" Kipp called out.

"Don't, Kipp!" I shouted back at him.

But in my mind, I could see it unfold from my ever present vantage point in the back of his head. Without hesitation, he took a running start and leapt at least fifteen feet from the creek edge before landing in the water, roughly parallel to my erratic and uncontrolled course. He began paddling frantically, trying to reach me as well as keep his own head above water. In less than a minute, he was next to me, pushing up against my exhausted body. I felt I would go under at any second; the dress was pulling me down to my grave.

"Put your arm over my back!" Kipp commanded. The sound of Elani, barking hysterically, filled the air in echoes distorted by the rushing water.

"Save yourself!" I cried. "Leave me!"

"Never. If you go, I go with you, Petra. Always." Kipp shoved up hard against me, and I threw my numb arm over his broad back.

I think sometimes amazing feats occur simply because we know we cannot fail. It happens with humans and apparently with symbionts. Kipp knew failure was not an option, and somehow he managed to tow me towards shore, only releasing me when my feet touched earth. The men, of course, were there to help me out of the water, and an amazed Andrews made certain Kipp was okay, too, as I sat, breathing heavily, my face covered by my dark hair which hung in damp tendrils.

"That was amazing, Miss Sam!" he said, staring at Kipp. "That's quite some dog you've got there."

I looked at Kipp and began to cry, almost uncontrollably. The men hovered uncomfortably, not sure how to deal with a weeping woman. They would have been amazed to discover the true reason I was crying. My love for Kipp had overwhelmed me; once again my partner had saved my life and his devotion to me, sometimes not deserved on my part, was beyond my capacity for words. Kipp sat close, quiet, his mind closed to me. He allowed me just to hold him close, his massive muzzle resting on my shoulder.

CHAPTER 23

Once again, I was a thoroughly wet, muddy mess. And here I was, almost to Atlanta, riding in the buggy, with Andrews behind the reins. Staring at the back of the head of my horse, which was bobbing along in rhythm with his steps, I wondered if he felt any remorse over my condition. If he'd just gotten clear of the creek instead of pausing mid stream, I'd be dry and presentable. As it were, I looked more than disrespectful. My dress was torn in the melee, one sleeve hanging by a thread. At some point, my underwear had crawled up as I tried, discretely, to shift on the hard seat of the buggy, to dislodge a wedgie that threatened to make me start crying again. The horse suddenly shook his head, harness bits jangling, as if he was responding to my accusatory thoughts with a little sassy reply of his own.

"When we get to Atlanta," Andrews was saying, "the men will go to a hotel." He paused and looked at me, his face reddening. The guilt he felt over what had happened was immense, and he was struggling with a way to repair the damage. "I'm gonna take you to my mama's house where she can help you get cleaned up and all," he said, delicately not mentioning all the layers and steps a lady might require for decent presentation.

I started to argue, but Kipp and Elani talked me out of it. All of us needed a good night of rest. I, in my current condition, would not be able to convince anyone of my sincerity or appear remotely as a respectable woman should in that day and age. Wearily, I nodded my head. Two hours later, Andrews pulled the buggy to a stop in front of a neat, brown brick dwelling that was located on a street lined with similar middle class homes. There was a tiny garden out front filled with spring flowers; most notable were early roses that grew in tight bunches, spilling over the white wooden fence and winding up an ornate iron trellis. The smell of the roses overflowed out into the street, mixing with the cloying, earthy odors of horses, manure and sweat that made up a busy thoroughfare. Honey bees hovered over the flowers, darting in and out as they went about their gathering of nectar. Butterflies, too, flew in chaotic patterns, lacking the organized work ethic of the bees, their wing colors flashing in competition with the flowers.

The sun was reaching the western horizon and soon would dip below visibility, ushering in twilight. The bees would seek out their hives, as would the butterflies look for shelter. The martins circling above would likewise find safe harbor, leaving only the night creatures, such as bats and owls, to begin to hunt. I'd always liked this time of day, just as I enjoyed sunrise. Dusk, as opposed to daybreak, seemed to be a moment when the earth held its breath, just for a second, before breathing a deep sigh of relief. There was something sobering and grounding about the earth's way of slowing down and reminding us of our need to regenerate.

Andrews helped me down while being mindful of my left shoulder which had become wrenched during my water adventure. Gritting my teeth, I smiled, not wanting to complain. But maybe some liniment would help.

"My mama has some liniment that really will help your sore shoulder," Andrews opined, startling me by reading my thoughts.

His mother was a short woman, comfortably round,

perhaps in her late forties. Charles, my dutiful Lieutenant Andrews, was her baby; tears glistened in her eyes as she embraced him on the front porch. She darted a glance at me and immediately nabbed polite control over her startled expression at my appearance.

"I'm Belle Andrews," she announced with her soft southern drawl as she lifted up a flour dusted apron to dry her hands.

"Mama, may I present Miss Samantha Keaton," Andrews said, with a slight bow and a serious voice. "I was accompanying Miss Sam here to Atlanta on the orders of the Colonel. We had a little accident north of town, and Miss Sam fell off in the water and hurt her shoulder." Andrews gestured to my left arm.

"Why, bless your heart, honey!" Belle exclaimed, her brows drawing together in worry. "You come on in here, and I'll get you a hot bath and find you something to wear." I followed her thoughts and recognized she would bring me clothing that had been left when her daughter married and moved to Valdosta.

"And, Mama, these are Miss Sam's dogs. Kipp saved her life by jumping in after her and pulling her to the edge of the water." Andrews sounded as if he was a proud father pointing out the athletic accomplishments of a son who ran the fastest or threw the farthest.

Belle Andrews stared at the two lupines, who did their best to look submissive and happy. They were about as much as mess as was I, but her kind heart won out over conventional sensibilities. Buddy, the house dog, had waggled his portly, short legged body out to the porch and was trying to engage the lupines, who responded in kind, leaving the poor dog completely confused.

"Charlie, you get to heating some water and take the doggies on the back porch and clean them up. Then, bring them on in to dry in front of the stove," she said, referencing the wood burning stove in the kitchen. Smiling, she looked at me. "I'll take Miss Sam to her room while I get the hip bath ready."

As always, I didn't like to be separated from my companions, but we were just talking about a temporary interval and a wall separating us. Kipp, knowing how much my shoulder was throbbing, nodded his head.

"It's good, Petra. Get a bath, wash your hair, and you'll feel better. We will, too, when we get our hair done," he concluded, trying to sound humorous.

I've had some physically pleasurable experiences, but that hot bath with Belle pouring warm water over my head while she scrubbed my hair with some lavender scented soap was a pinnacle in terms of happy, contented moments. After I was clean, she handed me a thick towel for drying, while she rubbed some sort of lotion into my shoulder. In about thirty seconds, it began to burn fiercely, and I felt my eyes water from the pungent smell. I didn't even bother to look at the white bottle and try to read the ingredients. The stuff probably contained turpentine or something equally toxic to flesh. I believe that the chemist who concocted it decided that one's mind would be diverted off of an organic pain by the fiery heat of the liquid which soaked into my skin like hot oil from a deep fryer.

"Are you hungry, baby?" Belle asked. Her forehead was wrinkled up in concern for me. I'd told her the story of Peter, and she was aggressively on my side.

"No, ma'am," I answered, keeping my best manners intact.

I followed her to the kitchen, wrapped up completely in a pretty, floral dressing gown that covered me from neck to feet. To my delight, the two lupines were drying in front of the wood burning stove, tails thumping at my entrance. A metal tray of golden biscuits lay on a table while a large, iron pot of what seemed to be beef stew sat warming on the stove top. I thought Kipp's eyes were gonna bug out of his big head in response to the aroma that wafted through the room.

Charlie, noticing the attentiveness of the lupines, retrieved a couple of large bowls and, with the nodding approval of his mother, broke a couple of biscuits into each bowl and ladled large portions of the stew on top. The lupines wagged their tails faster and faster as he placed the bowls on the floor. It might have been a new record because both Kipp and Elani were finished in less than sixty seconds.

"Oh, Petra, you need to get in on this," Kipp said, breathing heavily in between bites.

I realized Mrs. Andrews would not let me sit quietly with no food–such behavior was not in her genetic makeup—so I agreed to have a couple of buttered biscuits, on top of which she poured some dark, thick syrup that was just shy of qualifying as blackstrap molasses.

The spare room was one where her two daughters had slept. The double bed that was almost too high off the ground for a comfortable ascent had been left neatly made up as if it was expecting a guest any moment. I noted that a couple of dolls, reminders of her daughters' childhoods, were perched on little chairs in a far corner. It was a sentimental touch that revealed Mrs. Andrews' character; however, those immobile porcelain faces staring at me from across the room left me feeling uneasy. My hostess saw me safely to my bed and turned down the oil lantern on a bedside table as she left the room. Kipp and Elani, who by then were clean and dry, carefully climbed up, making certain their toenails didn't rip or pull the fabric of the sheets. As much as possible, we wanted to not incommode Mrs. Andrews, who had revived us. Yes, I felt I could journey forward.

"Petra, I was terrified when you fell into the water," Elani said, her head across my abdomen; Kipp's stretched heavily across my chest, as usual.

"Me, too," I said, moving my hand to thread my fingers through her fur. At the base, I could still feel a tiny bit of dampness, but only in spots. If she'd been a cat, she might have purred in response to my caress. The liniment on my shoulder must have contained a second, unexpected level of fire, because the heat flared again, and I squirmed against the bedding, trying to diminish the burn.

"I don't think I could be as brave as Kipp," she added, her voice sounding a little plaintive in the back of my mind.

"But you are," Kipp remarked, turning slightly to look at her, "You were ready to jump in the box car with Peter, despite the danger. The notion of saving yourself never entered your mind."

"I hadn't thought of it like that," she answered. After a moment, she sighed deeply, the action making her entire body tremble.

It was quiet in the room, unlike the modern day when televisions, radios and the like are constantly stimulating the senses what seems to be 24/7. The bedroom was on the back of the house, and only occasionally could I hear some noise from the street, but it was muffled and arrived as a gentle murmur. I got another whiff of lavender, which probably came from the sheets as well as my hair. The fragrant herb acted as a soporific, and between that scent and the syrupy biscuits in my stomach, sleep came with ease. I found I wasn't worried about the following day and whether or not we could find Peter. It was just nice to rest for a bit.

Charles Andrews picked me up out front in the buggy; my horse looked rested, bobbing his head energetically and even rolling his eyes a little to demonstrate he was back in the game. I politely but firmly declined Belle's offer of hoops and corsets but did allow for a couple of really full, stiff petticoats just to mollify her sensibilities. Charles appeared content from a night spent in his own bed and consuming his mother's superlative cooking; he assumed an officious pose as if he pretended that he'd not had a "mama" the night before who doted upon him and insisted he eat a second helping of stew and biscuits because he was looking "poorly". Overnight, he reverted to military man. Atlanta was not that large a town, so it only took a few minutes to find the Fulton County Jail, which was the logical location of Peter.

The raiders would not arrive in Atlanta for some weeks after being held prisoner elsewhere in horrible, humiliating conditions. I did recall reading about their incarceration, and the inhumane treatment was not warranted, no matter how seriously the South took assaults on her railroads. As we approached the jail, I gazed up at the neat, two storey building built in a square, with ornamentation that obviously was designed to give it a regal, intimidating appearance. Well, I suppose jails and prisons aren't supposed to look particularly inviting. From Kipp's studies, we knew the prisoners were held on the second floor while the jailer and his family lived on the first floor. A crowded omnibus passed us, drawn by a couple of large draft horses who looked bored with the business of pulling people around all day long. It was clear that they would have preferred trotting across a green field where the tall grass swept past their knees and the fluff from dandelions drifted up to tickle their broad noses.

"It's heading to the Car Shed," Andrews remarked, nodding at the omnibus.

For the first time, I realized the irony that I was being accompanied by a man named Andrews, when another man named Andrews–the leader of the raiders—had been captured and would be brought to Atlanta, hanged–rather unsuccessfully, since he really strangled to death–and buried in an unmarked grave. It would have been interesting to meet James Andrews, a man of courage and conviction, but that was not to be. Of course, nothing could prevent me from one day returning to meet him before the entire train adventure unfolded, but I knew I wouldn't. Such self-indulgent behavior could lead to unhappy obsessions with humans, and there was no good solution to that problem except to avoid it in the first place.

Charles secured the horse while I waited for his courteous hand, knowing he'd be horrified if I catapulted from the buggy on my own. The lupines hopped down to the ground, which was nice and dry for a change. We'd only left Atlanta a few days ago when the rain was unceasing and the mud was pilling up in thick, rolled banks alongside the well travelled roads.

Charles walked beside me; his gait was stiff and formal, telling me that he was nervous.

"He's worried if this isn't simple and easy that it will cause him conflict with Duncan. He has orders to return to his camp in Rome immediately upon getting you safely to your destination." Kipp chimed in.

We entered the front of the building; the inside was surprisingly cool and ample light filtered through the first floor windows. A man sat behind a desk; he had a copy of the *Atlanta Intelligencer* spread out on the scarred wood of the desk, which looked as if someone had taken to carving on the surface to offset boredom. It didn't require a talented telepath to immediately discern that the man, who was assigned as a screener of potential visitors, was unhappy in his vocation and used the opportunity to demonstrate his power and control by maliciously applying the rules.

"Yeah?" he asked, staring up at us with blood shot blue eyes. He'd been out carousing too late the previous night, only to tumble into his bed at four in the morning.

Andrew's neck began to redden in embarrassment over the man's rudeness to me as well as his insolent gaze. He'd not bother to stand, nod his head or even, might I say, kiss my foot. Of course, I was impervious to such slights and almost yawned. If this was the jailer's best, then he had just proved himself to be a rank amateur.

"We're here with a letter from Colonel Duncan, who is in charge of our company training outside of Rome," Andrews began. "This young woman's brother was brought here in error, and this letter begs for an accommodation to release him."

"And his name?" The man still sat as if his butt was glued to the chair.

"Peter Keaton," I replied. I knew that using my feminine wiles would not work with this man, so I didn't try any tactics to gain his sympathy.

"Yeah, he's here, but he can't be released unless by the order of General Thorpe," the man said as he fingered the edges of the newspaper. He obviously was keen to continue reading and be done with our intrusion.

"Shall I convince him?" Kipp asked, chomping at the bit to implant a thought.

At that minute, several men dressed in military uniforms descended the stairs, nodding at us as they passed. Andrews glanced at the castle guard, raising his eyebrows.

"We have a number of military prisoners here," the door man remarked, "and General Thorpe is using our jail as a temporary holding place. He's deployed several guards to stay here around the clock since there have been rumors of these men's confederates planning to break them out of here." He shrugged his shoulders. "They're supposed to be on our side but are spies and deserters all. They'll be hanged," he said, shrugging his shoulders as if the matter was not worthy of his attention.

"But I have a letter from Colonel Duncan…" I began.

"And you can show me a letter from the Lord Almighty, but you'll still have to wait for General Thorpe," he responded. "He'll be here tomorrow." The man knew the disrespectful reference to a deity would really rile Andrews, which it did.

Since there was a number of guards coming and going, any intervention by Kipp immediately became complicated. He could implant a thought in one mind, but to try and do so in several minds and have all of them arrive at the same conclusion simultaneously would be almost impossible.

"Leave it, Kipp," I said to my partner. He'd moved next to me and was staring at the man behind the desk in his most intimidating manner. "And quit staring at him. He already doesn't like us."

"May I see my brother?" I asked.

The man rolled his eyes up in his head but after a minute pursed his lips and gave a shrill whistle. He was obviously too lazy to stand. A young man in a neat, clean uniform descended the stairs from the second floor. He was instructed to take me upstairs; Charles Andrews, not thinking it was appropriate for a lady to be ambling around

a jail full of criminals, walked with me while Kipp and
Elani followed behind.

The second floor was dim and light only came from
small, box-like apertures sunk in thick wooden planks high
up along the walls. The smell of anxiety, fear, and
unwashed bodies assaulted my nose and almost caused my
eyes to burn. In a place such as that, open buckets became
latrines as men were dehumanized and broken down to the
most base level. The first cell to my right was home to
about five men; the same was true for the one across from
it. As we walked down the hallway that spliced the second
floor, the men's heads went up with interest at our odd
party, but they remained silent. At the far end of the
hallway, there were two more large cells. In the one on my
left side, I saw a forlorn figure sitting on a metal frame, his
head cradled in his hands. It was Peter! He'd been so
miserable and preoccupied that he was not focused on his
telepathy, and our arrival startled him; he jumped to his
feet, his eyes opening wide at the sound of my voice. Elani
barked with joy and dashed to the bars to lick his hands.
There were numerous soldiers in the hallway, all armed.
The men being held were obviously important and worthy
of such protection. The guards saw I was with a military
man and didn't rush to keep me from Peter.

"Oh, Petra, I didn't know if you could ever find me!"
Peter exclaimed, forgetting in his surprise to call me Sam.
"I'm so sorry I've put you through this." His dark eyes
looked down to meet Elani's; she stared back, her tail
wagging frantically. There was no time for regrets or
recriminations.

"Peter, I'll tell you all about it one day, but right now we
have to focus on getting you free. I have a letter from a
Colonel Duncan who is asking for your release, and per the
jailer, we are waiting on General Thorpe to arrive
tomorrow and make disposition on cases." As I spoke I had
an idea, one which gained Kipp's immediate approval.

"I'm going to go to the Car Shed and look for Murphy,
the man who helped us get this far," I said. "If there is any

way possible, I'll bring him back for the hearing tomorrow." My thought was that Murphy was a man of solid reputation, and that it wouldn't hurt things a bit to have his endorsement of facts since we'd ridden the pole car together and got to know one another. "Can I bring you anything?" I asked, looking carefully at Peter. He hadn't been deprived long enough to really feel it, but I knew the food must be horrendous. He had a large bruise on the left side of his face as well as a blackened right eye. Obviously, his captors had enjoyed roughing him up a little.

"No. If you bring decent food, it'll get stolen from me. I'm okay for another day or two, so let's hope I get free tomorrow." He looked dejected; his mop of dark hair fell lank across his forehead. I found I missed the cocky little sweep of bangs and was surprised to acknowledge my feelings of affection for him. Peter had become like a goofy, younger brother to me.

As we left the jail, I was monitoring Charles Andrews' thoughts and knew he was torn between doing the chivalrous thing and remaining with me or returning to Rome with his men as ordered. It was the decent thing to cut him free, and I was never concerned to be on my own, just me and Kipp.

"Charles," I began, as we paused under the shade of an enormous oak; its branches crowded a wooden sidewalk. "I can handle this situation, and I know you need to return to Rome. You are under no further obligation to me."

We'd said goodbyes to his mother that morning, and I had money for a hotel, thanks to the money-laden collars that both lupines wore. The carriage and horse were mine, so I had transportation around town as needed. With gratitude, I watched the young man make his way towards the hotel where his men were staying. They'd probably all be gone within the hour.

"I really do wonder what happened to him and Belle?" Elani mused. "They were so kind to us."

"Atlanta will burn, and Belle will be forced to become a refugee," I replied. It was a fact, and we could be sentimental about the woman who'd cared for us like we were her own or accept the harsh fact that history was just that. Looking down at Kipp, I recalled the gentle tribe of prehistoric people with whom I'd lived when I met Kipp. There was no doubt in my mind that none of them survived their journey when they traveled away from their homeland. I recall the despair I felt as I watched their party make its way south; they were hopeful for a new life, but I knew they were headed towards disaster, and there was nothing I could do to save them. Having the knowledge of people's futures gives us time travelers an unfair and unpleasant advantage, one I don't relish at times.

"Let's go find Murphy," Kipp suggested, eager to prod us from our funks.

CHAPTER 24

The Car Shed was just as chaotic at noontime as it had been at four in the morning and maybe even a little more so. As I entered, the crowded rush of people hurrying to catch trains, depart trains, and deliver and retrieve merchandise was almost overwhelming. So many thoughts were swirling that I purposely limited my telepathy so as to not feel like I was spinning in a tight circle. A couple of finely dressed women passed, their broad skirts swaying from the rigid cage of hoops; delicate lace shawls covered their shoulders in the manner of current modesty. Unlike my braid which was tied with a ribbon supplied by Belle Andrews, the hair of the women was smoothed and twisted in neat side rolls before being contained primly in the back. A whiff of some sort of pretty, rose based perfume followed their passage. One of them looked back at me and sneered. My hoopless, sassy profile was definitely out of fashion.

"You are a trail blazing renegade," Kipp remarked, nudging his head up under my hand. "I think you need to come back wearing a miniskirt and go-go boots."

"Go-go boots?" I asked, wondering where on earth he got that fashion suggestion.

"Oh, there was some woman in Durham at the café

where we were eating. She was reminiscing with a friend about when she was a teenager and got her first pair of white go-go boots." Kipp looked up at me. "You know, kind of short boots, mid calf, that were all the rage in the sixties."

"Thank you, Mr. Professor. I lived though the sixties and had a pair, complete with pink pom poms hanging off the zipper." I ruffled his fur.

"Look!" Elani exclaimed, drawing our attention from silly chit chat.

On a far siding, the *General* stood, magnificent, beautiful and looking none the worse for wear. A familiar figure paced along next to her, stooping to inspect some piece of machinery associated with the left rear driving wheel. It was William Fuller! As I approached, he stood, turned, and a look of surprise crossed his face as he recognized our little party.

"Miss Keaton," he greeted me, removing his slouch hat. A rare smile crossed his usually stern and stoic features. As if on second thought after he allowed me that one familiarity, he compressed his lips tightly together. Fuller's black hair was combed straight back from a receding hairline to lightly brush the top of his collar. He was not dressed as he had been before in his conductor's garb, but wore dungarees and a work shirt that was dotted with spots of oil and grease. "Just doing a final check on her," Fuller said, pointing at the engine. "She goes back on line tomorrow morning, bright and early." After a pause, he said, "I recognized your determined nature and knew you'd pursue your brother like a hound after a rabbit."

"Yes," I replied. "My brother is here in the Fulton County Jail, and I plan on securing his release."

"If anyone can do it, ma'am, I'm sure you can," he replied. His words were a compliment to my doggedness. Fuller could appreciate that quality since he was the man who would gain fame by chasing a stolen locomotive on foot.

"Do you know where Mr. Murphy might be?" I asked, looking around the large station. I'd had the fleeting thought of asking Fuller to help me tomorrow, but if the *General* was heading out, he'd be aboard and nothing would shake that.

"He's coming in on the *Texas* later this evening," Fuller replied. "I can get a message to him, ma'am, if you like."

"Yes, please. I'll be staying at Washington Hall," I said. "If you could ask him to meet me there in the lobby after supper, I'd be grateful."

He agreed, and we left him to his business. I led the way, the lupines trailing carefully behind me. The wooden platforms were very crowded, and the lupines were anxious over having their paws trod upon by careless human feet. We passed a vendor who was selling some kind of meat and vegetable pies—savory innards crammed inside a sealed pastry pocket. Both lupines gave me the look, and I paused to purchase four of the pies, much to the delight of the vendor, an old woman with a creased face and an impressive dowager's hump that consumed most of her upper back.

It was a relief to go outside and feel free of the press of rushing humanity. The hiss of engines, the thick smell of hot grease and oil as well as the occasional unwashed body was overwhelming. Outside, the weather was beautiful. The sky was an unblemished blue, with all semblance of rain having disappeared. The humidity was nonexistent, and I took a deep breath, feeling the inrush of clean, crisp air fill my lungs. Our little symbiont party paused under a tree where a wooden bench rested, a haven for travelers who'd had way too much fellowship within the confines of the oppressive Car Shed.

"You know, just when I think I've eaten the best thing ever, something else comes along," Kipp said, his eyes rolling in pleasure as he bit into the savory meat pie. "On this trip, I've discovered mashed potatoes, grits with lots of butter, fried okra and now this!" Elani nodded her pretty head. "And what have you had?" Kipp asked looking at me. "A glass of buttermilk; the smell of it is still caught in the back of my throat."

"Yeah," I replied, smiling. He was having fun poking at me, so I let him go on and on.

"I do miss French fries and early morning egg bacon and cheese biscuits at the Hardees in Durham," he said. "It'll be nice to get home and be in my own bed for a change."

"We are leaving tomorrow," I replied.

"Are you sure?" Elani asked.

"Yes. I will have it no other way. If General Thorpe won't release Peter, we will take him. And I don't care what rules we break to do so." In my mind, I was considering telling Kipp once again to insert a thought in the mind of Thorpe. Plan A would be to do things the up front, noninvasive way. Plan B would involve breaking rules and just getting the job done. I really didn't care which at that point. Neither did the lupines.

"Why does it matter so much that we stay true to the rules?" Elani asked.

"It's too easy to become corrupted," I replied. "And in any case, Kipp's ability to influence human thoughts is a little unique. We found, historically, that ability existed in our species but seems to have been lost over time." I didn't add that I'd recently found that I could influence dreams. "We are still trying to figure out what to do with that unique skill in the context of our species and how we interface with humanity."

Since we had time to kill, we took our buggy and did a little sightseeing of early Atlanta. It was difficult to imagine this town in terms of what it would eventually become in just a little over a hundred years. For Elani, who was on her first big time shift, it was especially amazing. Late in the day, we made our way to Washington Hall and found the same surly desk clerk that had been there when Peter checked us in days before. As I walked towards the man, flanked by the lupines, I suddenly remembered that the last time he saw me I was dressed as a man; the moment required some quick thinking and a convenient lie. He obviously recognized the lupines…who wouldn't?

"Yes, uh, ma'am?" he asked, trying to control a sneer on

his face. He'd been eating something with crumbs and a number of them still adhered to his facial hair and were liberally sprinkled on his stained vest.

"My two brothers stayed here a few days ago and recommended your accommodations," I began, trying not to laugh at Kipp who was projecting funny pictures in my head. "Quit messing with my concentration" I hissed at him in the back of my mind.

"Oh, yes ma'am," the clerk replied. "Always happy to have return guests." He pushed the register towards me quickly enough, but I knew he was still battling with some confusion. But after all, money was money.

"And they mentioned that I need to pay for the extra cost of the dogs," I added, smiling, in order to sweeten the deal.

"Oh, yes ma'am," he replied, almost gloating with joy. He would make a little extra that night for his generosity and permissiveness.

Since I had no baggage, save for a small, clean flour sack that contained a couple of apples, hard, crusty biscuits and Peter's watch carefully wrapped in a kerchief, I told the man I needed no guide, but mentioned I'd have a visitor later in the evening and to please alert me when Murphy arrived. The lupines and I climbed the worn, carpeted stairs and found our way to the same room that Peter and Elani had shared. It was early afternoon, and the sun's rays slanted in through the nice, street facing window, so there was plenty of illumination in the small room.

"I'll be glad to get home to a really hot bath and some clean clothes," I remarked, as I plopped down on the edge of the bed. A nap seemed like a good idea as I pulled off my boots, sighing as the leather left my feet.

"What was the roughest trip you ever took?" Elani asked, as she hopped up to nestle on my right side, Kipp on my left, as I stretched out.

"Oh, definitely the one where Kipp and I met," I replied. "My symbiont, Tula, was killed trying to protect me. I was stranded on a prehistoric tundra in the midst of a climatic crisis with no way home. It was a miracle Kipp and I connected."

"Do you think there are miracles or do amazing and inexplicable things just happen at times?" Elani asked. Her fur, since the last cleaning at Belle Andrews' house, was tangle free and fragrant; the scent of the lavender soap was still evident, and I inhaled the fragrance, enjoying the taste of it in my mouth.

"Oh, sweetheart, that question is one for philosophers and those who study religion," I replied. "Some humans believe such events are a part of God's direct intervention; others think that coincidences occur in life and nature."

"What do you believe?" she persisted.

"Kipp finding me was a miracle," I replied, as Kipp pushed harder against me, pressing his jaw down upon my breast bone until I almost gasped. "Our ability to bond was also a miracle."

Elani sighed softly as she processed what I'd told her. It was not my way to direct others' deeper beliefs; I'd not done it with Kipp, nor would I do it with Elani. A sign of respect, in my eyes, was to present facts, evidence, or even my point of view, if asked, and then allow others to pick their chosen path. The road to one's spirituality was best taken alone.

Given the stress of our recent journey, although we'd not been on that time shift for long, it was not surprising that we fell asleep. Kipp's head lolled to the side, and when I awoke to the soft knock on the door, his head was upside down, mouth open, tongue lolling out in his stupor. I jerked in response to the sound, and the lupines struggled to get their footing in the soft bedding before they jumped lightly to the floor. A young man with a cleanly shaven face and carefully pomaded hair politely alerted me to the fact a Mr. Murphy awaited me in the parlor downstairs. I glanced at the large window and noted it was dark outside. We must have slept for hours.

I tried to brush some of the wrinkles from my dress and glanced in the mirror which hung over the small, wooden dresser. With no comb or anything else, there was little I could do to help my appearance, so I pinched my cheeks a little to revive some color to offset my dull appearance and made my way downstairs, followed by the lupines. Murphy, who looked as grand and robust as when I'd last seen him, stood at my arrival. He smiled broadly at me and held out both hands for me to grasp.

"Miss Keaton, I don't know whether to say I'm amazed to see you here or tell you that I knew you'd complete whatever task to which you'd set your mind," Murphy remarked. He led me to a chair and then took one opposite. As I rested my back against the chair, the wooden supports pressed against my spine; the padding was worn thin from years of use. "And your doggies look none the worse for wear."

He demanded I tell him my story and so, just so I could entertain him and see his dark eyes round with amazement, I gave him the entire tale, including the moment of high drama with the highwaymen. As I spoke, I wondered what had happened to those two unsavory characters. Murphy was predictably horrified and inwardly struggling with whether or not to disapprove of my careless actions which were not the mark of a lady or give me a round of applause at my sheer audacity. Finally, he compromised and softly muttered that he was happy to see me looking reasonably intact.

"I need your help, Mr. Murphy," I said, leaning forward. "Peter was mistakenly brought here, and his fate will be decided tomorrow by a General Thorpe. I plan on meeting with the general to explain the situation, hoping he will believe me that Peter is no spy and was not a part of the group of raiders. If you could be there, too, and tell what you witnessed, it would help greatly, I believe."

Murphy was relieved since my request did not involve running for miles, pole cars, mud, rain or other strenuous tasks. Not that he wasn't truly game, but he was still recovering after the pursuit of the *General*. He agreed, even adding he was delighted to help me, and commented he'd meet me in the morning so that we'd be at the Fulton County Jail by the appointed time. We'd be on foot, since

I'd donated my horse and carriage to a small, growing Methodist church that we'd stumbled on earlier that day while exploring the northern boundary of Atlanta. The parson was out front of the neat, whitewashed, plain building, planting flowers when we rolled by. I asked him if he had a horse and buggy for visiting his parishioners, and he had replied no. My only caveat, as I turned over the noble steed that had seen me through so much adventure, was that he be treated kindly. Kipp, after plowing through the man's head, recognized him to be an animal lover and knew the horse would have a good life with no whips applied to his broad back. I even gave the parson some of my money, so he could buy extra feed for the horse.

Murphy left, and we returned to our room on the second floor. This time, I removed my dress and hung it carefully, so that some of the rumples would fall out and perhaps I'd look presentable the next day for the general. That left me in my thin, cotton shift. It was mid April and the nights were still cool, so I huddled under the chenille spread on the bed, dependent upon the warmth of the lupines to act like heated bricks on either side. We didn't wake until we were disturbed by the lusty crowing of an energetic rooster the next morning.

"I'm hungry," Kipp announced. "Some grits, ham and biscuits would be nice," he added, obviously placing his breakfast order.

I splashed water from the pitcher into the large basin and washed my face; the rough, almost threadbare towel was actually invigorating, since it scrubbed off most of the superficial layer of dull flesh until my skin glowed. Dressing took less than a minute since I had so little with which to work. There was a chamber pot, but I made my way to the water closet down the hall before accompanying the lupines outside so they could make a discreet trip to the back alley. While I waited for them, I asked the lad who was working as a porter at the hotel that morning if he could make a run to a nearby establishment and bring back biscuits, ham and whatever else might be portable. He cheerfully went about the task, knowing an extra coin or two would find its way into his pocket without the hotel manager knowing of our private exchange. The lupines and I waited in the room; as the boy ascended the stairs, the smell of food preceded him, and Kipp began to drool.

As the lupines polished off the mixed fare on the plates, I crumbled a biscuit, a little too nervous to eat. What if today went badly and we couldn't retrieve Peter as planned? Pouring a glass of water from the pitcher, I tried to swallow, but the crumbs of bread caught in my throat. Coughing, I felt my face turn red as Kipp stared at me between bites of ham.

"What are you worried for, Petra? You know I can direct Thorpe to do whatever we want him to do."

Well, in the past Kipp had demonstrated his ability to insert thoughts, manipulate dreams and other magnificent feats. But what if, for some reason, Thorpe was not easily manipulated or persuadable, and this time it didn't work? Peter could be sent to a military prison or even executed if Thorpe felt he was involved in the train abduction.

"Murphy being there will help," Kipp remarked with confidence. "Don't be a worry wort."

From outside, there was the rumbling sound of a large dray; I crossed to the window. The dray, pulled by two stout draft horses, was loaded to the brim with fresh cut lumber. I'd left the window open for some fresh air, and as the breeze fluttered the flimsy curtains inward, the smell of pine sap curled into the room. Atlanta, once again, was on the move, growing by leaps and bounds. Craning my head slightly, I gazed down the street to see the tall, well built form of Anthony Murphy as he strode towards the hotel. He walked with a pleasant swagger, the mark of a confident man. A felt bowler, on trend for men's fashions at that time, was settled upon his head.

Moving over to the small dresser, I took a moment to gaze at my reflection. My lips turned down at the dark circles of fatigue beneath my hazel eyes. Lacking a comb, I did my best to tame my unruly hair into submission; a neat braid was about all I'd have time for, and since I didn't even have a hair pin to my name, it would have to make do. My guess was General Thorpe was focused on his business, and my appearance, one way or the other, wouldn't influence him. The lupines hastily polished off the remainder of their breakfast and then, as a group, we walked down the carpeted hallway to the stairs and descended into the lobby. The day clerk nodded at me and motioned towards the small sitting room to the left. Murphy, standing by the large front window, took off his hat as I approached him.

"Are you ready?" he asked, his dark eyes bright and observant. Murphy looked at my face with concern, noting the same dark stains beneath my eyes that had irritated me. "You look tired, Miss Keaton," he remarked.

"I'm just worried about my brother," I said, with a dismissive wave of my hand.

"Then let's go and take care of that little problem," Murphy responded.

CHAPTER 25

The bright light almost blinded me for a moment, as I narrowed my eyes against the sudden change from the dimly lit hotel to the outdoors. Murphy had walked to meet us; none of us symbionts was opposed to that method of transport, so we ambled along happily, Murphy keeping a polite distance between his body and mine. I stumbled once on a tree root, and his hand automatically shot out to steady my elbow, for a second, before he withdrew it as if he'd been snake bitten.

"He's well known around here and doesn't want any nasty gossip," Kipp offered. "But he already shared your situation with his wife, and she is in full support of him aiding a damsel in distress."

"And how did you find your brother?" Murphy asked, tilting his head at me. When I hesitated, he clarified, "I mean, how did he seem? Was he well?"

"He was tired, scared, and someone had roughed him up," I replied. "His face was bruised," I added hastily. Murphy wouldn't understand my use of vulgar phrases not commonly put into play by ladies.

"I'm sorry to hear of it, ma'am," he remarked. "I'm sure the Fulton County Jail is not an accommodating place."

A carriage passed by at a high rate of speed and at an

alarmingly close proximity to our party. Murphy had taken the gentleman's position of being between me and traffic. He frowned at the departing carriage, his thoughts dark for a moment in consideration of the uncouth louts that seemed to be much too prevalent in the town. Then he laughed unexpectedly, the sound bright in the early morning air.

"I was just recalling the ride on the pole car as we started down that steep hill before the tracks ran out. We suddenly took to the air like a flock of birds…but without the accompanying grace and agility." Turning slightly, he gazed at me. "You are a brave and determined lady," he added.

"I've never been airborne in quite that fashion, Mr. Murphy," I said, knowing he'd find my reply humorous.

"Nor I," he agreed, tipping his hat. "And I have no wish to do so again."

I almost chorused "Amen" but feared he might think me irreverent.

As we approached the jail, I saw that a large tent had been set up on the lawn, with an extended flap propped up to provide a shelter from the sun or other elements. There were a few horses, unsaddled, tethered along a rope line. Obviously, Thorpe had arrived. A sentry in uniform stood stiffly outside the little encampment.

"Let's go meet the man," Murphy suggested.

We were stopped by a sergeant–who looked all of seventeen, his face pocked with acne scars—and were forced to wait until he discretely spat out a stream of tobacco juice before being compelled to speak with us. Murphy explained our business, and the sergeant excused himself for a moment, walking to the tent. In less than a minute, a tall man with a barrel chest which pushed against the buttons on his gray tunic ducked out from beneath the tent flap and approached. He had gray hair, worn long so that it curled up against his collar, and a full set of whiskers and beard, the latter reaching mid-chest.

"He's worked on that for a while," Kipp observed laconically.

"General Thorpe, I am Anthony Murphy, a supervisor for the W&ARR," Murphy began, removing his hat politely. "And this is Miss Samantha Keaton," he added, touching my elbow with a feather dusting of a gesture. Murphy was not one to waste words and quickly and efficiently explained our purpose. Thorpe's gray eyebrows drew together in a frown.

"So, Mr. Murphy, you were part of the party which pursued and retrieved the *General*?" he asked. Leading, he motioned for us to follow and invited us to sit in some camp chairs that were clustered beneath the tent flap.

"Yes, along with Jefferson Cain and Bill Fuller," Murphy replied. "This brave young lady, along with her dogs," he said, pointing at Kipp and Elani, "chased after us, running several miles and encountered extreme danger and risk to herself to try and find her brother."

Thorpe's gray eyes flicked down to look at the lupines, who tried to look bored and uninterested; then he looked at me. It was clear he had the same thoughts of other contemporary men and was torn between admiration for my boldness and extreme horror over the concept a lady might have done what I did. His lips tightened and turned down to become lost in the mass of facial hair that covered his chin.

"It was quite terrifying, General," I said, keeping my voice soft and my eyes wide open. It was helpful he not think of me as a kick butt type of ninja female warrior; yes, playing the role of vulnerable female seemed to be the route to take. "I beg you to forgive my current appearance, but all my belongings have been lost, and I've been forced to accept the charity and kindness of strangers." I blinked my eyes a couple of times for good measure, and hoped beyond hope I didn't sound too much like Blanche in *A Streetcar Named Desire*.

"You are just shameless," Kipp remarked, his muzzle pressed into the fragrant grass. His eyes crossed slightly as he followed the progress of a large beetle that was walking across his forepaws.

"Hey, good buddy, I've seen you pull out a few tricks, too," I replied lightly to Kipp, who rolled his eyes at me.

"May I have my sergeant bring you a beverage, ma'am?" Thorpe asked. "We have fresh coffee or perhaps some water?"

"What, no buttermilk?" Kipp interjected.

"Some coffee would be very nice," I said, folding my hands primly on my lap.

"I, of course, will have to interview your brother," Thorpe said, smiling in satisfaction as the sergeant put on his hostess hat and presented both me and Murphy battered tin cups filled with steaming coffee. The handles were almost too hot to touch. "The allegations of being involved in stealing the *General* are serious ones. And the fact the men were captured out of uniform, including your brother, compounds the injury." He didn't need to add that being caught as a spy was automatically a capital offense. It was clear he was trying to avoid upsetting me with the news. "But I plan on giving a fair hearing and will allow you and Mr. Murphy to contribute," he concluded, happy that he could be magnanimous in his little fiefdom. Perhaps I could have leapt out of my chair, given a curtsey and bowed over his hand but chose not to. Since we were present and ready for a disposition, he asked the sergeant to have Peter brought out first. While we waited, Thorpe commented on the growth of Atlanta as well as the nice change of weather.

"Traveling in the rain and sleeping in tents on soggy ground makes for unpleasant days," Thorpe remarked, smiling. His teeth, for a man of his advanced years, were surprisingly intact and only marginally stained from years of tobacco and coffee.

"I can't imagine the hardships," I said, leaning forward slightly. "Have you always been a military man?"

"Oh, for goodness sakes, Petra! Why don't you just tell him the very thought of it gives you vapors, and you just might swoon?" Kipp rolled on his back, arching his spine into the grass to relieve a persistent itch.

"Hey, I'm working this, so leave me alone," I replied, with a hard glance at Kipp.

"Yeah, Kipp. I think she is doing a grand job so don't distract her," Elani interjected in a rare moment of disagreement with him. She really missed the nuances of our relationship with one another. We played rough like brother and sister, teasingly critical, but in truth, not at all. It was a stress reliever, and maybe one day, when she and Peter were more experienced, she'd understand that.

"Being ganged up on by a couple of girls," Kipp muttered as he flopped on his side.

"Yes, ma'am. I actually graduated from West Point and have been military all my life," Thorpe replied, as he answered my query. "It is the only way I know."

The door to the jail opened, and two guards flanking Peter, who was shackled with leg chains and wrist cuffs, walked forward. I noticed the guards, in a fit of unkind humor, walked quickly, causing Peter to try and keep up with his manacled legs. He stumbled once, and the guard on the left used the butt of his rifle to dig viciously into Peter's ribs. Kipp drew slowly to his feet, his eyes taking on that primal, intimidating stare that was an attention getter. Thorpe noticed Kipp's actions, as did Murphy, who took a step back.

"Tell the guards to not be rough with the prisoner," Thorpe ordered, nodding at his sergeant, who trotted over to the trio. The guard who'd hurt Peter looked up and his face paled as he saw Thorpe, who looked a little like a king on a throne, staring back.

"Watch yourself, Kipp," I said, cautioning my partner. "It's about to end, and we don't want to complicate matters."

Kipp's sides heaved as he took a deep breath to settle his anger. Elani stood, too, and nosed him softly, her face close to his.

Peter finally arrived, and the two guards backed away from him. I noticed, as did Thorpe, that his face had acquired an additional bruise, and he was favoring his side, leaning slightly, where the guard had dug into his ribs. Peter's dark eyes met mine as he tried to smile.

"Had a rough night yesterday," he said, telepathically, so the humans would not hear. "They put someone new in the cage with me, and he wanted my piece of cornbread."

"Did he get it?" I asked, smiling back.

"No, but it cost me. I think I have a loose tooth," he replied.

"That's what dentists are for. We'll get you fixed up at home," I promised.

"And I think I picked up head lice," he added, miserably.

"Then I won't be touching you...not even a hug. Do you still want to travel?" I asked.

"More than ever," he replied, his eyes shining from the dirty mask of his face. "It's been fascinating."

It was an odd hearing. The only witnesses were Peter, Murphy and me. Of course, Kipp and Elani were, too, but their testimony was not required. I realized from the tone of Thorpe's queries that he believed our stories and was planning on granting Peter absolution. But it was his style to drag out the proceedings and make it appear as if he was doing all of us a big, stinking favor, even when he privately thought Peter was innocent. So we waited in the small grove of trees; there was no wind that day and all was still except for one horse who kept restlessly shifting from side to side, his feet softly striking the earth, from where he was tethered with the string of horses.

The shackles and irons clanked loudly as they were unlocked and removed from Peter's wrists and ankles. Elani leapt forward, rearing up to place her paws on his chest, licking his face frantically. I realized he was about to cry but managed to keep control. Thorpe smiled, pleased over the response to this, the ultimate gift. As we walked away, Murphy stayed behind to speak to Thorpe. Peter looked back, once, at the jail.

"Didn't care for that part of the journey," he remarked. "Actually, the Yankee raiders on board the *General* were very nice to me. They just wouldn't let me go earlier because they thought I'd talk, and up until almost the end, they believed they could make it through to Chattanooga."

I handed him the flour sack and waited, expectantly, for him to look inside. His grandfather's watch was safe, intact and back in his possession again. We heard rushed footsteps and turned to see Murphy running to catch up with us.

"On behalf of the W&ARR, I am authorized to offer you both a trip to Dalton, which, I recall, was your original destination. We are taking a special club car from Atlanta north on this line, and you and your doggies can ride in comfort and privacy." Murphy smiled broadly, his hat in hand as he spoke.

Peter looked at me, his eyes begging for my approval. I knew the lupines wanted to go, too. Personally, I was looking forward to the trip home and a good, hot bath. But with three pairs of pleading, brown eyes cast in my direction, what could I say?

"We need to get cleaned up and purchase some decent clothes, I think," I replied mildly.

The train would leave at four the next morning. It was not yet noon, so we had time to make some minimal preparations. After parting from Murphy, we walked back towards Lloyd Street where the Washington Hall hotel was located, intending to stay there again, since the management appeared to have pet friendly policies—if the bribe was right. There were a number of general mercantile stores, so our plan was to buy readymade outfits for the next day. Before we entered the first establishment, I took Peter into an alley and carefully inspected his thick hair, my fingers combing through the mass gingerly.

"I don't see anything crawling," I remarked, "but we'll buy some lye soap, and I'll take you into the water closet at the hotel and scrub your scalp 'til you beg for mercy." Mentally, I ticked off a comb and soap in addition to basic clothing.

Peter assured me, his face bright pink, that he was capable of cleaning his hair and would not need my services as shampoo technician. As the bell over the door of the dry goods store tinkled at our entry, a hopeful clerk looked up from the counter; a worn down pencil gripped between lead darkened fingers indicated he was working on accounts. His happy face changed to one that was more guarded, given our terrible, ragged appearances. Even more so, he frowned at what he thought to be dogs. Kipp and Elani, not wanted to be evicted, lay immediately by the door, curling up into unobtrusive balls.

"May I help you?" the clerk drawled, trying not to sneer. The lenses of his glasses were as thick and opaque as the bottom of Coca Cola bottles; his forehead, which was high and broad due to a receding hairline, puckered into deep furrows as he stared at us.

"We have been in a bit of an accident and are here from out of town," Peter began. He had a naturally pleasant, beguiling manner, and his polite tone helped the clerk to assume a more helpful attitude. "I need a new set of clothes, while my sister here," he said, gesturing at me, "needs a dress and all the, uh, accoutrements."

"Don't forget the lye soap and a comb," Kipp called out, helpfully.

If I'd had time, I would have spent hours wandering through the store, gazing at the shelves that stretched from floor to ceiling. Places such as that no longer exist…where one could buy hair pomade, a can of peaches, fifty pounds of flour, shoes, undergarments, a hunk of cheese accompanied by saltine crackers and a pickle served on a piece of wax paper, and leave wearing a new hat and new shoes. What an efficient concept, I thought. Yes, there were modern superstores where one could shop for hours for most items, but these little general stores were brutally efficient, selling the necessities of life in a concise package. Kipp, following in my brain as always, demanded I buy him a can of peaches, since he'd never tasted such a delight.

"Then we'll have to buy a knife for opening the can," I whined in response.

"Hey, are we coming back anytime soon? Don't be so cheap," Kipp chided me.

The clerk, after he moved past his distaste for our unsavory appearances, decided that a sale is, after all, a sale. So, after a short time of perusing, we eventually left with arms full of packages. We were so filthy, especially Peter, that we didn't try on our new things before purchasing but weren't particularly worried about exact fits. I confess, I self-indulged and purchased a pretty little bonnet to perch upon my head. In addition to the lye soap for Peter, I bought a cake of finely milled lavender scented soap just because I was female and wanted to smell nice.

Upon our return to the Washington Hall hotel, we explained our dilemma to the day shift clerk who was much more accommodating than the sour faced, greedy night shift fellow. He arranged for the water tank to be filled and heated in the small room adjacent to the water closet so that we both could have baths. I planned on combing out the lupines, who thankfully were not considered attractive bait for lice or fleas, while waiting on Peter. We'd purchased some cheese, biscuits, crackers and fresh fruit–as well as Kipp's can of peaches—so as I worked, the lupines snacked. A small mountain of fur was accumulating as I finished with Elani, her dark eyes closed in pleasure as the comb dug through her thick fur to scratch her skin.

"Mmmm," she muttered. That happy sound stopped when I took a damp wash cloth so that I could clean her ears. Kipp watched, his back slightly arched, lips drawn back from teeth, knowing his turn was coming. The door to my room opened, and Peter walked in, refreshed, clean, and wearing his new clothes.

"I'm ready to go again on another time shift," he pronounced.

"And I'm gonna need a few weeks of rest," I replied.

"Oh, come on. It wasn't that bad, was it?" he asked.

"We'll hold that discussion until I've had my bath."

The hot water on my scalp felt good, and I scrubbed my hair until it squeaked. Then, with a towel wrapped turban style around my head, I tippy toed down the hallway, hoping I wouldn't get caught dishabille in the thick dressing gown I'd purchased. Women's clothes were not particularly comfortable, and I had no plans to sit around all day in a dress that bunched up around my waist. Peter and the lupines were finishing off the food we'd purchased, happy to eat and not particularly concerned over the simplicity of the fare.

"Okay, we do need to talk before we go home," I began, taking time to review my thoughts. Sitting on the floor, I beckoned for Kipp to approach for his turn at grooming. "What went right and what went wrong with this time shift?" I asked, raising my eyebrows as I caught the attention of both Elani and Peter.

"Well, our timing and arrival was flawless," Elani began. "Peter's review of the history was spot on and his recall of details was perfect."

"I agree," I replied. Kipp stayed silent, his thoughts guarded. His eyes closed as he leaned towards me so that I could get to a particularly itchy place with the comb.

Peter's face began to redden as he sat silently, looking at the wall, which was covered in some outdated, stained wallpaper that featured bunches of tiny roses scattered haphazardly across a green field. Looking down, he crumbled a biscuit that was half eaten, making a little mountain of crumbs on a napkin.

"Your impulsivity, Peter, almost got all of us in serious trouble," I began. "In fact, it did get us all in serious trouble, no ifs about it."

"I thought you told me you've done stupid stuff before, too," he replied, his face looking defensive and a smidge pouty.

"Yes, that's true. And every time I have, I had to face up to it, usually with Fitzhugh or Philo or someone else who cared, chewing off my butt over that episode." Leaning forward, I reached out and touched his arm. "This is how we learn. Peter, you messed up royally and could have left Elani stranded forever in this time with no way to escape. You have to think beyond yourself."

"So, are you going to tell Fitzhugh and the others?" Peter

asked. His dark eyes met mine as a spark of hope ignited.

"No, I'm not. But you will," I replied. "If you can't face up to your mistakes, then you don't need to travel."

I looked down at Kipp, who was lying in patch of bright sun light thrown carelessly upon the floor as the afternoon stretched on. His eyes were half closed, his thoughts hidden from me as he pretended to be a statue. But I knew his mind was busy working, and if he disapproved of my words, he'd be all over my brain, flooding me with his opinions.

Maybe I was finally growing up, I thought. I'd been accused of being careless, short-sighted and one to break all the rules. And here I was with Peter, sounding like a grounded, old sage of my species.

"It's having to take responsibility for training him and Elani that did it," Kipp remarked privately to me. "I feel that way, too. Suddenly, it's bigger than the two of us."

"Glad you're back, buddy," I replied in our covert manner of speech to one another. "Am I too harsh?"

"No, let's see. Peter jumped on a train and was abducted. We chased him for miles and miles, putting ourselves at risk. Then, you were accosted by armed highwaymen, fell into a river and almost drowned. There's more, but that is enough for now. His behavior put you in danger, so I think you are within your rights to let him know about it."

I knew that Elani forgave Peter. She, too, was young and learning and recognized his eagerness and enthusiasm had taken over the judgment needed. She'd travel again with him, anytime, anywhere.

"We will only tell Fitzhugh," I said, sighing, "and trust him on what to formally share with the Twelve." That was a compromise on my part, but I'd done the same before and didn't want to set a totally different standard with Peter.

Finally, Peter managed a wan smile and nodded. Elani was next to him, her head in his lap. His fingers, bruised and stiff, combed her fur. The cuffs of his shirt pulled back to reveal the dark, purple bruises on his wrists from the manacles. The black eye someone had given him over a piece of cornbread was still vivid.

"Your mama's gonna ask about that eye," I pointed out.

"I may tell her you hit me," he responded, laughing softly.

"And I may tell her you deserved it," I replied.

Kipp twisted his big head to look at me. "Do you have to clean my ears? I don't think they are really that dirty."

In reply, I held up a damp washcloth.

CHAPTER 26

◆

I'll always remember that club car; I'd been on many train rides but never in a conveyance so finely apportioned. The windows, which ran uninterrupted down the side of the car, were adorned with velvet curtains, draped in a swag fashion. Along the edges of the velvet, which was a deep, burgundy shade of red, were little silky tassels that swayed as the car moved. Instead of the crush of passenger seats designed to maximize the number of people transported at any one time, there were a couple of circular tables with chairs as well as a couple of scattered, plush window seats. A large mahogany bar, with ornate, carved wood obviously done by a master craftsman, almost covered one end of the car, while a wood burning stove sat idle at the other.

Peter's mouth dropped open, slack, as he glanced around. In his imagination, he could not have conceived of riding in a club car pulled by the *General*. He glanced at me, and I knew his thoughts; I, too, was glad we'd purchased some halfway decent clothes. Murphy stood back, hat in hand, enjoying the expressions on our faces. The lupines showed their appreciation by frantically wagging their brushy tails.

"So, Mr. Murphy, how did you finagle this?" I asked, smiling up at him.

"Ah, what's the good of having strings if you can't pull 'em once in a while," he answered, his face reddening slightly. The words held the pleasant lilt and cadence of his ancestry.

I was personally saddened that he couldn't ride with us, and as he walked away, I had the satisfaction of knowing we'd made another friend. And, unless there was something I didn't know, we'd not changed the arc of history, except to leave a few memories of our having been present. Maybe Murphy would tell his grandchildren of the ride on the pole car accompanied by a woman dressed as a man and two extremely large dogs.

Peter began to explore and quickly found a carafe of coffee on the mahogany bar next to a plate of delicate iced cakes that were lightly dusted with powdered sugar. I heard the sharp steam whistle of the *General* reverberate in the confines of the Car Shed; a moment later, the brakes were released and the train began to roll out of the chaotic terminal building into the early morning darkness. I took a seat at the window and waited; Peter brought me a cup of black coffee and sat opposite me. From a little different viewpoint than a dirty boxcar, with cinders and soot blowing in our faces, we observed–in lavish comfort—the skyline of Atlanta, which was shrouded in threads of gray. The smoke from early morning fires threw a hazy cast to the lantern lit streets. The lupines decided to recline on a large circular, braided woolen rug, leaving us to fill their minds with the images we saw.

"Riding in the boxcar was okay," Peter said, "but this is infinitely better." Leaning forward, he lowered a window so that a rush of fresh air entered the car. I could smell freshly turned earth, the result of some farmer's labor. The fragrance of dark, moist loam was almost grounding, comforting in a basic, elemental way.

I closed my eyes as the car swayed gently along the tracks. In my mind, I replayed what I'd seen before. Small farmsteads dotted the landscape; lights glowed from within homes, indicating habitation and purpose. My hand drew to my neck, and I pulled the pearls free from beneath the high collar of my dress. Like beads meant to soothe the soul, I felt each one in sequence, searching, with my sensitive finger tips, for tiny flaws or imperfections and finding none in my cursory inspection. Opening my eyes, I saw Peter, his head tilted slightly to the side, watching me with curiosity written on his expressive face.

"How long will you miss him?" he asked, oddly perceptive for one so young.

"Always, I think," I replied with a sigh. "But this trip was good for me. I needed focus and to redirect my energies for a while."

He became quiet; even without using my telepathy, I knew he was wondering if he would ever have those type of romantic feelings for another. Given his youth, Peter was full of career energy and only could focus on traveling. But life for humans and symbionts involves more than just work, and perhaps he was thinking ahead to the next stage of his predictably long life.

"Tell me more about the pole car," Peter begged, in a not too subtle ploy to change the tone.

As we rumbled past Vinings and Marietta, I gave a humorous account of the harrowing pole car ride; Kipp and Elani chimed in for good measure. It seemed we'd just left the Car Shed when we began the climb up a gradually steepening hill before the sound of the steam whistle broke the early morning quiet to signify the stop at Big Shanty, the place where our grand adventure had gone awry. The white hotel with the green shutters was unchanged, as was the stream of passengers leaving the train to have breakfast. Peter and I left the club car last and were delighted to see Jefferson Cain back in service as engineer. He smiled broadly and pulled off his cloth cap.

"Good to see you in one piece again, young miss," he said. Clapping his hands, he leaned forward as a human would do and welcomed the lupines with vigorous pats and side thumping. Watching, I recalled he loved dogs.

"Not sure why humans think dogs want to have their sides pummeled, but whatever, I guess," Kipp muttered, looking up at me.

We managed to convince Mrs. Lacy to allow us to take some food to the porch for the lupines and enjoyed our breakfast there. At first, I thought she might ban us from her premises, since Kipp couldn't stop himself from rushing the ducks; I gave him free reign, since this was his last opportunity. I knew, of course, he wouldn't injure them, but Mrs. Lacy was not amused. The ducks were like children to her, and she'd even named them; she held a particular fondness for one named Roscoe, which had been abandoned as a baby only to be hand raised by Mrs. Lacy. The moment held a surreal quality, almost as if the other events had not occurred—maybe had been part of some bizarre dream—and this was our new reality.

"Yes, I've decided I like grits," Kipp remarked, from our perch on the wide front porch upon which we sat. Peter and I shared a round, ornate wrought iron table, while the lupines stretched out on the worn, wooden planks of the porch. "It's just the texture seems kind of odd, and I think I have a grit stuck between my back molars."

"I'll floss for you when we get home," I replied, laughing.

"No, thanks," Kipp said, rolling his eyes up at me. "I've seen you take that piece of string and dig between your teeth, and I'm not having any of it."

I admit, I forgot with whom we sat and was having an energized moment. Carelessly I remarked, "When you have no teeth, my lad, no sweet young lupine will look twice at you."

My comment inadvertently drew Elani's attention; her sentiments were such that she'd always have feelings–and strong ones—for Kipp. My partner, in the meantime, would have blushed, if he'd had flesh like mine. Kipp gave me a look of such savagery that I unconsciously raised my hand to my throat.

"Really sorry," I muttered in a private exchange between us two.

Thankfully, our brief break was at a close. Fuller signaled

it was time to leave and drove us all back to the train, herding us carefully like sheep. He was a man about his business with an ever cautious eye on his pocket watch. As I gazed out of the window of the club car, the men of the training companies that stretched off into the distance on the far side of the tracks were stirring. I saw the early morning sunlight glint off of bayonets and caught a tantalizing whiff of pork frying in skillets. The rows of tents stood out amongst the green of the grassy meadow and small, sapling trees. I thought of General Thorpe and the fact this had been his life since he was a young man. The train's brakes released with an accompanying hiss of steam as pressure was vented from the boiler, and we were off again, quickly picking up speed on the tracks.

"What draws humans to a military life?" Elani asked.

Since I was not human, I had little to contribute. Peter shared history of men who pledged oaths to follow warlords and the concept of people being called to protect their homelands in ancient times. "It is as old as mankind," he concluded.

As the morning stretched on, we traveled through Etowah, Kingston, Calhoun, Tilton—and all the small stops in between—for water and wood along the way until we arrived in Dalton. It was with hesitation that we departed the club car. Personally, I wouldn't have objected to riding to the end terminus, but our time in 1862 had drawn to a close.

"If we ever came back, would they remember us?" Elani asked.

We were walking as a group down the narrow, center street of Dalton. None of us was eager to time shift yet and were in search of a tea room or little café for coffee or tea and a snack for the lupines. People who met us stared in curiosity at our odd party; the lupines' tall stature and Kipp's unusual coloring was an attention getter.

"That's a good question, Elani." I considered my reply because such thoughts could strain the edges of reason and logic. "If you were to come back after these people had met you, then, yes, they should recall you." I reached my hand down to scratch the top of her soft head, smiling as my fingertips found the funny little point on her skull. "If your timing was such that you arrived even a second before we did this time, then, no, you would not be remembered."

Peter touched my arm. "So, we could come back, arrive just a little earlier and have a do over and no one would know the difference?"

I stopped walking and turned to stare at him. A breeze caught his heavy mop of hair and for a moment the old, familiar forelock fell across his eyes. With a slight shrug, he tossed it to the side and stared back.

"Peter, this trip is done. Yes, technically we can do a "do over" and revisit this trip so that Murphy, Fuller and all the others would not know us. But what purpose would be served by that?"

He turned and started walking again. I hurried and caught him, looping my arm in his. Kipp took his familiar place at my side, while Elani flanked Peter. I finally made Peter stop and turn again to face me.

"You did fine, Peter. Yes, mistakes were made, but we are able to go home in one piece. If you learned from this trip, then the purpose was served." His dark eyes met mine. "You know, it didn't have to be perfect, nor will it ever be. Humans and symbionts alike live in an imperfect world, and there will always be too many variables for one to be in control of the outcome."

"Let's get some tea," he suggested, gently putting a period on my dissertation.

We found a little café at the end of town, and the proprietor brought us a pot of rather bland, uninteresting tea to a round table on the front porch where we could sit with the lupines. A plate of sugar cookies accompanied the pot; alas, there was no honey for me but there was a little crock of cream and some sugar. The chipped plate which held the stack of sugar cookies caught my interest. If I'd found it trying to hide on a dusty shelf in an antique store, the delicate pattern of wildflowers on the border would have compelled me to pick it up and examine it further. The hallmark on the reverse side would have hinted at its age. The little chip off the edge of otherwise perfect porcelain would have convinced me to take it home and give it a new family. Kipp, always fascinated by my sentimental and irrational side, smiled at me, his tail thumping the floor.

"Not quite like Fitzhugh's," Peter said, frowning as he gazed as his teacup and the amber liquid. He spent a full minute stirring his tea, the spoon making a sound as it scraped gently along the sides of the porcelain vessel. "I really do get it, Petra, in case you think I'm just being dull. I see what I did wrong, and I have learned. I guess what bothers me is…"

"Yes?" I prodded.

"I wanted to be really good…I wanted to be the best, I suppose." He ducked his head, his face blushing pink.

"Peter, when Petra and I took our first trip together to Land's Point Colony, she was accosted by the man who was responsible for murders that had terrorized the small group of humans who lived there," Kipp said. "I was a distance away but realized, telepathically, she was in danger. I began running towards her, determined to rescue her." Kipp looked up at me, his eyes large with the memory of that day. "She kept warning me off, telling me to stay clear, to let her handle it, but I wouldn't listen. I felt driven, compelled to reach her and protect her. The man hit me with a club, striking my shoulder, fracturing it. My pain was so great that it almost prevented us from being able to focus on our bond and travel home." Kipp paused for a moment. "I know all about messing up and doing exactly the wrong thing at the wrong time."

Peter took a sip of his tea and grimaced slightly. It was bitter, even with the addition of the cream and sugar. Leaning forward, he took a sugar cookie and broke it in half, offering a piece to Elani, who took it delicately in her massive jaws.

"Thanks, Kipp," Peter said, smiling at my partner. Looking down, he saw the gold watch chain that stretched across his vest. With slender fingers, he pulled his grandfather's watch from the little pocket and pushed in the stem, watching as the lid popped open. "At least I got the watch back."

"And you weren't hanged or sent to a military prison," I added, narrowing my eyes at him. "You're not going home with a head full of lice, either. Things can always be worse." After a moment, I added, "But there is the trip to the dentist to address that loose tooth. Things are worse, after all."

When we finished the tea and the lupines polished off the remainder of the cookies, we decided to walk down the street. Peter's shoulder brushed mine; he was of average height but still taller than was I. His hand drifted down to capture mine; Peter's fingers curled up to intertwine with mine. I smiled up at him. To others, we could have been a pair of young lovers, perhaps a bit too overt in our affections for the sensibilities of a small, Southern town. Continuing to walk, we left habitation and continued until we found a pleasant meadow that stretched to meet a heavy growth of trees to the east. That seemed to be as good a place as any to stop, so after a look around to make certain no one was observing–Kipp also conducted a mental sweep–we sat down, enjoying the scent of the thick meadow grass as well as the sprinkled clusters of wild flowers. Overhead, the honeybees buzzed and a few blue jays cawed loudly as they flew towards the forest.

I took my place with Kipp stretching out next to me. Peter no longer felt the need to copy our postures and was developing his unique style with Elani. My usual pattern was to lie on my back, with Kipp's head across my chest, my hands tangled in his auburn fur. Peter sat upright, knees crossed, Elani's large head on his knees.

"I think I'm more comfortable like this," he said, slightly defensively, as I watched.

"Whatever you want to do," I replied dismissively with a wave of my hand.

I was grateful to be heading home and had no plans for another shift anytime soon as the landscape began to blur and the sound of movement rushed in my ears.

CHAPTER 27

───◆───

"**P**etra, did you forget to pick up my Earl Grey when you went shopping?" Fitzhugh's tone was whiney and quarrelsome. He'd been that way ever since I got home. The sound of his house shoes scuffed loudly on the bare wooden floor of the hallway as he approached the kitchen where I sat, trying to enjoy my first cup of coffee for the day. Kipp twisted his head and looked up at me, his tail thumping; Juno, too. I rolled my eyes and took a loud sip of the hot brew, which was black and probably a little too strong; my heart rate surged in response to the caffeine.

Kipp was using a stylus, firmly gripped between his teeth, to read a new book on his Kindle, which was propped between his front paws. Peter downloaded another Civil War book, this one on Gettysburg, and Kipp was, as usual, focused in his primitive, unique way–which meant he was reading and concentrating on the text before him while simultaneously communicating with me.

May had arrived; our timing for the trip home was impeccable, and we only lost a couple of days in our natural timeline. Kipp had to assist Elani a little on the return so that she would hit the mark. It quickly became evident that her skills at such were superior to Peter's, much as Kipp's were better than mine. Partners usually balance one another out, and Peter was learning that Elani's talents were an asset and didn't imply he was without skills of his own. I assured him that Kipp was stronger in all things than I, and that it was wise to simply appreciate and enjoy a powerful partner. Envy and feelings of inadequacy had no place in our traveling teams. A lovely spring storm was just passing through our area, and the early morning sun began to radiate a pretty, diffuse glow of light from behind a blue-gray cloudbank. Outside, the water was dripping from the leaves, making a soothing pattering noise on the roof that echoed softly in the kitchen. My thoughts drifted back to the night spent in the barn with the metal roof when I lay in the straw listening to the storm rage outside.

Fitzhugh entered the kitchen wearing his old, tattered robe cinched around his waist. Despite the fact we'd lived together for a while, he still maintained his proper reserve. I figured I'd never see his bare chest at this rate, but that was definitely okay with me. His gray hair was uncombed and a long strand fell forward over his forehead. I resisted leaning forward and brushing it back for him.

"I mean, really, Petra. Is it that difficult to remember one little thing?" He obviously was not ready to let the issue go.

Kipp, always ready for subtle humor, began to sing in his brain the Carpenter's song "Close To You", getting louder as he got to the part when moon dust was liberally sprinkled in someone's hair. Narrowing my eyes, I darted a savage look his way, not wanting to burst out in laughter since Fitzhugh would undoubtedly misunderstand my humor.

Sighing, I set my coffee aside. "I'm sorry, Fitzhugh. There's been a lot going on since we returned and I forgot." He sat across from me; I reached out to gently touch his forearm. "I'll get it today."

Occasionally, I am granted the rare epiphany of valuable insight, and I was struck with the notion that his irritability had to do with the fact he'd missed me and the disruption my absence caused to our new, bizarre, nuclear family. Trying not to smile, I ducked my head to sip my coffee.

"Do we have any Pop Tarts left?" he asked.

I hopped up and retrieved the box from the counter–fortunately it was strawberry, his favorite–and put the pastries in the toaster. He preferred his warm; I was more of a heathen and ate mine straight out of the box. While the toaster hummed and clicked, I poured him some coffee, adding just the amount of cream I knew he liked. Once the feast was before him, his mood began to lighten.

"I've still been considering how to document what occurred during your time shift," he said, his brows drawing together. "Or if I should say anything at all," he added. Crumbling a corner off the tart, he put it in his mouth and chewed as he considered. The whole idea of team travel was still a little novel. "I think what you managed to accomplish with such a young pair as Peter and Elani is pretty amazing." His dark eyes met mine and he frowned. "But I suspect it had more to do with Kipp's skills than yours."

I knew I'd never get much credit thrown like discarded scraps of food from his table. But there was no arguing that Kipp had subtly managed the trip in ways I probably would never know. Looking across the kitchen, I stared at Kipp, who paused in his reading to gaze back at me.

"What?" he asked, acting innocent, which he never was.

"I realize," Fitzhugh continued, "Peter is worried if the Twelve learn of his impulsivity, it might cause them to rethink his request to be a traveler. But the other side of that coin is to prove that despite adversity, he managed to survive, and he and Elani returned home safely."

"Yes, but that wouldn't have happened if Kipp and I had not been there. Peter would have been taken to jail and who knows where that would have led? Elani would never have been able to find him or, if she had, get to him for a bond. They both would have lived out their lives in another time, stranded, and unable to return home." Oddly, I found myself on the opposing side of the argument.

Fitzhugh pursed his lips and stared across the small room to the window which offered a view of the backyard.

"Margaret Shelton is leaving us," Fitzhugh announced, his change of subject abrupt and startling.

"Really?" I asked. Standing, I walked to the coffee maker and brought the carafe to the table. This might be a two cup discussion.

"Apparently, she reestablished a romantic connection and is wishing to relocate near her, uh, paramour." Only Fitzhugh would use such antiquated words. "So, it will be just you and me again," he added, not looking at me.

"Okay," I replied cautiously, not certain where this discussion would lead.

"Which is exactly why I was so disturbed over your oversight regarding the Earl Grey. The workplace just won't seem the same without the fragrance of the tea." He raised his eyebrows and broke off another piece of Pop Tart. "Next time, I wish you'd buy blueberry, just for a change."

"Okay," I said, again, trying not to smile.

"I'm glad to see your pearls came through the trip intact." Fitzhugh nodded at me. "The stick pin you lost was one of Suzanne's favorites from the vault, and I'm led to believe she is pretty agitated over its loss." He ran a hand up through his hair in irritation, to subdue the long strand that stubbornly refused to be displaced. "I heard she wants your pay docked for the item."

Lily chose that moment to saunter in and crouch at the base of the table before gracefully making the leap to land on top without disturbing any object, which was pretty amazing considered the cluttered condition of the surface. Fitzhugh didn't look at me as he neatly scooped the willful feline off into his lap. I narrowed my eyes at him since it was clear that Lily was accustomed to taking gross liberties in my absence. Sighing deeply, the old symbiont began to gently stroke the cat, who purred with sufficient volume to crack the sheetrock walls.

A week later, I found myself stopping to tie my shoelace, which had come undone as Philo, Kipp and I walked along one of the lesser trod paths in Duke Forest. Philo paused, in no hurry on that lovely day. A busy little Carolina wren scolded us from his perch above; it was clear he and his lady were busy building a nest, and he didn't care for our proximity to his home site. Underneath our feet, the forest floor was quiet, unlike the noisy swooshing sound our feet made dragging through the fallen leaves during autumn. Small pockets of wildflowers were clustered around bright green ferns; some feathery moss grew, indeed, on the north facing side of an ancient oak, its surface damp against the ridged surface of the bark.

"Silas called the other day and asked me to say hello to you from him. Vashti's doing well, too. I think I mentioned they are no longer travelling but are working in their collective as teachers." Philo looked at me, his face carefully neutral, waiting for a response.

I'd never told him my true feelings about his son, who lacked his father's ethics and warmth. And I would never divulge all that occurred during my time shift to Victorian London where I found Silas and his lupine in a terrible predicament due to Silas's poor judgment, which led to necessary involvement by Kipp and me.

"Oh," I finally responded, trying to be diplomatic and noncommittal. "Well, experienced travelers can make excellent instructors, so I hope Silas has found a happy niche."

Philo stopped walking and took a deep breath, obviously enjoying the elemental feel of the air moving in and out of his body. After a moment, he sat, choosing a large boulder that rested next to a stream that ran through the forest. He patted the rock with his hand, indicating I should join him. Kipp, who'd been quiet, found a bunch of ferns near the water and circled before plopping down on them, letting the vegetation serve as a pleasant bed.

"I know more happened with Silas than you will tell," Philo began, looking off at the water. As it flowed past us, the light was caught and glinted like silver shards of mercury glass, shattering over and over again, as the water broke over the rock stream bed. The water murmured, as if it was speaking to us, as it traveled to curve off out of sight around a bend. "Just in the same way, I know more happened with you and Peter than is being told."

"I'm not hiding anything about Peter," I responded. The fact I'd not mentioned doing the same for Silas was obvious but Philo chose to not pounce on that omission. "I told him he'd need to make a truthful report, and as far as I know, he did so."

"Except he left out the parts where you were placed in danger," Kipp said, his thoughts only heard by me.

"And I told him to do that," I replied to Kipp. "My response to assisting Peter was not a part of the report."

Philo turned to me, his dark eyes slightly shadowed. I wondered if something else was bothering him and finally asked.

"Well, Margaret Shelton resigned, so we are looking for someone to take over that position to assist Fitzhugh. I'm getting pressure to make a decision about Peter and Elani, too."

"What kind of decision?" I asked.

"Whether or not they are ready to hit the streets on their own," Philo replied.

He must have seen the look cross my face because he smiled. "And that is exactly why I've been hesitant. Even though you've not said anything, you don't think they are ready to fly solo."

I knew my responsibility to give an honest assessment was needed, but I didn't want to rat them out. Kipp stared up at me; his sides heaved as he sighed.

"Philo, Peter and Elani show great promise" Kipp said, after a moment's hesitation. "Elani seems to have some natural gifts that will benefit them. But Peter is still a little impulsive and got the team in trouble, as you know from the report he gave…which was honest and factual. But, at Petra's insistence, he left out a couple of times where Petra was placed in great danger in her efforts to find him." Kipp looked at me and tilted his head to the side. "If you're gonna be a mentor, you have to be honest, right?"

I looked up; the sun had sidled behind some brilliant cumulous clouds, the white fluffiness turning to a honey-toned amber for a moment. There was no need to look at Philo to know that he was staring at me. Finally, I gave more information…from the pole car, to the highwaymen who waylaid me and mine on an isolated patch of country road, as well as the river adventure. When I had concluded my story, I actually felt better.

"Is that all?" Philo asked.

"All? I could have drowned!" I retorted, feeling my face grow hot.

Philo threw back his head and laughed, a sound I'd not heard from him in quite some time. The laughter rang out into the forest, echoing softly off the surface of the stream.

"I'm glad you finally confessed," he said. "Actually, I didn't draw the conclusion before today that Peter and Elani were ready to work without a net. There is more maturing needed there, to be sure. But I do recognize their talents and think they have a good future. So, I believe when they've rested sufficiently, it will be time to send them out again…with supervision, of course."

I felt my shoulders creeping upwards and twisted my head from side to side to relieve the tension. Kipp was staring at me; his jaw opened as he began to pant.

"And who, uh, do you plan to be the supervisors?" I asked, not wanting to hear the answer.

"Why you and Kipp, of course!"

*Turn the page for an
excerpt from*

TITANIC, 1912

The Symbiont Time Travel
Adventures Series

Book Five

T.L.B. Wood

As I passed people, some of whom were on their way to their cabins, others who were heading to one of the various post dinner locations on board, it was impossible to meet their eyes. Keeping my head down, my chin tucked on my chest, I moved on, feeling resolute and single minded. There was no other choice...we were committed and would see this out as long as possible.

Kipp and I made our way forward on the Promenade Deck until we were located beneath the Bridge Deck and the wheel house. Kipp looked up at me and nodded. "This is good," he said, nuzzling my hand for comfort. Sitting, he closed his eyes, tilting his head slightly. We were alone; the blackness of the seemingly endless expanse of water stretched ahead of the *Titanic*. It looked benign, even welcoming to the humans on board who lacked our regrettable vision which gave us foresight but no ability to act.

"First Officer Murdock is on duty," Kipp said. "His thoughts are organized but with mild concern over the number of iceberg warnings. They started receiving them early this morning from the *Caronia* and since then have received messages from several other vessels noting field ice, icebergs and growlers." Kipp looked up at me. "I know that a short time ago, McBride in the Radio Room was supposed to have received some type of warning from the *Californian*, but there is too much, uh, static for me to find him in all these people," Kipp concluded, his tone apologetic. "He's unfamiliar to me and that makes it difficult."

"It's okay, Kipp. Don't worry about it. You're doing great."

"But Murdock, like the captain, has steamed through similar conditions—or at least he thinks they are similar—before and believes that the necessary caution is applied." Kipp took a deep breath and stood, shaking himself from nose to tail, before seating himself again. "This deck is a little cold on my backside," he grumbled.

I didn't know how to reply since I thought my nose would freeze and fall off any moment. A man passed, tipping his hat, as he went aft towards more pleasant environs. He paused to give me the accurate time from his watch before departing again. It was 11:25 pm. The iceberg was fifteen minutes away.

"I want to go forward, as far as we can, to the open bow, so I can see what the crew are seeing," Kipp demanded. With that, we hustled back to the stairs, taking us down to B Deck where we moved quickly forward, ignoring the stares of people as we hurried along. The outside air was brisk, cutting into my skin like shards of glass. I'd left my hat in the suite, thinking it would be an encumbrance; for a moment, I missed the clumsy warmth it provided. Normally, the forward part of the deck that led to the sharp point of the bow was not for casual strolling, but there was no crew to politely redirect us, and we made our way past the upright support holding the crow's nest and the two men who were watching the black water until we had a clear view, my hands gripping the railing. Although I was wearing gloves, the cold from the metal was not put off by the barrier; my fingers ached.

In the words of Lightoller's description, there was a flat calm. No moon hung overhead, but there was an unusual canopy of bright stars stretching from horizon to horizon. I've rarely seen anything to match in the brightness and clarity... it was as if someone had taken a length of black velvet cloth, punched holes in it from one end to the other, and shone a bright light on the other side of the fabric. The effect was disorienting, at least for me. Kipp's feet were planted wide, his eyes blinking against the numbing cold as he strained to see what lay ahead.

"I see it!" he exclaimed, his thought hitting the back of my head like a hammer. Kipp turned, looking at me. "Can't you see it?"

I couldn't, and neither could the two men in the crow's nest. Maybe it had to do with lupine vision, which was superior to mine as well as humans, but all I could see was the dark void ahead as I strained to find the massive object bobbing ahead of us. My heart thudded heavily in my chest and for a moment it felt as if my throat was closing.

"The speculation about a mirage must be correct," Kipp said, his sides heaving; his breath was visible as clouds of white mist eerily visible in the darkness. "The cold, dense air has created a situation so that something that large and apparent has melted into an optical illusion and has been rendered invisible."

"Why can you see it and the rest of us can't?"

"I guess my eyes are different, as well as my instincts," he replied. "But we are headed right for it!"

The horizon was neither soft nor was there haze; it was a sharp horizon, and the stars seemed cut in two by the definition, their radiance shining onto the water, causing pinpoint spots of iridescent sheen on the ocean.

A minute later, I heard the thoughts of Fleet in the crow's nest as he recognized the danger, finally, first ringing the alarm bell three times, before calling the bridge to alert the crew. Turning, I stared up at the bridge and saw Murdock peering forward, his face pale from cold and shock. The fear he felt as he, too, finally saw the enormous iceberg floating heavily in the water ahead, flooded over me in a nauseous wave; swallowing hard, I twisted around to watch the iceberg ahead.

◆

TITANIC, 1912

available in print and ebook

THE SYMBIONT
TIME TRAVEL ADVENTURES
SERIES

The Symbiont
Tombstone, 1881
Whitechapel, 1888
The Great Locomotive Chase, 1862
Titanic, 1912

T.L.B. Wood began her appreciation of literature at an early age, encouraged by her mother who was an English teacher. T.L. is a certified adult behavioral health clinical nurse specialist and works as a case manager as well as a clinical instructor at a school of nursing. She and her husband share a love of nature, and more than one rescued dog or cat in need of a caring family has found a forever home with the Wood Family. When not feeding and caring for her menagerie, T.L. can be found at her desk, writing, or taking long walks as she envisions new stories to be told.

You can contact T.L. through her publisher at
TLBWood@epublishingworks.com

www.ingramcontent.com/pod-product-compliance
Lightning Source LLC
Chambersburg PA
CBHW030938260626
47169CB00002B/531